THE END OF THE WASP SEASON

Denise Mina

WINDSOR
PARAGON

First published 2011
by Orion Books,
an imprint of The Orion Publishing Group Ltd
This Large Print edition published 2012
by AudioGO Ltd
by arrangement with
The Orion Publishing Group Ltd

Hardcover ISBN: 978 1 4458 8678 7
Softcover ISBN: 978 1 4458 8679 4

British Library Cataloguing in Publication Data available

Printed and bound in Great Britain by
MPG Books Group Limited

For Louise

For Louise

ONE

The silence startled Sarah from a hundred-fathom sleep. She opened her eyes to the red blink of the digital alarm clock: 16:32.

The yips of small dogs came from one of the gardens downhill, insistent, ricocheting off the ceiling and around the curved room.

Quiet. The radio was off. Sarah routinely left the radio on in the kitchen when she was here, tuned to Radio 4. The conversational coo took the edge off the emptiness. Heard from another room it gave the impression that the house was full of charming, chatty people from Hampshire. Burglars might find that strange in Glasgow but it was plausible in the exclusive village of Thorntonhall. Sarah left strategic lights on too: hall, stairs, anywhere that couldn't be seen into. She had a talent for making things seem.

Quiet. This was not the burgling hour. The house was at the top of the hill, visible in daylight, especially at this time when neighbors were out in their grounds, critiquing the gardeners' work or goading fat pedigree dogs around. A thief would have to be very confident or very stupid to break in now.

Exhausted and desperate to sleep, she considered an innocent explanation: either a fuse in the kitchen had blown or the old radio had finally stopped working. Everything in the house was old and needed fixed.

So she decided that the radio had died, smiled and shut her eyes, curling up under the crisp duvet, almost glad to have woken up for the delicious tumble back to sleep.

Her mind slid softly into the dark warm.

A sudden crack of floorboard at the bottom of the stairs. Her eyes snapped open.

She raised her head from the pillow, the better to hear.

A shoe scuffing over carpet, amplified by the stairwell and a hissed two-word instruction. A high voice. A woman's voice. *"Go on."*

Sleep-befuddled, Sarah sat up, imagining her mother on her stairlift, her whirring, inexorable rise to the landing. Her mother, pinch-mouthed and imperious. Her mother wanting answers: why did they fix on that care plan? Why was Sarah never there to bathe her? Why didn't Cardinal Geoffrey conduct her funeral service?

Nonsense.

She threw the duvet off and swung her feet to the floor, attempted to stand up but her drowsy knees failed her and she toppled back, landing awkwardly on the bed with an undignified bounce.

Exasperated with herself, she realized that she was vulnerable because she was at home. Sarah had been in strange places, scary places and managed to stay alert and calm. She always mapped the fire exits on the way in, arrived in charge and stayed in charge, but here she was defenseless.

But this was different to those stranger rooms because here she was a normal householder. She could call the police, ask them to come and help her.

Relieved, she flopped forwards over her knees, reached into her handbag at the side of the bed. Her nervous fingers fumbled past tissues and receipts and passport to the cold metal back of her iPhone. She pressed the button as she pulled it out and was delighted to see the face light up. She had turned it on as she stood in the aisle of first class, waiting to get off at Glasgow Airport. She didn't always. Sometimes she left it off for twenty-four hours until she'd had a sleep. Now, using both hands to concentrate on the screen, she unlocked it, selected phone, selected keyboard, jabbed 999 and pressed call just in time to hear movement outside her bedroom door.

It was more of a sensation than a sound, air shifting on the landing. A body brushed the wall by the door, low down, as startling as cold fingers to the small of a bare back.

She shoved the iPhone into a little cave in the duvet and stood up.

The door moaned softly as it fell open.

It was not the ghost of her mother but two teenage boys, gawky, awkward. They wore baggy black jogging trousers and matching T-shirts, inside out, the seams showing all the way down the legs, along the arms. They wore the same black trainers too. The strange uniform made them look like the members of a cult.

Tentative at first, shuffling, they occupied the doorway. Not desperate but confident, boys on a dare.

She almost laughed with relief. "What are you doing in here?"

One of them was tall, shaven-headed. He couldn't look at her and squirmed slightly at the sound of her voice, stood sideways in the door, his shoulder out on the landing as if he'd like to leave.

"Look," she said, "get out of my house. It

isn't empty, this house . . ."

The other boy had longer hair, black and thick, but he wasn't tentative. He was angry, standing square to the door frame, looking straight at her, taking in her face.

Sarah knew she wasn't very pretty but she made the best of herself, was slim, had a good haircut. In a kind light she could be thought attractive. This boy wasn't finding her so. He was disgusted by her.

The taller one elbowed his friend. The angry boy didn't break eye contact with her but answered him with the jut of a chin, ordering him into the room. The tall friend flinched, giving a half shake of his head. They continued their conversation in micro-gestures, the angry boy holding her eye, hating her.

"My mother died," she said, voice fading as it dawned on her that they weren't surprised to find her here. "I still live —"

"Where's your kids?" asked the angry boy.

"Kids?"

"You've got kids." He seemed very certain.

"No . . . ," she said, "I haven't got kids."

"Yes, you fucking have." He glanced around the room as if her children might be hidden under the edge of the duvet, in the armoire, under the bed.

His voice was high, the voice from the

stairs, but the accent was what she noticed: not Glaswegian, not west coast at all. It wasn't even the tempered, indeterminate Scottish of the local kids. He sounded east coast but English: Edinburgh and London maybe. They'd come here, not stumbled across the house, but had traveled here. She suddenly had no idea what this was.

Sarah tried again. "You're in the wrong house."

But he looked at her and said firmly, "No, I'm not."

The money. They must be here for the money. It was the only thing in the house they could have come for. And yet the cash was in the kitchen and this room was through a door, along a corridor, across a hall, upstairs. They had come here looking for her.

A little more confident now, she looked at them afresh. They weren't getting the money. She'd deny all knowledge if they asked because she'd called the police now, and they would come and take the boys away and question them and she needed to sound innocent.

"Look," she said, trying to sound reasonable, "you should go. I called the police a minute ago, they'll be on their way. You could get in a lot of trouble being here."

The angry boy held her eye as he slid his foot into the room, his toe touching the edge of the yellow Persian carpet, invading the sacred neutral space between them. He saw her bristle with alarm, she saw a spark of empathy on his face before it hardened and he jutted his jaw defiantly. He moved his foot forward again, half an inch, until it lipped over the fringed edge, telling her that he could come over to her, that he would come over.

Irritation shocked her awake and she took charge. "I know what you're here for," she said, stepping towards him, waving a hand towards the stairs. "You don't know who you're dealing with, you've made a mistake —"

"*STOP.*" The angry boy bared his teeth. "Get *fucking* back." He took a firm step towards her, smiling now. His teeth seemed unnaturally dry and that scared her.

Sarah stepped backward to the bed. She could see the corner of the phone peeking out of the duvet. She flexed her fingers, a quickdraw gunfighter rehearsing.

His eyes slipped from her face, snaking across her T, down to her thighs, and he looked away, suddenly repulsed. She had no knickers on, she realized. She had been so tired when she got in that she'd pulled her coat off, dropped her shoes in the hall and tramped up the stairs, shedding her dress and knickers on the bedroom floor. The old T-shirt she slept in only came down to her thighs, barely covering her. She hadn't slept for twenty-four hours. She was sore. Her mum had died. She deserved to sleep.

She shouted as loud as she could: "GET OUT OF HERE THIS INSTANT!"

The tall friend flinched but the angry boy didn't even blink. His lower jaw jutted forward as if he'd like to bite her. It was the anger, the tinge of deep-rooted bitterness that she recognized and she suddenly knew his face.

"Who are you?" she said. "I *know* you."

The tall boy was thrown by that, afraid, and looked at his angry friend.

"I definitely know you." She wasn't sure though: it was a grainy memory, as if he had been on television or in a newspaper. "I've seen a photo of you."

The angry boy's face pinked in blotches and he spluttered when he spoke. "Photo? You saw a *photo?*"

She shrugged awkwardly and saw that he was clenching his fists.

He raised one and punched himself hard on his heart. ". . . showed *you* a fucking photo of *me?*"

His voice was cracking on the upper register. The friend jerked his hand across, pulled the fist free from the chest and yanked him backwards. "Stop. Stop, man. Breathe, take a breath."

Sarah stole a glance at the iPhone, looking for a glow of hope but saw nothing.

The angry boy sputtered still: "Fucking handbag! Fucking get her phone!" He was changing color, paling, looking at the floor by her feet. His friend followed his eye and let go of him, stepping long-legged, colonizing the precious distance in two careless steps. He dropped to a crouch by her feet, shoving a rude hand into her favorite handbag. He was less than a foot from her thigh and Sarah uncrossed her legs, baring herself at him, shocking him into a freeze.

But the angry boy was unmoved by the sight of her. "Squeak, fucking *move*."

The crouching boy tore his gaze away, pulled his hand out of the handbag. He was holding a cell phone. It was a brick, the sort of phone a pensioner would have. Red plastic with big buttons, small screen with a picture of a palm tree on it. It did look puzzling up close because the screen didn't light up — it was a phony phone. Dismayed, Sarah realized that she had forgotten about it. She always forgot about it and she should have used it.

The boy held the phone up over his head to show his friend by the door. The angry boy's face twitched. "What else is there?"

The crouching boy shoved the brick phone into his pocket and reached into her handbag again. He seemed pleased to find her purse. He stood up, held it up triumphantly.

Sarah almost laughed with relief. "You want money?"

But they were focused on the purse, the tall finder stepping back to his friend, still holding the purse high. They were little more than muggers, stupid kids wearing inside-out clothes and she realized that they were hiding a school logo.

She watched the angry boy yank at the zip on her purse. She knew that nose, the short splay, the wide, round nostrils. She knew it very well. She guessed:

"I know your dad —"

She was right: he hesitated in tugging the zip open so she said it louder, *"I know your dad."*

The tall thin boy looked from her to the angry boy, panicked, and she raised her voice: "You'd better get out of here. What do you think he's going to say when I tell him you've broken in?"

A dad. That could be anyone. A sniveling dad, powerful or a pathetic drunk. Maybe Lars had decided he didn't trust her and wanted it back. Lars. It was Lars's nose.

"Lars!" she blurted. The angry boy looked hurt.

For a moment she expected him to drop the purse, give it back, apologize, back out. For a moment her blood slowed and she caught her breath. Bitter Lars, hurt, thrashing Lars who despised her but needed her and had never needed anyone. Lars wouldn't flinch from killing her if it suited him. But it didn't suit him. Lars hadn't sent these boys.

The angry boy was looking at her, that self-same deep hurt in his eyes, his lids lowering to hate. He kept looking at her as his rude fingers fumbled inside her purse, scissoring around a couple of big notes and a taxi receipt, drawing them out.

Sarah took her chance and lunged for her iPhone. As she toppled onto her side, her fingers found the cold metal, wrapping hard around it because she knew it was slippery. She held it up, stabbed at the face, it had locked itself while on the call and she tried to slide it open, missing twice:

"POLICE! HELP ME! TWO BOYS ARE IN MY HOME —"

The angry boy was next to her. He grabbed her clenched hand, pulling her upright, easily yanking the smooth phone from her fingers, but Sarah continued to shout at it: "— IN MY BEDROOM. ONE — I KNOW HIM —"

They all froze, looking at the phone, imagining themselves heard, suddenly conscious of an audience in their play. The angry boy was the first to break out of it: slowly he lifted the phone to his ear and listened.

A smirk erupted on his face. He jabbed a finger at the screen, hung up and threw it on the bed.

They stood close together, a tight clump of animosity in the rambling husk of a house.

Behind her the tall boy shuffled a foot, moving close until his breath was hitting her hair. She felt the moisture from it settle on her ear. The angry boy read the desolation on her face and she saw his eyes brim with fury at it.

Behind her shoulder the breathing was getting faster, more shallow.

Once, in a hotel in Dubai, Sarah had met a client and had dinner with him. He was a fat man. She remembered the sadness about him, desperate, distant, and though she tried to make conversation, he remained quiet throughout the meal and drank a good deal, which wouldn't help. In the lift up to the room she rehearsed her speech: it happens to everyone sometimes, isn't it just as nice to touch and talk, the next time they could use a pill if he wanted . . . On the bed, facing down into a pillow as instructed, she heard that same breathing behind her, rapid, suddenly animal, and she turned around to glimpse a flash of metal in his hand. She'd kicked him off the bed, grabbed her clothes and run. She only got away because he was too fat to chase her.

"I've got money . . . ," she said to no one.

"Money?" said the angry boy quietly. "You think *this* is about money?"

"Then what *is* it about?" she shouted as loud as she could, hoping it would make them back off. "What the hell are you doing here? This is my fucking house."

But neither backed away. The angry boy's eyes met hers.

She was crying now, her hands out in entreaty. "Have I done something to you? I'll tell, you know, I will."

He broke eye contact, looked around the room, unconcerned.

Sarah understood abruptly: he wasn't afraid that she would remember his face

19

because he had come here to kill her. She would never get to leave this house. She would never get out of here.

She couldn't die here, in a cold, run-down house she had been fighting to escape her whole life, with a bare backside and two insolent kids coming into the room that was once her nursery.

Through a shimmer of tears she saw the space between them, the open door beyond.

Sarah put her head down and ran.

TWO

Kay sat by the window, looking down at the bowl, smiling at it. It was worth a lot, she was sure. She shouldn't really be using it as an ashtray. If she took it on the *Antiques Roadshow* she would be the last one on, the high value surprise that drew a gasp from the crowd when the expert revealed the price at auction, just for insurance purposes.

She sighed and looked out over the gray city. Castlemilk was built on a hillside that afforded a view of the whole of Glasgow. In any other city that view would have been reserved for the rich, the Cathkin hillside would be scattered with big houses and fancy gardens, but not here. She never really understood that. Too far out of the town maybe.

The city looked gray from the window, street lights were starting to blink on, dirty yellow, but maybe it wasn't the city that was gray. The kitchen window was gray, a sheen of dirt she could never wash off because it was on the outside of the glass on a window that didn't open far enough. She often looked up to the windows as she hurried up the hill from the bus stop and saw the matte coating on the glass and wondered at windows that could never be washed. Who the fuck thought that was a good idea? On a good day it was an oversight by the planners. On a bad day they hated the would-be residents, thought them filthy and low and beneath having clean windows, begrudged them the greatest view in the whole city.

She tapped the ash from her cigarette, slow, tap-tap-tap, punctuation points in a conversation with an invisible adversary across the table. Two seats, one on either side of the table top. Five of them in the house and table space for two.

She took a deep draw of her cigarette, felt it scratch down her throat and fill her lungs, and smiled to herself, realizing that it was the one. Every day, twenty cigarettes a day, six, maybe seven, draws in each and she only ever enjoyed one of them. One draw out of a hundred and twenty every day. It was a smoking cessation exercise, to show her how little she enjoyed smoking and how pointless it was. It wasn't working. She just enjoyed that one draw all the more for knowing how rare it was. Tap-tap-tap. She smiled at the ashtray. Tap-tap. A bit of burning red tobacco fell off and she stopped, rolled the tip into a neat little cone around the gilded silver slope.

The doors were hanging off the cupboards, the chipboard worktop swollen with water where the plastic had come off. They'd been promised a new kitchen, had been down to the housing office and picked out the worktop and doors from a choice of three, but that was months ago.

Kay heard a bedroom door open in the hall. Marie stepped over to the kitchen, looking away from Kay, as if she happened to be passing. At thirteen, Marie was so self-conscious she was almost housebound. She was wearing yet more nail varnish, blue this time, and a matching hair band. Her cheeks shone, pink circles on her chubby face.

"Have you got make-up on, pet?"

Marie was suddenly, inexplicably embarrassed. "Shut up." And she stormed back into her bedroom.

Kay bit her lip to stop herself laughing. Marie once cried with shame because Kay said she liked Ribena in front of a boy from her class.

"Darlin'," she shouted, "we've crisps."

Marie hesitated, strode back across the

hall with her head down, looking away from her mother. Feeling blindly on the worktop she found the multipack somehow, took out a packet of salt and vinegar.

"Like your nail varnish."

Marie glared at her. "Well, then, I don't."

Kay sighed, "Give us a fucking break, Marie. Or my crisps back."

Marie resisted a laugh, snorting through her nose with a bit of snotty follow-through. Shocked, she touched her wet top lip and looked at her mother accusingly. "For God's sake."

She left in a huff, remembering to take the crisps with her.

Kay took another draw. A bad one, sour, sore. One of the ones that made her wish she didn't smoke.

"Where's my trainers?" Joe was standing in the doorway, his skinny frame in silhouette. "Is that crisps?"

Without waiting for an answer he padded into the gloomy kitchen, rummaged in the multipack bag and pulled out two packets of cheese and onion.

"ONE!"

He dropped one packet on the counter. "Where's my trainers?"

"Why don't you *look* with your *eyes*."

"Because it's *easier* to look with my *mum*."

He opened the packet of crisps, took some out and shoved them into his mouth.

Joe was charming, that was his trouble; he charmed people into doing things for him all the time. Kay didn't want to encourage it. "Fuck off, I'm having a menopause."

"Seriously, where's my trainers?"

She turned back to the filthy window.

"Mum?"

She slumped over the table, defeated. "Where did you take them off?"

"At the door."

"Have you looked at the door?"

"No. Will I?"

She didn't answer.

He turned and looked at the laundry bin that sat behind the front door. She kept it there to put in all the shit they dropped. It was clear plastic and she could see the trainers smashed into the side.

He spotted them too, grunted, and padded over to the bin.

He'd be out for hours now. He was that age where standing on a street corner was irresistible, fascinating, the company of his pals hypnotic. Kay remembered that herself. It wasn't even that far in the past, four kids ago, but still not beyond her memory to recall the excitement of it, the pull of it. Hormones. Now she had four kids, all steps and stairs, all of them hitting their teens at the same time. They were all bouncing off the walls.

"Hey," Joe called to her from the hall. She looked and found him sitting on the floor, pulling his trainers on, legs sprawled.

"What?"

"You look fed up sitting there in the dark."

Blindsided by his charm yet again, she brightened. "I'm all right, son. Just chilling."

"Sure? I'll bring you in a bag of chips if ye like."

"Nah, I'm all right."

She watched him pull his jacket out of the laundry bin. He slipped it on in one of his improbable moments of grace, and opened the front door, stepping out to the yellow gloom on the landing, leaving a puff of cold drafting through the hall.

She liked Joe best. It was wrong to have favorites but she did. They were all teenagers but he was the only one who noticed she had feelings. He tried to cheer her up sometimes.

Kay took another draw. It was getting dark outside the windows but she couldn't be bothered getting up to put the light on, so she sat in the gathering gloom, enjoying the quiet pause before starting the tea and the

26

next round of chores. Down on the street she heard the noise of boys shouting and running, the leather slap of a football. She imagined an audience of girls clustered to the side of the concrete. Out beyond that she saw the city, the barrier of tall flats in the Gorbals, the bright city center and the jagged tower of the university.

The light from the hall caught the side of the ashtray, the red enamel petals glinting, catching the snake of coiled silver wire that master craftsman's hands had formed in Moscow. She sighed, savoring the colors. Gustav Klingert — she'd checked the hallmark on the internet; 1880-ish.

Kay sat back to see it better. It was a small bowl, tucked in tight around the rim. The inside was gilded silver, slightly worn so that the watery sheen of the cold silver showed through the warm glow of gold. On the outside the enamel background was yellow, with red flowers and white and blue leaves picked out in wire. A small line of blue dots articulated the rim and base.

She reached forward and touched it with her fingertip, feeling the rims of the twisted wire around the little pools of luminous enamel. It was the red that caught her the most. The red enamel was clear, transparent, like the inside of a fruit jelly. She didn't even know how to say the name of the style, Ros-tov fin-ift. She liked that it was unpronounceable. It made it feel as if it came from another universe, like Obi-Wan Kenobi.

It was not for the likes of her at all. But the patterns of Russian enameling came from peasant embroidery. Poor women had designed those patterns and the color schemes, they sewed them onto their own tablecloths and the hems of their clothes, working hard in cold, dark houses, pricking their fingers. They were poor women with a deep aching need for beauty to keep them moving through the dark, make them feel alive.

And then, hundreds of years later, jewelers took their designs and made them into expensive things like this bowl, clasps for belts, tea caddies when tea was a luxury, items so expensive the sewing women could never afford them. She was one of those women, those sewing women, sitting in the gloom, and the intricate patterns spoke to her of the beauty to be made from nothing, of the importance of seeing the beauty in things and appreciating it, even through a dirty window.

Kay knew that of all the people who had owned or used or seen this bowl in the last one hundred and thirty years, none of them had loved it as much as she had, stroked it in the long dark nights when she couldn't sleep, tracing the little coils of silver wire snaking through the pools of brilliant color.

THREE

In the freezing early morning rain Alex Morrow stood by a raw grave, holding the tasseled end of a golden rope.

The fiction of it bothered her. They weren't lowering him eight feet down with these curtain ties, the real work was being done by the motorized straps under the coffin. But the funeral director had ordered them in hushed tones to take an end of rope each: herself and Danny, a grizzled man who was her dad's cellmate for years, two cousins, a childhood friend, and one of the funeral directors. They stood around the hole they were putting her father into and went through the charade, while the other funeral guy operated the machine that actually lowered the box into the ground.

When the box reached the bosom of the earth they all looked up for guidance. The funeral director at the graveside dropped his rope into the hole sadly, waiting as the rope snaked away and dropped with a dull *thunk* onto the coffin below. He nodded into the hole, solemnly, as if he had finally come to terms with the death of a man he didn't know existed until he got the job of burying him. He looked at the other bearers, saw them wondering what the hell to do and swept his hand to the hole, telling them to follow his lead.

One of the cousins straightened his arm and dropped his tassel straight in, not touching the sides. He watched it fall, his mouth open in a slight smile, enjoying the drop. The cellmate chucked his in dutifully, turning away before it hit the wood. Danny flicked his wrist, as if he was chucking away a sweetie wrapper, knew littering was wrong but didn't give a shit. Morrow just opened her fingers and let it fall into the hole, trying to give the gesture no meaning, fully aware that her studied carelessness was an eloquent summary of her feelings for her father.

Behind her, Crystyl whimpered loudly. She was wearing a gigantic black hat with black silk roses sewn all around the rim, staggering occasionally when her stilettos sank into the muddy ground. Danny was embarrassed by her. She'd never met the dead man.

Morrow turned to walk away but found herself kettled in by the long mound of loose earth covered over with vibrant green AstroTurf.

It was a small turnout, pathetic, but more than he deserved. They weren't there for him — most of them were men and most of them were there out of loyalty to Danny. She despised the lackeys. They dressed like Danny, did their hair like his, supported his team. It was a loyalty born from mutual greed and self-serving ambition. The enmity was mutual: they knew she was a cop.

Danny caught up with her as she walked carefully through the mud to the path.

"Thanks for coming," he said formally, falling into step with her though she was striding fast and brisk away to the path.

Morrow pulled her coat closed against him. "He was my dad too."

"I know, but just — thanks."

"Well, you know, thanks for organizing it."

"Aye, no bother." He was shoulder to shoulder with her, walking up the steep hill to her car as if they were together, hurrying over a path deep with black granite chips that demanded a slow gait. Danny wanted something.

"What?"

He gave her the look, the heavy lidded

watch-your-fucking-step-with-me look. "Brian didn't come?"

Danny had never met Brian and she never wanted him to either. "Couldn't get the time off work."

Danny nodded, smiled at the ground. She sensed that he knew Brian still wasn't working. She had asked Brian not to come. She did it because he was a good person, not fit to resist the snaky charms of Danny. Two minutes in his company and Brian would be doing him a favor, getting sucked in. That was how Danny roped people in: ask a small favor, give a small favor, lend a bit of money to a needy cousin and then, before they knew what was happening, a perfectly good-living person was driving a car packed with heroin from Fraserburgh. Safe contact was no contact. They arrived at her car, a tired old Honda Brian had bought in a moment of romantic nostalgia for their past, and Morrow fumbled for her keys in her bag.

Behind them, down the hill at the graveside, Crystyl struggled loudly with her grief, and a henchman of Danny's, dressed in a funereal tracksuit, stood an arm's length away and handed her a packet of Handy Andies.

"Crystyl's taking it hard," said Morrow,

allowing herself a dig as she pulled her keys out.

She could see his jaw flex out of the corner of her eye.

"Alex, a woman's going to phone you. A psychologist. About John."

Morrow stopped and looked at him. John, not Johnny, not JJ, not Wee John. Sunday name. Serious. "You gave someone my name in connection with John?"

Danny sucked his teeth and looked hard at the granite chips around his feet. John was the son Danny had at fourteen. The mother was eighteen, a sex symbol on the South Side, a trophy for a young thug. Alex remembered hearing about it when she was at school and feeling strangely proud of Danny. She was fourteen herself and someone her age having a baby seemed ludicrously sophisticated. But John's life had not been a credit to teen parenthood. He grew up fast and brutal.

"Is he having a hard time inside?" she said, trying to care.

"Hmm." Danny was grinding his jaw so hard he was having trouble speaking.

He looked away and managed to open his mouth. "That thing . . . with that woman —"

"Fifteen isn't a woman, Danny."

34

He looked straight at her and she saw the hate in his eyes. His breathing was short, fast, as if he'd hit her if he could. "You never fucking stop, do ye?"

She looked at her car key.

"He's my fucking *son.* Isn't that why we both hated him" — he pointed back to the dirty hole in the wet ground — "because he never gave a shit about us? John's my son and I'm fucking *trying.*"

The back of his neck flushed pink and Morrow looked away, begging him not to cry. Danny cleared his throat and whispered, "I'm *trying.*"

Trying to care about a rapist son who carved open the milk-white thighs of a fifteen-year-old girl with a Stanley knife. At a party. That was the part of the story that the newspapers couldn't get over: that a party was going on outside the door while he did that to her in the parent's en suite bathroom. A middle-class girl at a private school. A clever girl who drank too much and let bad boys in. They had run the gamut of social panics: teen drinking, gangs, knife crime, teen sex. It felt as if the story would never run out of juice, until John was arrested and all the coverage became prejudicial to his trial.

Danny might be trying to help John but

he was the problem too: everyone in the city knew John was guilty because Danny was his father. If Danny had a speck of doubt about John's guilt then the boys who had named him to the police would be missing. The guilty verdict had been a foregone conclusion.

"Is he going to get help in prison?"

Danny shrugged.

"Why did you tell them to contact me? I'm not going to lie about him, Danny. His previous'll be listed in the trial papers anyway."

"It's not because you're polis, it's because you're family. They want a history, it's just facts they're after."

Morrow tutted as she fitted her key in the driver's door. "Danny, we're hardly a family."

He nodded at that. "But you're all I've got."

"Can they not talk to his mum?"

Danny shook his head. "Hospital. Nuts."

"What about his granny? She's alive, isn't she?"

"She's . . . not keen."

"Hmm." Morrow didn't say it out loud either: JJ had kicked his granny about and been charged with it. The granny would have even worse things to say about him than Morrow did.

Together they looked down at Crystyl again, still crying as she was led away from the graveside. The smattering of men standing around looked away, embarrassed, thinking perhaps that even dead psychopaths deserved more decorum.

"If I speak to her," said Danny, "it's going to end up being all about me. I'm trying to stay away from it all, create a distance, or else he'll get killed in prison by some wee prick making his bones. It's too messy. The woman just wants a bit of background."

"What does she want to talk about?"

"Background about John's life. Information about his life. Where he lived and who with and that." Danny swiveled on his heel, facing away from her, his breathing short and hesitant. "I'm not dodging it, Alex. I'm trying to do the right thing. It's harder for me to ask you for a favor."

She'd slag Danny off. That was what he wanted, it would help John. But most of the information she could offer would be on his young offenders' record anyway. They must have done social reports when he was charged with assaulting his gran. She looked down at her hand. The key was in the door, her hand was on the key, all she had to do was turn it, get into the car and leave. "I don't know all that much about his back-ground —"

"It's not about treatment, it's for sentencing — how likely he is to do this again to another lassie. We don't want him getting out if . . ."

Morrow paused for a long deep breath. Danny really knew how to work her: save the girls, don't kill JJ, be better than our dad. He knew where her buttons were and how many times to press them. For a moment it occurred to her that maybe this time their interests were the same, that it was the reasonable thing to do. She considered it until the exotic sense of filial warmth set off an alarm. She hadn't come out of all of that chaos and joined the police by being reasonable. She hadn't stayed out of it or married a man as nice as Brian by doing what Danny thought would be best.

She turned the key, opened the door to her own world and put one foot into the car.

"No. I won't. And Danny, after this . . ." She opened her hand, repeating the gesture she had at the graveside, letting the golden tassel fall. She dropped into the driving seat and shut the door.

Danny looked at her through the windscreen, for just a moment. Heavy set, shaved head and square shoulders, his style was intended to intimidate. And now he stood there with his small teeth bared in a tight slit of a mouth, his chin down, glaring at her.

She'd never seen that expression on his face before and felt a pang of fear run through her, through the twins in her belly, through her nice old car. Danny broke jaws and slammed car doors on hands. Danny stabbed a man in the face with a bottle. Danny did those things when he felt he was owed or when he wanted something. Alex felt strongly that this was the last time they would speak kindly to one another, and she was aware that the choice to move away had been hers.

Keeping her breathing steady, she started the engine, and drove past him, carefully taking the high path down the far side of the cemetery, glad when the funeral party disappeared from her rearview mirror.

She made it to the gates before her work phone jingled a vulgar cheery tune. It was Bannerman. She pressed a button on the hands-free and his voice crackled into the car:

"Where are you now?"

No hello, no preliminaries, just a bark. She hadn't spoken to him yet and he already sounded pissed off at her. "Leaving the cemetery."

"Good."

"Sir, you need to ask me how it was."

"Do I?" It wasn't a challenge, it was a genuine inquiry. Bannerman had been promoted above her and, though the move wasn't unexpected, it had a surprising effect on him. They had shared an office for months and Morrow knew he was insecure, she'd guessed that from the phony persona he seemed determined to act out, the tousled hair, the sun-kissed cheeks, from his aching need to be popular and appealing. What she hadn't expected was for the opinion of those beneath him to mean so little so suddenly. He shed all that, was acting for a different audience now. Now he was angry all the time, was heavy handed, harsh and haranguing. The men on their crew loathed him, a fact which he bore with a degree of pride. Even more bizarrely she had suddenly become very popular with the men, possibly on the basis that her surliness was at least sincere.

"Why do I have to ask you?"

"Because it's good manners to pretend to care about a family funeral."

"OK: how was your auntie's funeral?"

"Fine."

"How old was she?"

"Um, quite old. Eighties, I think."

"Fair enough, then . . . ," said Bannerman.

"Yeah." She glanced in the mirror and saw an old lag, hands deep in his pockets, limping up the path behind her. "Suppose so."

"Well . . ." He stalled, as if stale platitudes about death were hard to come by. "Great. Anyway, we've got a murder in Thorntonhall, if you're finished there."

She looked in her rearview mirror and smiled. "I am finished here, sir."

41

FOUR

Thomas sat down on the pebbled beach, waiting, hoping Squeak would know to come here. He should have been here by now. A chill wind came off the long stretch of water ahead of him. Thomas could see sheep on the hills ahead, tiny dirty-white dots on the exposed grass. They'd been for a visit to a farm once, long time ago. The annual day out was to a farming show as well. It was a holdover from a time when most of the boys at the school would be inheriting an estate and cared about sheep. No longer. They were a different crowd now. The talk in the bus on the way back from the farm was all of whether you could actually shag a sheep and how smelly and greasy they were.

The pebbles on the beach were black, not of the soil around here, dumped by a landscaping lorry. He picked one up to chuck it at the rippling water but stopped himself. Kids did that. He wasn't a kid anymore. He put it down and heard a footstep behind him.

Squeak sat down next to him, a little bit away.

They both had their jackets zipped up to their chins, their hands tucked tight into the pockets. Lunchtime in the big hall followed by free association. Twenty-one minutes and counting before they were missed. They had arrived by different routes, Squeak through the woods because he was coming from the chapel, and Thomas by the cemetery so that if anyone saw them they could say they happened upon each other.

Though they hadn't been to this bit of beach together for ages, Thomas had known Squeak would find him. They knew each other.

When they both started school at eight they were the only two kids in their year. Most families, most boarders, waited until later. Thomas's dad had started at six but that was regarded as too young now, damaging. They started at eight and everyone pitied them, knew that either there was trouble at home or their parents didn't like them. So they grew close to each other, grew into each other, developed a language almost, blinks and looks, names for kids who picked on them and words for why they picked on them. Games with rules no one else understood.

Squeak sighed at the water and Thomas glared at him. They had a lot to talk about but neither could find the starting point. They were each in their own private torrid stream, rolling through resentments against each other, secret worries, and shame, not of what they had done so much as what each thought of the other.

They hadn't spoken since they got into the car at Thorntonhall, Squeak driving and smoking, Thomas busying himself with wet wipes for the entire two-hour drive. He'd used two whole packets and now smelled like the world's biggest baby, the sickly perfumed oil stuck to his face, leaking into his eyes, under his nails. His bath day was two days away and the smell of the wipes made him want to vomit, made him think of Nanny Mary, disgust so intense it felt like his gut was rotting.

"There weren't any kids," said Squeak.

When they got back after the drive, Squeak had parked in the village. They scaled the school wall and crept through the grounds, coming through the back field, staying away from the trip-lights around the back of the boarding block. Thomas didn't care if they were caught. He wanted to be caught. But Squeak insisted that they climb in Thomas's window, left open for the purpose, and they stood in the dark, looking away from each other until Squeak muttered "g'night" and left for his own room.

They had seen each other at breakfast this morning, across the refectory floor. Squeak looked tired, red eyed, spooning porridge into his mouth mechanically, his blank eyes roving around the room, stalling on Thomas's face, just for a moment, and then moving on.

Now the water lapped softly at the stones. Squeak pulled his tobacco tin out of his pocket and opened it, taking out a small smoke, lighting it and drawing hard. He held his breath, rolled his eyes back with relief and exhaled before offering it across.

Thomas took it, unable to refuse. He faked a draw, holding on to it for long enough, taking in a little but not breathing deep down. He handed it back.

"Not into it?" said Squeak, letting him know he'd noticed.

"Nah." Thomas leaned back on his elbows, his quick furtive glance at Squeak's back belying his relaxed posture. Suddenly convinced that Squeak knew he was pretending to be relaxed, he sat up. "You sleep?"

Squeak glanced back over his shoulder, looking down, in a way that seemed despising, or maybe it was just his position. "Not bad." He looked away and took another draw. A deep draw, like he was stopping himself from saying something, swallowing it down.

Thomas couldn't stand it anymore and snapped at him, "You got something to say to me?"

Squeak turned slowly. "Me? Have *I* got something to say to *you?*"

Blindsided by the strength of his reaction, Thomas flinched. Squeak flicked the spliff into the lake. "What the fuck would I have to say to you? *There weren't any kids.*"

Abruptly, Thomas's eyes brimmed. His chin convulsed into a tight ball and Squeak was in his face, fingernail an inch from his eyeball. "*Don't you fucking cry.* You fucking took me there. You said it was her, you said you knew. Don't you dare fucking cry."

He let go and sat back, looking furiously over the water.

Thomas whispered, "He told me —"

"Did he say her name? Mention that house?"

He hadn't. He hadn't said any name in particular. Thomas got her number from his dad's desk, tracked down her address from

46

an old text.

Shocked into taking a deep breath, Thomas stopped his crying pang. His chin relaxed and he rubbed the wet off his eyes roughly as he imagined someone walking past the lakeside and seeing them and thinking it was some sort of lovers' tiff.

A rumor like that would stick to you, follow you for the rest of your life even if you fucked every bitch in Fulham.

He was walking in a London street with his father once, last Christmastime; it was cold and everything had started to go wrong.

His father was being named publicly, on the internet first and then in the papers. They were shopping for gifts and they ran into a man his father knew.

The man was impressive, handsome and fit for a fifty-year-old. He was smug. Thomas remembered him pointing out a sports car and saying it was his Christmas present to himself. But his dad was dismissive of him, condescending. When they walked away his father said that the man had been in the year below him here and once got an inadvertent erection in the showers after rugby. He snickered about it, said they never let him forget it. He was called Stander forever after. Thomas laughed about it because his father said "erection," and it seemed funny, but when he thought about it afterwards, really considered it, the story scared him. It wasn't the suggestion of being a homo that frightened him, no one really cared about that, it was the vulnerability, being so raw in front of everyone, a private thing made public. Now he tried to avoid games when he couldn't have a wank just before it, didn't want to get that sort of name for himself.

Squeak took another smoke out of his tin and lit it, a cigarette this time, drawing hard, pulling his cheeks in, opening his mouth and letting the smoke curl into a fist outside his mouth before sucking it back in again.

"That's how you get cancer, throat cancer," said Thomas, he'd heard it somewhere. "Right?"

"Letting the smoke linger in your mouth. Cig smokers get lung cancer but cigar smokers get face and throat cancer. Because they do that. My dad told me."

Squeak looked angry again. "Does he know yet?"

Thomas shook his head. "He wouldn't call until study anyway. He knows the rules."

"Didn't have mobiles when he was here, I suppose."

"They used to ring the two big black

telephones in the back corridor and a passer-by would answer it and then run off to find you, like a mug," he smiled, knowing he sounded like his father. "Other end of the school sometimes but they'd do it."

Squeak didn't care. "Tastes nice, though, when you blow it out and suck it back."

Thomas smiled, tentatively, sad really but a smile nonetheless. Squeak talked through a mouthful of smoke, "You should smoke. You'd look older if you smoked."

"Hmm." It wasn't a dig. Thomas didn't care that he looked so young. Squeak was more ashamed of how thin he was and how his ribs stuck out at the bottom. They knew everything about each other. Thomas suddenly realized that it explained why yesterday had thrown them so much. For the first time since they were eight they had surprised each other. Surprised by what had happened.

"Shock and awe," he pondered aloud.

Squeak had to look at him to see if he was taking the piss or starting something. When he saw it was neither he smiled. "Shock and awe?"

Thomas nodded sadly at the lake. "Was though, wasn't it? Yesterday."

Squeak drew on his cig again. When he exhaled he was grinning. "Fucking A."

FIVE

All the houses in Thorntonhall were big and lonesome. Even the smaller cottages were nestled in ostentatiously large gardens or had massive extensions hidden at the back. The hedges along the road were groomed into immaculate angles.

The arrangement of the village didn't make sense to Morrow, looking out of the passenger window. On the outskirts the houses were tall Victorian villas, but towards the center they had seventies flair, angled roofs and big picture windows. She wondered if the center of the village had been bombed in the war.

Her driver took a sharp left down a tree-lined avenue towards the incident address. Away from the main road the houses were even newer, beige brick mansions monkeying the style of the older villas but with double garages, double glazing, double everything.

The avenue forked into two driveways at its end; a brand-new road of yellow chevrons led downhill to a modern ranch-style mansion and the uphill fork was a strip of raw-edged tarmac, leading up to a crumbling gray flint country house.

"I don't get this place," she said. "Where's the shops round here? Why would you build a mansion down the hill from that mess?"

"That'll be the original estate house," said the driver, quietly nodding uphill.

"The estate?" Morrow sat forward.

The driver seemed embarrassed suddenly and Morrow had to strain to hear her. "Well, this one, the house we're going to, it's the oldest house on the highest position. See how the older houses are further away? All the land would have belonged to this house once. They've been selling it off in bits, furthest away, then closer, finally these giant new houses."

Morrow looked at the gloomy old mansion, saw what the driver meant. She felt a shivering thrill of realization, saw the village grow up in her mind.

"How d'you know that?"

But the driver was reluctant to show her cards. "Just . . . watch a lot of architecture shows . . . TV."

They craned forward as the car pulled up

the steep incline, Morrow eager to be there and re-feel the synaptic twang. This was not the original driveway, she thought, trying to add to the driver's conclusion, because a horse and carriage couldn't have taken the sharp ascent. It was a new access to the property, built when the real driveway was sold off for the mansion with the chevron road. She looked at the driver for the first time. She was a new recruit but older, thirties maybe, had a just-out-of-uniform formality to her. She was pretty and dark with a fantastically Persian profile. And she was English.

Morrow didn't press her. At the top of the hill the tarmac gave way to gravel, the car losing pull. They came around the front of the house and saw DC Harris, looking worried, standing next to two squad cars and a big forensics van.

The façade was pleasingly symmetrical and solid, built of gray stone, small windows and a big green front door at the top of a short flight of steps.

"What style is that then?"

The driver glanced up. "Georgian."

"How can you tell?"

The driver frowned and looked at the house. She knew the answer, Morrow could tell, and she could see where the reluctance to admit it came from. A broad knowledge of architectural forms wasn't much of a bonus in the canteen, and being a woman, older and English would already set her miles apart from the rest of them. The force was all about belonging, about them and us.

The woman blushed a little. "Um, well, everything's kind of square and the windows are a giveaway. See the three windows on the first floor?" Morrow looked up, saw three small windows equally spaced along the first floor with sash openings. "That's typical, but it's late Georgian." She pointed to the green front door in a square porch, sitting at the top of six steps. "That's Georgian. You get doors like that in Bath and Dublin. Did you see the oval rooms at the back?"

"Where?"

"The middle rooms at the back of the house come out in a semicircle. That's Georgian. That extension there," she pointed to a block attached at the side, built in the same stone but with long tall windows in a set of three, "that's neoclassical. That's later. Victorian."

Morrow looked at her. She was wearing a suit too expensive for someone of her rank. "Where the hell are you from?"

"Surrey. East Molesey."

"What are you doing up here?"

"My partner got a job up here and I applied. Late recruit."

It showed. She wasn't intimidated by Morrow's rank, had none of the schoolyard politics about her. "What did you do before?"

"Had my own business, electronics."

Morrow grunted. They were dangerously close to making pleasant conversation. She wondered if "partner" was code for "lesbian partner" or just a common term in Surrey. She didn't seem butch but then lesbians didn't anymore. "They treating you OK?"

She shrugged a shoulder and looked away, blinked. In short no, they weren't, but she wasn't letting it get to her and she wasn't going to tell on them.

Morrow was impressed. "Good for you. Ambitious?"

She looked at Morrow, gave a sharp nod, eyes cautious behind. No one admitted to being ambitious nowadays.

"Good. When you get promoted over their heads they'll say it's because you're female. You're smart, that's against you, so's being a bird and being English and — well, yeah."

The driver pretended not to understand the unspoken but her mouth twisted in a thwarted smile as she pulled on the hand-brake. They sat together and watched Harris walk over to the car. His skin was as Scottish as it was possible to be without actually being tartan: white on the brink of blue. He had small eyes, black hair and a ridiculously small mouth that barely met the width of his nostrils.

"Look," muttered Morrow, as Harris walked over to the car, "I won't tell anyone you said that, about being ambitious."

"Thanks, boss," she said quickly.

"You're smart though, so you know, keep close and, um . . ." Morrow was suddenly aware of how short her time was, how soon she would be irrelevant. She wanted to be helpful but had nothing concrete to offer. "I'll take your ideas and pass them off as my own."

She meant it as a stupid joke but the driver thanked her again, their voices overlapping.

They opened the doors and stepped out at the same time. Morrow was relieved Harris was there so they couldn't speak to each other anymore.

"Aye," Harris frowned at the driver, "you — on the door-to-doors. Specifically: saw anything? Knew the residents here? And whether they've been up recently. We need to know whether anything was stolen. Wilder'll take you."

The driver nodded and walked over to DC Wilder lingering by the cars.

"Who is that?" Morrow asked when the woman was out of earshot.

Harris looked. "DC Tamsin Leonard."

"She smart?"

Harris grunted noncommittally. Morrow could have slapped him. Since the last round of pay increases DCs were getting a better wage and overtime for every extra minute over their shift. It was a disastrous decision. The men were making more than the DSs and didn't need to stay on for days at a time until a case was resolved. Now, fingering someone for a promotion would be a betrayal and the smart ones were hiding among the donkeys. But the disenchantment went deeper than that. Bannerman's rudeness had made it a point of pride among the men to hide their lights, as if being good at their job was helping Bannerman be a prick. The belligerence was bedding in. Morrow felt that she was watching it harden from a habit into the culture of their team.

She looked up at the roof of the Georgian house, pretending to check the property over, glad of the excuse to arch her back.

"Been in?" she asked.

Harris nodded uncomfortably at the ground. "Hmm . . ."

"What?" she said. "Mess?"

"Bad mess," he said quietly.

"Since when?"

"Last twenty-four hours. Probably yesterday evening."

Morrow looked up. The roof tiles were clustered, sitting not quite true. Lumps of dead leaves peeked out over the gutters around the roof. Standing in full view at the side of the house, a septic tank slumped on rusting stilts. On the far corner, above a window, a tiny yellow hexagon housed the alarm, but the plastic was sun faded and the blue lettering no longer legible.

"This is one of those worth-a-fortune/cost-a-fortune houses, isn't it?"

Harris nodded at his notes. "How was your funeral?"

"It wasn't *mine*."

"No, I know —"

"It was my auntie's."

She'd had to lie. She'd already said her father died because she couldn't bring herself to admit that her son had. Not for a long time. Eventually, she admitted that Gerald dying was the cause of her depression, but she'd still pretended her dad died around the same time. They made her sit for session after pointless session with a counselor in the welfare unit. She did her time, knowing nothing would help and all her bosses would ever see was the time sheet. Her father's death was one lie she wasn't prepared to admit to. It freed her, broke the link with the infamous McGraths and she felt triumphant, claiming he was dead when he wasn't. It made her feel as if she had killed him.

"Yeah," said Harris, "your auntie."

"It was all right, anyway."

"Yeah, good."

She looked up again. The house had been dearly beloved of someone at some time: an apple tree in the front garden was overloaded with fruit, unpicked, dropping and rotting in the overgrown lawn. The flower beds had been turned but not replanted.

She found it depressing — it made her think of Danny and John and the frailty of family, how easily, despite all the parts being in place, everything could suddenly turn to shit. "Where's the cash?"

Harris looked at her, the little "o" of his mouth like an undelivered kiss. "In the kitchen." He raised his eyebrows. "There's more than we thought. It's in euros."

"High denominations?"

"Five-hundreds."

They smiled up at the house. Five-hundred-euro notes usually meant money laundering, usually meant drugs. It was the highest denomination note available in a dependable currency and needed far less space than hundred-dollar bills. "How much?"

"God, I don't know, hundreds of thousands?" He grinned. "Wait till you see it."

"Someone in there with it?"

"Aye, Gobby. He's glad of the sit down."

She felt herself warm to the house. "She had the money but she's not spending it? Is it someone else's? Maybe she didn't know it was there."

Harris shrugged. "Possible, not likely. Wait till you see where it is."

If it was drug money it could lead them to a team, a big international operation. It could make for a nice tidy case, give them extra clean-up.

"It's something well organized anyway 'cause it's not loose cash. It's got bank bands on."

"You know this area?"

He shook his head. "Been in and around for an hour or so, haven't seen a soul in the streets but workmen and gardeners."

"Ma'am?" Leonard had hurried over from

standing with Wilder. "Boss called. Says your phone's turned off so he called him." She pointed back at Wilder, standing a hundred yards away holding his work mobile and looking shifty. He had been wise enough not to come over with the news. "Wants to talk to you."

"Does he now?"

At her shoulder, Harris coughed a wry comment.

Leonard didn't understand what was going on. "Yes?" she said uncertainly.

"Say you couldn't find me." She turned her back abruptly and asked Harris, "So what's the story?"

"Female, twenty-four years old. Her mother died here recently —"

"That hers . . . ?" She pointed to a steel ramp leaning against the steps to the front door.

"Yeah, mother was in a wheelchair."

"Carers coming in and out?"

Harris checked his notes. "Round-the-clock care. Found a set of accounts in the living room."

"Expensive?"

"God, aye. Makes me want to save up paracetamol for my own mother, looking at that."

"Maybe the money was for that?"

"You'd keep it in a bank then, wouldn't you? If it was straight."

In their peripheral vision, they saw Leonard edge away.

"Check the agency they used, find out who was coming, who had keys and so on."

They watched Leonard arrive at Wilder's side and say "I can't find her" to him. Wilder held the phone out to her. Morrow was glad to see Leonard hold her hands up and back off.

"Shit runs downhill," observed Harris pleasantly.

Morrow allowed herself a smile. "So, victim's name?"

"Sarah Erroll." Harris paled slightly.

"You look ill, Harris."

"Oh . . ." He tipped his head up the stairs to the green front door, cringed and glanced down at her stomach. "I dunno . . ."

Morrow tutted at him. "For God's sake, don't start that."

She looked back at him. Harris was genuinely not sure that she would be all right. It bode ill, she thought; Harris was fairly hardened.

She looked up the steps to the open front door. A white-suited scene-of-crime officer was kneeling inside, examining the lock, but the house yawned black beyond him. "Who found her?"

"Lawyer was expecting her at his office, a meeting about the estate details from her mother's death. She didn't arrive so he came here . . ."

It didn't sound right. "That was sinister enough to warrant a visit?"

"Very out of character, apparently. She was steady, always where she said she'd be. Important papers. He came to find her and did. He's still inside."

They had been there for nearly an hour. Morrow wasn't just late because of the funeral, she'd had to drive back to the station to dump her car. Officers were not allowed to use their own vehicles on police business, in case they ran someone over or got followed home. "Still here? Get him out. Get him to the station — why's he still there?"

Harris drew a sharp breath. "Intruders came in around the back. We're doing forensic there but also trying not to bring him out past the body. He's kind of trapped." He cleared his throat. "The men are calling her 'nice legs.' "

"Who?"

"Sarah Erroll."

"Something happen to her legs?"

"No — 'shame about the face.' " He

hissed a breath in through his teeth. " 'S a mess."

Morrow groaned. It was bad for a victim to have a dehumanizing nickname just one hour after the start of an investigation. It was hard enough as it was to get the men to admit that they cared. There was only one thing worse than a violent death, she thought, and that was a humiliating or funny death. No one gave a shit then and it impacted on the quality of the investigation.

But there must be some pity in it: Harris looked pale, sad, and his eyes searched the gravel as if he'd lost something and it worried him.

Morrow looked away and muttered, "What, is it sexual?"

Harris paused to draw breath and she flinched. She hated sexual murders. They all hated them, not just out of empathy with the victim but because sexual crimes were corrosive, they took them to hideous dark places in their own heads, made them suspicious and fearful, and not always of other people.

"No," he said, finally, sounding unsure, "not superficially. No sexual assault. She was fine-looking though. Slim . . . there's photos. We should think about that as a possible motive, maybe." Harris took a deep breath and tipped his head sideways to the house, eyebrows raised in a question. "Not joking, it's bad, boss."

She was suddenly very angry. "You keep saying that, Harris — yes, you have managed to get that over."

He smiled at the ground. "OK."

She slapped his arm hard with the back of her hand. "Talk about a bloody buildup. You should do trailers for the movies."

As they set off for the steps Morrow was affecting barely contained fury and Harris was smiling, no longer worried for her.

Anger was her trump card, the sole emotion that could sweep sorrow to the curb. Stay angry, stay detached. Everyone was worried about her doing the job because she was pregnant. She could feel herself fading in the eyes of the big bosses, becoming an invisible factor, dying in their eyes. They made ludicrous suggestions that her pregnancy might make her forgetful, emotional, incapable. Actually, the pregnancy had sharpened her mind and brought her into the day. She never wanted it to end. She knew her dread was partly about her son's sudden death, but she had spent time in the special care unit once, as a cop, when she was sent to guard a newborn awaiting adoption. The mother had tried to stab it through her own stomach and they were afraid she would get out of her room and come for it. While Morrow was there a nurse had told her the statistics about twins. For now she lived moment to moment, enjoying it while she could, savoring the visceral minutiae of this time before, the taste of food, the depth of sleep, the intimate wriggles inside her skin. She had never been more acutely in the present than she was now.

They took the steps up to the house together, watching the ground for traces. The stone was spotted with lichen, the balustrade moss-covered. A rotting cast-iron boot scrape was sunk into the bottom step, lions rearing on either side, their noses and ears eroded to stubs.

The door at the top of the steps was green, heavy, solid, and a forensics guy was kneeling down, taking scrapings from the brass lock. The intruders hadn't come in this way, but they would have to prove that no other method of entry had been used. A recent home-invasion case had failed because a wily defense had created reasonable doubt by suggesting a possible second entrance by an unknown crew. It came as an order from the top: they had to use their limited resources proving negatives while hairs and fiber traces got blown around hallways.

Harris followed behind her and when, for a moment, she tottered on the doorstep, she felt his palm brush her back. She was only five months gone but she was already enormous. Her center of gravity was shifting every time the twins moved. She smiled back at him and heard him give a little snorting laugh.

The shallow porch inside the door had a black stone floor. A worn oak bench sat on one side beneath a series of coat hooks, empty, apart from one gray woolen jacket on a hanger. It was unusual, chic, with round lapels, a tight waist and a flare at the hips. A red label with gold writing was just visible. On the door jamb a holy water font hung on a string from a nail, the little semicircular sponge inside dried up and yellow.

"Papes?" she said, wondering instantly if the word was offensive.

Harris nodded. "Suppose."

She shouldn't have said that. She was sure the word was insulting. "That's unusual, isn't it? I thought you couldn't be a landed toff and a Catholic. They couldn't inherit land or something . . . ."

Harris shrugged. "Maybe they're converts."

Morrow expected to see a line of muddy

wellingtons in the porch. Instead, a pair of elegant black velvet high heels were casually discarded on the floor, one upright, one collapsed on its side. They were new: the scarlet sole was barely scratched. Next to them lay a small Samsonite wheelie bag: a molded white plastic oval with a crocodile-skin pattern punched out on it. It was a hand-luggage bag, very new, and clean, with a first-class British Airways luggage tag looped through the handle. She stepped over and looked down at it. Glas Intl from Newark, dated yesterday, in the name of Erroll. It was a very small bag to take to New York.

She pointed to the handle. "It's hand luggage but she checked it in. What did she do that for?"

"Heavy?"

"Maybe. She have other bags with her?"

"Not that we can see."

She pointed at it. "Get that dusted and take it in, I want to see what's inside. Call US immigration. Her visa entry form will have a note of which hotel she was going to stay in and how long for."

Harris scribbled in his notebook.

"What have we got on her so far?"

"Not much at all. Next of kin on the passport is her mother, who's dead. We

67

found her national insurance number but it looks like she's never worked."

"Might be right. She could be living on family money?"

"Still pay income tax, wouldn't you? On interest or something?" Harris looked at the first-class luggage tag. "She had money."

"Could she have worked abroad? Or be married? Have another name?"

He shrugged.

Morrow looked into the dark hall. "The kitchen cash could be her inheritance, hidden for tax reasons."

"In new five-hundred-euro notes?"

"Aye, right enough." They were in it now, talking in shorthand, half voicing half thoughts, seeing through the same eyes. She thought again that it was a shame Harris wouldn't put himself forward for promotion. For him it wasn't just about the money, it was personal: he loathed Bannerman. She saw Harris flinch when the man's name came up in his company, and when any routine humiliation was visited by Bannerman on one of the troops they looked to Harris. She was hoping to be out of the department when it came to a head.

Through an inner door the reception hall was imposing but windowless. Two large oak doors led off it; one into a giant empty living room with faded blue silk wallpaper, one to a shabby library. The right-hand wall was punctured with a large flat arch leading to the Victorian extension and the stairs.

The darkness was exacerbated by wood paneling up to waist height and deep chocolate wallpaper flecked with gold. All the light in the room came from the arch. The brown wallpaper on the left of the hall had faded to a striking orange diagonal where the sun hit it: a pale smear of time across the wall.

The black and white tiled floor was pitted and grimy. Like the porch, the hall was curiously devoid of furniture and effects. She could see empty spaces, lighter tiles, darker wallpaper, where furniture had been removed and pictures had been taken down. She pointed at them.

"Burglary?" Harris suggested.

Morrow looked at a six-foot-high square of brighter paper on the wall. A giant dresser had stood there for a long time. "They'd have needed a hell of a big van."

It caught her eye because it was clumsy: through the opening to the stairwell, lying against the wall, was a red mobile phone. It was a chunky, inelegant handful that lay comfortably on its side. It didn't match the velvet high heels in the hall.

"What is that? Her mother's phone?"

"That," smiled Harris, "is a taser disguised as a phone: 900,000 volts."

"They left it?"

He shrugged. "They left it or it was hers, we're not sure. They're available in the US." He nodded back to the suitcase. "She went there a lot, nearly once a month according to her passport."

Morrow was surprised. "The money coming from there?"

"She didn't seem to be going anywhere else."

The taser phone could have been left there by the intruder. Traceable objects left at the scene were sometimes hidden, fell under car seats, slid under heavy furniture, dropped down the side of settees but sometimes they were found in full view. Most people scanned a room as they left it, but in the heightened state of awareness after the commission of a crime people sometimes remembered to take their cigarette butts but forgot they'd left their car outside.

She stepped back and looked around the hall again, bringing her eye to the phone afresh. Very visible. It seemed unlikely that they dropped it and didn't spot it on the way out. All it would take was a backward glance. There was nothing in the hall to lose it behind. "I think it might be hers. Has there been a threat, a recent break-in?"

"I'll find out."

She filed it away, aware of the soothing sense of calm that came over her when she spotted an incongruity. She noted them and waited patiently for the meaning to make itself known. This looked complex and distracting, the sort of case she'd mull over in her bath, as she rubbed the baby oil on her belly at night, as she dodged calls from a psychologist assessing her rapist nephew. She warmed at the prospect, as others would in anticipation of a football match, a concert, a drunken night out. It was the promise of utter absorption.

Morrow approached the arch that led into the Victorian extension and a big room so light it was slightly dazzling after the darkness of the reception hall.

The forensic team were still processing the scene; she could see their shadows shifting on the wall, hear the crisp crumple of their paper suits around the corner.

She led Harris towards the body and felt him staying in her blind spot, trying to hide behind her. He was bracing himself for what he knew was coming up.

It was another large, empty room, this time papered in time-yellowed cream, veined with blue, speckled with birds faded

71

to an almost invisible pink. Turning the corner, they saw the edge of a white plastic stairlift chair folded flat against the banister at the bottom of a wide wooden stairwell. It was new, clean and the remote control was perched on the armrest, ready for use.

"Careful . . . ," muttered Harris behind her.

She was about to turn and reprimand him when she saw the woman's feet, far apart from one another, toenails painted scarlet. Morrow's weight shifted half an inch and, confronted with the full sight, she lost her breath. She had expected disgust, had defenses against that, but against sheer, suffocating pity she had nothing.

The woman had come down the stairs, in a hurry, holding the banister maybe. She must have fallen backwards and they killed her where she lay. Her legs had fallen open at the knees, the orchid of her genitals assaulted the eye. The neck was still intact, the rest of the body apparently untouched. It was a nice body. Slim brown legs, slender sun-kissed thighs.

But the worst of it for Morrow was that she had clearly not been positioned like that: her feet were uneven. Sarah Erroll had dropped there, died there and had been left. The killer had not looked at her, thought how to demean her and set her in a way that was undignified. They had left her there carelessly. Her vulnerability was unbearable. Morrow understood the distancing joke about her legs now: it was only a matter of time before the officers came to despise Sarah Erroll, as if she had chosen to be found like this, because the reality of it was too pitiful.

She stepped over, took a breath and tried to look at the injuries but she found herself examining the banister: delicate struts, deep warm wood. SOCOs were taking fibers from the dried pools of blood on the stairs, white-suited, their little boxes of kit, white plastic vanity cases, littering the steps.

Morrow tried again but her eye would not stay where she put it. It skitted off the face to the window high above the stairs, to a painting of a greyhound hung on the wall, to a bloody footprint on the stair next to her.

It was natural, she knew that: the need for order in a face. When injuries were this catastrophic there was nothing to anchor the gaze, no starting point for the human map. It took an act of will to force your eyes over it, a cold determination to orientate yourself.

She remembered a scene-of-crime photograph from a helicopter crash on a hillside on the Western Isles. The front of the chopper had been cut off so the pilot's body was clear and crisp in the picture when it was projected onto the cinema screen in the dark room in Tulliallan Police College. He was sitting upright, his right hand still resting easily on the throttle. She remembered the confusion she felt looking at that face: red but not bloody, no eyes, no lips but the teeth were there, a strangely shortened nose. She remembered the feeling of disorientation as her eyes slid around the picture until she suddenly saw Munch's *The Scream* hanging down at the pilot's side like a deflated balloon. His face had been sliced off by the rotor blades.

Morrow took a breath and forced herself to look at the red pulp at her feet, made her eyes stay out of respect for the woman, to set an example. The lobe of one of her ears had become detached and nestled under the shoulder, a fleshy comma, speckled pink.

It was easier to look at photographs back at the station, often more effective for finding patterns or traces, but the officers in the hall would see her looking closely at the woman, tell each other and it would set the tone. No nonsense, no hysterics, look straight at it and say what you see.

74

The effort of looking made her breathing shallow, her heart rate slow and the blood drain from her extremities. She was standing so still that the twins in her belly mistook horror for sleep and performed sinister somersaults around each other.

She was looking at a blunt-trauma split in the skin, feeling the babies dance a slow sensuous ballet in honor of the mess, when the flesh pulsed suddenly and Morrow lurched back, thinking the thing alive.

She looked up. A SOCO ghost stood at the top of the stairs, face obscured, eyes guilty. A door had been opened on the first landing and the light had shifted on the body.

It began as a nervous titter. Someone in the hall laughed and she looked around. Suddenly everyone in the hall was laughing, embarrassed in the circumstance, and the laughter became relief, a normalizing expressing of shock and disgust, puffed out in great hearty gusts, echoing around the hall and snaking up the stairs, punching through the oppressive silence in the old house.

Morrow tutted. "Calm down, for God's sake. As if you've never seen a bit of pudding before."

Six

Thomas was watching a wasp die on the window ledge when Goering came for him. The sun burned hot through the windows, a shaft of yellow like a pathway to heaven, lying low over the long lawn in front of the old house, burning in through the glass that gravity had warped and two hundred years had tinged yellow. The wasp was struggling to get onto its stomach, antennae writhing, the little comma body contracting, the essential shape of it the trap that killed it.

End of the wasp season.

They all died, it was natural. At this time of year, when the rain set in and their time had come, the wasps found their way into every room at the front of the old mansion house, through rotting window frames, burrowing under stones and through vents, making their way inside to die.

He watched the insect struggle and wondered whether they knew death was coming. Maybe they understood its inevitability and chose not to drown, but to curl up in the dry. Or maybe evolution afforded them the luxury of self-delusion, that they genuinely thought they could escape in here.

He watched the wasp contract like a small child over a tummy ache, curl up tight, still struggling, hoping for a future. Thomas wanted to get up and step over and use a ruler to flip it onto its side, give it another minute or so of delusion, a final sense of triumph before it died. But Beany was invigilating library time, his skinny limbs dangling from his long thin body, making sure their faces were pointed at the page they were supposed to be reading. That's as much as they could control you. Make you point your face at the front of the chapel, at the book, at the massive angry boy thundering towards you down the rugby pitch. But they couldn't control what you thought about it. Not unless you told someone else and they reported you.

Beany, thirty-something but still boyish, willowed between the tables in the library. He nodded at favorites, flicked fingers at the inattentive, making them pretend to read the books they had chosen. Library time. It said in the prospectus that it built a lifelong thirst for self-education. Lack of staff. It used up a small portion of the end-less study time they had. They only let them watch TV once a week and then it was in a giant hall with a hundred other boys and the TV tuned to such a fucking weak pro-gram that no one wanted to see it, *X Factor* or some shit.

Thomas liked this room. The library was in what would once have been the drawing room of the house. The ceiling was so high that the seven-foot-tall bookcases hardly made it halfway up the walls. Two enormous sash windows looked out over the lawn towards the trickle of a burn and the rolling Perthshire hills. A big vista. He liked to imagine he owned this house, that this was his drawing room, that everyone else would fuck off and he could do the cornicing justice, fix the windows and be alone.

It was pseudo Adams. The cornice plaster-ing had been repainted during the summer, different colors picking out the grapes and leaves. It was just like the estate's manage-ment to get it so wrong: the grapes were green and the leaves coiling around them yellow. Thomas imagined that they'd made a mistake at the beginning, started with the grapes and only realized their mistake when the pot of yellow came out. No one else seemed to have noticed.

The room was quiet, apart from the shuffle and fidget of boys, jumpers being pulled off, discreet sniffs. Pages fiddled with. Beany whispered *"stop that"* and everyone looked up to see Donald McDonald grinning. He'd been cleaning his nails on the edge of the pages again.

Abruptly, the big black door to the drawing room opened, not quietly, not creepingly careful, anxious not to interrupt, the way the library door was usually opened, but flung open so it bounced on its hinges. Hermann Goering caught the back bounce with the flat of his hand, intimidating the door to a dead stop. He filled the doorway. Everything about Goering was big and square, from his giant rugby shoulders to his oddly geometric head. Adamant black eyes scanned the room, stopping on Thomas.

"Anderson," he said and stepped back, staring straight at Thomas, ordering him to come.

Thomas stopped breathing. He fumbled his jumper, balling it into his satchel, shoving it in so that the arms hung out like spaghetti over the edge of a pasta pot. He turned to his books but Goering spoke again, louder this time: *"Leave it."*

"Yes, sir, Mr. Cooper."

Thomas blushed, not because he was embarrassed, just in a sort of panic. People didn't hate him the way they did some boys, though they had every reason to. It was because of his dad that three boys from their year had been forced to leave the school. Somehow, his old man being in the papers all the time had countered the shame of that, and he was a bit of a celebrity.

"Anderson." His voice was more commanding this time and Thomas jumped.

They called him Goering because he was Doyle's number two. Goering did nothing himself. Goering was here to take him to Doyle's office.

Realizing he was blushing, that he was being watched and looked a fool, Thomas stood up tall, looked around at his classmates and felt furious with them. Fuck them, he thought, they'd fucking hear about him and he didn't care. It was between his father and him, not them. He didn't even tuck his shirt in. He dropped the bag messily on its side, letting the books and folders tumble out, walked over to Goering without catching Beany's eye or asking. He just went.

Nosy, desperate to know, Beany followed him out but Goering cut him off at the door. "No," he said firmly. "Just Anderson."

And then gracefully dipping a meaty knee, he swept the door shut between Thomas and his classmates, listening for the big brass mechanism to click shut before standing and looking Thomas in the eye.

Until recently Thomas would not have thought that Goering knew him by name. All of the staff probably knew him by now. Probably read the papers out loud to one another in the staffroom, savoring the misfortune of the pupils.

"Thomas, Mr. Doyle would like to see you in his office."

Would like to. Not *Move.* Not *Get.* Thomas couldn't work out what it meant. Goering acting respectful was so unfamiliar he felt sure it was very, very bad. They'd found the car. They were angry. He and Squeak were being sent away.

The library door led into the central hall, an oval balcony above, roofed by a matching glass oval. It was freezing. Below, at the bottom of the stone steps, was the drafty front door, and the large double doors on either side of the hall channeled cold but still Thomas was sweating. He clenched his fists, telling himself he would unclench them when they went numb and that was something to think about, a different thing to think about other than how much trouble

81

he was in and what old man Doyle's face would look like when he stepped into the office and who would be with him. Squeak, probably, and police officers. His mother. Not Nanny Mary. Please God, not Mary.

Cooper pointed at Thomas's belly and half smiled. "You'd better tuck your shirt in. Don't want to get into trouble."

For a moment Thomas stared at him, flummoxed. He managed to unclench his hand and tuck the shirt front into his trousers, tucking the end of his tie in too. It was a style they had, a mark of defiance, untucked at the front, tie worn low, but Goering was telling him kindly to fix it instead of giving him a talk about civic responsibility and setting an example for the younger boys. He was being uncharacteristically kind, trying to soften his face, attempting a smile. It was eerie.

Before Thomas had a chance to look up and read his face again Goering had turned his back and was leading the way through the network of drafts to the chapel corridor that led to Doyle's office.

Thomas followed him, aware of his silly slouching walk that the other boys teased him about. Imagining himself seen by Doyle, he was aware of every error on his person, every problematic aspect of his appearance and manner.

They moved from the freezing hall, through a side hall, past the infirmary and the music room, passing into the mouth of the chapel corridor, a quiet area of dull lighting where talking and running were strictly forbidden. The corridor was long and windowless and smelled of stale benediction incense. The only door off it led to a choir balcony above the chapel, rarely used in case idiot boys threw each other off, saved for visiting parents on holy days of obligation.

Cooper's footfalls were quiet, regular. Thomas's leather soles shuffled and skipped to keep up. At the far end, through a double door set in an arch, stood Doyle's office door.

Goering knocked, heard a call and opened it in time for Thomas to arrive and be swept straight onto the nylon carpet. He hesitated, surprised to find himself in the office with no one but Doyle there. Doyle stood up to meet him. He had an impenetrable expression on his face: annoyance or distaste.

"Sit down please, Mr. Anderson."

Hypervigilant, watching for clues, Thomas sat down in the uncomfortably overstuffed chair. He was alarmed to find Doyle step out from behind his desk and come around behind, lowering himself into the chair next to him. Doyle was wiry, slim, hangdog face. Goering stood behind the desk, not sitting down, hands clasped behind his back.

Doyle leaned forward and softened his voice. Thomas heard him as if through a tunnel: something has happened. Athome. Andyourmotheraskedustotellyouaboutit-ourselves. Sosorry. Deadisyourfather. Hanging. Verysadsuiciding. Areyouallright. Thomasareyouallright?

But Thomas was stuck behind a gathering *bzzbzz* in his ears and eyes, a dulling of the lights as his lids lowered to shut out the room. End of the wasp season. Burrowing in out of the cold and the rain, their death callously witnessed by bored schoolboys. Boys watching as wasps thrashed and died.

Hanging. A hanging. A sudden bolt of empathy shocked him awake, imagining his father's body in the garage and how cold it would have been. "Is he dead?"

They looked at each other, Mr. Doyle and Hermann Goering.

Mr. Doyle said, "I'm afraid he is."

Thomas nodded over and over; so much it was as if he was confirming what Doyle had said: yes, you are correct, yes, yes, very correct. He couldn't seem to stop his head bobbing and he looked at the desk jumping in front of him, at the oak legs and the blotter and the pens in the school pen holder and the telephone. "She could have phoned . . . ?"

"Your mother?" asked Doyle.

Thomas didn't answer.

"Your mother thought it might be better coming from someone who was actually here, rather than on the phone, from her, at home . . ." He had that voice on, the one that told the boys not to mess with him or question him and just shut up or someone would be in trouble. She was wrong to do that, they all knew it was shoddy of her, but staff weren't allowed to speak against a parent. That was the whole point of the school, to do the parenting duties she couldn't be fucking bothered with.

" 'S . . . he's *dead?*"

"We had to tell you before you set off for home because the newspapers have got it and they'll be reporting it from this evening. Your mother is sending your father's airplane —"

"Which?"

Doyle was not used to being interrupted. "Which *what?*"

But Thomas was so angry he couldn't stop himself. "Which plane? It's the Piper, isn't it?"

85

Goering stepped in. "We don't know which of your father's planes she's sending for you but it will be at the airstrip in an hour. We'd like you to go to your room and pack a bag."

Weedy tears stung his eyes, spite-drizzle down his face. "It's the Piper. She's sent the Piper."

"Thomas." Goering had run out of sympathy and it told in the sharpness of his voice. "It doesn't matter which plane she's sent —"

Abruptly, Thomas slapped the wet off his face. He stood up and looked at the two men.

"My father came here," he said, looking down at them, not saying what he meant: when my father came here there were religious brothers running this school, monks ran this school, not just fucking teachers who couldn't get another job or work in industry actually making things and doing things. "You're teachers." And my father paid for the fucking extension to the sixth-form halls and the computer lab and you couldn't do that because you're just fucking teachers, so don't look down on me as a sad, lost fucking kid whose own fucking mother won't bother phoning and she's sending the fucking *Piper*. "Ella?"

86

"Your sister, Ella?" Doyle stood up to meet him.

"Ella? Does she know?"

"I believe that Ella is on her way home now too."

"In the ATR-42," said Thomas. "I believe she is on her way home in the ATR-42."

Doyle reached across and did something Thomas had never seen him do. He touched a boy, placed his hand on Thomas's shoulder. It felt warm, the heat prickling his skin. It felt threatening. Thomas expected Doyle to push him down and touch him and humiliate him. He flinched, shuddering out from under the hand. He looked at Doyle. The man had a kind, sad look on his face, seemed perplexed at Thomas pulling away.

"Sorry." Thomas'd got it wrong again. He didn't trust himself suddenly. "Sorry. Sorry."

"Don't worry," said Doyle, dropping his hand to his side.

Thomas lost himself in the carpet. He had tried to get his dad to look at him, to see him, but Lars rarely made eye contact. He had to look at the company prospectus to see his eyes. His father only spoke to him when they were standing up, looked over the top of Thomas's head and made pronouncements, not conversation: You are stupid; Business is a battle; Spread your bets; Never show weakness. Thomas had tried to get to him, past his mother and over Ella, through Mary, but nothing worked. Nothing. "When . . . did he die?"

"Your father?"

"Today?"

"Yesterday. At lunchtime."

Yesterday at lunchtime, when Thomas was in the refectory eating spongy white bread saturated with golden syrup, when Thomas was drinking a pint of brown tea and looking over the rim to Squeak, holding his eye too long so that he knew to come to his room after lunch. He asked Squeak because he had a car. He thought he knew Squeak but he didn't. They had soup with carrots in. Stock cube clumps at the bottom of the serving dish.

"Mr. Cooper will take you to your room and help you pack."

Thomas stood straight and remembered himself. "Thank you. Both. For telling me. It cannot have been easy for you."

They liked that a lot, not so much that he had remembered his manners in such a fraught moment but that he was making it easier for them. Doyle smiled kindly. Goering nodded and pressed his lips together tight, sympathetic. They stood for a moment in the stillness, the clock on the wall ticking softly, counting down their allotted seconds on earth, and then Doyle shifted his weight. He moved towards the door and Thomas turned with him. Doyle stopped in front of him.

"Thomas," he said, uncertainly, and Thomas had the feeling that he was talking off the cuff, "we are very sorry for your recent troubles. We know how difficult things have been for you but rest assured, whatever happens, you will finish your education at this school. Grants are available and we can make inquiries into replacing the funding so that you can stay here."

Goering almost expressed an idea. One of his eyebrows bobbed a fraction. Doyle ground his teeth and looked through Thomas. They were all thinking the same thing.

"That's very kind of you, Mr. Doyle," Thomas spoke carefully, "but I think it would be inappropriate when the collapse of my father's business has been the cause of several other boys having to leave the school. It would be . . . unfair."

Goering agreed with him, he could see that. Doyle accepted it graciously. "We don't hold our boys liable for the sins of their fathers, Thomas. God forbid. Your behavior here has been exemplary."

Thomas looked at him. Doyle believed that. He actually believed that he knew anything about him. Thomas opened his mouth to speak and a sob barked out of him. He clamped his hand over his mouth but the sudden sound was like a shout, a bark, a howl. He pressed his fingers into his cheeks, pushed hard, cramming it all back in again as his mouth flecked spittle and let off little screams. He caught his breath and held it.

They stood, frozen, until it passed. Cautiously, Thomas took his hands away.

"Sorry," he said. "About . . ."

Doyle tilted his head sympathetically but Goering stepped in. "We should go and pack."

Thomas shuffled towards the door, slipped back into the dull gleam of the chapel corridor and a world forever changed.

SEVEN

Morrow and Harris stepped carefully past the body as they made their way upstairs. The splatter was everywhere, shoe prints, crisp and bloody, like a child's stamper set.

The staircase was straight and wide, carved from beautiful wood, fitted to the wall.

The steps themselves were wide and deep, Morrow's size fives could have fitted twice on the tread. These were not stairs to hurry down, they were for sauntering. The carpet was well fixed to the back by rods and the pile was thick, rugged enough to exclude a slip at the bottom and a head injury on the banister. If the woman had died from an accidental head injury and the intruder then mutilated the body, they'd be looking at a different charge, for a different kind of man altogether.

When she got to the top of the stairs she looked back down. The body was almost hidden behind the fat newel end, just the bare knees visible. Despite the paper shuffle of the forensics guys and the muttering of the coppers, she felt an ache of quiet, a throb of history pressing the house inwards. This was not a house many young women would live in alone if they had a choice. Too big, too old, too heavy.

At the head of the stairs, between two doors, sat a small table with a series of silver framed photographs propped up on it, crowding each other: a program for a play with a cast of three. An elderly man and slightly younger wife at weddings, in gardens, on a boat. There was only one young person in the play: she was seen once as a girl and once again as a young woman.

As a girl she smiled miserably in a pink dress with a tight orange cummerbund.

As a woman she was slim and tall, statuesque, but not pretty. Her jaw was weak, her nose squint at the tip, her eyes small. She stood outside on a sunny day, possibly on the steps in front of this house, holding a glass of piss-yellow wine, smiling awkwardly. From the chic jacket and shoes in the porch, Morrow guessed it wouldn't have been Sarah's favorite picture of herself and she thought it telling that the unflattering photo had been chosen by her family to represent her.

She turned to the SOCO and found him staring at a small green object on the floor. A leather cube with three heavy duty zips across the top, each with a distinctive green leather tag on it: one with a silver hoop, one with a big square stud, one a riveted hole. On the front, punched into the leather, a large D&G logo. It was a purse, open and empty, discarded on the hall floor.

"Dust it?" she asked and caught herself. "You have, I know, just running through . . ." He nodded, appreciative. "It's empty?"

"Aye."

She gestured to Harris. "Cards?"

"Phoned in," he said. "They haven't been used."

Morrow frowned. "Don't think this is about money, somehow."

"Aye, too much." Harris wrinkled his nose and nodded back downstairs at the bloody body.

Together they turned towards the bedroom door. A rosy pink glow came from inside. The door was ajar and she pushed it open from the hinges, avoiding possible sites of fingerprints.

The oval room was low and cozy. Small windows sat all around the curve, white wooden shutters closed, pink flowery wall-paper and a tiny white fireplace with a black iron grating. Across from it was a rumpled double bed, a luxurious white duvet thrown back. The air felt thick in the room, as if someone had been sleeping in here moments before and had sucked all of the oxygen out.

On the floor lay a dropped-and-stepped-out-of black dress with a racer back. A pair of shocking-pink lacy underpants with a pale blue ribbon threaded around the waist, the legs perfect circles where they had slipped down perfect thighs.

This woman made no sense in this house. She looked at Harris and he shook his head, bewildered too, but also slightly enchanted by the prettiness of the underpants.

"Those're . . . kind of whory, aren't they?"

"What," she said, "the knickers?"

"Aye. Could give the wrong impression." He couldn't seem to take his eyes off them. "Or not."

Morrow looked at them. She had knickers a bit like that, she wore them to cheer herself up on grim days, give a kick to her walk when she felt beleaguered. "You thinking she was . . ." She couldn't think of the word for prostitute now. Prostitute was wrong, sex worker was wrong too, for some reason. Frustrated, she pointed at the knickers. "Working?"

He stared hard at the pants, his eyes circling the thighs. "Maybe. Maybe where the money comes from?"

She looked at the jolly knickers again. "Lots of women wear cheeky pants to cheer themselves up."

Harris blushed, looked quickly away from the pants on the floor. "OK, ma'am."

She had hinted at her own underwear habits, breaking the sexless rule of the force. Wrong. It might have been hormonal, it could have been the realization of how stupid it was that she couldn't share an insight about underwear without causing an incident, but she smiled quietly where before she'd have been angry at herself for getting it wrong. "Or they might have been the only clean pants in the place. Could be a few things, is what I mean."

Harris nodded and looked nervously around the room, willing her to move on. She liked Harris, but he did seem to put a sexual connotation on everything possible. She couldn't work out if he was very repressed or had a crippling libido.

Turning back to the bed, she could see the twist on the sheet where a bottom had turned to the side and feet had dropped to the floor. She looked at the duvet. The cover was very clean and expensive. As she looked at it, wondering whether it was one of those high-count linens and what the count was actually of, she spotted a dull silver glint in among the folds. She stepped forwards, pinched the edge of the cover and pulled it back. A mobile phone, silver backed, broad but slim, lay face down on the bed.

"iPhone," smiled Harris. "That'll have her whole life on it."

Morrow frowned at the silver. "I thought they were black or white?"

"It's an original." He pulled out a plastic bag for it, thought better of it and called in the SOCOs to fingerprint it first.

As they busied themselves dusting the phone, Morrow looked down at the handbag on the floor. Again, good leather, good deep mustard color, quirky design with big zips and slightly outsized fastenings. Morrow bent down awkwardly and flicked the top of the bag open with her pen. A set of keys sat at the bottom: four keys clustered around a simple silver hoop. She was pleased to see shop receipts littering the bag. Most tills printed the time and date and their shop address. They'd be able to retrace Sarah's movements from them.

Morrow stood up and watched as they

dusted the iPhone carefully, flicking black dust all over the white linen.

She looked back at the door to the room, thought her way down the stairs to the porch and imagined Sarah Erroll coming into an empty house. Her face was a hazy cloud of blood, her body slim and lithe in the fitted black dress.

Sarah left the suitcase by the wall, dropped her keys into the mustard bag and pulled her shoes off by the heel. Morrow imagined the gentle *pwup* as the hard heels fell to the tiled floor. She saw Sarah reaching into the baggy handbag, feeling around the rubble in the bottom for the taser phone, stepping across the hall to drop it carelessly by the other wall. Or stand at the top of the stairs and throw it down.

Morrow started again with the taser: it was near the site of her death. She'd been going for it or someone else had it and dropped it there. It could have been in her handbag and someone had taken it, thought better of it and dropped it on the way out. "Check the taser for prints."

"Aye."

"Check it for fiber traces too," she said. "See if it came out of this bag."

She saw the faceless woman drop her shoes and climb the stairs, imagined the aches and strains of sitting on an airplane for seven hours, imagined her pleasure at taking off the lacy underpants, pulling on a T-shirt and being swallowed by the big bed.

They walked back downstairs, holding the wall as they stepped carefully past the body. Harris was in front this time and she saw him actually look straight at the mess for a moment, not flinching, and hoped it was because of her example. He tiptoed between the red footsteps and stopped at the bottom, holding out a hand to help her. She brushed his hand away.

"Shoe prints?"

"Aye," he said. "Found black fibers in them, probably made of suede."

Harris tipped his head and looked back up as Morrow came to stand by him. The footsteps were a mess of red, smeared over steps, some crisp prints, some spaces where the deep green carpet showed through.

"They about a size eight?" said Morrow.

They looked for a moment, angling their heads, stepping one way and another to discern a pattern.

Finally Harris said, "Two sets?"

"Is it?" She stepped over to where he was standing and saw a perfect print next to another, both right feet, one bigger than the other but the same sole markings. "God, you're right. *Shit.*"

Two was bad. If there were two it wasn't enough to show that they'd been there and been splattered with blood. It meant they would have to show a jury that each of the co-conspirators had been actively committing the violence. They'd have to charge them with conspiracy to commit murder, which had a lesser tariff. It was unsatisfying, especially if one of them had been standing at the side shouting at the other one to stop. If the defense could plant a doubt they could both walk. Morrow felt it reduced the process to trial by combat: that the stand-off was usually won by the stronger party, not the innocent one. The best they could hope for was physical evidence that proved the case.

She squinted at the footsteps again. "Shit. They're the same. We need to find something, marks on the sole or something."

"They're the same though, is it a uniform?" said Harris.

"Mibbi." She waved at the stairs. "Can we break these steps down, reconstruct the movements? Take out the interview roulette."

"Dunno. I'll ask."

Morrow shook her head and looked closer. Both sets of soles had the same pattern on them: three circles on the pressure points and straight stripes leading towards them. "Can we trace those soles?"

Harris didn't seem convinced. "We can ask in shoe shops."

"Let's see the cash."

He led her past the body, turning away from the main hall, taking her through a small door and down a step to the kitchen. A cast-iron cooking range sat in a chimney breast. The room was cold because the walls and roof were solid concrete and the back window long and wide, looking out onto a tangle of naked bushes.

A white-suited scene-of-crime officer was shuffling around, picking fibers off the window sill and the sink and bagging them up. Gobby was parked in a corner, staying out of the way. He greeted her with a silent nod, keeping his eyes steady on the table.

"Right, Gobby?"

He didn't say anything. Gobby didn't talk much.

Morrow looked around the kitchen.

It was a large room, bigger than they would build now but not at all grand. Tired red linoleum covered the floor, rips carefully mended with silver electrical tape. The units were workaday as well: a solid pine dresser, painted white but badly chipped, one of the glass panels mended with the same silver electrical tape: another job for another day. An old-fashioned fridge gave off a hard, high whir. The cooker was unimposing and electric, immaculate but the glass cover slightly dusty. No one cooked in here. The center of the room was occupied by an old teak kitchen table, cup-stained and knife-sliced, a seam across the middle where it could be extended. A smattering of chairs were pushed up tight against it except at the sink side where they had been pulled out.

Harris gave a dry cough behind her. She turned to see him nodding a gentle warning at a corner of the room.

She hadn't seen him there, the man sitting in an armchair by the range, hugging his briefcase and facing into a corner. He was young, in his thirties, but dressed old in a dark pinstripe with a mustard waistcoat and red tie. His body was formless, flattered by the clothes but still portly, and his face was round too, his eyes wide and watchful of her.

"Hello," she said.

He stood up quickly, stepped across to her and held his hand out, leaning hard towards her, as if he was hanging over a cliff and wanted her to pull him up. "Donald Scott."

She took his hand and shook it. "DS Alex Morrow. You've had a shock."

He panted a yes, glancing to the hall, to the table, back to her, pumping her hand, holding tight.

"You knew the victim?"

"Yes, yes. Yes." He considered the question and added, "Yes?"

"You were her solicitor?"

"Mmm." He looked wildly around the kitchen, panting, building up to an outburst of emotion that they didn't need. Morrow took charge. "OK, we're going to take you to the station and speak to you there. When you get there I want you to have some biscuits, something with sugar in it, for the shock. Understand?" She wasn't sure sugar did help with shock but knew that giving people a task did, something to focus on, a small thing to achieve. "Understand?"

"Yes." But he was staring over her shoulder to the doorway, afraid they were going to make him go out that way, pass the body again.

"Out the back," she told Harris.

Harris led the man out by the elbow, careful that he didn't stagger on top of anything important, pulling the back door shut behind him.

Everyone in the kitchen relaxed, coming out of character. The raw horror of an outsider shamed them into reverence. It was uncomfortable, it reminded them how scarred they all were. Morrow rolled her head back to relieve the tension in her neck. Her shoulders had been creeping up to her ears since she turned the corner and saw the mess at the foot of the stairs.

She looked around. A window above the sink had been jimmied open crudely, bending the metal outwards at the fastening, and it had been left hanging open. Not a professional job. Not even a careful job. A housebreaker with any experience would attempt to cover the mess and make it look as if the window was shut once they were in. Outside in the overgrown garden, she could see the top of a copper's head, checking below the window for footprints. It was one of the benefits of having coppers who weren't seeking promotion: they were brighter than the left-behinds used to be, thought of things before they were told to.

She took a breath and stood back against the wall, taking in the room and imagining the path of the intruders: through the window, over the metal sink and draining board, clamber down to the ground. If they knew the house they'd go straight to the hallway but the pantry door was ajar, and next to it a door sat open into a shallow utility room with the washing machine, dryer and rusting mangle. Across the room another door sat open into a deep-shelved cupboard full of tins.

Morrow approached the pantry and stood in front of the doorway. A cold room for keeping food in before the advent of refrigeration. She could feel a bitter draft licking her ankles. The person who lived here would take care to keep that door shut. The intruder had been looking for the door out of the kitchen.

On the worktop near the cooker an old radio had been unplugged from the wall, a flex dangling over the edge of the worktop, not sitting under the wall socket the way someone who was about to plug it back in might leave it. The radio had been on, they'd turned it off to orientate themselves.

"Dust that plug," she said to the SOCO.

As if aggrieved, she turned to Gobby and demanded, "Where is it, then?"

He grinned and pointed to the table.

Morrow looked at it. "Under?"

"Aye."

"Shit." Morrow looked at the table, planning her route. Her body was changing so quickly every new position was an experiment.

She asked the SOCO, "Is it all right . . . ?" She put her hand out to the table top, asking if she could lean on it.

"No, better just . . ." He held out his own hand and Morrow reluctantly took it, leaned on him heavily as she got down first onto one knee and then onto the other. She couldn't bend to the side without her ribs digging into the babies: she had to go down on all fours and peer up like a dog asking for a biscuit.

She didn't think it could get more humiliating but then Harris came back into the kitchen — she could see his feet behind her.

At first the beam of light from her torch caught a slab of roughly cut plywood. It was sitting on the two struts of the table legs, balanced there, looking like a shoddy repair job. But she saw something on top of it, sandwiched between the top of the table and the rough wooden plank, pink as a flesh wound.

"Let's get that out."

She shuffled back up onto her feet as Gobby and Harris stepped forward and bent down, taking an end of the plank each, sliding it out so that Harris could hold one end until Gobby came around and helped him. It was heavy and they worked hard not to tip it or move the money around.

They sat it on a worktop OK'd by the SOCO and looked at it. Morrow smiled: purple and purple and purple, like a patchwork quilt, the blocks of notes next to each other echoing the pattern over and over.

The money had been laid out carefully in the middle of the plank. Sarah must have set it out before sliding it under there but Morrow could see that the bundles around the edge were messy, as if Sarah had developed the habit of kneeling down and shoving the bundles in as she got them, fitting them in blind.

A great purple delicious flurry of money. Morrow realized that her mouth was hanging open, she was salivating. The currency being unfamiliar made it seem infinite, how money looks to a child, and the notes were large, almost the size of a paperback book.

"You," she barked at no one in particular, "who's keeping the book on this?"

Gobby grinned. "No one yet."

Morrow looked along the plank. It was four feet long, the bricks neatly stacked in six rows, eight columns long. She tried to work out how much was there, to remember how many zeros there were in a million.

"Gobby, you're not getting paid to just

stand here. Start the book and put me down for a tenner."

"What's your guess?"

"Could be nearly a million."

Gobby licked his pencil tip. "Is that in euros or quid?"

Harris was suddenly animated. "Let's make it the value in sterling, the exchange value on the day we get the count."

Morrow nodded. "Yeah, I'm changing mine then: make it seven hundred and fifty thousand quid."

Gobby jotted it on a receipt he had pulled out of his pocket and Harris watched. "Yeah, put me down for six fifty at a tenner."

Gobby frowned at the plank. "Right, I'll take the bald seven."

"Yeah, yeah, good, OK," Harris was smiling. "How soon will the count be?"

She had never seen Harris so abruptly animated before and knew the look of a gambler. "Probably tomorrow."

"Tomorrow, right." Harris nodded to Gobby. "See who else is up for it, yeah?"

Gobby had noticed as well. "You're not having a Gamblers Anonymous slip here, are ye?"

Harris flushed a little. "Don't know what you're on about."

Gobby grinned as if he'd found a cat to torture.

The sight of the cash had been so distracting that Morrow had to start from the beginning again: they came in through the window, over the draining board, checking the different doors. The doors all looked the same size, all blank paneled on the back, a sixties improvement to the doors in old houses to stop them gathering dust, make them more hygienic. They'd tugged the plug of the radio out and listened, hadn't seen the money —

"Ma'am." It was Tamsin Leonard at the back door. "DCI Bannerman —" She held out the phone and Morrow heard Harris give a dismissive little grunt at the name.

Morrow turned and gave him a reproving look, making him cast his eyes down. Gobby raised his eyebrows innocently, as if it was nothing to do with him.

Slowly, she took the mobile from Leonard's hand. "Sir?"

"What's going on over there?"

"One dead householder, stacks of cash hidden in the kitchen. Lots of oddities about it —"

"Like what, like what?" He sounded excited. He wouldn't have sounded like that if he'd seen the woman at the bottom of the stairs.

"Face smashed in, obliterated really, clumsy break-in, not professional at all —"

"Someone who knew her, then." It was obvious. Detection 101, obliterating facial injuries usually meant the assailant was known to the victim, but Bannerman wasn't showing off to her, he was using her to rehearse his conclusions for the bosses.

"Well . . ." She watched Harris order Leonard to make a bet on the tally, explaining the rules of currency exchange. Leonard seemed reluctant. "Still piecing it together really."

"Sex murder, then?"

"Still gathering evidence, sir." She liked the idea that he'd be jealous of her, being there, seeing. "There's a shitload of money. Cash. In euros. I don't know if it's real or not but we need an armored car to come over here and take it away."

"How much?" He sounded disinterested, implying that a lot of money to her might not be a lot of money to him.

She could already see Bannerman at the photo op with a table full of purple money, looking solemn but handsome. "I don't really trust my maths, sir. Are there six zeros in a million?"

"I'm coming. I'm bringing an armored." And he hung up.

"Goodbye," Morrow said to no one, out of habit. She was a bit dazed herself. She handed the phone back to the copper and caught Harris's eye, holding it steady as she gave him the news. "Bannerman's coming."

"Fine. Fine by me," he said, keeping his face neutral. "Is he a betting man?"

EIGHT

Goering loomed over Thomas's shoulder as they walked the dark corridors to the residents' block. He stayed in Thomas's blind spot, his face a soupy blur, down dark corridors, into a part of the building forbidden to the boys during school hours. His presence was well meant but a portent of disaster, like a bodyguard.

Thomas tried not to think, just to walk, one foot, then the next, open a door, one foot, then his father hanging from a beam, then a woman's vagina and scarlet blood splashing onto Squeak's shin, turn the corner, open the fire doors, a heel crushing a nose, the bleached white cartilage and scarlet freckles. He wanted to stop and concentrate on breathing, to get into a scorching bath and slough off the oily slick, but he kept thinking of Stander. Stander in the showers, not of his erection but his face, young, spotty, dismayed. One moment of weakness stamped onto you forever. Thomas should just get home. Swallow it down and not think until he got home.

A connecting corridor to the dorms, a long cold strip of concrete floor with windows on either side. Glancing up he saw into the science labs, a group of boys in safety glasses gathered around Mr. Halshall. A face looking at him, mouth open, eyes warped by the thick plastic lens. Toby was in the year below them but he was an altar boy with Squeak. Toby's magnified eyes strayed behind Thomas to Goering: it must have looked as if Thomas was being frog-marched to his dormy.

He walked through the fire doors, punched in the code to the security door and onto the nylon carpet that sparked against slipper soles in the dark. Up three stairs, past four bedroom doors to his own room. He opened the door.

It smelled funny. He always got a waft of it when he opened the door and he was aware that it was his own smell, the smell of his body and his hair and his habits. He usually liked it but now that Goering was here he was suddenly conscious that it was disgusting and pathetic. The cleaner hadn't been yet so his bin was full of wipes and they looked like tissues he'd been wanking into. He glanced back as he walked in and snapped on the light. Goering had no expression on his face but he knew he was taking it all in.

"Just the basics, Thomas. The plane will be ready to take off in half an hour."

Goering held the door open, fitting the rubber doorstop under it. School rules: the door was to be left open if more than one person was in a bedroom. Failure to comply meant instant suspension and it applied to staff and pupils. They were always watching.

The room was tidy, the bed was made, nothing was out that shouldn't have been and yet Thomas felt naked. He pulled out his desk chair and stood on it, reaching up to the top of the cupboard, yanking at the canvas handle of his duffel bag and dragging it over the edge, pulling a shower of dust on himself. He stepped down and threw it on the bed.

Goering leaned over and undid the zip, quite tenderly, sitting the bag open as Thomas watched. Thomas looked at him and Goering almost smiled.

"Now you can just put your stuff straight in," he said.

Suddenly Thomas couldn't remember what they were doing here, or what the stuff was or why the dormy was so quiet. He looked at Goering for guidance.

"Get your underwear from your drawer."

Thomas did as he was told and Goering pointed him at the bag. He put in the pile of pants and vests, still stiff from the laundry, still with their scratchy ironed-on identification tags on the front.

"Now toiletries."

The bathroom was at the foot of the short boxy bed. Thomas opened the door, felt for the light switch and found himself startled by a blaze of white light from the bare light bulb above, as if he had woken in the dark, come in for a pee and blinded himself. He shut his eyes and opened them to the mirror. An angry kid with wide eyes, flushed. Vulnerable, Stander. He hadn't been able to look at himself this morning. It wasn't psychological, it was a physical inability to raise his head and look at himself. But now Lars was dead and he was looking at himself. He blinked, looked again and found his stance improved: harder, cold, mouth tight, better.

"Toiletries." The edge was back in Goering's voice.

Thomas reached forward and grabbed his toothbrush, his soap, his spot cream, the inhaler he never used. He walked out of the toilet and dropped them into his bag.

"Books?"

"No," said Thomas firmly.

Goering was surprised by the change in him. "Games? Address book?"

"No."

Goering hesitated. "OK. You have a look around and see if you want to take anything else with you. I'll go and get your mobile phone from the housekeeper." He stepped out of the room, taking out his own phone, walking off down the corridor with a little tinny ring tone sounding from it. He was calling ahead, calling a car, making some arrangement. Thomas wished he hadn't gone. The fire door slapped shut behind him and Thomas was left alone in the hissing quiet. He looked at his bag. Jumpers.

His home clothes were in the wardrobe. He heard his father's voice angrily ordering him to put his home clothes on. Thomas stood still, staring at the floor. Lars had killed himself. He couldn't give orders to anyone anymore.

Thomas looked up at the window and his throat let out a tiny squeal of joy.

Across the gray concrete forecourt, in the gathering dark, stood Squeak. Thomas had his eager hand on the window before his eyes adjusted and he saw Squeak properly, the stern look on his face, the clenched fists at his sides.

Squeak must be between classes. He'd have skipped off from the crowd of boys meandering slowly through the school, he'd be late but say he'd gone somewhere for something, wouldn't be missed. He must have heard that Thomas had been taken out of Library. That was all he knew, Thomas had been frogmarched out of Library and Goering took him to the dormy. He must be shitting himself.

Without a signal, Squeak bent over, running but keeping below the windows of the long corridor, his fingers touching the ground, galloping on all fours like a gangly monkey. He skirted the building, keeping low until he reached Thomas's window.

Thomas saw Squeak's crown appear at the edge of the rectangle of light on the concrete, stop, look up. Thomas broke eye contact immediately but reached over to the window latch, unscrewing the lock and swinging it open as little as possible, flicking the lock on to let Squeak know he couldn't come in.

"Goering about."

He reached under the sill to the books on the shelf and lifted them out, putting them on the sill and separating them into two

116

random piles, pretending to choose between them.

Thomas and Squeak spoke then, simultaneously, in the same mumbled undertone. "My dad hung himself and I'm going home." "I won't tell what you did to her."

Shocked, Thomas looked up.

Squeak was on all fours below the window, leaning on his fingertips, looking up at him, a dog ready to spring. His lips were damp and slightly parted. He looked as if he was smiling.

Squeak was a complete stranger to him. Thomas knew him as well as he would ever know another human being and yet he didn't know him at all.

Now Thomas stood with a book in each hand, poised over the meaningless piles of meaningless books and looked down at the corner of the window. Staying out of the rectangle of light from Thomas's room, Squeak craned his neck up and met his eye.

Thomas looked out and saw the dog that he was bonded to, wet-lipped and smiling up at him out of the dark.

NINE

Kay was almost finished. She was catching up on the twice-a-year jobs, the washing and buffing of glassware that was never used. To her almost certain knowledge Mrs. Thalaine hadn't touched these wee red vases in three years. But she'd been given them by one of the kids, and she liked them. Kay pressed them down into the hot water and watched the grease lift and the sheen return to the glass. Her hands were pink to the wrists. She smiled at the steam settling on her face like artificial perspiration, cooling her down before her body had time to respond to the need.

The doorbell rang all the way across the house. Kay turned to see who it was. The kitchen window looked out onto the courtyard and the front door.

A man and a woman stood looking at the door. Both in suits, but not sorry the way salesmen were. They looked confident, weren't swinging their briefcases nervously or letting off weak practice-smiles.

Mrs. Thalaine's lady-trot clip-clop hurried to the hall followed by the sound of her unlocking and opening the door. Kay turned back to the sink and her washing, taking the vases out, putting them on the draining board, her meditation broken by curiosity. She craned to hear the muted conversation in the hall.

The man and woman introduced themselves. Kay couldn't hear the details but Mrs. Thalaine mumbled some questions and then she heard footsteps coming this way. She resented it because she still had bits to do and then she'd promised herself a smoke and a sit on the bench before she moved on to the Campbells'.

Margery Thalaine sounded nervous, her voice high and a little shaky. Whoever they were, if they were hassly salesmen, she would surely know to bring them into Kay so she could tell them to fuck off. They came to this area every so often because of all the money and the polite old people. It took the staff to tell them where to go.

Sure enough, steps through the hall, low voices making conversation but now Mrs. Thalaine quite chatty, not sounding irritated the way she did when she was being made

119

to do something she didn't want to.

A pause outside the door and then it opened. Mrs. Thalaine stood there for a moment, the suits behind her, and Kay read her face for clues. Calm. A little excited. She wasn't supposed to get excited.

"Kay? These are the police."

At that Kay turned towards them, looked them up and down, getting their measure. The man looked back at her arrogantly, tipping his nose up, squaring up to her. The woman leaned forward and held her hand out.

"I'm DC Leonard."

Kay would not shake hands with a police officer. She held her hands up, wet. The female dropped her hand. Kay didn't respect many people and the police were low on her count.

Her wet hands dripped suds onto the floor she had just cleaned. Another thing to do. "You want me to . . ." She sounded cross, she knew she did, and she didn't want to upset Mrs. Thalaine.

Mrs. Thalaine smiled weakly. "If you wouldn't mind . . ."

Kay dried her hands, knowing she looked cross and promising herself she'd come back and explain on her way to the bus stop, that she didn't like the police or trust them, that she'd had trouble with them.

She softened her voice. "Well, I'll just leave it there today, if that's all right with you."

Mrs. Thalaine's chin twitched anxiously so Kay touched her forearm as she passed on her way to the door, letting her know she wasn't angry with her.

"Actually," Kay turned back at the sound of Margery's voice and saw that she had been comforted, "could you take the recycling with you?"

Suddenly angry, Kay pinched her mouth. "Can't you take it round yourself, Margery?"

Margery pinched her mouth back. She didn't like Kay calling her by her first name in front of visitors. They looked hard at each other for a moment until Margery broke off and sat down on one of the kitchen chairs. "I'd rather you took it."

Kay left the room and slammed the door behind her. She stomped through the long living room. Bright sun streamed in the long wall of small windows, hitting her pupils like a series of slaps.

She opened the door to the hall cupboard. There was the bag she had set out nicely for Margery: a bag for life, Waitrose, to take the poor look off her. Kay had set it there for her, near the door, handles up, ready to go.

Kay always arrived half an hour early, thirty minutes that she insisted she didn't get paid for, just to listen to Margery moan and weep because she was lonely and so much had gone wrong and she couldn't talk about her worries to her clubhouse ladies because none of them ever admitted to having troubles. And this morning over those stupid wee cups of tea that wouldn't wet a mouse's tongue, it took her twenty minutes to get Margery to promise she would leave the house at least once a day, and today's expedition was to the recycling bins a hundred yards away.

Kay felt foolish and tricked, as if all the intimacy they had shared meant nothing, as if she had been kicked back into her place. But her sadness was too deep and she knew it was really about Joy. She didn't love Margery. She was trying to replace Joy, that soft, kind intimacy, sometimes mother, sometimes child. Looking at the bag of recycling, she remembered a tiny withered hand touching her forearm. She had to clear her throat to chase the tears.

She glared at the bottles in the dark cupboard, called them bastards under her breath, cursed herself for being a mug. She turned and looked out of a living room window into the kitchen.

Through the French windows she could see the policewoman filling out a form on a clipboard. It'd be some neighborhood snoop scheme. Margery could run it, she could invite all her phony fucking pals into her house and feed them Markie's biscuits and daft wee sandwiches and pretend that she wasn't flat and fucking stony broke or scared to leave the house, that she didn't wake up in the night and listen for her husband's breathing just to make sure he wasn't dead.

Kay took her coat down from the peg and threw it on. She took her handbag and slung the strap over her head, lifted the Waitrose bag and her own poly bag and then realized she needed the loo. She slammed the cupboard door, put the bags down in the hall and went into the bathroom.

Washing her hands, she looked at herself in the mirror. Her roots were showing. She could see specks of gray. She looked more than tired; she looked defeated. She stepped back, turned to the side slightly so the harsh daylight wasn't on her. Holding her eye in the mirror, she smiled softly and liked what she saw.

"I'm nice," she whispered, thinking about

listening to Margery's complaints. She nodded, knew she was right. "The gift's to the giver."

Becalmed, she unrolled some toilet paper and wiped the watery splashes off the basin, buffing it to a shine, threw the paper in the toilet, flushed it and walked out to the hall, picking up the bags on her way out.

She knew Mrs. Thalaine would see her walking away from the door, stepping awkwardly across the badly spaced paving-stone path set into perfectly raked white gravel chips. Kay didn't look back but thought to herself that she should go home and get the photos of Joy out and she wasn't going to kid herself anymore. She wouldn't come early tomorrow. She'd come on time. And she decided to buy a hair dye on the way home and maybe some cream for her hands.

She kept her head high until she was sure she was out of view of the kitchen window and then she reached into her handbag for her cigarettes, lit one and sauntered around the corner, enjoying it, knowing she was early for the Campbells and needn't hurry.

It was breezy, rain threatening, too windy for an outdoor smoke to taste pleasant but she enjoyed it anyway because it was her time. That's all she got for herself nowadays, the spaces in between, but it was enough for her.

The wheelie bins and recycle point was a source of much local dispute. No one wanted to see the bins or have them near their house. A compromise had been reached. A space the length of two cars had been tarmacked and surrounded by high box hedging. It always made Kay smile, the prudishness of it, as if they were ashamed of needing to use a bin. It was a natural windbreak. She leaned into the cushioned hedge and took another draw on her cigarette. It was a nice one. She felt the anger at Margery sucked deep down into her lungs and dissipate through her stomach.

The sound of a car engine came over the hedge so she dragged one last draw, a nasty scratchy one, and dropped the cigarette on the ground, crushing it with her heel and stepping away from it. There had been complaints about cigarette butts left by the bins. Picking up the Waitrose bag for life she thought "fuck Margery," lifted the lid for the household rubbish and threw it in just as the car came past.

The car stopped behind her and she turned to it, expecting to be ticked off by a local for dropping her smoke there, but it was the police from Margery's.

The male officer was driving. He rolled down his window, a stupid big grin on his face, and he was nodding slowly as if she was a bit simple.

"Should that not have gone in the recycling?"

The grin was big, open-mouthed, she could see his tongue twitch and glint inside.

"If she cares so much about the environment she can bring it back herself," said Kay sullenly.

Undeterred, he carried on grinning and talking slowly, his accent muted as if she wouldn't understand. "Do you not care about the environment?"

She saw his eye stray to her tits and that he wasn't even respectful enough to be embarrassed when he saw that she had noticed. She folded her arms over them.

"Did you just stop here to blind me with your wit, or was there something I could help you with?"

Scolded, he slunk back in his seat. The woman officer who had tried to shake hands with her leaned over to the window. "You Kay Murray?"

"Yeah."

"You used to work up at Glenarvon?"

"Sure, up until a couple of months ago when Mrs. Erroll died."

"Could you come up and tell us if anything's been taken?"

"Was it burgled?"

"We don't know. We don't know if anything's missing."

Kay frowned. "Ask Sarah Erroll. She's home, I think."

"I'm afraid Sarah Erroll was killed last night during a break-in. Mrs. Thalaine said that Sarah was selling off items of furniture and crockery and stuff but we don't know if the intruder took anything. Could you come up and tell us if you think anything's missing?"

"Killed? Sarah? In the house?" Kay was aware that she was slurring.

"Oh." The woman seemed to realize suddenly that Kay was upset by the news. "I'm afraid so, sorry for telling you like that . . ."

"Who's killed her?"

The man wasn't grinning now. "That's what we're trying to find out."

"She's twenty-four . . ." Kay was calculating the difference in ages with her own kids, eight years between her and Joe.

The woman officer tried again. "I'm sorry, were you close?"

She was about to light another cigarette to blunt the shock when she realized that Margery was alone in the house, sitting with

127

news of another sudden death, another reason to be afraid. "You never told her, did ye?"

"Told who?"

"Marg— Thalaine, Mrs. Thalaine?" They looked at each other and she knew they had.

"Oh, for fuck's sake." She hurried around the bonnet of the car, touching it, finding it warm.

"You'll come up?" the woman called to her through her own window.

"After," shouted Kay as she sprinted back along the road. "I'll come after."

TEN

The cushioned rings around Thomas's ears were hot and itchy as the Piper rattled down through gray clouds to Biggin Hill.

It was small, little more than four seats and an engine, a go-cart of a plane. He never liked landing in the Piper. The plane was so small he always had an image of a balsa wood collapse on landing, the plane caving in on itself like a soggy cardboard box, crushing him. He took deep breaths to calm himself, sucking in the stale smell of Captain Jack's sweat. They were inches from each other. Thomas couldn't even pass the time reading because the cabin lights had to be out and the plane juddered so much it made the letters jump. All he could do was think.

Now he was alone and unseen, he wasn't haunted by images of the dead woman or the smell of baby wipes. Now all he could think of was his parents.

Moira. Distant, stupid, no-longer-pretty mother. She'd be fainting away every half hour, unable to cope with the loss of a man who'd been phoning his mistresses from the breakfast table for years. His grandmother used to say of her that she made a meal of everything, that's why she never ate. She was a suffocating, empty vacuum. She didn't even like him. Everything was reserved for Ella.

Squeak was right: there were no children. Just a plain woman in a tumbledown house. His father wouldn't stand for that. He insisted on immaculate decor, perfect clothes, appropriate dress always. It was shock and awe but in the wrong house, and the mistake was his. It was a foolish mistake. People would find out and think him foolish.

In the rumbling dark his mind ricocheted between the messy old house and the image of Squeak on all fours, staying out of the light, looking up at him. He couldn't blame Squeak but took it on himself, as if Squeak was a part of him that he had allowed to grow and fester unchecked. One small rational part of him recognized that it was wrong to be so loyal, and he was astute enough to know that he had picked Squeak randomly, because they had been physically close for a long, long time, because his parents weren't fulfilling the roles they were supposed to and he needed to attach himself to someone. He was Squeak. It was irrational how much he was Squeak. These were not rational times. Every time he looked up everything had changed completely.

The headphone cushions were really itchy. He worked his index finger up under the leather cuff and scratched the skin around his ears hard. Moira wouldn't come to the airport to get him. She'd probably be hiding in the house, in her own apartments, with Ella.

They were suddenly below the clouds, low enough for Thomas to imagine tumbling out of the plane, remaining conscious while hurtling towards the ground. The pilot took instruction from the landing tower again, their conversation crackling suddenly in Thomas's itchy earphones. Captain Jack had flown him many times and spoke in that strange stay-calm voice they used on commercial airlines. He sounded like a bad radio DJ.

Whatever Doyle said, Thomas wouldn't go back to St. Augustus's. He tried to imagine his life now, how it would be day to day, what he would fill the day with. He wondered if his dad dying meant that the creditors couldn't take their house. Thomas would still have his rooms, away from the main house, on the ground floor. It was a granny flat really. The last people used it as a granny flat. Two large rooms onto the garden, with a small kitchen and a bathroom. When they moved in his dad let Thomas have it for his own because he was smoking a bit and they wouldn't allow it in the house. It was bad for Ella's asthma.

He imagined himself in the bed, lying in the dark, finally, properly alone and free to think. He didn't feel grief or sadness like he was supposed to. What he felt was bewildered and so angry that he wanted to reach forward and strangle Captain Jack.

Alarmed by his thoughts, he clasped his hands together on his lap. He looked out of the window.

His father was gone.

He had filled every room he walked into.

"Look at them, looking at me," he said to Thomas and Ella as they walked into a restaurant once. Ella hugged her father around the waist and said something pathetic. But Thomas looked at the man, at his white hair, silvered with mousse, and knew that everyone was looking at him because he looked so moneyed. His jacket had never been rained on, his collar was new-white, he was bringing two children to a three-starred Michelin restaurant full of financiers in dark suits. It was not for the benefit of the children, nothing was ever about them. They were eating there so that people could see him squander two-hundred-quid meals on an awkward teen-ager and a soppy kid. His father wasn't special, he was just rich. Now he was dead. Thomas kept thinking he had killed him, that he'd heard about her and hanged himself. It was as if he was hoping that. He had to remind himself over and over that his father had been swinging from a beam before Squeak even started the engine.

Thomas looked out of the window. He should hang himself too. He'd like to see them then, the creditors protesting outside the security wall of the house, throwing eggs and burning newspaper over it, when it could land on anyone, Ella or a dog or someone. He'd like to see the headlines when his fifteen-year-old son was found hanged. They'd make it all about the money and the public pressure. They'd feel terrible. The newspapers that had gone for his father would reverse their position, denounce oth-ers for attacking, call for calm. He smiled at the back of Captain Jack's head.

They were coming down, circling, lining up to the landing strip. Thomas looked out to the horizon. He could see Bromley on the far right, Blackheath maybe, sinking down, down, disappearing, being swallowed by the earth. They were coming down fast.

His breathing was so loud it made the voice activation start up and the pilot asked him to repeat what he had said.

"Nothing," said Thomas, sounding urgent. "Just breathing."

They were lined up with the landing lights, a perfect straight-on landing. Coming straight at it, dipping down, nose low. Thomas abandoned the deep breathing and began to pick at the edge of the seat covering.

The plane bumped onto the runway and slowed, tipping a little so that they could feel the weight shifting alarmingly to the nose. It righted itself, slowed to a crawl and Captain Jack spoke into the headphones, using the stupid voice, telling the tower that they had landed.

Slowly, the plane taxied to the brightly lit mouth of the hangar, a slit of fraudulent yellow warmth. The doors were pulled back waiting for them. It was empty as they rolled in slowly. Usually there were a few aircraft in there and they had to wait and get a tow but the pilot had been told to drive straight in. Thomas looked for the ATR-42 but couldn't see it. Captain Jack performed a perfect stop, no heavy jolts forward, no bumps. The engine died.

He shut down the engine and lights, switch by laborious switch. Somewhat inappropriately, he thanked Thomas over the headset for his company this evening. Definitely a failed airline pilot, Thomas thought, drunk at the departure desk or something like that.

Testing his knees for steadiness, Thomas undid his seat belt and stood up a little, pulling the headset off and dropping it onto the seat. Outside a man in a boiler suit wheeled some steps up to the plane. Thomas waited for Captain Jack to open his door, scrabble out and help him down.

Then he saw her.

She was standing in the freezing cold of the hangar, on a concrete platform in front of the office door. She knew the plane because she'd often met him coming off it, coming back from school. Dark hair, and holding her long green sheepskin shut. Nanny Mary. Thomas felt a burst of love for her, a need for her and, as always, the follow-through: a feeling of disgust and self-loathing, slimy, like her juice under his fingernails as he lay in bed at night, the smell of her on his bedsheets, her hard runner's body lying next to him, unyielding muscles in soft skin. She caught his eye, sensed his mood and smiled uncertainly. Thomas looked away.

The pilot opened the door to a shock of cold and stepped out. Thomas pushed the chair forward and stepped down to the freezing ground, ignoring the pilot's out-stretched helping hand, not making eye contact. Mary came towards him, reached out a hand too and Thomas ignored that as well.

"Where's the car?"

"Tommy, you're bleeding." She reached forward to his ear but he yanked his head away, cupping his hand over it. Cold wet dampened his palm. He had scratched too hard.

"Where's your luggage?"

Captain Jack climbed back in and found his duffel bag in the back, behind the seats. He handed it down and Mary made a big show of getting it for him. Thomas watched her reach up, look into Captain Jack's face — though she had made jokes about him many times behind his back — and smile a snaky smile.

She carried the bag to the car for him,

holding the weight easily, swinging it into her outside hand at one point, making him panic. Afraid she would take his hand, he tucked both deep into his trouser pockets until he could feel the hole forming in the bottom of the lining and a patch of stiffness from a burst biro.

Jamie, his mother's favorite driver, was standing by the car, rubbing his hands to keep warm. She had sent Jamie and he hoped for a moment that it was out of affection, an attempt to give him a warm welcome, but it wasn't. Jamie was only here because she didn't need him. She was indoors, in the warm, with Ella.

Jamie smiled nervously, nodded and opened the door. Thomas said, "All right?" and got in before Jamie answered. Mary climbed in after him. Behind them the boot popped and Jamie put the bag in, slamming it shut, jogged around to the front and got in.

She had set it out before she came to the hangar: two Starbucks' cups, plastic not paper, sat in the cupholders between the two seats. Steam rose from the sip hole, the smell of chocolate. She pointed to them as Jamie started the car and pulled out.

"Hot chocolate."

Thomas looked out of the window next to

him. "No."

She smiled and picked hers up, wrapping her big hands around it. "Thought you might be cold."

"I'm fine." He could see her reflection in the dark window, saw her eyes stray to his belly and his groin. He had a shuddering need for her and felt sick. "Don't want anything."

She looked away. "You're still bleeding."

He caught his own eye in the smoked glass window. "Shut the fuck up, Mary."

ELEVEN

Cold rain speckled Morrow's face. The top step was exposed and the soft shower swirled around her, engulfing, wind tugging at the hem of her coat like a child, making her smile as she listened to Bannerman shouting through the phone, "Turn that off! Turn it off and listen to me!"

The phone was inches from her ear but she could still hear a woman's voice in the background, talking slowly, sounding medicated: "Follow the course of the road."

Bannerman shouted, "Turn the fucking thing off!"

It was out of character for him to swear. He was desperate to get here. It was the lure of the money, unknown quantities, unimaginable provenance, a sea of pink possibilities.

"Turn around, *right now.*"

They trained them to be impervious though, the drivers of the armored vehicles,

139

trained them not to respond to shouting or threats, just to ignore, stay calm and get to the assigned destination. Some officers were easier to train than others. She could hear the driver answer in monosyllables, no, yes, here, not here, while the GPS lady sounded her gentle course and the wipers shrieked across the glass.

"Morrow? Morrow!" Bannerman was shouting at her.

She considered hanging up and claiming afterwards that the signal had been lost but he would only phone back, shouting more requests for directions that the driver wouldn't follow.

"Still here, sir."

"Right. We're coming. Slowly, but we're coming."

Looking out from the top step Morrow thought about Sarah Erroll. Younger than her and living here alone. Strange to have always lived in one place. The house must have been so familiar that she didn't see it anymore, the stones and grass and steps and walls superseded by the cumulative memories of her life, small incidents, vignettes, images retained in forensic detail for no discernible reason. Morrow hoped it was happy, the cloud of impressions, until the last. She saw a black shoe, stamping. That was all they'd harvested from the shoe prints, black suede. The sole looked like a trainer, with deep grips and no heel. Two different sets in almost the same size. "Go up, take a turn here!"

She held the phone further away from her face.

It was only four thirty but it was dark already. There were no street lights up this high on the hill and every light inside was on, supplemented by the bright white spotlights from the science lab. Twenty feet beyond the bottom step the dark was impenetrable.

Her phoned beeped, another call, number unknown. She told Bannerman, "I've got another call coming in," and switched to it. "Hello?"

The voice was soft, girlish. "Hello? Is this Alexandra Morrow?"

It wasn't someone from work, but no one else had this number. "Yes?"

"Hello, um, my name is Val MacLea. I'm a forensic psychologist. Daniel McGrath gave me your number?"

Morrow dipped her chin and dropped her voice. "Danny gave you *this* number?" She wondered how he could have found the number for her work mobile. It wasn't listed anywhere. Brian didn't even have this number.

"Yes." The woman hesitated, sensing all was not well. "Sorry, are you not at London Road Station right now?"

He didn't have it, the call had been redirected from her work. "Sorry, sorry, no, I've . . . you're calling me on my work's mobile, the call's been redirected."

"OK," said the woman patiently. "Is there a better time to call you?"

Morrow looked down the road, saw no signs of headlights on the avenue. "No, not really."

"Well, I hope I'm all right phoning you, it's with regard to John McGrath, he's your nephew?"

She waited for an answer and Morrow kept her eyes on the avenue. "Mmm."

"Well, I'm conducting a risk assessment on behalf of the court and I wondered if I could speak to you for a bit of background?"

"A risk assessment?"

"It's a way of looking at John's past, it's a way of determining the likelihood of future offending."

"He *will* do it again."

She stalled at that. "Well, would it be possible for me to speak to you personally?"

She sounded pleasant and reasonable;

Morrow would have liked to talk to someone about her background without having to censor herself or explain. But if she did Danny would hear about it. He'd read it as a favor.

"I don't want to."

Owning up to John was the responsible thing to do. She had seen from afar what was happening to him, passed from nutter to nutter, knew the chaos he grew up among and she did nothing. Once, when she was at college and he was a small child, she saw him. It was summer and he was in a buggy, strapped in, parked outside a pub, alone. He looked poor. His toes were dirty in his sandals. He didn't know her but she could have taken him, anyone could have taken him. Morrow stood at the corner for twenty-five minutes, watching over his buggy. As she stood there she considered stealing John, taking him home, washing him, feeding him. But she was young and had no money, nowhere to take him. His mother stormed out of the pub doors, yanked the pram brakes off, never looking at or speaking to the child who was smiling up at her. Morrow watched her walk away, and felt her childhood conviction that she would be more responsible than her own mother evaporate.

A yellow tinge of headlights showed through the trees at the end of the road. "I need to go," she said.

"Would it be possible to meet you?"

"You know I'm a police officer — no one knows my background, I don't need to be associated with that —"

"I could interview you at home if you like. Or you'd be welcome to come to my office."

The lights were approaching, slowing at the fork in the road, choosing the incline and turning, penetrating the soupy dark as the van took the sharp slope.

"No." She hung up on both calls.

Guilty as a schoolgirl caught with a cigarette, she fixed an awkward smile on her face and watched the armored van pull up in front of her.

It didn't look like anything special, just a small black van with a camera on top. It was inside that it was different. The back doors opened to another door, a safe door with a timed lock. The box was welded to the floor so that robbers would have to cut the van in half to get the box out. It was used to transport drug hauls and big money. Even training the drivers was costly.

The van cringed as the handbrake was pulled on. Bannerman opened the passenger door and climbed out, slamming it behind him, furious. He stomped over to her, as if she didn't already know that he was angry, stopped at the bottom of the steps and muttered a curse at the driver.

"He took me to a cashmere shop called Glenarvon in the next village."

Morrow didn't give a shit. "I see."

"Where is it?"

"The body?"

"No, the money." Typical Bannerman, he'd climb over a dead woman to get straight to the kudos item. Even if the money wasn't drugs-related he'd get a spot on the front page of the Strathclyde Police newsletter. Bosses read the newsletter, they were the only people who did. They felt it kept them in touch with the men and Bannerman liked being seen in it.

They heard a door open as the driver stepped cautiously out of the van. His visor was down, he had his gloves on and he scanned the area for robbers. Just off training, guessed Morrow. Taking it seriously. She felt sorry for him. He looked across at them standing on the steps and faltered, reluctant to come over while Bannerman was still there.

Morrow gestured impatiently to him. She couldn't leave for the office until she handed over responsibility for the money. He

145

stepped slowly, stopping ten feet away. Bannerman glared, daring him to approach.

They were wasting time rattling their bollocks at each other and she still had Sarah's solicitor waiting to be questioned at the station, needed to get through some of the preliminary reports before she went home. For a moment spite made her consider taking them past Sarah Erroll without a warning, but she caught herself: "You should both go in around the back — they're moving her now, it's not nice. There's a kitchen door round there and they came in through the window."

"What, go round the back because the body's up there?" Bannerman took one of the steps. "I can take it, I know it's bad —"

"No, you'll disturb the scene. The money's in the kitchen." She looked over his head. "Driver, you, what's your name?"

He told her but his voice was muffled by the visor and Morrow wasn't listening anyway. She was congratulating herself on her courtesy to underlings.

"OK," she said, "well, you go around the back and have a look at the money. I'd like it taken in as it is, on the board."

"Round here?" It was dark around the side of the house now and he seemed reluctant to go.

"Aye, follow it around to the back. The lights are on, you'll see the door open."

He walked off, wading through the long wet grass, disappearing behind a tree.

Bannerman looked up at her. "How are you? You OK?" he said, sounding intimate.

Morrow feigned confusion. "Fine, yeah."

"Not too much for you?" He nodded to the house.

"No, no, 'm fine. Although I do feel," she stroked her stomach as she dropped down the steps to his side, "that I could do with a long lie-in tomorrow."

Bannerman laughed joylessly. "Ah, I think I like you better pregnant. Hormones are making you mellow." He touched her then, patted her on the upper back in a way he would never have dared to before.

She was changed, she knew that, but it wasn't chemical. That she was about to have twins was life-changing enough, and he knew that Gerald had died. He seemed to think she wanted to talk about her feelings now, wanted to be touched and have allowances made for her. To avoid saying anything stupid she turned her face up to the open door.

"The men don't give a shit about this," she said quietly.

"How come?"

She sighed back up at the house. "Big house, no close relatives to cry over her, loads of obviously shady money in the kitchen. Her face is gone."

"They'll come around, we'll find some pictures of her as a kid."

"Boss, they've already got jokes about her."

"I heard that." He smirked a little. "The legs . . ."

Morrow didn't know how to say it to him but the men were offended because the dead woman's genitals were on display. They were old-fashioned, sympathetic to women who kept their knees together and their underpants high. The merest hint that a woman was promiscuous could negate their sympathy. Morrow tried not to think about it too much but wore her shirts done up to the neck.

"Crisis of commitment," he said loudly. "A lot of them just want their paycheck."

She *hmm*ed vaguely. Bannerman wasn't really making an observation, he was repeating an indignant conversation he'd had with a golf buddy. The men had every right to be in it for their pay but the problem was deeper, their lack of engagement was becoming entrenched, a badge of honor, something they boasted about to each other.

The deeper it went the less they'd get out of them and the bosses were despairing, trying to tackle a problem of hearts and pride by starting rumors of a bonus scheme.

The driver reappeared around the side of the house. He had taken his helmet off, revealing his big bonny baby face. "Boss, we'll need another few vans. There's too much."

Morrow saw the van he'd arrived in. It had plenty of space for what was under the table. "Nah, you can fit that in."

"No." He held his hand up and shut his eyes conclusively. "Under the regs we're not allowed to carry more than seventy-five k at any one time. By my calcs we'll need nine vans."

Bannerman looked back at Morrow and they smirked.

"So," he continued sadly, "we haven't got seven vans avail. So we're gonna need to unload, come back, return and come back." He saw them smile and misunderstood. "Yeah, massive. Drugs, is it?"

Morrow frowned to stop herself giggling and leaned back into the house, shouting in for DC Wilder to come. "I'll let you sort this out," she said to Bannerman. "Make sure nothing's moved —"

"— until it's photographed, I do know

that, Morrow," grinned Bannerman.

Wilder came out of the front door, guilty when he saw Bannerman and Morrow laughing together on the step.

"Wilder," she said as he nodded hello to Bannerman, "drive us up the road."

Morrow and Bannerman sniggered their goodbyes, as Wilder tripped down the steps to the car. Morrow followed him, got in and they pulled on their seat belts, driving past the front door in time to see Bannerman and the driver walking up the steps to the front door.

"Good luck," muttered Wilder.

Morrow appreciated him saying that; it softened her to him. She'd never liked him very much. He was a bit beige, even for a policeman. His hair was the same color as his skin and he never said anything interesting. She suspected him of being at the heart of the belligerent donkeys on his shift, him and Harris, though she had no real reason for thinking that of him, other than she didn't like him much to start with.

He pulled the car carefully past the parked mortuary van and down the steep dip of the tarmacked drive.

Along the avenue the headlights licked big trees and picked out bushes. The houses were set back from the road, each with lights along their driveway like landing strips. They were nearly at the end of the avenue when they saw a woman in a raincoat walking at the side of the road, her head down, a handbag slung on a thin strap across her body. She looked up at the headlights and Wilder tutted, pulling into the side of the road in front of her. Morrow saw an inch of roots, brown and wild gray mingling, the weather-warp on the shoulders of the coat and the leatherette flaking off the strap of the handbag.

Her face was bleached by the lights and she looked up at the car, cocked her head at the shadow of faces and squinted, before walking over to the car.

Kay looked in the window, her mouth open to speak but she smiled, open-mouthed, genuinely delighted. Morrow caught her breath: Kay Murray, unchanged.

Morrow opened the door and stepped out, slamming it shut behind her.

"God Almighty," said Kay, "you look about twelve."

"Kay," Morrow wanted to touch her face, "Kay."

"What are you doing here?"

"I'm in the police."

"No!"

"Aye."

"I hate the fucking polis. How did that happen?"

"I tripped."

They had been young together, hung about street corners together and Morrow had often wondered what had happened to her. She wasn't the sort of person to keep in touch though: a person was either in Kay's life or they weren't; she wasn't the catch-up-coffee kind. She was someone to see bands with, chase boys with, do things with.

They grinned at each other, until Wilder revved the engine for no reason. Kay squinted in at him. "Oh, him. That boy's a prick." Morrow looked through the windscreen to Wilder's beige face. "He was talking to me like I was fucking Mrs. Mop or something earlier."

"Where'd'ye meet him?"

"Down the road, one of the houses I clean. I used to work up there." She pointed back to Glenarvon on the hill. "I said I'd come up and see what was missing."

"Would ye?" said Morrow, conscious that they were moving the body. "Will ye wait until tomorrow? I'll be there after ten."

"And I can see ye again." Kay nodded, almost hiccupping with glee. She looked at Morrow's stomach. "When ye due?"

"Five months."

"You're very big."

"Twins."

"Nightmare," Kay said lightly.

"Got weans yourself?"

"Four." Kay smiled tenderly. "Four bastard teenagers. Make my life hell." It was very old manners, talking negatively about your children while oozing pride, as if complimenting them would be self-aggrandizing. "I was thinking about you recently. Heard about your John. What a nutter."

"He's not *my* John —"

Kay interrupted, "Aye, he is."

"No, no, nothing to do with me."

"Aye, your arse. He's yours. Ye get who ye get." Kay looked up the road at the brightly lit house, apprehensive. "What — eh — what's happened here?"

Morrow shouldn't say anything but she knew Kay and trusted her. "Battered," she said, pointing at her face.

"Sarah?"

"Aye."

Kay's forehead wrinkled suddenly and she bowed her head. "Holy God."

"Did you know her?"

"Aye."

"What was she like?"

153

Kay kept her face down. "Nice enough. Quiet." She smiled a little. "The mother was mad as a brush."

Morrow saw the fat wet tear drop from Kay's face. She thought it was the rain until she saw another drop. It occurred to her suddenly that Kay knew the mess in the hall when it had been a living, moving thing, that they might have been unlikely friends. She reached forward, touched Kay's shoulder, as if trying to grab back the offense. "Sorry."

Kay stepped away. "No," she was too embarrassed to look up, "no, it's not —"

"I didn't realize you were close."

Kay turned back guiltily. "We weren't. I'm just . . . teary. The lassie died. It's sad."

She turned and stomped off, keeping close to the trees. Morrow watched her walk away.

"See you tomorrow?"

"Aye," called Kay.

Under a warm street light, Kay reached her hand behind her head and scratched the back of her long neck with a hooked index finger. Morrow caught her breath. The gesture was so familiar as to almost be her own, from a different time, a softer time peopled with flawed angry women and uncertainty and warmth. It struck Morrow very suddenly: Kay was right. Sarah Erroll wasn't just a battered jigsaw puzzle. She was a young lassie and she was dead.

It was sad.

TWELVE

At the right time of day the drive only took half an hour, but this was the wrong time. It was rush hour and the cars crawled along, suspicious, selfishly sticking close to the bumper in front in case anyone tried to cut in. He could always tell when they were getting close to Sevenoaks because the cars seemed to be bigger and cleaner, like his father somehow. Sleek and clean and powerful enough to run you over without stopping.

Thomas hated Sevenoaks. They moved there six years ago when his father was at the zenith of his career and the money was rolling in. Lars came home every night looking happier and happier with himself. He put on weight, Thomas remembered, had a whole new wardrobe of bespoke clothes made to disguise his swelling arse and belly.

It seemed inconceivable that he had hanged himself. He was not a man given to dark reflections on his own character. It wouldn't have been over the public scandal because he despised his investors. He said you couldn't trick an honest man.

Moira changed when they moved to Sevenoaks. Thomas never knew why. He was just a kid at the time. He didn't question the dynamics between them, but it felt as if his father was sapping the life from her, that the more animated and fun he became the more she melted into a soft-eyed victim. She stopped attending company parties, company holidays, company wife-bonding days. She began to take pills that made her mouth infuriatingly dry. Thomas remembered the disgusting rasp of her tongue moving inside her dry mouth. Her blinking stopped being expressive and became slightly slow, as if, sometimes, when she shut her eyes she wasn't altogether certain that she ever wanted to open them again.

Thomas was holding the armrest below the window with both hands, looking resolutely out of the window. He could feel Mary's presence burning behind him, could feel the vague disinterest of Jamie, his mother's proxy, in front. He stared at the glass, at his reflection, his round eyes and stupid big Moira-lips, faint over the watermark of Sevenoaks. Mild hills, not rugged

157

or massive like at school. Big houses hiding away down roads, skulking behind trees.

Moira moved into the Sevenoaks mansion Lars had bought without consulting her and she did it without an objection. She moved miles away from her friends and neighbors and all the shops in north London. It'll be great, they were told — possibly by her, maybe by him — it'll be great there because we'll have acres of our own land and a big fence all around it and a top-of-the-range security system. We'll have electric shutters and a panic room and a safe.

They moved, and then Thomas was sent away to school, before he even had the chance to find out what was so great about a panic room. Moira didn't complain about that either. When Ella's turn came she fought for her though, insisting she stayed at the local school until she was twelve. Thomas asked her about it, why she fought for Ella and not for him. She got teary, slacking her tongue from the dry roof of her mouth, guilty maybe. Boys are different, she said. That's all she said. Boys are different.

Moira didn't look vacant in the papers. She looked good actually, a couple of the boys had mentioned that she did. She had stayed thin and his father paid someone to come and do her hair a lot, dye it and set it.

But even in the papers as she bustled through airports, drove through waiting protesters at the gate, even then he could see the emptiness in her. She was all he had left and there was no one there.

They were drawing near the turn-off, edging along with the other big cars, Jamie indicating early to let them know he was trying to get out. The sky was dark, the fields were fallow strips of turned mud. There might be nothing on the earth but this strip of tarmac, this line of cars.

He could hear Mary next to him, thinking of something to say, opening her mouth and shutting it. She kept quiet. She must be worried about her job, they must all have been worried. They couldn't afford to keep all the staff on. If he met Mary and she didn't work for them, he wondered, would she be different? He knew she thought things and didn't say them, everyone did that. Jamie would probably be the same as he was now. The exact same. Silent, pleasant, a bit vacant. Moira loved Jamie for that. She liked him because he had nothing going on either.

Jamie took the turn, followed the road along to the gates, new gates, faux Victorian; his father loved faux things. Jamie pulled up to them, pressed the button on the dash and the gates swung slowly inward, giving Thomas time to take in all the graffiti on the walls. LIAR, said one. Thomas had seen it before, it had been pictured in the papers. SCUM BANKERS, said another. Ridiculous. He didn't work for a fucking bank. Other than that the protests seemed to be very mild. A bunch of cheap supermarket flowers had been left propped up with a wooden cross. People knew about the suicide.

Through the gates, the drive was sheltered from the wind off the hill by a long arcade of gnarled old trees, naked, mournful and looming. The glass roof over the swimming pool looked dirty. Thomas could see dead leaves on it.

It was a nasty house, an asymmetric façade, plastic Arts and Crafts, supposed to look like a squat cottage with a heavy roof, but much too big for that. It looked like a sports center, had a big hall, big rooms. His father got it cut-price from a bankrupt trying to minimize his losses by selling for cash. The stench of panic clung to the place. Moira had redecorated. In a dry-mouth rasp she ordered the decorator to do it all in frosty blue and white, Swedish, completely inconsistent with the Voysey-esque exterior, but consistently so. Thomas's quarters were full of spindly-legged tables and white chairs and strings of painted love hearts.

As they stopped at the bottom of the steps Mary finally thought of something to say. "We are all very sorry about your dad."

She watched the back of his head for a reaction but Thomas didn't move. He was looking at his father's lawn.

The house was set up high, not on a steep hill like the house in Thorntonhall, but elevated, with a balustraded terrace along the front of it, stairs leading down at the side, to the top of a long gentle slope of lawn. He was looking at it and his mind was blank. Thomas should get out of the car now but he couldn't move, his muscles were slack, he was afraid to let go of the armrest.

"Shall I go and see if your mother is in?"

If she's in? She wasn't even in the house. She'd gone out. Home to nothing. Still looking at the lawn he realized very suddenly that his eyes were dry, they were open wide as if he was being hit. He could hardly draw breath.

Mary took his silence for a yes and stepped out of the stationary car. She hurried up the steps to the door.

Thomas's eyes were on the lawn. His dad loved the lawn. He loved that he owned it and the shape of it, that it dropped at the end so it looked as if it went on forever and he owned it. When they moved in Thomas and Ella wanted to play on it, run and roly-poly down it but Moira said no, it's your father's, he owns it, it's not for playing on.

He owned it and no one, not Moira or even Ella, was allowed to run on it or step on it and the gardeners were sacked if they let an inch of it fail. Thomas's nose was hard against the window, it hurt how hard it was against the window, and he looked out at his father's lawn and pressed harder until his nose clicked and he saw a heel crushing a nose and saw the inside of the broken nose and the blinding white of the cartilage and perfect round bubbles of blood on it and Squeak on all fours, looking up at him with blood running from his mouth, smiling in the dark —

"You all right, Tommy?" Jamie had turned in his seat, his face a quarter visible, a vague, awkward smile on his face.

Thomas let go of the armrest and threw both forearms around Jamie's throat, choking him as he dragged him backwards into the passenger seat.

THIRTEEN

Wilder drove Morrow to London Road in silence, and she was glad of it. She kept her notebook on her knee, glancing down at it every so often, pretending she was making sense of the details and time lines. All she could think about was a younger Kay Murray, standing on a street corner outside the AJ Supplies in Shawlands, wearing a lot of lipstick. JJ had just been born and Morrow was jealous of Danny, resenting the tender way he talked about him, the softness in his eyes, his pride because she thought having his own family now meant he would move on from the mess they were born into.

She felt her phone vibrate before it rang out and fumbled for it in her pocket, pulling it out at the first tone chime. The screen said "Office" not "Bannerman" and she answered with an element of relief.

"Ma'am, Harris."

"Right?"

"iPhone's last call was a 999."

"Did she get through?"

"She didn't answer the operator."

"Shit. I can hear the papers banging on about that already. Look into that. Be thorough. OK?"

"Aye, ma'am, no stone and that."

"What else is there?"

He covered the mouthpiece and asked someone, came back on the phone: "Still looking through the emails and photos."

"Any word on Mrs. Erroll's carers?"

"Made up a list of names and addys."

"I'll be there in fifteen minutes." She hung up.

They could have saved her. They could have been standing outside the door and caught the arseholes on their way out. Or arrived in time, stopped it happening at all. What might have been. She yanked her thoughts away to happier things.

Kay Murray had children, four children, teenagers. It was jarring. Morrow couldn't think of Kay as anything other than a teenager herself, even though her face was older and her hair graying, even then she couldn't imagine Kay doing anything other than standing around lampposts late in the summer, too late for the little she was wearing, young enough to suffer high heels bought in a charity shop because she was self-conscious about her stubby legs.

Morrow looked at her notebook. She hadn't turned the page for two miles. "How did you get on at the door-to-doors?"

Wilder had been in a world of his own too and started at her voice. "Sorry?"

"Door-to-doors, anything?"

"Oh," he indicated for a turn, "nothing much. Erroll kept herself to herself. She was selling the house though."

"Really?"

"Big deal," he nodded, agreeing with himself. "Big deal because they've been there for a hundred and fifty years. Neighbors thought it was a big deal."

"Bad time to sell too."

"And the house is in a mess."

"Yeah, she wouldn't have gotten a very good price for it." She ran her fingertips across a line of notes. "The woman that we met there in the avenue . . ."

"Kay Murray?" He was smiling. "You know her?"

"At school. Where did you meet her?"

His smile fell to a smirk. "Down the hill, the old stables is a house now, Mrs. Thalaine. Your pal's her cleaner. Quite a character."

He meant it as an insult. Morrow grunted,

smiling on the side of her face that he would see out of the corner of his eye. "Get her address?"

He shrugged. "In the notes."

It would take him a day to get around to writing up the temporary report. She felt suddenly exposed and changed the subject. "Did Erroll have a boyfriend?"

"Not that anyone saw."

Wilder's shift ended in twenty minutes and she could feel him zoning out.

"She wasn't friendly with the locals then?"

But he was gone, already working out what he'd do when he got home, how he'd get home. "Dunno. Kay might know."

She warmed at the mention. "How would she know?"

"Apparently Sarah Erroll paid ten quid an hour and everyone's cleaners and staff went to work for her when her mum was ill. That Kay, the cleaner, she worked up there until the old lady died. Then she moved back. Mrs. Thalaine said Kay's got a lot of problems."

"Kind of problems?"

"Lives in Castlemilk."

"How's that a problem?"

"Mrs. Thalaine seemed to think it was."

Morrow snorted. "She ever been to Castlemilk?"

"She said she'd driven past it."

"Stupid cow."

They skirted the grim grandeur of Glasgow Green and Bridgeton and took the London Road down to the station.

It looked like a normal office, three stories of shit-brown brick, but had the architectural features of a fortress: windows punched well into the façade, buttress pillars all along the front. Two giant concrete boxes full of wild bushes in front of the main entrance, a device to foil spiteful ramraiders who were more of a threat than terrorists. Around the back a high wall topped with broken green glass formed a yard for squad cars and drop-offs to the booking bar and the cells.

The street outside was full of cars for the shift change. They were parked along the road and on the pavement, but there was order in the chaos; not one was touching a double yellow or blocking an entrance.

Because they were in a squad car they had to park in the yard. Wilder drew slowly in, navigating carefully around the vans and walls, around the cells in the middle with their high barred windows.

He pulled on the handbrake and she opened the door, adding as a parting shot, "Give us Kay Murray's contact details before you leave."

She slammed the door, cheating him of the chance to protest that he had other things to do. As she walked up to the ramp she worried that she was thinking about going to see Kay Murray on her own. No copper should ever go and see a witness alone, not just because they could make allegations against them, Kay wouldn't do that, but because of the corroboration rule: not a word they told them would be usable in court without another officer there to witness it. Single-officer testimony was worse than hearsay: it was unprofessional.

She walked up the ramp to the door, stabbed the security code into the pad and stepped back to let whoever was on the bar have a look at her on the video camera. The door fell open.

The processing bar was empty but she could hear screaming in the cells, the voice muffled by the door. It was a plaintive scream, a man's voice worn thin from a rough day and a lot of shouting. John looked out from the back office. "Just yourself?" he said, knowing she never drove if she could help it.

"Wilder's out there. Who's that?" She nodded her head to the cells.

"Street fight. Off his face. Crack."

She frowned — most of the junkies they brought in were there for being a nuisance, for sleeping in the road or incompetent thieving.

"Had a spate of crack users today. Because of the anthrax."

A batch of heroin had been contaminated and users were seeking solace elsewhere. "They causing havoc?"

John shrugged. "Be more of a danger if any of them weighed more than seven stone." He glanced at the clock. "You got a briefing to do?"

"Oh, aye." She'd been so distracted by thoughts of Kay that she'd forgotten.

She pulled her coat off as she hurried through the lobby to the CID door. She caught it as Harris was coming out.

"Ten minutes," she warned, pointing in at the briefing room.

"Ma'am, the lawyer who got trapped in the kitchen, Donald Scott, he's still upstairs."

"I know, I know, I'm getting to him. I'll see him after the briefing. Tell him twenty minutes."

"He's getting arsy."

"Well, that's fine," she said, and let the door fall shut between them.

They were gathering in the incident room,

the night shift and the eight-to-fives, ready to go home and forget all about it, leave her alone to care about Sarah Erroll. She let herself into the office for a minute, didn't bother turning the light on, dropped her coat and bag and, standing in the dark, took her personal mobile out.

Brian answered immediately. "Hiya."

"OK?"

"Yeah, you OK?"

"Yeah."

She opened her desk drawer slowly and pulled out a notepad and a pen, took the lid off.

"How did the funeral go?" asked Brian after a pause.

"Well, he's definitely dead." She doodled a spiral. "Got any dinner in?"

"That soup's in the fridge."

"Oh, aye." Troubled by the trap of the spiral, she drew an outward spiral next to it. "Be a bit late maybe."

"Well, I'll be here." He was smiling, she could hear it in his voice. "Everybody OK?"

She touched her stomach. "All fine, aye."

In the dark, a mile away from the bustle behind her in the corridor, they smiled at each other down the phone, two people readying for their own year zero.

She sighed a reluctant, "Bye."

Brian reciprocated and hung up.

She smiled at the phone. He always did that, no see-you-later or messing around. She checked her desk voicemail messages. One. She pressed play. The psychologist had called and left her number. Please call back.

Morrow had already said no. Smarting at the gall of the woman, she glanced at her watch and found she had two minutes to go. She gathered her papers together, pulled her clothes straight and turned to the corridor, out of the calm dark office, blinking into the harsh stream of noise and light and over to the incident room.

Chairs were being dragged about to face the back wall, coppers chatting to each other, their voices dropping slightly as she came in and passed them. She saw a few of them drop their eyes to her belly, always the same ones, some disgusted, some wistful, happy fathers themselves.

She dropped her papers noisily on the table, giving them a thirty-second warning to sit down and shut up. They did so before she turned back to face them. Seven men, all coppers, four coming on, four going off: one missing.

She welcomed them, looking over at the door for the latecomer, Routher, letting him know with a twitch of an eyebrow that he'd been spotted. For the benefit of the new shift she gave the rundown on Sarah Erroll and the house and the money. She told them they were looking for two people with black suede trainers but she left out the grotesque details of the injuries, leaving it to ferment as a rumor. They'd see the photos soon enough anyway. The image would lose its power as they walked past day after day, but she was hoping that the shock of it would help them to engage a little.

The next day would give them a better sense of who the hell Sarah Erroll was.

Looking around the room as she spoke she noted that a rich woman, just back from a weekend in New York, dying in a house full of money wasn't eliciting a lot of sympathy. When she told them Sarah had no next of kin to inform she saw the shift about to finish flick their eyes to the clock behind her. Those coming on were listening to her, following her face, not looking through her and imagining how the dead woman must have felt. They didn't give a shit about Sarah.

She finished up, handed over to Harris to allocate the night jobs, and looked around the room: the men looked bored, the day shift tired. They were waiting to go home and get on with their real lives.

The room dispersed and Harris came over, hoping, she felt, that she'd tell him to go home, get a good night's sleep.

"I asked around about the footprints. DC Leonard," he pointed over to Tamsin, "she knows someone at the Caledonian who's developing a program for something like this. She's a PhD student on the forensic sciences course."

They both smirked. The F.S. courses were churning out graduates, twenty for every vacancy. The C.S.I. effect, they called it.

"She's doing forensic mapping of crime scenes. Said she might be able to show who was where doing what if there's a lot of blood."

"Well, that's one thing there's enough of. Has it been tested in court?"

"No, it's new."

"Oh." She started to think through other limitations. "If you're giving her access to any photos make sure she'll keep it all confidential. No faces. Pictures like that end up on the internet all the time."

"There isn't a face."

She didn't like him joking about that. "You know what I mean."

He brushed over the rebuff. "Also, we've got the 999 recording. They're cleaning it up for sound."

"Good."

"It looks like a big file." He sounded nervous.

"She didn't get through, did she?"

"Don't know."

They grimaced at each other.

"Go upstairs to Scott and I'll be up there in a minute," she said.

Harris didn't voice an objection but his mouth contracted to the size of a penny.

FOURTEEN

Thomas felt like an aberration in this grand, pristine room. Two enormous white sofas were facing each other and between them a white table with white things on it and the walls were white and the curtains. Opposite, facing him, Moira had her arms crossed, her skinny legs coiled around one another, her lips thin and twisted. She was sitting very still, staring at him. She stared for a long time before she spoke.

"I'll tell you anything you want to know about it and then I never want to speak about him again."

Thomas had expected a talk about Jamie. He had prepared some excuses, was going to blame Mary or grief, and was thrown by her opening gambit. "Oh."

She ground her teeth. "Ask me."

He didn't want to know, hadn't wondered about many of the details. It was the consequences he was worried about but he said,

175

"What did Dad do wrong?" Moira rolled her eyes.

"You said ask anything."

"I did, I did." She took a breath. "He invested other people's money and they lost it all."

"After the market crashed?"

"No." She sighed. "Everyone was very angry because the investments he was selling sort of caused the crash."

"How?"

"This is very complicated, Thomas, I meant you could ask me about your father's suicide, not about this —"

"I want to know this, I'm reading about it in the papers all the time and I need to know what he did. *Then* I'll ask about the other stuff."

She cleared her throat: "Lots of people stopped paying their mortgages and the investments failed."

"Why did they stop paying?"

"Because they're silly. And now everyone's angry because Daddy's company bet against them paying."

He looked at her. Lies for a child. "The mortgage rates shot up after two years," he said. "He knew that and bet the houses would be repossessed. Don't you understand it or do you think I won't?"

"Well, it's terribly complicated."

It was fitting that his father owned an empire of empty homes. Thomas recalled walking around the National Gallery, stopping in front of Monet's *Water Lilies:* a huge, fluid wall of beauty filling his vision, and his dad behind him, telling him the monetary value. Even aged nine Thomas knew his father was missing the point.

"Do you have any questions about your father's death is what I meant."

Thomas thought he should ask something. "Where did he do it?"

"On the lawn." She gave a bitter little smile, acknowledging the significance. "From the oak. Used a rope."

"When?"

"Yesterday at lunchtime, about twelve thirty."

She stared hard at him again. Conscious that they weren't talking about Jamie, Thomas thought he should ask another, bigger question:

"Why?"

Moira uncrossed her arms and took a deep breath. "He left a note. Want to read it?"

Thomas shrugged, though he did want to read it very much. She reached into the pocket of her slacks and pulled out a folded

177

sheet of paper, holding it out to him by her index and middle finger.

Thomas took the sheet and opened it. It was a photocopy.

"He left you a photocopy?"

"No. The police did that before they left. They had to take the original with them."

Thomas read his father's big bombastic handwriting:

Moira, you *bitch.* You've finally got your way & I hope you're happy, finally, as if that was possible, you dried up *cunt.*

Thomas looked at Moira, sitting placidly on the opposite sofa, watching the paper as he read it. It was Lars all right. It was him angry and a little bit drunk, alternately shouting and hissing at her. They could both hear his fighting voice coming off the page.

"Are you sure you want me to read this?"

She shrugged, rolling her eyes back for a languorous blink. "The police have it, they'll read it, someone will leak it. Everyone in the country will know." Her eyes reddened. Thomas read on:

I gave you everything, I worked night and day for you, to give you *everything.* I was a great husband. And in return you

178

sucked the fucking *life* out of me. You fucking wizened bitch. I hope you're happy, L.

Thomas looked at the back of the page and found it blank, and then at his mother. She was weeping.

"I didn't even get a mention," he said, and let it fall onto the table.

They both looked at the letter, at the giant hateful letters and sloping lines, at the fury that had made the pen puncture the page at the full stops.

Thomas started laughing first, a titter, covering his face, and then Moira joined in, laughing and crying, pointing at the note, trying to speak through sputtering tears:

"Would you . . . would . . . would you want one!"

They were rocking with laughter now, struggling for breath and Thomas stood and screwed his face up and jabbed his finger at her and shouted, "Yaaaw dried up CUNT!"

And Moira fell face down into a cushion with mock shame, still laughing and crying because he did a good Lars. Then Thomas puffed his chest out and looked down at her as if he was disgusted and, still laughing, used one of his father's lines:

"Get out of my fucking sight or I'll pick

you up and throw you out of that fucking window!"

But Moira had started coughing, choking on her laughter because it had gone too far down and she was red in the face, but still she couldn't stop laughing and she stood up and pointed in Thomas's face:

"You fucking loser prick, I'll teach you to be a man," and she faked a wide-armed slap because it was too complicated to mime taking him to a brothel in Amsterdam.

Thomas stopped laughing at that memory but he wasn't sad. They were both panting and smiling. He sat back down, falling onto the sofa, looking at the door to the hall.

"He's not coming back," said Thomas simply.

Moira opened her eyes wide, incredulous at their good fortune. "I *know.*" She sat back on her own sofa and combed her hair with her fingers, wiggling them through the crunchy hairspray. She looked young and excited and her chest heaved.

"I watched them cut him down." She stared out of the window to where the oak was. "His . . . They cut the rope and held him by the legs and put him on . . . a bed thing."

"A stretcher?"

"A stretcher, yes, and his hand fell off it

— and I jumped!" She mimed a little bunny-hop jump and laughed again, at herself this time.

Thomas didn't laugh. "He's not coming back," he said again, serious, staring at his hands. He looked up suddenly, realized that the house was very quiet. "Where's Ella?"

Moira's eyes brimmed again, not happy at all, panicked, her head bobbed forwards, and Thomas suddenly knew that Ella was dead and his dad had fucked and killed her and stamped on her nose and left her in her room with her gash on show. He stood up as Moira covered her face and spoke.

"At school, still, Thomas —"

But Thomas's heart was racing and he couldn't bend his legs to sit back down. She looked at him with big wet eyes.

"Thomas, I wanted to see you first because —" and she broke off to sob into her hands again, her fingers curling into her hair. He could see the blood drain from her nails as she dug them into her scalp. When she took her hands away he could see bloody dashes in the parted, unmoving hair.

"Thomas. I know that sorry isn't enough, I know it isn't, but I was standing with that note in my hand and watching them cut him down and all I could think of was you and how you —"

181

Again the nails in the head, the shoulders convulsing, silent, like a cat bringing up a hair ball.

She sat like that for quite a long time. When she looked up her face was scarlet and wet, the wet from her nose running all over her mouth until she wiped it with a bare hand. Her hair was standing on end. She couldn't look at him.

"I have always known, Thomas, that I should have protected you and didn't. And I wanted . . ." an aftershock shook her chest, "to apologize." She found her rhythm and caught her breath. "I'm sorry. And I know that isn't enough but I'll do anything . . ."

Thomas felt nothing. The most vivid emotion he felt was mild surprise at her letting him see her cry, at the mess of her hair. She never came downstairs without her make-up and a full set of matchy-matchy clothes on. He wondered if she was drunk but she wasn't.

She looked up at him, a straight stare, not chin dipped down, supplicant and looking for favors. Not mouth twisted and annoyed or reprimanding.

Moira looked at him as an adult would another adult, with respect and with love and with honesty and she said, "I love you, you know."

182

FIFTEEN

Morrow stopped at the door to the remote viewing room to watch Donald Scott before she went in to speak to him. On screen he looked perky and restless; he had been there for a few hours now. He had eaten some biscuits, drunk sugary tea and seemed revived, knowing the interview was coming and he'd get home soon. He sat looking across the table at Harris, his briefcase on the floor, his hands clasped on the table as if he was about to start a negotiation.

His suit was new and smart, charcoal gray wool, his shirt clean. Smaller than she remembered from the kitchen, he was neatly put together, tighter, but she supposed the shock had scattered him.

The viewing room was empty, everybody busy downstairs, collating the door-to-doors, retracing Sarah's trip to New York from the documents and the receipts in her bag, mapping her life from the mobile phone. No one was expecting anything interesting to come out of the interview with the person who found the body.

She turned out the lights in the viewing room and shut the door on the gray glow of the screen, straightening her clothes before she set off for the interview room around the corner.

Her hand stroked her stomach and she smiled faintly to herself, allowing herself another stroke and a smile before she set off. Four months pregnant and no miscarriage and the scans said both were growing and all was well. She felt happy, content for them all three to stay here together forever on this cusp of disaster and worry and sleeplessness.

She looked again at the green floor, at the scuffed walls of the corridor where terrified and half-mad men and women had been dragged to interview rooms, angry, sad, kicking against officers, pathetic and passive or swearing revenge. The walls were lined with grief and fright and worry and she felt suddenly that she might be the only person in the short history of the building to find such a measure of absolute contentment there.

Knowing how few of these moments there might be, she shut her eyes, committing it to memory, before she blinked away her mood and moved on.

When she walked in and greeted Scott he stood up, formal and polite, smiling, as if noting the details of the day for the story afterwards. He was a frustrated criminal lawyer, Morrow suspected. The lawyers they dealt with were the rock stars of the profession, had interesting lives, knew tasty characters, had stories to tell at parties. Conveyancing and executory lawyers like Scott were heroes to no one except the firms' accountants.

She put the cassette tapes in the machine and turned it on, told it who was here, the date and time and gave Scott a prompt for the events of the morning.

Scott looked at the table top, stroked it carefully with the edge of his hand as if sweeping away crumbs, and began to speak in a strange, distancing form of legalese:

"This morning, at nine thirty, I returned to my office, on time, to await the arrival of Miss Sarah Erroll. I removed my overcoat, spoke to a colleague, Helen Flannery. Further to this, I entered her office on a matter irrelevant to this matter and returned to my office —"

Morrow rolled her eyes rudely and interrupted him: "What was she coming to see you about?"

But Scott wasn't to be put off. "We were meeting for the determination of two matters: primarily for Sarah Erroll to be a signatory in the finalization of her mother's estate settlement. Secondly, for her to authorize my firm to handle the sale of Glenarvon —"

"The house?"

He brightened. "Yes. The house. Yes. Yes. It was in furtherance of these matters —"

" 'Finalization of her mother's estate settlement,' what does that mean?"

His eyes slid around the table top, his mouth contorting at the edges. "Just signing some papers —"

"What papers?"

"Authorizations." He smiled, patronizing, and explained, "It's a technical term."

"Yeah." She looked hard at him. "What does that technical term mean?"

"In what sense?"

"Don't be slippery with me, Mr. Scott, what was she signing?"

"Finalizing an account. Further to this —"

"Paying a bill?"

"Further to this —"

"Shut up."

Scott looked a little stunned. Next to her Harris shifted on his buttocks eloquently. He was right. They'd left him too long and

186

he'd prepared for his interview. "OK," she tried to reset the tone, "Mr. Scott: this is a murder inquiry, I'm expecting your co-operation. All this 'further to this and that,' you're making it sound as if you have something to hide."

He looked very small suddenly. "I have nothing to hide."

"You saw the state of the woman. We need to find who did this very quickly. They could do it again, d'you understand?"

He nodded.

"I'm sorry." She sounded formal and blunt and not sorry at all. "For the benefit of the tape could you say that rather than just nodding?"

"Yes," he said obediently.

"How long were you waiting in the office before you set off for the house?"

"About forty minutes."

"After forty minutes you were concerned enough about it when she didn't turn up that you went all the way from the city center to Thorntonhall to find her?"

"It's not that far. It all gets billed to the client."

"You went looking for her to pay a bill and were going to bill her for that too?"

"It's common professional practice."

Morrow looked hard at him. "How much

187

was the bill for the settlement of her mother's estate?"

"I don't know, I don't know. I'd have to look it up."

Morrow smiled. She had a knack for smoking out lies. She could read a subtext as well as she could read a newspaper and she knew that spontaneous insistence was a virtual double negative. She sat back and looked at Scott and noted the glint of sweat on his forehead, the rapid blinks.

"So," she leaned forward and smiled, "to recap: you were waiting for forty minutes with the papers in front of you and you don't know how much it was for?"

He didn't answer.

She whispered, "I can find out."

Scott smiled unhappily. "Eighteen thousand."

"Eighteen grand? That's a lot of driving back and forth."

"Not really."

"When my mum died it didn't cost anything."

He smirked, supercilious, looking at her cheap nylon-mix suit jacket. "Well, no offense, but it's contingent on the size of the estate."

"I see." She touched her lapel with her fingertips, feigning defensive. "I happen to like this suit."

He blushed, uncomfortable at having the unspoken answered aloud. His own suit was expensive and his shirt looked professionally starched. She wondered at him going to all that trouble for a meeting with a client in his office.

"So, do you get a commission on the estate?"

"Commission?"

"A cut," explained Harris, "like, if you worked at Comet?"

Morrow smiled but Scott looked puzzled, as if he didn't understand the reference to the cut-price electrical shop.

She pressed him. "You don't shop in Comet?"

He mimed a thought. "I don't really think I have . . ."

She watched closely. "You've never driven past a shop with a big black banner and yellow writing that says 'Comet'? They're everywhere."

"There's a picture of a comet above the writing," added Harris.

"Well, we tend to go to John Lewis."

Scott was pointedly trying to tell her something about himself, something that mattered to him and it wasn't that he didn't read shop signs while he was driving.

She ignored it. "She was planning to sell the house?"

"Yes."

"Her family have lived there for a hundred, hundred and fifty years. That must be quite a wrench."

"I suppose."

"Was she selling it to pay your bill?"

Scott came out of his corner fighting. "Look, I resent the implied suspicions being mooted here. I wasn't doing anything wrong. It was a difficult estate to manage, but all of the expenses are documented and verifiable. Her mother needed around-the-clock care. That's very expensive as I'm sure you can imagine." He let them sit with that for a moment, as if it would take a thirty-second pause for them to comprehend the concept of things being expensive.

Harris sat forward. "Mr. Scott, things being expensive is just about all we can imagine."

The two of them smiled and Scott feigned confusion again. Morrow found it an interesting tactic. Telling.

"Yes," he said, when the moment had passed, "it was Sarah's sole aim to meet her mother's desire to stay in Glenarvon and die there, which she did. I wasn't tricking money out of Sarah, I had the greatest

190

admiration for her. She was an amazing young lady."

Morrow watched his face. "Did she live off family money?"

"There was none," he said, seeming sad for Sarah.

"None?"

"I'm afraid it had been a sizable estate but the three generations before were rather feckless. True what they say: we can't choose our ancestors . . ." He smiled at that, as if it was a pleasing cliché they had all employed at one time or another when referring to their own diminished estates in the colonies.

"What'd she live off then?"

"Sarah had to work, I'm afraid."

Harris affected a mock gasp.

"What did she work at?" smiled Morrow.

"Financial management. Gave pensions advice and did consultations on investments."

"For a company?"

"No, she was a consultant."

"Who for?"

"Big companies."

"Mm." Morrow felt suddenly very tired. "I'd like to ask more about that but you've been so bloody long-winded, I'm afraid to 'cause I want to get home tonight."

Scott smiled at that, taking the suggestion

that he was combative as a compliment. It wasn't meant that way. It was difficult for police and lawyers not to get on, they shared so much of the same world view, but Morrow gave it another try: "Were you tempted to rip her off over the carers for her mother as well?"

But Scott had unilaterally decided they were getting on well. "I handled the carer payments and most of the arrangements, if that's what you're asking me."

The twins were tickling her lungs, just gently, and she found herself smiling. Back in the real world Scott smiled back and she had to make it look deliberate. "Was it all through the books?"

"Absolutely: Carers Scotland is a certified company, all the payments and payroll done through the books. It all came out of the same account and she paid it all faithfully."

"We'll be looking at those accounts." She meant to sound threatening but she was still warm from her dip into the other world.

Scott nodded. "You're welcome to. I'll happily make them available to you. And the bills for the settlement of the estate, if you wish. I have nothing to hide."

"Yeah, fine." She took a breath and whipped the carpet out from under him. "Sarah had about seven hundred thousand quid in cash hidden in the kitchen."

"Maybe nearer six and a half," muttered Harris.

She watched Scott pale. He struggled to speak. "In the kitchen?"

"Yeah. On a false shelf under the table."

He looked to the right, thought his way back into the room. "The small table . . . seven *hundred thousand?*"

Harris chipped in playfully, "Possibly six and a half."

But Morrow was serious. "You didn't know she had that kind of money?"

"No. I didn't know that."

"Where do you think it came from?"

"I don't know."

"Why didn't she put it in the bank?"

Scott swallowed hard. "Don't know, I don't know, maybe she was avoiding income tax on it? She was careful with income tax."

"How do you know that?"

"Well, we had conversations, professional conversations about income tax . . ."

"Like what?"

"Oh," he shook his head and she knew he was going to be vague about it, "just, you know, what was deductible, what was an allowable expense, stuff like that."

"See, that's odd." Morrow flicked through her notes. "Because as far as we can gather

Sarah had never paid income tax."

He considered it for a moment, sitting very still, and then shook his head. "No. That's wrong."

"I can assure you it isn't. We used her passport number and got her national insurance number from it. She wasn't even registered."

"No, sorry, but she did pay income tax. She paid me to give her advice about income tax, specifically about what was and wasn't deductible from income tax. She sat in front of me in the office and listened for forty minutes just a year ago. If she had told me she wasn't paying income tax I'd have been obliged to report her . . ." His voice trailed off as the alternative explanation occurred to him.

"Hmm." Morrow nodded at him. "Who initiated that meeting?"

"I did. I said, you must ensure that you are maximizing your income. She had so much to pay out for the care plan, for her mother. She didn't understand taxation, she said. Bewildering, she said it was. Why would she . . . ?"

"She was a financial consultant who didn't understand income tax?"

He could see how stupid it seemed now. Sarah had let him lecture her, paid him to lecture her about income tax to stop him prying into her affairs. "She sent me a Fortnum's hamper to thank me for all my help . . . the money in the kitchen was in cash?"

"In euros," she said, watching his face to see if he registered the significance. It didn't. "We may have missed her tax records, she could be under another name. Did she use any other names?"

"No."

"Never married . . . ?"

"No."

"Why would she not bank the money?"

Scott had paled. "Dunno," he said, looking distant.

"You look worried."

He cringed. "Maybe she knew something we don't know?"

"About the financial situation? What could she know? That we're all doomed? It's not a secret."

Scott looked genuinely haunted. "Sarah, she knew people, a lot of people, she gave me tips sometimes . . ."

"Like shares tips?"

"No, no, no, *deals*. Money deals, buildings going up, where to buy flats for resale, things like that."

Morrow was looking at his mouth. The

accent was so well hidden she had missed it until now. She mouthed the give-away word to herself. "Dee-uulz," working class, South Sider. Not *deellz*, not middle class, not the world he professed to be of.

"Dee-uulz," she said, watching his expression wilt as he realized he'd given himself away. "Mr. Scott, where is it you're from?"

"I live in Giffnock."

"No," she said carefully, "where is it you're *from*. Where did your parents live when you were born?"

"South Side." He blinked.

Morrow cocked an ear. "Priesthill?"

"No," Scott said carefully, "Giffnock."

"Aye," she nodded, "Priesthill."

He sat back, his mouth twitching with disgust. "Giffnock," he said quietly.

She put a consoling hand on the table. "Listen, we won't tell anyone, ye don't need to lie to us."

He chewed his cheek unhappily and Harris added, "We can find out . . ."

"Kennishead high flats," he said quietly. They would have laughed at him but his shame was so raw that it took the fun out of it. "What's that to do with anything?"

"What university did you study at?"

"Glasgow Uni Law School."

Morrow nodded again. She'd been to the

Law School to interview someone once. If she'd been a student there she'd have lied about her background too. "Sarah was as posh as you can get, wasn't she?"

He blinked defensively at the table top, adopting his posh voice again. "As I say, she was a well-bred young lady."

Morrow watched discomfort and conflict ripple across his face, as if his idea of himself was melting. "Sarah asked for you specifically?"

"Yes."

"D'you think she knew you were a bit impressed by how posh she was?"

"I was always respectful —"

"No, no: d'you think she spotted you passing for white? Knew she could intimidate you?"

Scott sat back in his chair and glared at her. His eyes flicked to the cassette tapes whirring in the recorder and he narrowed his eyes and mouthed at her — fuck off. A criminal lawyer would have known not to do that.

Morrow looked hard at him. "I'm very sorry, Mr. Scott, could you just repeat what you said for the benefit of the tape?"

"Didn't say anything," he smirked.

Slowly Morrow raised her hand to the corner of the room. He followed the trajectory of her finger and froze when he saw the red light on the camera.

Morrow leaned across the table to him. "Did Sarah Erroll seem bright to you?"

"No," he told the camera quietly, "not really."

"Violent?"

"Violent?" Still looking at the camera. "God, no."

"Talk to me, please, Mr. Scott."

He turned his remorseful face to her but his mind was on the watcher. "Sarah was harmless. Horsey."

"We found a taser gun in her house disguised as a mobile phone. The initial forensic traces suggest she carried it in her handbag."

He forgot the camera then. "A *taser* gun? What, like an electric shock gun?"

"Yeah."

"That's dangerous."

"Nine hundred thousand volts," said Harris and left it hanging in the air.

Scott shook his head at the table. When he spoke his voice came from the high flats, "I'd her down as a diddy."

Morrow watched him, reading his confusion, seeing him rerun every meeting with Sarah Erroll, looking for clues, wondering if he could have known. She watched him and saw yet another person lose sympathy for Sarah Erroll.

She watched him until a tiny heel, no bigger than her thumb, karate-kicked her heart and stole her away from the world.

SIXTEEN

Moira and Thomas were in the big freezer room below the kitchen. Neither could remember the last time they came in here. Usually the kitchen was full of staff, or the threat of staff, and had been a public space, but Moira had dismissed almost all of the live-ins.

She had kept Nanny Mary on for Thomas's sake but they talked about it and Thomas said she needn't have. He didn't want her anymore. As he said it Moira watched the curl on his lip, not his eyes. He couldn't be certain that she knew about Mary's midnight creeping, but she agreed and called Mary in and said they couldn't afford to employ her now. Mary seemed relieved, said she'd pack and be gone in the morning before they woke up. Then she shook both their hands, cold and professional, not searching Thomas's face for anything or trying to look him in the eye.

He watched her leave the room, her buttocks pert through her silk skirt, and he was struck suddenly by the impression that his father had ordered Mary to fuck him and she was glad it was over too. He did think it odd that she didn't ask for references.

Jamie had taken two grand cash as an *ex gratia* payment. Moira hadn't mentioned the choking incident and Thomas felt she probably wouldn't now.

So the hall, the kitchen, the whole of the house was empty. They hadn't had any supper and Moira had suggested an expedition to the kitchen.

The freezer room was warm and windowless. The whir of the motors bounced off the subterranean walls. It took them a while to find the light switch, a cord hanging down at the very bottom of the steep stairs in the pitch dark. Three big sarcophagus freezers purred quietly. One of them was padlocked shut. Moira went straight over and fingered the lock.

"This must be the meat freezer," she said.

Thomas thought suddenly of a bed of meat, of a body in the locked cabinet, but it was just a spooky, unfamiliar room. That was all it was. It was dark and quiet and spooky.

He lifted the lid of the freezer next to him,

looked down and found the contents were well ordered. Clear plastic tubs full of handmade gourmet meals prepared by their cook before he left, individual portions, each dish marked clearly on the lid in thick curly writing.

Moira had opened the other freezer and found it crammed with loaves of different kinds of bread, ingredients, frozen herbs and cheese, frozen juice. She held up a frosted cylindrical bag triumphantly by the tail. "Look!"

Mini pizzas. Cheap mini pizzas. "This must be what they eat," she said, "the staff. Let's have them!"

"What do you do with them though?"

"Put them in the oven." Thomas was impressed until Moira explained, "It says it on the packet. I can do it."

She hurried past him, up the stairs to the kitchen proper to cook a meal for him and prove she was able. But she had left the freezer lid leaning against the wall, the smoky cold crackling out of it into the warm room. Thomas waited until her ankles disappeared up the steps into the brightness of the kitchen then stepped over and shut it. She heard it slam and bent down to a crouch, smiling. "Sorry. Fell at the first fence." She stood up and vanished into the kitchen.

Thomas looked at the locked meat freezer again. There was no one in there. Sarah Erroll wasn't in there. Ella wasn't in there. It was just a spooky room.

He took the steps up to the kitchen, emerging to find Moira with her head in the oven. For a moment he thought she was trying to gas herself, in an electric oven, thought of her gone and he found he didn't move to yank her out.

"Oh, there it's . . ." She pulled the top of her head out and smiled at him. "Electric. Silly me." She pressed the button and turned the knob.

Thomas considered himself with a kind of horrified wonder, his capacity for callousness, and then changed the subject. "Mum, where did Cookie keep the keys?"

She pointed to a small metal cabinet on the wall behind the kitchen door. He opened it and found six key hooks, each occupied, each labeled. "Freezer 3" had a small key on a loop of pink string. He took the key, stepped carefully back down the steep steps to the freezer room and looked across to the padlock.

Small. Brass. He didn't want to open it. Never wanted to see a mess like Sarah Erroll again. But the longer he left it the more frightened he became. Forcing himself to walk over, he stood in front of it, looking down at the white coffin. Blindly, he fumbled the tiny key against the hole, feeling for the lock, missing, feeling there was something sexual about this and it was terrible and soiling and filthy, but making himself go on because not knowing was worse and he wouldn't sleep for thinking about it.

The padlock sprang open and dropped into his open hand.

He flicked the hinged shackle up, stood, looked and lifted the lid. A bed of frosty meat. Steaks, chops, venison, joints. A giant leg of lamb. No bodies, no blood, no dead Ella.

"Meat?" Moira had followed him down.

"Yeah." He slammed the lid shut. "Just meat."

"Did you think he'd hidden money in there or something?"

"No, I just . . . I wondered."

As they waited for the pizzas to cook he cracked open a beer from the fridge and they enjoyed the quiet of the house. Moira explained that Lars's business collapse had left them with no more than three hundred thousand a year. They'd need to sell the house and live somewhere else. The ATR-42 was owned by the business, as was the house in South Africa that Thomas had never even been to because they always went in term time, and most of the cars and the central London office space and the Stamford Bridge memberships, so they wouldn't be seeing them again. Thomas didn't care. He didn't even like football much.

She took the pizzas out and put them on a chopping board to cut them up. They were delicious.

Thomas watched Moira eat. "Your mouth isn't dry anymore."

She looked back at him and knew what he was asking. "You're right. It's not. I came off them."

"When?"

"Five weeks ago. Your father hasn't been home much."

Thomas wondered if she knew where Lars had been. Thomas knew exactly where he had been. With her, the other wife.

It was the last conversation he had with his father. Lars took him out the day before autumn term started, to Fortnum's ice cream parlor, where every second table had a distant-eyed father in a city suit escorting an estranged brat. Thomas was older than the other kids, wondered if his father had even noticed how much older he was.

Thomas looked at Moira. She might know. She might not care.

"Why did he really kill himself?"

Moira shrugged. "They disqualified him. I think he knew he'd never be the big player again. He couldn't live without the game. He'd no friends left, no other interests, I suppose." She looked dreamy. "You didn't know him when he was young. He was fun. Funny. He had a sense of humor back then. And early on, we really loved each other. We had *friends.* We could have been happy, instead of, you know what happened. God . . . it's such a lot to squander."

Thomas listened, nodding, until Moira looked at him and saw his eyes were red and told him to go to bed.

"I need a shower," he said quietly. "I really need a shower first."

SEVENTEEN

Morrow was in the office, pulling her coat on, checking her bag for keys and phone when Routher knocked gingerly on the open door.

"DCI Bannerman would like to see you in his office, ma'am."

"Thanks, Routher."

He slipped back into the corridor and she called him back. "Why were you late for the briefing?"

Routher would never have made a spy: his face was so expressive she could see the whole story unfold in the tiny shifts of his facial expression: eyebrows meeting because he had been late for a good reason and it wasn't his fault, a sudden recollection that lateness was bad and not being promoted was good, a half smile congratulating himself on being so fly and finally the lie: "Sorry, I slept in."

"At five in the afternoon, you slept in?"

He looked confused. "It won't happen again."

She stared at him, watching him redden. "Get out of here."

He did and was glad to.

She stepped down the corridor and found Bannerman's door half open. He was talking to someone, yeah-yeahing. She knocked and walked in and found him on the phone, agreeing with someone. He eyed the chair in front of him and she took it, waiting while he finished, looking around his desk.

When they shared an office he had the desk laid out in ham-handed messages, loudly advertising The-kinda-guy-I-am. Morrow didn't believe any of them. She found it interesting to read though, to hone her skill at looking behind the stated to the obvious. Bannerman didn't eat health bars for lunch because he was health conscious but because he was afraid of getting fat. She wasn't taken in by the surfboard paperweight either: he didn't enjoy an outdoor life of adventure but an occasional sunbed. She hated him because she saw him trying to stand out from the tone of the force, knowing he could afford to because he was so intensely of it; his father was a police officer, he knew the game inside out.

Promoted, Bannerman wasn't concerned

with appearing anything but in charge.

He hung up the phone. "I'm taking this investigation over a bit, Morrow," he said without apology. "Because of the money. It's a worry, not just that it's there and there's so much, but because it's in euros."

Another lie. The money was part of it but he wanted more than the glory. He was up to something else. "Have they checked it for traces of drugs?" she asked.

"Yeah: it hasn't got any traces on it. Little or nothing. An unusual amount of nothing, these seem to be straight from the bank. Which bank we're not sure yet, they're not sequential. We're checking for large withdrawals of euros in this country but they could be from anywhere."

"My guess is New York."

"Yeah, there's enough floating about over there for that to be feasible."

She didn't know how to broach the fact that the men wouldn't work for him. "Sir: morale. They're competing to see who can be most useless — it's not supposed to be like this."

Bannerman checked behind her and dipped his voice. "I know. I've noticed. I'm coming in tomorrow morning to give them an earful."

"No, please —"

"Morale is my job as much as yours. If they can't bring it with them I'll have to use the heavy hand."

The heavy hand: a boss phrase, as if the men could be slapped enthusiastic. These men were older, more confident, not straight out of Tulliallan. "They're not that kind of crew, sir."

"I don't want Harris taking on too much." And here it was, his downcast eyes, signaling the significance. "Why don't you use Wilder a bit more?"

"Because he's a dick."

He gave her a look, a warning. "You going home?"

"Trying to." She gathered her things together. "I think Sarah Erroll gave the impression that she was a daft Sloane but was actually double wide. We interviewed her lawyer and she'd —"

"I know, I was watching."

She stopped and looked at him. He really was taking over and there was nothing she could do about it. "OK," she said testily. "I'll see you tomorrow."

"Good night."

She allowed herself a small curse at him under the click of the door.

Routher was outside in the corridor again and she turned her venom on him. "Are you planning to hang about the corridor all night, Routher?"

Startled by the strength of her annoyance he spluttered, "No, I'm . . . I'm waiting on you. Prelims are on your desk and McCarthy's been looking at her phone. She was an escort."

"Oh, shite." Morrow stepped over to her office and opened the door, swinging her bag in, bowling it to her desk. "Come on."

Mark McCarthy had the face of an underweight hemophiliac. He was the unhealthiest-looking specimen Morrow had ever encountered in the force. She was always amazed that he hadn't been seconded by the drug squad for undercover work.

He smiled up as she approached his desk. "Got some good stuff, boss. These phones have got your whole life on them."

She pulled a chair over and sat down. "Give us it."

"Okayyyyy." He pulled the phone out of the plastic productions bag, the black dust from the fingerprint search sticking to his fingertips. "First off, we got prints on the face of it and they're not hers. They're good 'uns as well."

"Anyone with a record?"

"No matches so far."

"Fuck," said Morrow with more force than she meant to. What she really wanted was a home address of someone with previous in the same sort of crime so she could go home right now.

McCarthy looked hurt. "It's still good though, eh?"

"Oh yeah, yeah, what else?"

"The last call made was 999. This is what they sent us."

He had set it up to impress her: he shook the mouse back and forth and his computer screen opened to an audio file. He selected "copy" from the menu, dragged it to the memory stick, let it download and clicked the stick out, handing it to her. After all the pronounced disinterest of the day Morrow was quite touched.

"Can you hear Sarah on it?"

"Yeah. Also . . ." McCarthy clicked up a list of emails, each headed with the sender's name. Most of them were from Scott and headed either "Glenarvon" or "Settlement of Estate" but as he scrolled down a series of older emails appeared, all from "Sabine." "See how the messages are headed 'Re: . . .'? That means they came from another email account. And they're all the same sort of thing."

McCarthy opened one. P would be in London on business, had heard about her from a friend. He knew the score and the prices and hoped they could get together for some fun. He gave his hotel and a phone number. It was an internet hook-up.

"Did she reply?" asked Morrow.

"No. If there's a wee arrow at the side," he shut the email and went back to the listings, "that arrow tells you it's been replied to. These don't have one. She stopped replying about two months ago."

"When her mum died," Morrow said. "And she stopped having to pay for the carers. Her mum had around-the-clock care in her house. It's very expensive."

McCarthy nodded, but she could tell he was realizing it for the first time. She didn't care whether he knew or not, she just wanted him to mention it to the other men in passing.

"This phone got a camera?"

"Yup." He went back to the main menu and selected the pictures file. "It's an old iPhone though. She must have been an early adopter: tiny memory, holds about a hundred photos, tops. We're looking through her laptop," he pointed to a tiny silver notebook on another desk, "but she's got passwords for everything and they're all different."

There were eighty-seven pictures on the phone. Some were of people but many were of odd items. They opened them and could see that they were Yellow Pages listing for roofers and septic tank engineers, photographed presumably so she didn't have to jot numbers down. The rest were recent. Many were of New York street scenes, the park, badly framed images of other passengers on a sunny-day boat ride off Manhattan.

"Was she downloading the photos regularly?"

"Yeah, far as we can tell."

"I never remember to download. My phone's polluted with old photos." She frowned at the phone. It seemed strange.

"Show me the dates on the New York ones."

McCarthy moved the mouse over them and the dates came up. They were taken within the past week. "They're all new."

Morrow chewed her lip and looked at it. "She'd been there seven times in the past year. Doesn't it seem strange to be thrilled enough to take photos? It's like she's pretending to be a tourist."

"Maybe she was a tourist."

"But she'd been there seven times in eleven months. Who still takes photos like that after the seventh time?"

"She was doing touristy things when she was there, for definite. She was going to museums and that." He pointed over to the suitcase on an exhibits table. "She's bought a museum catalogue. Must have really enjoyed it because the book weighs a ton. Tripled the weight of her luggage."

Morrow looked over at the small white suitcase from the hall. It lay unzipped and open next to the contents: a small pile of neatly folded clothes and a transparent toilet bag. A massive cellophane-wrapped book sat by it.

She stood up and walked over to the table, looking down at the contents of the suitcase.

The huge pale green catalogue for the Museum of Modern Art was still sealed in cellophane, the receipt sellotaped onto it. The purchase dates were right for her last trip. Also in the case were a change of underwear, a blue version of the pink lacy camiknickers they had found in the house, a silver dress, a toilet bag with all the creams and lotions transferred into flight-friendly small bottles and gathered in a transparent plastic ziplock bag. She'd been on the pill.

There were no traces of an individual in

the suitcase. No home address in case it got lost, no photos or magazines she was in the middle of reading, no notes-to-self or old tickets, nothing extraneous.

Morrow looked at the catalogue. She tried to pick it up with one hand. It was so heavy that it strained her wrist. She took hold of the suitcase lid and shut it, looked, opened it again, put the catalogue in and shut it again. The catalogue took up almost half of the case. She took it out again and sat it on the table, looking at it. There was something wrong with it, the cellophane was slightly loose and the seams inconsistent, wavering.

She took out her car keys and caught the edge of the plastic, scratching at it to start a rip and pulling it off. She used the edge of the key to flip the book open.

Morrow smiled. Inside, off center, in among black-and-white photographs of tatty cubist collages, someone had cut a perfect bed for the fat brick of crisp purple five-hundred-euro notes wrapped in two elastic bands. Sarah could have taken the same catalogue through time after time, rewrapping it, buying a new one for the receipt with the right date. And it explained why she checked it in. If she'd taken it through hand luggage the catalogue would look new to the naked eye but the security

216

X-ray would show a gray rectangle and the inconsistency in the paper. The photos of New York were part of her cover as a gallery-visiting tourist.

McCarthy was standing across the table from her, staring down at the money, hypnotized. Routher came over too and a young DC stood up at his desk, standing on tiptoes to see.

Morrow looked around at them, at their mouths hanging open, eyes locked on the money but their minds far away, in bookies, in car showrooms, wherever their yen took them.

The night shift was fractured after that: McCarthy and Routher had to guard the cash until the armored van driver could be roused from his bed. Bannerman insisted on taking the catalogue over to the lab himself for processing, even though traces of anything relevant to the murder investigation seemed unlikely. Morrow was left alone in her office looking through the files from the phone.

In among the photos she found three of a man, a silver-haired man, and made a note to herself to check whether his photo was in Glenarvon somewhere. The older photographs were of Sarah's mother, a tiny tortoise of a woman wearing out-of-date dresses that had belonged to her in a heftier time. The later ones showed her peering at the camera, cross, wearing brand-new nightclothes in pale blue and powder pink, blankets over her knees, in the armchair in the kitchen, in her bed, by a window. The photographs were very tender. Sarah had crouched to take them at her mother's eye level and the light was soft in all of them. Kay was in the background of some of the kitchen photos, smiling over her shoulder at the late Mrs. Erroll, looking plump and motherly. Morrow touched Kay's face on the screen and smiled to herself.

The emails on Sarah's phone nearly all concerned the house. Scott seemed determined to write to her about every detail of the sale and the estate settlement, doubtless charging every time. The emails were so overwritten and obsequious he sounded kickable. She could well imagine the level of deference would make Sarah despise him, feel a certain glee about tricking him.

Many of the other emails were addressed to Sabine, arrangements to meet up in specific hotels at very specific times, promises of hearty fun but ambiguous as to the exact nature of it. It was a disaster that she'd done that. Cops had little sympathy for sex workers, however many courses they were sent on. They were too much trouble, too chaotic, magnets for nutters. The only way most cops could summon up sympathy was to frame them as children who'd been tricked into it, call them "girls" and "boys." Or else they made it an accident of addiction: they did it for drugs, because of drugs, needed drugs to do it. Either way they couldn't help themselves. Sex workers, in the habit of telling people what they wanted to hear, always agreed. Few did it for the money, she'd noticed. Few admitted it was an economic option.

Morrow covered her face and thought of Sarah on the stairs. At some point she must have known what was happening, and the job would have made that moment of realization even more appalling. Sex workers blamed themselves, however appalling a crime against them. Half the battle when taking a rape report or the details of a brutal assault was getting them to admit that they had been a victim. They needed the illusion of control. Morrow rubbed her stomach. They all needed that. She imagined Sarah lying on her back as a foot came towards her face and her last conscious thought being a personal reproach.

She sat back and knuckled her hot eyes. It was getting late. The room was dark and the corridor outside was quiet. She wanted to be home, in front of the telly, seesawing the settee with Brian. As a final chore she put in her earphones and called up the audio file for the 999 call.

If Sarah had just spoken five seconds earlier they could have saved her life.

But that wasn't what happened.

The pause between Sarah dialing the number and speaking made the operator tag it as a silent call and put it through to the recorder. Silent calls were usually made by drunken teenagers or attention-seeking idiots, or by five-year-olds playing with the phone while their mum went for a bath. The recorder was a pragmatic, statistically based system that nearly always served to weed out time-wasters. Nearly always.

Morrow listened and heard Sarah's soft voice in the far, foggy distance. She saw the cold, blank eyes of the coppers at the brief, waiting to get to their warm, safe homes.

She listened to the end of the 999 and then listened to it again. She found herself crying in the dark, not just for Sarah Erroll but for her own dead father and for JJ, for all the unloved and the unlovely.

When she had finished she dried her face, listening for noise outside in the corridor before slipping out of the front door of the

220

station. She walked around the back of the giant planter pots, following the wall to her own car, parked in the black street.

She slipped into the driver's seat and locked the door, flicked the cabin lights off and sat, ashamed, feeling raw and porous and stupid and pregnant.

EIGHTEEN

Thomas was exhausted but wired. He'd had a shower and felt clean now, sitting on the sofa in his living room, watching TV in a towel, changing channel every thirty seconds, looking, for what he didn't know. *Family Guy.* Something short. His burning eyes were busy on the TV, vague thoughts half-formed in his mind, thoughts he couldn't have dealt with if he'd been alone with them, focused on them.

He watched a video of a rap collective, ugly guys in a mansion poolside, batting away beautiful strippers. He thought about his parents. To Thomas, Lars had always represented a great aching need to impress, an imminent performance that was doomed to disappoint. It had taken up a lot of his head space because he wasn't great at anything much. Lars had told him many times that the biggest thing he'd ever be was Lars's son. But now Lars was gone. All that head-fuck was over with. And Moira had been cold and distant, but she was here now, warm. If they never spoke again, if she took an overdose tonight in her rooms, Thomas knew he couldn't have asked for more than this evening, chatting, making eye contact, her apologizing.

He knew he didn't deserve either her warmth or the delight of Lars leaving. Two incredible strokes of luck, just after what he had done. It wasn't right. Like Hitler winning the lottery.

He shifted a buttock on the damp itchy towel and changed channel. Sharks in murky blue water, mouths open, coming straight for the photographer, and he thought of Sarah Erroll at the top of the stairs, looking at her bare buttocks as she held the banister and dropped her foot to the first step, and the bump to his shoulder as Squeak came past him, his hand outstretched for her hair. Blonde hair. Lots of different colors of blonde, dark, yellow, traces of white and then pink and scarlet through it, clumps of hair hanging from Squeak's fist where it came out when he pulled her back.

The trilling made him sit up and look around before he registered what it was. His mobile. Still in the duffel bag sitting next

223

door, on his bedroom floor. Nanny Mary had dropped and left it, because she'd been called to see Moira and told she was sacked. Obeying the trilling, he padded through to the bag, lifted it out and saw the name on the screen: Squeak.

Thomas held the phone and looked at it as it rang. Squeak wanted to threaten him. It was pathetic. He was going to run through all of that again: you took me to the wrong house. Thomas didn't want to talk to him. And yet the need to obey the ring tone made him stay looking at the phone, imagining Squeak in the toilet in his room in the dormy, sitting in the dark because it was after lights-out. He'd be sitting on the toilet: the bathrooms were small and it was the only place to sit down. They had to hand their mobiles into housekeeping at the start of term and got them back at weekends but Squeak had an illegal phone, an extra phone that he just used for looking up porn. He'd be sitting in the dark on the toilet, calling on his porn phone, waiting for him to answer.

Thomas pressed the green button and lifted the phone to his ear. "Man?" He was whispering too because Squeak could get in trouble having a mobile.

"Yeah, you there?"

"Yeah."

"Sorry about your old man?"

"Not really, no."

"Hung himself?"

"Yeah. On his lawn."

Squeak breathed a laugh at that, he knew about the lawn. " 'Kin hell."

"Yeah. Twat."

"Twatster."

Thomas looked into the next room, to the shark show: bloody water. "Twatmeister."

Squeak breathed deep into the receiver. "Sorry about earlier."

"Yeah."

"I didn't know, thought you'd 'fessed up to someone. Put me in it."

"Fuck off," Thomas said gently, picking at a mark on his bedroom wall.

"Yeah. Got a fright."

"Nah, it was just . . . you know." Thomas nodded, didn't want to say it as if it was a big thing because it wasn't to him. "Lars gone bye-bye."

"Hmm." Squeak understood. "We all right then?"

"Course. Happened today?"

He could hear Squeak smile. "Got eighty-nine percent in that Social Sciences prelim."

"Fucker."

"I know. Want to know what you got?"

"What?"

"Forty-six percent," said Squeak, and laughed because it was pathetic. And Thomas laughed too. It didn't matter. Social Sciences was a piece of shit subject anyway, but that's not why Thomas was laughing. He was laughing because Squeak was giving him a hard time, taking the piss and it meant everything was all right.

"You smug fuck," said Thomas softly. "I was dreaming of becoming a social scientist and you're crushing my dreams."

"Yeah," Squeak smiled. "Anyway. Ella home yet?"

"Tomorrow morning."

"Yeah, tell her I was thinking of her . . ." Thomas shut his eyes and cringed, knowing he was going to say something about her. "Just don't tell her what I was doing while I was thinking about her."

"Yeah," warned Thomas. "Twelve fucking years old, man."

"Hey." Squeak sounded annoyed at being corrected. "I could marry her in Texas."

"Still not right."

"In Holland —"

"Not right, man." Thomas took a stand. "She's my sister. I hate her but she's still my fucking . . . you know."

"Yeah, well, fuck off." He sounded a bit

annoyed.

"Fuck off yourself," said Thomas, telling him to drop it.

"Yeah," he let it go, "fuck off . . ."

Squeak didn't mean anything by it, he didn't have a thing for young girls at all, Thomas knew that. If anything he had a thing for Nanny Mary's age, and he meant it as a compliment. Fancying a bloke's sister meant he wasn't stuck with a pig or someone fat. But it bothered Thomas, Squeak talking like that, because he'd seen the things Squeak had on that phone, animals and anal and stuff, and he didn't want any part of him in real life associated with that shit.

"Better go," said Squeak and hung up before Thomas had the chance to say goodbye back.

Thomas dropped the dead phone onto the bed and looked at it, reproachful, as if it was Squeak's porn phone. He spun on his heels and his eyes fell on Sarah Erroll's bare buttocks as she held the banister and dropped her foot to the first step. He felt the bump to his shoulder as Squeak came past him, his hand outstretched for her hair. And then the hand in her hair, knuckles white because Squeak was holding so tight and her feet moving on despite her head staying where it was, and her falling back and slaloming down the stairs to the bottom, and Squeak crouched, still holding her hair until it came out in his hand, following her down to the bottom and looking back up to Thomas, excited, happy, as if he couldn't believe his luck, as if every Christmas he'd ever had had come at once and he didn't know how he had managed to be such a good boy as to deserve this.

Thomas looked at the phone on the bed and he felt sick again, a small echo of the sickness he'd felt looking at Squeak at the bottom of the stairs. A kind of heavy sadness, sickness that made the world sway and his head feel as if it was full of oil.

He had resisted the realization when they were on the stairs but he faced it now: if they got you down, anyone would do that to you. Anyone.

NINETEEN

It was nudging eleven, too late for a visit, but Morrow was searching for a spark of comfort in a melancholy day and so she drove on.

The roads around Castlemilk were broad and straight, designed for the age of the automobile, but with a population who could only afford the bus. The wide streets weren't used for anything other than mowing down toddlers and racing stolen cars so the planners had sprinkled them with deep speed bumps and extended the pavements to create traffic-calming swerves in the road. Morrow was taking it at ten miles an hour and it still felt reckless.

Passing the local police station, another solid fortress in brown brick, she pulled up a short steep hill and parked in one of twenty parking spaces. The flats looked scruffy and ominous, three high blocks watched the city. The glass column of each stairwell was lit in a different color, electric blue lights in the middle, orange and purple on either side. The vibrant-colored lights clashed with the winsome time-drabbed pastel of the outside walls: mustard, pea green, brown.

She stepped out of the car, thinking to herself that as well as visiting a witness alone, she had parked her private car in full view of the flats. She looked around. CCTV cameras were pinned onto lampposts at every corner. From where she was standing she could see more than ten and they all looked operational.

If anything happened tonight the bosses would know she'd come here alone in her own car. Still, she didn't turn around and get back in but walked over to the middle block, checking her notebook for the flat number, pressing the buzzer before looking through the doors. The lobby was tiled white and as clean as an operating theater. Haranguing signs on the wall ordered the residents not to have dogs in their flats, not to dump rubbish in the lifts, not to graffiti. They didn't seem to need much ordering around. Even the signs were nice and clean.

A young girl's voice crackled "Hello?" on the intercom.

"Hello, is this Kay Murray's flat?"

The girl turned from the intercom and shouted, "Mum! For you!"

Morrow smiled as she heard Kay's voice approaching, ". . . bloody ask who it is instead of just bawling at me."

But the girl stomped off and a door slammed shut.

Kay cleared her throat and spoke, "Aye?"

"Kay? It's me."

There was a pause.

"Alex?"

"Yeah."

"Oh. Come up . . ."

The entry door buzzed angrily and Morrow pushed it open. Across the lobby she pressed the call button for the lift and the doors slid open into a warm orange light. The floor was clean, none of the plastic buttons were charred with lighters and there was just the faintest tang of disinfectant. It was an unthreatening environment but still, as the doors slid shut in front of her and the lift took off, Morrow felt a jolt in her stomach.

The doors opened again onto cold strip lights and a lingering smell from a takeaway curry bag left hanging on a door handle. The floor was vibrant pink with turquoise diamonds set out in a path. All the doors were turquoise with mottled glass panels, some lit, some dark. Morrow walked down to number eight.

Kay's window had a ruffle of pink nets inside. It was an old door, a good sign: it meant she'd been there a long time, had paid her rent and no one had kicked it in. A shattered and patched door was a classic signifier of a problem household.

Morrow chapped and stepped back, waiting. Behind her, the lift doors beeped and she turned and watched the orange light narrow to a slit and disappear.

Without preliminaries, the front door flew open and a tall thin boy stood there, looking her up and down.

"Hello!"

Morrow forced a smile. "Is this Kay Murray's house?"

He grinned at her polished shoes. "God, you really are a polis." He leaned out and took her elbow, tugging her gently into the small hall and shutting the door. "She said she'd met an old pal from school and you'd became a polis. You really the same age as her? You look younger."

"Oh, I'm all puffy because I'm pregnant," she said, but she was pleased nonetheless.

The hallway was busy with empty cardboard boxes for detergent, washing powder, crisps, crackers, empty trays for washing-up liquid bottles and shampoo. They were stacked messily on top of each other, four or five high and shoved against the wall. Morrow thought briefly of shoplifting, truck hijacks and theft from employers. She stopped herself: she was here to see Kay, it wasn't supposed to be official business.

The living room and kitchen doors lay open to her right. In front of her were three more doors, each decorated by the occupants: one was matte black, one painted pink with randomly placed glittery butterfly stickers and a greasy, balding bit of pink marabou wrapped around the door handle. The third was split down the middle, half Celtic green and half Rangers blue. The Celtic fan had used a felt tip to reclaim part of the border lands but the Rangers fan had smeared the green intrusion off with a wet cloth.

The bathroom door opened and Kay stepped out, her wet hair swept harshly back from her face. She had a tired purple towel around her shoulders, frayed at a corner, splattered with old spots of hair dye, and one of her ears was rimmed brown. She looked angrily at the boy and kicked at an empty box. "I keep telling you to take these things down but you just walk past them." She smiled nervously at Morrow. "My pal's got a Costco card."

"Lucky you," said Morrow.

"Aye, it's great." She clutched the towel at her neck and lifted an empty crisp box, sitting it on top of the others, kicking them against the wall. "We've got a club, buy in bulk and then split it up when we get back here. I don't know if I'm saving any money or just buying more." She gestured at the boy who had answered the door. "They're right gannets. Just eat whatever I bring in. Food just evaporates. They've been necking a bucket of gefilte fish."

The boy rolled his tongue out. "They're disgusting."

Kay rubbed at her hair with the towel. "Still eating them though."

The boy was dark and handsome, had a commanding unibrow and blue eyes. Morrow could see faint traces of Kay about him but not much. Suddenly earnest, he asked Morrow, "Listen, seriously: how would I get to be a polis?"

Kay shook her head at Morrow. "Fuck's sake."

Morrow shrugged, not certain he was being serious. "Just apply. Phone them and ask how. You have to apply a few times though, so don't get discouraged."

He thought about it, seemed to arrive at a

234

resolve: "I wouldn't get discouraged."

Kay looked embarrassed and said to Morrow, "As if they'd take you, anyway."

"Why, what's wrong with me?"

Kay tutted and stepped across the hall to the kitchen, rubbing her hair with the towel as she walked between them and flicked the kettle on. "Ye know fine."

"Seriously, what's wrong with me?"

Kay ignored the question. "Alex: tea?"

No police officer on duty would accept a cup of tea from a member of the public. It made the stay longer and you never knew what they would put in it, but Morrow said, "Aye, thanks." As if to prove to herself that it wasn't official.

The boy was still talking to her. "Defo. I'm gonnae phone and get a form. Mum, will ye help me fill it out?"

The pink bedroom door opened and a young teenage girl looked out accusingly. She was her mother's double at the same age but chubbier than Kay had been and prettier for it. Morrow smiled warmly. "Hello."

The girl looked suddenly shy and shut her door a little, half hiding her face.

"Your mum and I were pals when she was your age."

"Oh." Clearly not interested but too well

brought up to let it show, her eyes strayed to the wall.

"She looked exactly like you, only not as pretty."

The girl blushed, panicked and slammed the door shut. Her brother smiled and looked at the pink door, knowing his sister was listening. "She's gorgeous, isn't she? She doesn't even know she's gorgeous."

Morrow was touched. The custom of complimenting children was relatively new in Scotland. She had never been complimented on anything until she met Brian, and it was far too late by then, she never really believed him.

Kay looked up and sighed. "Right, Joe," she said gently, "you fuck off. We're gonnae have a chat."

"Oh, aye." Joe raised his eyebrows suggestively at Morrow. "Old times? Gentlemen callers?"

"Sarah Erroll." Kay looked sad.

"Oh." Joe couldn't think of anything funny to say about that. "Terrible." He backed off to his wee sister's door, knocking and walking in without waiting for an answer. They could hear him speak and the girl's squeaky voice responding.

Kay reached into a cupboard. Morrow saw her take out a mug, look into it, flinch and put it back. She chose two from the back. The worktop was littered with giant packets of crisps and cakes, the sink clogged with used tea bags and everything smelled of cigarette smoke.

Morrow slumped in the doorway to the kitchen. "I hope it's OK, me coming here?"

"Aye," said Kay, "no problem." But she was embarrassed and gestured at the mess. "I don't get much more prepared for company than this."

Morrow's insincere response about the mess in her own house was lost in the rumble of the kettle.

She knew she shouldn't feel sad for Kay. This house was a good house. The kids were talking to each other and to Kay, but she felt that they both recognized it as a depressing replay of the places they had grown up in. Homes full of ciggie smog and broken biscuits and unspoken anger, of reluctant affection and ridiculed ambitions.

Kay took two tea bags out of a giant packet of Tetley, dropped them into the cups and poured water on them. Morrow felt she had to say something positive. "He's lovely, your Joe. Handsome."

"Too charming. Gets in trouble." She corrected herself, "No, they're good kids. They're nice to each other. Bodes well, I suppose." She added the milk from a six-liter carton and put it back in the fridge. "Sugar?"

Morrow shook her head and Kay handed her the cup. " 'Mon."

Morrow followed her into the living room. A scuffed leather settee was stacked with clean, folded clothes arranged in neat rows. An ironing board was standing up in front of a boxy old television. Hung around the walls were a collection of clip frames of family photos. A lot of them had slipped behind the glass, giving the impression of an avalanche of family events and parties, school plays, of lives passing in a great, hurtling blur.

Morrow saw Kay's eye flick anxiously to marks on the floor, to a greasy strip around the light switch where hand after hand had swiped it on their way out and in.

Kay put her cup down on the floor and looked for room for Morrow to sit down. Then, resentment telling in the jerky speed of her gestures, she carefully stacked the separated piles of ironing on top of each other, putting them on the ironing board, making a space for her.

Morrow kept her coat on, put her mug down on the floor and sat down.

Kay took the armchair, looked at her,

238

seemed annoyed and looked at Morrow's mug. "Is that too wet for you? Fancy four gross of shortbread with it?"

Morrow smiled. "Not really."

"Multipack of Hula Hoops?"

"Naw, 'm fine."

Kay held her hand up and waved a rainbow arc in front of her face. "All the flavors . . ."

"No thanks, I'm going home to my dinner anyway."

"Late . . . aye." She looked at Morrow's stomach. "Important to eat right, eh?"

They ran out of things to say suddenly and Morrow felt awkward in a way she never did when she was on business. Kay gave into her mood and asked, "What's really going on, Alex?"

"How d'ye mean?"

"Why are you here on your own?"

Kay knew the police always flew in twos. It troubled Morrow that she did. "I wanted to ask you about Sarah, what kind of person she was, stuff like that."

"Background stuff?"

"Yeah, you know, background . . ."

But Kay narrowed her eyes at Morrow, staring too long, trying to read her.

Morrow kept her face straight. A smile would have looked sly. Morrow was working, she lived in a bought house, had a car. She had gotten away and Kay hadn't. Morrow was worried that this was what she had come here for, not for comfort or nostalgia or to find out who Sarah Erroll was, but to measure herself against Kay, looking for cheap confirmation that, measured and weighed, she was doing better than her old friend.

Kay watched her unmoving face, seemed to recognize that she was being stonewalled and why. She blinked and began reeling mechanically through some facts: "Sarah was nice. She loved her mum, even though Mrs. Erroll was a cheeky cow. I liked Joy. That was her name, Mrs. Erroll. Joy Alice Erroll. Everyone called her Mrs. Erroll." She put a leg straight out in front of her and rocked her bum off the seat, reaching up to the ironing board for her cigarettes and lighter. She opened the packet and looked at Morrow's belly. "Mind?"

"Wire in."

They smiled at that, each away from the other, because it was word-for-word a conversation they'd had a hundred times, a hundred years ago. Kay lit up, puffed hard and leaned down over the side of the chair for a dirty glass ashtray. She cradled it on her knee.

"Did Sarah have a boyfriend?"

"Never brought a boyfriend home. I know she was going with someone though. She'd get texts and . . . well, the way she smiled at the phone . . ." Kay remembered quietly. "Mother of teenagers. Makes you kind of psychic. Probably didn't want him to meet her mother."

"Was her mother difficult?"

"Auch, doesn't take a difficult mother to make children secretive. They just are. Natural, isn't it?" Kay thought about it and smiled. "But Joy was difficult, yeah, and bananas. Bad combination. If she didn't hate him, he'd have hated her." Then she squealed in a posh old lady's voice, "Kay, you look absyolutely dredful! How very fat you are!"

"Did Sarah like her?"

"She loved Joy to bits. Even though she was confused Sarah loved her, and that's unusual. She was an only child, you know?" Kay dropped her eyes, remembering, Morrow thought, that Alex herself was an only child, but that her relationship with her mother had been less than happy. "When it works it really works."

"How do you know she loved her?"

Kay smiled. "Face lit up whenever she saw or talked about her. 'I'd do anything for my mum.' She said it over and over. God Almighty, I miss Joy." She blinked valiantly against sudden tears. "Just — her company, know?"

"You were close?"

"Probably not." Kay smiled at her ashtray. "It's different with Alzheimer's. The personality changes. Their family don't recognize them. But the person she became, with the dementia, I was awful fond of that person."

"Did you ever see anyone else up the house? Any pals of Sarah's?"

"No."

"When did you last see Sarah Erroll?"

Kay exhaled a stream of smoke and frowned at her. "Hmm. Not being funny, Alex, but that's a real polis question. Should we not wait until someone else . . . ?"

"Oh aye, aye. You work in another house there, now?"

"Yeah."

"They all rich there?"

"Not as rich as they used to be . . . They lost a lot of money — you should ask them, they all had their money invested in shares."

"You work for Mrs. Thalaine?"

Kay shook her head. "See, that's a polis question." She looked hard at Morrow. "You shouldn't have come here alone." Feeling herself too harsh, she softened. "Tell me it

242

wasn't a sex thing?"

"Why do you ask?"

"You were asking about boyfriends."

"Just for background."

Kay nodded at her cigarette. "Good. I'd hate to think she was interfered with. She was a nice person, you know, proper and that."

"Proper?"

"Ladylike." She touched her wrist. "Always had a hankie . . ."

She was lost for a moment, head tipped, eyes damp. Morrow let her find her own way back and wondered if they could be wrong about the sex work. But then being very proper could have been a selling point.

Kay looked at her hopefully. "It couldn't have been an accident . . . ?"

Morrow didn't answer her. She didn't want to sound too adamant.

Kay sipped her tea and they fell silent again. Out in the hall the front door was opened and a boy's voice called, "Hiya, it's me!"

Kay called "hiya" back but the boy who had shouted didn't come into the living room. Joe and the girl had shouted back too and they could hear the bedroom door open to a rumble of voices.

Kay dropped her voice and asked urgently,

"What are you really doing here, Alex? Don't get me wrong, it's nice to see ye and everything but you shouldn't be here on your own and we both know that."

Morrow nodded. "Yeah."

"Yeah." Kay tapped her cigarette fast, rat-tat-tat on the side of the ashtray, suddenly very angry. "Yeah, I'm a bit annoyed at you for coming here alone, to be honest. 'Cause if you find the guy that did this, and he gets off because you've asked me something here, and there's no one to corroborate that and then the case fails on account of that —"

Morrow's voice was hard and loud: "How do you *know* that?"

Kay froze, staring at her. She raised her cigarette and took a draw. Her hand was shaking as she lowered it to the armrest: "I'm the chair of the Crimespotters up here. We organized a campaign. Against the police across the road." The smoke began to seep out of her nose and mouth, rising slowly up her face, sticking to her wet hair. "They were sending single polis up to interview people who'd been burgled so everyone else on the shift could get their dinner." She looked at Morrow and narrowed her eyes. "The clear-up rate for burglaries is so low, I don't think they'd ever have been found out. A lot of the people up here didn't know that a single copper meant they weren't going to do fuck all. So I mounted a campaign to tell everyone about the corroboration rule. I leafleted everybody in the block. Go over to the station and ask them about me if you like. *They know me.*"

If Kay was right it was an outrageous allegation. It not only meant that the senior officers were giving up the possibility of solving the burglaries, it also meant that junior officers were being put in danger by coming over alone with no back-up. But Morrow had listened to complaints from the public before, recognized the odd sensation of her consciousness retreating slowly away. It was a reflexive familial defensiveness, rehashing worn excuses: they don't know the pressure we are under, they don't understand, they-they-they versus us-us-us. She had already chosen a side.

Kay leaned forward, as if she saw Morrow shutting down. "You better get the guy that killed that lassie."

"I will."

" 'Cause she was a nice lassie."

"I will." She was surprised to hear herself saying that. She had no way of knowing whether she would or not.

"Ma?" The door opened and Joe looked

in. His brother was behind him, a different kind of boy, chubby like his sister but not good-looking, his hair dyed black, several piercings on his ears, a large plug in one, and a black T-shirt with white writing on it. He was shorter as well and smiled at Morrow, nodding a greeting as he looked her up and down. "Ma," said Joe, "Frank's bought a DVD, can we use the telly?"

Frank smiled, proud. "Just been paid."

"What is it?"

"Paranormal Activity."

"It's very late. Anyway, isn't Marie a bit young for that?"

"She is a wee bit."

"I heard it's very scary."

The girl shouted in from the hall, "I'm not a baby."

Kay shouted back, "Aye, Marie, you're not fifteen either." She dropped her voice, "Frank, put something else on, there must be something else she can watch with ye."

The conversation swirled around her but Morrow wasn't listening.

She was looking at the boys' feet. And she was feeling sick because they had the same Fila trainers on and they were black suede.

It was stupid but Morrow felt as though she was betraying Kay as she drove into the

246

police station across the road.

She parked around the back and locked the car, walking around to the front. The automatic door swished open, and she stepped in, walked over to the unmanned front bar and rang the bell attached to the desk. They were watching her from beyond the mirrored wall, she knew, so she nodded at her reflection and took out her warrant card, holding it up until the door opened and a middle-aged officer came out and checked it properly.

"What can I do for you, ma'am?"

"I'm over here talking to someone. You know the high flats?"

"Aye."

"Kay Murray? Joe Murray? Frank? What can you tell me about them?"

He raised his eyebrows and kept them there, looked down at her warrant card again and lifted the bar. "You better come in and speak to DC Shaw."

He left her waiting in the back bar while he phoned around for his colleague. She found it interesting that, although it wasn't shift change, he seemed certain Shaw was in the building, as if that was his habit or he wasn't allowed out. When Shaw finally arrived she found he was old-fashioned police: smart hair, clipped manner, same age as her

247

but less chippy and awkward.

"The Murrays are a pest. The mother ran a spite campaign to discredit this station, drove quite a wedge between us and the local populous of the high flats. Has taken months to get them back on side."

"Really?"

"Yes, quite the rabble rouser."

"What are the kids like?"

"Oh, listen, they were taking the leaflets around for her. Putting them through the doors of the people who —" and here he broke away, looked shifty, shuffled his feet.

He glanced up at her, suspicious, wondering if she was investigating the practices at the station. Morrow let him think it.

"These CCTV cameras everywhere around here — they all working?"

She saw his eye flick to the side as he thought through the playback, of the officers being seen traipsing up to the high flats alone . . .

"Look," she said, "I'm going to huckle you up to London Road in a minute if you don't just answer the question."

"Yes," he said automatically.

She pulled away from him, opened the door to the front bar. "You worry about the safety of junior officers at this station?" She saw a spark of shame in his eye. "Young,

248

inexperienced officers, out in a hostile environment? Needing back-up? And you're down here reading *The Digger*. Even if nothing happens to them, they get to think it's acceptable practice, then *they* send coppers out and something happens." She was getting close to making an allegation so she stopped. "If I hear anything else about this station I will come back and I will fucking huckle you, understand?"

His mouth tightened when she swore, so she did it again, "I fucking will, as well."

She walked off and slammed the door shut behind her, walking quickly through the front bar to the door.

Outside the air was threatening frost. From the side of her car she looked back up to the high flats.

Shaw had told her a lot about the Murrays. Everything he didn't say was a volume. He didn't have anything concrete to discredit Kay with, the kids didn't have any previous offenses. She wasn't in dispute with an ex-partner or neighbors, wasn't screwing the brew or prone to drunken parties. If she had he would have brought it up.

The Murrays were nicer than her family anyway.

TWENTY

It was freezing cold in the hangar. They were standing with their gloved hands in their pockets, shoulders hunched against the bitter cold, waiting. Morning frost had formed on the floor and the stairs but Thomas and Moira didn't wait in the office. Instead they stood on the raised platform Nanny Mary had been on the night before, waiting for the Piper to pull in, standing tall so that Ella would see them and know immediately that she wasn't coming home to an atmosphere. It was Moira's idea: a show of unity.

Thomas felt the vibration before he heard the ring. He struggled to get the phone out of his pocket with his gloved hands, smiled along with Moira at how clumsy he was being and finally yanked the gloves off and pulled the phone out. He expected to see "Don McD" on the screen, or "Hamish," one of the boys who'd be in study hall this morning. It couldn't be Squeak, he served mass in the mornings. It'd be Hamish, calling to ask him how he was, was he OK, had he fucked his nanny again since he'd been home. The caller ID said "Squeak." Thomas felt his fingers weaken around the handset. He let it drop back into his pocket without answering.

"Who was it?"

"Someone I don't want to talk to." He looked away to the hangar door but could feel her eyes still on him.

His phone vibrated against his thigh and stopped.

"A journalist?" she suggested.

"No." He couldn't look at her.

She felt his discomfort and tried to make conversation: "They've been phoning me nonstop. I don't know how they get my numbers."

The phone sprang to life again in his pocket and Moira rolled her eyes. "Just don't answer, Tom."

"No, I won't. Have I got time for the loo?"

"Hurry."

Through the door the office was slightly warmer. A butane gas fire burned close to a man sitting by a desk with his feet resting on a bin. He was reading a newspaper, a red top, a cheap rag, the sort of paper that only did headlines in four-letter words.

Thomas wouldn't even have noticed the front page if the man hadn't blanched when he saw him, sat up straight, hurriedly tucked the paper under the desk and out of sight.

Thomas held his hand out. "Can I see?"

The man looked to the pocket with the insistent phone in it. Thomas shrugged and reached again for the paper.

The man gave it to him.

The photo was a large white square of gray sky. In the center was a small grainy figure, limp, dangling like a deflated party balloon: Lars hanging from the oak on the lawn. Thomas knew that view of the lawn, the low basement angle. It had been taken from Nanny Mary's bedroom window.

He felt nothing at all looking at the picture of Lars, at the limpness of his neck, at his barrel body and thin legs. He told himself that he should feel something but all he could find in himself was a spark of compassion for the oak tree. It didn't look like Lars. It didn't look threatening at all.

Thomas let the paper slide back onto the desk. The man dropped his head and muttered "sorry." Thomas shrugged.

Feeling colder than before, Thomas asked for the loo and the man pointed him to the back of the room.

Through a door to a small room with bare concrete walls that seemed to ooze cold. He locked the door and stood still, looking at the bare damp surfaces.

The phone in his pocket began to ring again. Thomas reached for the phone. He used a fingernail to pick the back off, took out the sim card to shut the fucking thing up. He looked at the little gold panel and held it away from him, revolted, as if Squeak was in it. He dropped it into the toilet bowl and flushed. The little gold square circled twice and then was sucked down the pipe.

He was staring into the toilet water when the headline next to Lars's photo registered in his consciousness. Three words only, all equal size. HEIRESS'S BRUTAL MURDER.

Thomas stopped still. He shut his eyes tight and tilted his head to the side, as if he could dislodge the words, make them drop out of his ear and stop being on the front page. That's why Squeak had phoned. It wasn't to threaten him, he was phoning to say did you see it. He'd gone to serve mass and seen the paper. Father Sholtham served Thursday morning mass and he read the *Daily Mail.* He must have left it in the vestry. But Thomas was glad the sim card was gone, that Squeak couldn't phone him. He didn't care if he never spoke to him again.

He pulled the door open and stepped into the office, looking at the headline again. HEIRESS'S BRUTAL MURDER.

Without asking he took the paper from the man's hands. He turned it around and looked at the words. *Full story inside pages 3–7.* Thomas opened at page 3. A picture of her, younger, blonder, wearing a red bikini, with a clashing blue sea behind her. She must have been on a balcony, standing with her hips twisted away from her body to make herself look slimmer.

Sarah Erroll had been at an exclusive girls' school Thomas had never heard of. An old school friend said something meaningless about her — she was helpful. The article pointed out that she was an only child, had no kids, no husband and had devoted herself to caring for her elderly mother. *Brutal,* said a senior policeman who looked like a movie star and was featured on several pages. *Whoever did this will strike again unless they are found,* said DCI Handsome. *I have never seen a more appalling crime.*

"You take it, mate," said the man, "if you want . . ."

"Thank you." Thomas took it, not because he wanted to read it, only because he didn't want the man to read about her, to have that in his head. But when he got to the

254

door he remembered Lars was on it and Moira was outside. He turned and stopped at the door, looked at the paper, turned back to the man for guidance. "Don't want my mum . . ."

"Fold it up."

He did that, but it wouldn't bend enough so he took out the sports supplement in the middle and gave it back to the man and then folded it small and tucked it into his inside pocket before he stepped out into the cold hangar and shut the door carefully behind him.

Moira looked up at him, bright eyed, kind and warm. When she saw his face the smile slid from her face.

"Who was that on the phone?"

"No, it's fine." He craned forward to look for the plane.

"Tommy, who was it?"

"No one. Nothing."

"You look ill, suddenly."

He reached into his pocket and took out the paper, held it out to her. She unfolded it and sighed. "Oh no. Oh, Nanny Mary, for heaven's sake, what a snake. Those confidentiality clauses aren't worth a thing . . ."

"She didn't ask for a pay-out, did she?"

"No." Moira examined the picture. "Wonder what else she's got up her sleeve . . ."

It sounded like an insect, an approaching buzz. The plane came into view around the corner, taxiing towards them slowly until they could see Captain Jack's face in the window and the little bump of Ella's head in the back seat.

"Hide it, Mum."

Moira folded the paper away quickly, handed it to him and Thomas hurriedly tucked it back into his pocket.

They watched the plane slow in front of them and Thomas knew it wouldn't be all right. He thought of Lars in Amsterdam shutting a bedroom door, leaving Thomas with a depressed girl from Kiev. They passed the half hour whispering about how neither of them wanted to be here. Thomas didn't want to be here either. It felt the same.

He held on to the railing to steady himself, his fingers clenching the burning cold metal, glad of the searing pain. Sarah Erroll had no kids. She was not Lars's other wife, not his pride and comfort. She was like Thomas, just a footnote in his life.

"Smile now." But Moira was angry with Nanny Mary and her smile had dried on her face.

The Piper taxied into the hangar, crawling slowly through the open doors and Ella's little round face appeared at the window, hopeful, looking to see the first signs of how things were at home. Thomas watched her eyes flick from Moira to him, from Moira's brown lipstick slit of a mouth to his sad and guilty eyes. She slumped back into the dark cabin.

The plane stopped. Captain Jack waited until the engines had died before he opened the door, climbing down and helping Ella out.

She was wearing her gray school overcoat and matching cloche hat, little black shoes with beige rubber soles. As she waited for her bag Thomas saw her struggle not to cry, clenching her eyes shut and opening them, fighting the frown at her mouth.

Moira stayed where she was on the platform and carried on smiling, baffled that them being here was no reassurance at all.

Thomas walked down the steps and over to the sister he had hated since the moment she was born. He walked over to her and lifted her off her little feet in a tight hug and said kind things into her heaving shoulder as she hung limp on him.

"Don't cry, Ella." His voice was as flat as a petrol spill. "Don't cry. I'll make it right. I swear I will."

TWENTY-ONE

The early morning station was always nursery-warm and Morrow was already tired, sweat prickling at the nape of her neck and her oxters as she dumped her coat and bag by her desk and shut the door behind her.

She looked at her in-tray, took a deep breath before sitting down and pulling it over in front of her, placing a hand on either side of it on the desk, a pianist centering herself before a recital. Looking down at the neat stack of green and yellow papers she admitted that she didn't want this case. She didn't like it. She was losing her compassion for Sarah Erroll, finding her a trickier victim than she'd expected. And she didn't want to meet the killer.

She looked up at the room. Ugly brown wood, plain tables, gray plastic chairs. Greasy Blu-tack dots on the wall from absent pictures and posters, an empty desk across from hers. The room felt sterile compared to the garish chaos in Kay's kitchen, the sink full of squeezed tea bags.

She began to plow through the reports, planning her morning briefing.

Prelims on the door-to-doors. She looked through them for the notes of the visit to Mrs. Thalaine's; Leonard and Wilder in attendance. Nothing of note about money. A small mention of Kay and her promise to come up and identify anything missing.

Sarah Erroll's accounts book for the carers: she kept meticulous accounts of wages and expenses. She had written "Mum" on a sticker and put it on the front of the book. Morrow glanced at the total. It came to thousands of pounds a year. The entries weren't all in Sarah's writing though, someone else had been filling it in for her, a careful hand.

Some of the lab reports were in too, photos of the footsteps on the stairs, bloody, but the photographer had deadened the color so that it looked brown. The imprint was distinctive: three circles on the instep, two sets. There were no suggestions for brands on the report but a suggestion as to sizes: one pair an eight and the other a nine or ten. Morrow jotted "Fila?" down, looked at it and then scored it out. She looked at it again, asked herself what her motive was for ruling out Kay's boys, and then rewrote "Fila?"

They had fingerprints from the window frame, the iPhone, the banister. Two sets of fingerprints actually, both intruders, although the money in the museum catalogue had no fingerprints on it at all. They had photographs of an unidentified tire mark in the mud at the front of the house.

They had everything and they had nothing. None of the evidence could be used to find a suspect, only to confirm one. They had no one in the frame yet.

She could hear the day shift gathering outside, swapping morning greetings with the guys going off. She steeled herself and had a look through the incident photos again and found herself shocked afresh.

A sharp knock at her door was followed by Bannerman opening it, still coated and scarfed. "Morning."

"Morning, sir."

"I'm giving them a talk after your briefing."

"That's not necessary, really."

He stood and looked at her, raised his eyebrows in a challenge and left, shutting the door again.

She had to give more than a briefing this

morning, it was a sales job: she had to find a way to make them care about a posh, rich prostitute with no living relatives and horrific injuries. And then Bannerman would come in and make them uncare.

She stood up and opened her office door, shouting for Gobby, and waited, hearing the men pass the order around until Gobby came to her door. She handed him a report from her in-tray.

"Make ten photocopies of that. Staple them and bring them to the briefing. Harris . . ."

Harris was early, always early, and came around the door when he heard his name. "Morning."

"Aye," she said, "good morning, yourself. Get me some speakers for my laptop."

Harris huffed helplessly and walked away. Equipment was always a controversial issue. It could either not be found, or made to work, or else the wrong thing altogether had been bought. By the time an officer was senior enough to control the budgets for equipment, they were often hopelessly techno-blind. It was telling that when they talked about the recently acquired computer equipment they boasted about how much it cost, but never what it might be used for.

It was eight o'clock. The troops were filtering into the incident room across the way. She gathered her papers into a tidy pile, took a deep breath and walked out into the corridor.

Routher was standing there with a grin on his face that wilted when he saw her. "Get in there," she said.

The incident room was small, another ugly room with tables for everyone to hot-desk around, an incident board at one end and a whiteboard on the facing wall.

The night shift were slumped in the front row, nearest the door, pointedly ignoring Bannerman, who was three feet away from them. He stayed in everyone's line of sight by the whiteboard, letting them know who was really in charge but he looked lonely and lost over there. He saw Morrow come in and nodded to her needlessly, signaling that she was welcome and might begin. She stopped herself from nodding back.

"Right," she said, and they settled. "Sarah Erroll was rich, pretty, young and leaves no family. Who cares? I do, but I think I'm the only one here." It was an unconventional start, surprising enough to make them sit up and listen. "My job is extra hard today because I have to try and manipulate you into giving a toss." She looked at them. "That's *annoying.*"

She saw them smirk at the tables in front of them, guilty but honest.

She clicked her laptop and the picture of Mrs. Erroll came up, sitting in the kitchen in her nightie. "This is her mum, Mrs. Erroll." They sniggered at that because Joy Erroll looked so old and so cross. "This is Sarah."

She clicked on a profile picture of Sarah. She was standing in the street looking back over her shoulder, smiling so the apple of her cheek stood in stark profile, eyes brimming with love. Morrow left the picture there, making them look at it while she rolled through the briefing, telling them what she knew, about her mother's expensive care plan and recent death. She told them about the sex work but said it had stopped when her mother died, letting them put the two things together themselves, hoping it might prompt a spark of compassion.

Without warning, she brought up a scene-of-crime photo, watching the eyes widen and the heads tilt, the confusion as to what the fuck they were looking at, the piecing it together.

Sarah Erroll's face had been stamped on repeatedly, with the full weight of the assailant on it so that the nose was nothing but a pearly white stub of bare cartilage, the eyes burst black and unrecognizable, the hair a matted mess of blonde and blood. It was more than confusing — the degree of anger that had been spent on the face was repulsive. Someone had stood on the step next to the head and brought their foot down and down until no part of her remained. One ear was missing, the skull was caved in at the mouth and the teeth were jumbled into the back of her open throat. Somehow, her lips had remained more or less intact.

To give them a moment to hang on to, she said, "Whoever did this held on to the banister for balance, raised one foot and stamped . . ."

Then, dispassionately, she began to run through the incident chronologically: two young men came through the kitchen window, went upstairs, checked her purse, found her taser phone. She flashed onto an image of the phone lying in the hall, and then back to Sarah as she told them that all three had come downstairs and the two boys battered Sarah to death at the bottom. No weapons, just feet. She showed them a slide of a footprint, a close-up of the black suede fibers taken in the lab. She showed them the muddy tire prints from outside.

Harris was assigned the job of identifying the trainers — she mentioned Fila specifically — and Wilder got the job of looking through all the carers' names and records. She split the other jobs of the morning between the rest of the day shift DCs.

DC Leonard put her hand up to ask a question and the men sniggered at her breach of protocol. Questions were usually kept to the end, when the DS had finished rolling through their pre-prepared speech, but Morrow was surprised that anyone was listening and glad of the break. She nodded at her to go ahead, hoping the question wasn't about the shift rota.

"How do you know it was two young men?"

She nodded to Gobby to hand out the photocopies. He gave one to Bannerman who glanced at it and looked up, angry that he hadn't been asked. Morrow was taking a chance. Someone in the room might go home and tell the wife about it. Someone might have a pint with a journalist that night and let slip important details.

When Morrow was sure they all had one she called a hush. "OK," she said loudly, "listen. The last thing Sarah Erroll ever did," she pointed at the whiteboard and made them all look at the photo, "was call 999. The call was silent and she was put through to the automatic record."

They woke up. Suddenly they were being trusted with evidence, facts that needed to be unpicked and pondered on.

Morrow pressed play, turning the volume up as high as she could without the crackle becoming oppressive.

Blunted static filled the room: the sound had been enhanced to bring out Sarah Erroll's voice but it hadn't been properly cleaned up yet, not court-clean.

Sarah Erroll: What are you doing in hair?

They were nervous but they smiled at the typo. The transcript they held seemed to have been made by someone who had never heard an English accent: anything pronounced in an unfamiliar way was written phonetically.

There was a pause, no movement and Sarah must have turned towards the phone because the next sentence was very clear:

S.E.: Look get out of my house.

Annoyed, but not threatened. Her voice was girlish, her accent drawling estuary English, still tinged with a nasal twang of sleep.

S.E.: It isn't empty *[indistinct]* house.

Another pause but Sarah's tone was much

266

changed when she spoke again:

S.E.: My mother died. I still live.

And then a boy's voice, broken but not steady and low yet. He sounded loud and he sounded confident.

Accused 1: Where's your kids?

Everyone in the room sat up.

S.E.: Kids?
Acc 1: You've got kids.
S.E.: No I haven't got kids.
Acc 1: Yes, you fucking have.
S.E.: You're in the wrong house.
Acc 1: No I'm not.
S.E.: Look you should go. I called the police *[indistinct]* they'll be on their way. You could get in a lot of trouble been hair.

No one smiled at the typo this time.

S.E.: I know what you're hair for.

She seemed to move away from the phone at that point but they could still hear her:

S.E.: You don't know who you're dealing with, you've made a mistake.
Acc 1: Stop. Get fucking back.

Morrow pressed pause. The men looked around, startled at the interruption.

267

"Where's his accent from?" she asked.

A guilty silence, an unexpected spelling test when they were all dozing.

"English?" It was Leonard, new, enough of an outsider to offer an opinion. Everyone around her nodded to show that they had been listening.

"No," said Morrow, exasperated, "I'm not testing you to see if you're listening. It's a strange accent, it's a mix. I want you to think about it. Analyze it. See if you can place it or parts of it."

She rewound and pressed play again:

Acc 1: Stop. Get fucking back.

Now they were really listening, their facial expressions as responsive to the conversation as if they were in the room with Sarah and about to interject.

Footfalls, *dwump, dwump, dwump* of bare feet on the hard floor, coming closer to the phone and suddenly Sarah took command:

S.E.: *[shouting]* Get out of here this instant.

Morrow kept her face to the floor but smiled, proud of Sarah. Victims might incur sympathy but they always lost the respect of the officers. Real cops saw it all too often to keep caring.

S.E.: Who are you? I know you. I definitely know you, I've seen a photo of you.
Acc 1: Photo? *[indistinct]* a photo?

They were all sitting upright, a Pavlovian copper response to the strangled, angry voice.

Acc 1: Showed you a fucking photo of me?
Acc 2: St *[indistinct]* Stop, man. *[indistinct]*
Acc 1: Fucking *[indistinct]* phone.

A pause.

Acc 1: Speak. Fucking move.

Morrow watched them listening until the end, saw them cringe as Sarah insisted that she knew one of their dads and called the boys liars.

She watched them flinch at the crash on the bed, as Sarah shouted out to the briefing to help her, that there were two boys in her bedroom and she knew one of them. Then the line clicked dead.

Morrow heard them draw their breath, look anxiously around for confirmation that the threat was over. She looked at Bannerman for permission to dismiss. His mouth was tight but he nodded and Morrow turned to the front row.

"Thank you for your attention, gentlemen. I believe that's the end of your shift."

As they stood up she could see she had moved them, told them a story they could hold on to, given them the excuse they needed to admit they cared —

"Stop." Bannerman stepped forward, hand up, lip curled. "Sit back down."

He sounded like an angry headmaster. The night shift hesitated, looked to Morrow for direction. She shut her eyes. Bannerman was going to fuck it all up.

"It has been brought to my attention, *men,*" he saw Tamsin Leonard and corrected himself, "and *woman.*" He sniggered at that, for some reason, possibly because he was nervous. "That you are all clock-watching." He was flicking his finger at them and she could see them withdrawing, all the benefit of her briefing draining away, their eyes retreating to the table tops. "If I don't see an improvement in your commitment to this case we'll be looking at transfers and redundancies. Is that clear?"

No one answered and no one was looking at him. Except for Harris. He was at the back of the room, arms crossed, mouth tight, standing square to Bannerman, meeting him.

"Is that clear?"

"Yes, sir," they answered in a ragged

chorus, except for Harris, who said nothing.

"All right, then." And he raised his hand to dismiss them.

"Thanks for your help there," said Morrow, sarcastic and loudly, before the noise of the chairs had gathered enough to drown the comment out. The men heard her, looked at each other and laughed at him.

Bannerman gave her a look that was beyond angry. He was going to make her suffer for that and she knew it.

TWENTY-TWO

Before they even got to the outside gate Thomas hated Ella again.

She was working hard to keep crying. Every so often her grief would wane to a whimper, then she would catch her breath, give a forced wail and begin afresh. It was uneven, dramatic and stagy, as if she had something to say and was sobbing so she didn't have to make conversation.

Moira stroked Ella's hair with rhythmic sympathy, hushing over and over as Ella bawled so hard that her voice began to fail. She ran out of tissues. The limo driver from the hire firm handed a box back to them when he stopped in a traffic queue. He avoided Thomas's eye in the rearview mirror, embarrassed.

Ella let Moira hug her, which was unusual. She was clinging to her when they stopped outside the house. The driver of the hire limo pulled on the brake and, in that quiet moment before anyone could speak, Ella lurched across Thomas's lap for a sight of the oak, shouted, "Daddy, my daddy!" and began to howl uncontrollably again.

Thomas looked out over the lawn. It seemed familiar: "Daddy, my daddy," and then he remembered that it was a line from *The Railway Children.* Jenny Agutter on the smoky platform and her father stepping down from the train.

He felt a spark of indignation until he remembered the newspaper in his pocket and that he had done things that were significantly more shameful than borrowing a line from a movie.

The driver opened the car door for Moira and she peeled Ella off her bosom, gently shoving her back into her own seat. Her silk blouse was stained with smeary tears. She got out of the car, put her hand back in to help Ella out.

It was a telling moment: Ella's face was convulsed with misery but her eyes were calculating. She looked at Moira, looked at Thomas briefly, and reached over, taking Moira's proffered hand, leaning heavily as she shuffled out of the car. It was a cold look, as if she was assessing them and chose Moira as the safest.

Thomas must seem unsafe to her, he must

seem like Lars. For the first time he saw how things must look from Ella's perspective. Lars took him away shopping and to Amsterdam. He ostentatiously donated the sixth-form wing to his school. He even gave him a flat of his own away from the main house, and his own nanny, long after Ella's had been dismissed. True, Lars and Moira visited Ella at her school all the time, but her school was closer to the house, he was all the way up in Scotland. He had never thought her the loser but it must have seemed unfair to her too sometimes.

As he watched her scramble along the seat and climb out, he saw that Lars and Moira had set them against each other, not always deliberately, and how it was a shame. She was all he had and they didn't know each other, had never spent time together.

Thomas's door wasn't open.

He looked at it, looked for the driver who should have opened it but the driver was carrying Ella's suitcase from the open boot to the door. He didn't know that it was his job to let everyone out first and then get the luggage. Hire driver for a limo firm. He was fifty or so, white-haired, probably a failed estate agent who'd been given a big car and someone else's uniform.

Moira and Ella were up by the front door,

Moira looking through a set of keys, watched by Ella, no longer crying, just confused at her mother carrying keys for the house around with her. The housekeeper should have let them in. She should be standing by the door to take their coats.

Thomas opened the car door himself and stepped out. He left it open and sauntered, to give them time to get back into the house and disperse before he got there. He came level with the driver on his way back from dropping the suitcase off.

The driver thought he had come to talk to him and smiled, kindly, and said, "I'm sorry for your sister. Is she not well?"

Thomas looked up and shrugged. "She's upset."

The driver glanced up to the door, saw Moira putting the keys in the lock and Ella crying, straight-faced. "She's more than upset, son."

Thomas tried to explain. "Our dad just died."

"Oh," said the driver, shocked. "I'm sorry."

"He hung himself. Over there. From that tree," continued Thomas, realizing that the man was right. Even a truly terrible shock didn't really, fully explain Ella's behavior. "She's young."

The driver *hmm*ed, muttered "terrible" but Thomas saw him glance back up to Ella. She was following Moira in the door but her hair had not been brushed at the back and the way she held her head, dipped sideways, mouth hanging open, she really did look odd.

He didn't like the driver talking about a member of the family like that. He couldn't discount it on the grounds that the man was being nasty. He wasn't nasty. And he didn't seem stupid either.

"Well, goodbye, sir." The driver shifted his feet to move and Thomas held his hand out. The driver looked at him and hesitated. They weren't supposed to shake hands but Thomas wanted to meet his eye, like an equal, to show him they weren't all broken.

The man hesitated and then took Thomas's hand, pumped it, looking him in the eye and smiling.

"Goodbye," said Thomas, hoping he sounded as authoritative as Lars but nicer. "And thank you for your service." He backed off, taking the steps up to the open front door.

Inside, Moira and Ella had dropped their coats on the floor next to the suitcase. It looked as if they'd melted out of them. Thomas picked them up and looked around for a place to put them.

He stepped over to a big door and opened it. The light came on automatically. He'd never been in here before.

It was a small, square cloakroom with hanging rails around three sides, grouped by person, outdoor shoes on a rack and a high shelf with neat wooden boxes, each with a handwritten label: "Lars's gloves," "Moira's hats," "Scarves."

As Thomas hung the coats up the door fell shut slowly, sealing him in. He listened for the click, thankful when the light went off. And then he stood still and enjoyed being there, in the windowless dark.

A phrase formed in his mind, slowly rising to his consciousness:

We should not be seen.

His head dropped slowly forwards to his chest and he stood like that until his neck began to hurt. Still he stayed there, his breathing constricted by the bend in his windpipe, a deep burn on his neck and shoulders, spreading down his arms. He never wanted to raise his face to the world again.

And then Lars spoke to him. *You fucking wet cunt. Stay there, you useless cunt. Do nothing. Just fucking stay there.*

Thomas lifted his head, pushed the door

ajar, tripping the light on again. Slowly he reached into his pocket for the newspaper.

On another page Sarah Erroll was photographed at a party, flanked by other girls with pixelated faces. She smiled, uncomfortable, wishing, he felt, that the photo was over and done with and she could stop being seen. She didn't look very nice. Thomas thought she looked a lot prettier in real life.

It said that Sarah was twenty-four, younger than Nanny Mary. After leaving school at eighteen she worked in a champagne bar in the City of London, the Walnut, but she had left to go home to Scotland and care for her mother.

Lars drank in the Walnut. He ran up a legendary bill for wine one night: fifty grand or twenty grand or something. She must have met him there. Sarah may have looked up as Lars came to the bar, looked up with a dreamy smile. Maybe Lars saw that she wanted to be invisible and he liked that about her.

He looked at her picture and felt, for the first time, that she was a real person who existed independently of Lars, or him, or Squeak, or any of this. He saw her standing in a cupboard in her own messy old house, with her head down, then she looked up and her face was a bloody pixelated mess.

He threw his shoulder to the door and scurried out into the hall. He couldn't face being alone so he picked up Ella's suitcase and climbed the stairs up to the first floor, walking along the corridor, keeping his gaze down to avoid mirrors.

He rarely came up to this bit of the house. He'd forgotten it was nice and warm. The doors were tall and solid, the panels around the door handles were made of warm russet copper, etched with winding flowers and little sun motifs. Ella's rooms were right at the end, next to the door to the master suite. He knocked formally, unsure if Moira was in there with her. He heard a sniff and stepped around the door.

"Your bag, ma'am."

Ella's rooms were high ceilinged; a living room with a deep bay window, a bedroom and a large bathroom beyond it. She had chosen the furniture herself, everything in pink. Even the widescreen TV above the fireplace had a pink surround.

She sat alone in the middle of her rose-patterned sofa, legs folded prettily under her, looking out of the window. She seemed tiny all the way over there. She was slim, winsome, had straggly blonde hair and an elfin face. Her eyes were red from crying. Looking at her Thomas thought he could see what Lars had liked about Moira once.

He set the suitcase flat on a footstool, ready for unpacking.

"You're a fucking creep," she said, very loudly. "I fucking hate you, you creepy fucking creep."

Thomas froze by the wall. She was looking at the window and he tried to see if she was talking to his reflection. She turned, abrupt, and shouted adamantly, "Thomas! I know you're here!"

"OK," muttered Thomas.

She smiled and turned away. Thomas moved along the wall, coming to a table display of small china ballet figurines. He was puzzled and hurt. "Am I creepy?"

She gazed over at him, considered him. "No. Put that down."

He looked at his hand, a little relieved because her comment was appropriate: he was holding a figurine. He wrapped his hand tighter to get a reaction. Ella chewed her cheek and looked at it. Evidently it wasn't one of her favorites because she shrugged.

Thomas put it down again. "All that sobbing in the car, bit put on, wasn't it?"

She shrugged.

"Lars tell you about his other family?"

Ella's mouth twitched in a smile. "Knew

anyway."

She waited, making him ask.

"Why?"

"Oh, he'd take me to Harrods, buy eight dresses, give me four. Stupid fucking creep. She must be my age, then. Or my size anyway."

"He's definitely my age. I needed to be told . . ."

"Hmm." She seemed pleased to have that over him.

"Think Moira knows?"

She shrugged one shoulder carelessly. Now that he was closer and could see out of the window he realized that she could see the oak and was probably talking to it and to Lars and not to an invisible man or anything.

"How did you hear he was dead?"

"Oh, that fucking chump Mrs. Gilly called me out of French and told me. Took her fucking time about it as well, dancing around the fucking bushes, 'prepare yourself, my dear.' Really fucking ominous."

They were both thinking that Moira should have been the one who told them. Ella looked at him hard and whispered, "She off the . . ." she nodded at the door, "you know?"

"Yeah. Well, her mouth isn't dry."

281

Ella nodded. "She can see properly as well." And she did the face Moira used to do, shutting her eyes and opening them superwide, as if her eyeballs were drying out. "When did she . . . ?"

"Past few weeks, she said."

Warily Ella watched the door and whispered, "Because people can go bonkers when they come off them. Kill their family and so on. Have you heard that?"

Thomas couldn't remember if he had or not. "Don't know."

"They get, like, shotguns, go around the house and blast your face off while you're sleeping." She looked worried. "I mean I'd be first. You're all the way downstairs but I'm just next door . . ."

"She seems OK. Ella, that was all an act earlier, wasn't it? You're not mental."

Ella smirked at the door. "We still got guns here?"

"Some. In Lars's office safe downstairs."

She chewed her lip. "Hmm."

It was quite pleasant, speaking to each other.

"Housekeeper's gone. All the house staff have gone," he said. "She sacked them."

Ella frowned. "That's stupid. Who's going to do everything?"

"You are. We had a vote before you got

282

here and you've to do it all now."

She smiled at that. "Really, though, who's . . . ?"

"We've got to sell. We've got to move."

Ella looked around her little world, at her little armchairs, her pink mini-fridge, the telly. She set her face to the window and when she spoke again her voice was very low. "Will we get to go back to school?"

Thomas didn't think so. Three hundred k a year was bugger all. You couldn't pay for schools out of that. He didn't have to say it. Ella's well-practiced eyes brimmed again.

"I've only been there for a fucking year. I've just got used to it there." She became suddenly very angry. "I'm not going to a fucking comprehensive, anyway, I'll get stabbed, or raped or something. I want a home tutor."

"Don't talk shit, Ella, we're *broke*. There's no money for a home tutor. There's no money for *anything*."

"They can't make me go to a comprehensive, I'll get bullied."

He looked at her. The sunlight was behind her, making a halo of her hair, picking out the blue in her eyes. Her school skirt had ridden up her leg, baring her downy thigh. She looked pretty and posh and slim. "I don't think you will."

Ella sensed a compliment coming, tipped her jaw coyly to catch it. "Don't you?"

"No."

She waited for him to elaborate, but he didn't, so she prompted, "Why not?"

He walked over to the window bay, skirting the arm of her sofa, and pulled the curtain back, looking out over the front lawn. "Just don't. Think you'd be top fucking dog in a new school. They don't board, the other family. They go to day school."

"Fuckers. Lars tell you that?"

"Yeah."

"Lucky." Day school when boarding was an option meant your parents wanted you at home, it meant local friends and a social life, it meant normal. "Which schools, do we know anyone there?"

"Never said. He was supposed to come to St. Augustus's, though. Next term."

Ella's eyes widened. "*With* you?"

Thomas couldn't meet her eye but nodded.

"Was she coming to my school?"

"Yeah."

She looked at the oak again, gave a little choking gasp of indignation. "Prick!" She looked at Thomas. He'd been there already, that black lake, and it had taken him bad places. He didn't want to go back.

"They didn't like me at school," she whispered. "Wasn't top dog at all. Lot of those girls were bitches . . ." Her voice faded. In a sudden change of mood, she grinned and flipped onto her knees, looking at the oak tree with Thomas. "I saw the newspaper," she said. "Him hanging there like an idiot."

Thomas looked at the tree. Poor tree. "It's nice to have you home," he said, blushing because he meant it so much.

Ella smirked at the window.

"The crying in the car, was that for Moira's benefit?"

She looked around a bit and shrugged, as if she'd been caught in a lie. "Picture was taken from Nanny Mary's room, wasn't it?"

He nodded, though rightly he shouldn't know what the view was from there. She smirked. "You were fucking her, weren't you?"

"Shut up."

"Just asking." She looked sly.

"Hey," he said, "let's go and walk about on the lawn."

Her jaw dropped. Thomas monkeyed her, taking the piss. "Oh-my-GOD," he said in a big doomsayer voice, "don't-go-on-the-lawn."

Ella giggled and did it back. "Stay-off-the-fucking-lawn."

"The-lawn, the-lawn." He dropped his voice: "Hey, we went in the freezer room last night and got some mini pizzas and Moira made them for dinner."

Ella jolted back and stared at him.

He grinned. "Mini pizzas. We ate them in the kitchen. I had a beer."

She held her thumb and finger together to make a small circle. "*Mini* pizzas? Like mini burger canapés at a party?"

"No." He held both hands up and made a bigger circle. "Cruder than that. Actual supermarket mini pizzas. Moira made them in the oven."

Ella looked out of the window and disbelief rippled across her face. "Where is the freezer room?"

"Under the kitchen."

"Wow." She nodded, taking it in, understanding a little, he hoped, of the joy there was in this new life, out of the shadow of Lars.

She gasped suddenly and held her hand out for his, even though he was behind the sofa. "Come on," she said excitedly, being another person, someone in a movie, someone breathy, Helena Bonham Carter, probably. Or Keira Knightley.

Thomas looked at her hand distastefully.

"Fuck off, Ella."

She didn't start a fight with him, she just dropped her hand and said, "Come on, though, let's go and run the length of the fucking lawn."

Thomas looked out of the window at the sea of vibrant forbidden green.

Moira had had enough. She was at her window smoking a cigarette, mid-morning, which she never did, even in the dark days, smoking, fretting about the children being home all the time and talking all the time and having incessant needs. Ella was just managing. They were so noisy. When they moved to a smaller house they'd have friends over and she wouldn't even be able to pay for much help to look after them. She'd have to cook for them and mini pizzas wouldn't do every night.

She was smoking and worrying when she heard the commotion at the front door below her window, steps, shouting. She leaned forward to see what on earth it was but the front of the house was hidden under the window ledge. It wasn't until Ella and Thomas appeared on the driveway that she saw them. They were running, Ella breaking into little leaping skips sometimes, her heavy woolen school skirt swirling around her bare legs.

They ran over to the lawn and stopped at the edge, Ella dipping her toe into the grass as if she was testing the temperature in a swimming pool, and then they were on their marks–get set–go! — they bolted down the lawn, laughing loud to each other, their paths weaving away and together, away and together. Moira watched until they disappeared over the steep drop and came back up again, puffing but still smiling.

They walked over to the oak and found the branch that Lars had hanged himself from, each of them standing under it, taking turns. Thomas reached up to touch it, jumping the last two inches, slapping the rope-raw branch.

Ella looked so young and small. She was looking at nothing, staring straight towards the house, a big blank grin on her face and Moira began to cry.

TWENTY-THREE

The lobby in London Road Station was drafty. The floor was tiled brown, lined by chairs screwed to the floor, all of them overlooked by a two-way mirror. As if to provide an illuminating counterpoint to the bitter welcome, an absurd, life-sized cut-out of a smiling female officer stood to the side.

This morning the chairs were occupied by a group of women, and every one of them was pissed off. By the time Morrow passed through on the way to the interview rooms they had formed a committee to air their complaints: one of them stood up when Morrow came out of the CID wing. The other women watched expectantly as she anticipated Morrow's trajectory and stamped over, blocking her path.

"Hey, you. You in charge here?"

Hands on ample hips, she tipped her head back, looking down at Morrow, ready for a fight. She was very round in the middle, wearing a gaudy purple top over black trousers. Her hair was short, dyed a shade of burgundy that didn't flatter her yellow face.

"Are ye? You in charge?" She was looking for a fight.

Morrow wouldn't have fought her with ten cadets and a stab vest on. "Do I look as if I'm in charge?"

She examined Morrow, saw that she was pregnant and feeling it. "We've all been called in here at the same time —"

Morrow interrupted. "You understand that this is a murder inquiry?"

She craned into Morrow's face. "And are you getting that we're all missing our work to sit about here, waiting on you?"

The chorus of women watched, nodding.

"OK." Morrow stepped around her and spoke to the women, "You'll all be seen in good time."

But the purple woman felt she was winning and it made her confident enough to step in front of her again. "What does *that* mean?"

"What does *what* mean?"

" 'In good time,' what does *that* mean?" She leaned in, determined not to be put off in front of the others.

Morrow saw the light shift behind the

two-way mirror. The duty sergeant was behind there. If the woman looked like raising a hand over an officer, he would be out in a heartbeat, glad of the excuse.

Morrow didn't have time for a scuffle, or to fill out the forms for ancillary charges. A little overconfident from the triumph of the morning briefing, she held a hand up at the mirror, telling the sergeant not to come out. She sensed that the gathered women didn't really want to leave, so much as have something concrete to do; she walked straight over and addressed them directly:

"Right, ladies," she said, and she saw them note that her accent echoed theirs. "Here's the deal: Sarah Erroll was killed the day before yesterday —"

"We know that already," said a woman from the back.

"What you don't know is how she was killed." She looked around them, let them imagine it. "Now, I can't tell you that but what I can tell you is this: we have got to find this person and we have got to do it quickly."

"Are we getting paid?" It was the purple woman, coming up behind, trying to reassert her authority.

Morrow was indignant. "For finding a murderer?"

291

"She's right enough, Anne Marie," another woman called to the purple leader from the sidelines. She looked at Morrow. "But see, we've never even been spoke to. Just told to get in here. And we're all missing work and we were all asked to come at the same time. You can't interview us at the same time."

"OK, right." Morrow nodded at the ground. "Right. We're going to try and get you all seen before lunchtime. There's a takeaway café two blocks down." She pointed out the door and to the right. "You're welcome to send one or two of you for teas."

Some nodded, some murmured. Purple Anne Marie slunk towards her seat, defeated. "Aye, you," Morrow pointed at her, "don't you order anything, 'cause I'm taking you first."

Anne Marie had worked for Mrs. Erroll for less than three weeks. The money was good, make no mistake about that, she liked the money well enough, but the old lady was a lot more disabled than she had been told by the agency and the daughter never took to Anne Marie at all.

She told Morrow and Leonard this with a degree of disbelief, while reaching down the neck of her top, into her sleeve and yanking a stray bra strap back up to her shoulder.

During the three summer weeks Anne Marie was there, Sarah Erroll went away twice, once to New York and once to London. She never had any friends over. No one called her on the house phone or left a message.

"What sort of person was she?"

Anne Marie shrugged. "Well, I didn't like her."

"Why not?"

"Thought she was a bit wet. Bit vague." She wobbled her head. "Head in the clouds."

"In what way?"

"In what way what?"

"How did she have her head in the clouds? Did she have ambitions or talk about what she wanted to do with her life?"

"Nah."

"How did she seem wet?"

"Well, when I got the sack I went to her and said, 'Look, that's not right, I gave up a job to take this one and now she's saying I'm out on my ear —' "

"Wait, who's she? Who sacked you?"

"Her. The other one. Said I was lazy and I'd been sitting on the bed when she came in and said Mrs. Erroll needed changed, but I was just —"

"Who's the other one?"

"That Kay Murray." She screwed her face up. "Her."

"Kay Murray sacked you?"

"Well, she never actually sacked me. She just kind of trapped me. She made us a cup of tea and said, 'Oh, I can see you're not happy here.'" Anne Marie was waving her arms about and making an angry face, as if Kay had been unreasonable, when she sounded perfectly measured. "And I'm like, 'well, I'm not' and she's like 'well, maybe another position would suit you better and you've said about the traveling and that' and I'm like 'well, if you could pay my travel —'"

"Yeah." Morrow cut her off. "So you went to see Sarah about it and what did she say?"

"Kay's the one who decides."

Morrow was surprised by how much power Kay'd had. She wasn't trained as far as she could tell and she'd specifically said that she wasn't close to Sarah.

"Did you have a key?"

"No. Kay Murray let us in and out. She had a key."

"Who else had one?"

"No one. Just Kay Murray."

"So Kay and Sarah were close then?"

294

"No. Just Kay and the mum, Mrs. Erroll."

"Joy Erroll?"

"Aye."

Leonard chipped in, "I thought she had Alzheimer's?"

"She did. Doesn't mean ye cannae have pals though, eh?" She gave Leonard a superior look.

"How were they pals?"

"The mother lit up at the sight of her. Loved her. Cried when she left for the night. Couldn't remember her own name but she knew when Kay Murray wasn't in the house." She twisted her lips in a bitter little smirk. "Nice for us, if you're the one left looking after her, eh?"

"Do you remember the big square hallway just inside the porch?"

"Yes."

"What was in the hallway when you were there?"

"Just that big black cupboard. Like something out of a horror movie. Big knobs on it, hanging down."

"Big . . ." Morrow nodded, prompting her to describe it.

Anne Marie nodded. "Big, aye." Seeing that Morrow was looking for more she added helpfully, "Cupboard . . ."

■ ■ ■ ■

The next woman had worked there for five months until her granddaughter had a baby and she had to give up working to stay home and look after it. The baby was premature and the new mother had postnatal depression. She nodded at Morrow's stomach. "You know how it is."

She was small and fit and fantastically messy. Even the three buttons on the side of one of her boots were done up wrong. She was wearing a black T-shirt with a gold ABBA logo and the left shoulder was faded to gray. Morrow smiled when she realized that it was washed-out baby sick.

The woman remembered the black cupboard and said it was a dresser, at least ten feet high, which was wrong. They measured the height of the mark left on the wall and it was seven feet. She didn't know what had happened to it. Sarah Erroll was a lovely person and was very good with her mum, even though her mum was quite confused and not always very nice.

"In what way wasn't she very nice?"

The woman giggled and blushed. "Used a lot of language."

"Did she?"

The woman pressed her lips together, as if afraid that she herself might suddenly blurt something filthy. "It was the confusion," she confided in a whisper, "being confused. She spoke like a lady but put dirty words in it. You got some right laughs with her, right enough."

"Was it a nice house to work in?"

She thought about it for a moment. "It was lovely. I do this job, ye know, and it's a bit sad sometimes, the way people get treated."

"But this wasn't?"

"No. The pay was very good and Kay was her pal, I mean really her pal, and because of that Mrs. Erroll was still treated like a person. I mean, right at the beginning Sarah sat us down and said that the house had always been a happy house and she wanted the people who worked there to be happy too. She said her mum was confused but she still knew when folk were happy or not. She said if I had any complaints or some-thing was worrying me I should speak to Kay about it."

"Did you have any complaints?"

"No."

"Was Kay easy to work with?"

"Fine. She was all about the old lady. Dressed her in all her favorite clothes, they didn't even fit her anymore but she'd do it. She'd find old movies for them to watch together. If Mrs. Erroll was upset she used to tell her she'd just met the Queen and it would cheer her up. They did cooking together and that. Made bread and scones."

"Kay and Mrs. Erroll liked each other?"

"Oh my God." She rolled her eyes for emphasis. "Loooved each other."

Two more of the women had nothing much to say, had stayed for only a few months before they had to leave, one because of the traveling, the other because her back went wonky and she couldn't lift. Kay kept her on as a cleaner because she liked her but her back condition deteriorated and she couldn't do that either, then.

Morrow was about to call in another one of the women when Wilder came into the interview room and told her that Jackie Hunter, the head of the carers' agency, was downstairs.

Jackie Hunter was fifty and looked divorced. Her black bob was streaked with chocolate stripes and so shiny and well conditioned it looked as if she'd stolen it from a younger woman; ditto her magnificently white teeth. She spoke in a soft voice, her accent very definitely Giffnock, resting her hands on her lap, one on top of the other, nodding and listening carefully. Morrow could well imagine her radiating sympathy at clients as they wept, making them feel heard.

Jackie explained that Sarah had come to see her three years ago when her mother first had a minor stroke. Sarah had been working in London, in the City, living with girlfriends from school. She hadn't realized that her mother was becoming confused. Mrs. Erroll was a proud woman and, like a lot of people with Alzheimer's, she hid her illness well. Sarah had realized that her mother sounded different on the phone, but thought that she was angry because Sarah had moved to London.

Jackie arranged for Mrs. Erroll to be privately assessed. It was immediately clear that she would need a lot of care and it would be very expensive.

"How did Sarah feel about that?"

"I remember that Sarah was quite upset about it. She said she couldn't afford it, they had no money left. Either Sarah had to do all the care herself or they sold the house. Mrs. Erroll would never settle anywhere else. Then a few weeks later she contacted me and said could we send people for interview. Someone else had agreed to pay for her care, a relative."

"Who was the relative?"

"I don't know. The relative was never mentioned again." She set her face firmly to neutral.

"How much was it, roughly?"

"Round-the-clock care can cost up to twenty thousand pounds a week, depending on the number of staff and the level of their qualifications."

"What level was Sarah interviewing for?"

Jackie sat back and crossed her legs carefully, doing the calculations in her head. "Two full-time carers, auxiliaries, and a night auxiliary. That would cost about five thousand pounds a month."

It tallied with the amounts in the accounts books. "About sixty grand a year?"

Jackie Hunter nodded. "That's just for the carers. That's not for equipment or food or for overtime. It's a heavy, heavy bill. She was working in a bar in the City of London. I think she knew a lot of people with a lot of money . . ."

Morrow didn't want to tell her where Sarah Erroll got the money from.

"Did you like Sarah?"

"I didn't really see her after that. I mostly dealt with Kay Murray."

■ ■ ■ ■

Morrow was in the canteen eating the packed lunch Brian had made for her. Ham and cheese on brown bread and an apple. It was busy but she found a seat alone by the window with a couple of pages of notes open in front of her so she could pretend she was reading them if anyone tried to talk to her.

She glanced around. They called it the canteen but it was just a room with drinks machines and tables, used for eating food they brought in themselves. It had been a real canteen once but the kitchen had been shuttered for as long as she'd been here. As well as clumps of uniforms around the tables, some of her own crew were on their piece break. And she noticed them come in, see her and sit well away. The more socially skilled caught her eye, smiled, invited her over, knowing she wouldn't move, but others were blatantly shifty and couldn't look at her. Routher stared at his packets of crisps as if he might cry. There was a shift in atmosphere in the department, it felt different. A war was about to break out over Bannerman, and she would have to choose a side. But it was different for her than the

301

others because she was right in the middle of all of them, wouldn't be here to try to control the outcome and would have to deal with whatever the fall-out was when she got back from her maternity leave. It wasn't much of a choice: either the men would hate her or the management would.

She looked at the uniforms: their faces uncomplicated, resentful, hungry, laughing. At least they were clear about their motives. They were thinking about the money.

Her eyes strayed across the page of her notebook. Sarah Erroll's laptop password had been bypassed and they were in. She had kept meticulous spreadsheets charting her income. At the height of Sabine's working life she was earning a hundred and eighty thousand pounds a year. The payments were entered individually and ranged from eight hundred to three thousand. It seemed very naive to Morrow, keeping a tally like that. There must always have been the possibility of arrest, of her files being found.

She took a bite out of her apple and tried to imagine allowing herself to be fucked by an unattractive stranger in an unfamiliar room. She found it hard to imagine allowing someone to even touch her without seeing herself punching a nose. When she was still in uniform she'd arrested men who used sex workers and knew they weren't all unattractive, some of them were even quite nice people. It was the interaction between the buyers and sellers that was ugly. Even between fond regulars there was an edge to the interaction, like a marriage gone bad, a despising undercurrent.

She imagined herself as Sarah lying on a luxury bed, looking up at a luxury ceiling as a man who faintly despised her lay on top of her, pressing his cock into her for money. She knew then why Sarah kept her records: when she lay on the luxury bed she was thinking about the money.

When she sat on the airplane home she was thinking about the money. When she got home and filled out the spreadsheet and wrote in the amount, she was writing over the memory of a despising man.

How she developed that skill was what bothered Morrow. How Sarah had learned to keep her hands by her sides and think of the money. She'd learned it somehow.

Morrow looked up to shake the image of the ceiling. Routher was headed back downstairs with his cronies. Busy. Lots to do. They were reaching a critical stage in the investigation: the story had been on the news last night, papers were full of it this morning and the householders in the local area were pro police. The quantity of information coming in was on the verge of being crippling. Old school friends and nutters were contacting the police with tiny scraps of apparently irrelevant information. If any one of the tips turned out to be significant or crucial and they did nothing with them they'd be pilloried. Now they were using their limited staff to sift through the notes for relevant stuff, when they had nothing to go on.

The double door opened and Harris came in with Gobby, spotted her and came over looking pleased with himself. The other CID eyes in the room followed them to her table and she thought of purple Anne Marie.

"So," he said, "we're not including the money found in the museum catalogue: today the grand total is £654,576."

"Oh, I dunno," said Morrow, grateful to be out of the luxury hotel and back in the scabby canteen. "Is that if you changed it in a Bureau de Change though? 'Cause I think the banks give a better rate."

Gobby grinned at Harris's back.

But Harris was unfazed. "Any high street bank will put the total closer to my guess than yours."

"You're a fly wee monkey, Harris." She reached into her handbag and took a tenner out of her purse. "Were you up the house all morning?"

"Aye." He pocketed the tenner and he and Gobby sat down opposite her. "All the forensics are done now."

"I'll go back for a final scan."

"Found some slips from auction houses for some of the furniture as well."

"Selling it off?"

"Aye."

Morrow took another bite of her sandwich. "Did Kay Murray come up the house today?"

"No. Was she supposed to?"

"She was, yeah."

Harris looked at his watch. "Well, it's only three o'clock. She might pitch up yet."

"She was very close to them, it turns out." She took another bite. "I'd no idea. She never let on."

Harris nodded. "More significant than she seemed?"

"Much more."

The door opened to the canteen and a distinct chill settled in the room, the chat dampened down, Harris sat upright as a cat. Bannerman stood in the doorway, looking around, looking for Morrow and found her at the table with Harris and Gobby. She watched with interest as he came over, saw Harris reel back from the table top, saw Bannerman look from her to him.

Bannerman stood at the end, fingers on the table top to steady him. "So," he said stiffly, "she was a *working* girl."

Morrow nodded reluctantly.

"Could be anyone then," he said, and shrugged.

TWENTY-FOUR

Morrow stood with her bum on the still warm engine and looked up at Glenarvon. It was a brighter day today and the house looked less creepy and faded. Gray stone glinted in the patchy sunlight. The solidity of it gave the house the air of a firm elder, playful in parts but stolid and benign.

She didn't want anyone to talk to her, and had sent Leonard off to the officer on duty to quiz him about who had been and to check his record-keeping of entries to the house. Leonard was being left out of whatever was going on in the department and Morrow found herself drawn to her company, to the balm of neutrality. So she stood facing the house, clearing her mind as she approached the steps and walked up, letting her impressions of before flood aimlessly in. She needed to get to know Sarah but she was slippery. Bannerman had booked her on a flight to London for the next day, to interview the people from the bar Sarah had worked in, to get a fix on her and try to get her national insurance details. She needed to know what sort of person she was.

Carers coming and going, through the front, always through the front door. No one had a key because Kay Murray was always there to let them in and out. She must have worked long hours. Morrow was pleased Kay had a key: it made it less likely that she had anything to do with the break-in through the kitchen window.

As she walked past and went in through the door she heard Leonard asking if Kay Murray had been up and being told that she hadn't. Morrow would have to go and look for her.

Dark porch, the suitcase gone now, but the jacket still there. Dark porch, the shoes, one upright, one on its side. Darker hall, imposing. Through the arch to the stairs. Her shoulders crept up to her ears at the memory of Sarah's body. The dried, black bloody stamp of her mess still there, on the floor, rising up two stairs as if it was crawling up to the top of the house to hide.

She glanced to the side. The taser phone had been there, but even as she was thinking it she knew she was avoiding looking at the stairs.

She turned her head deliberately.

The blood on the ledge of the steps was still scarlet and tacky but the spills down the side had dried black. Two sets, one very slightly larger than the other, both facing her now. The smaller prints were nearer the black hole where Sarah's head had been. They were consistently nearer. The bigger feet had made impressions further along the step, away from Sarah.

Morrow stepped back. They were definitely next to her head. On one step she could see that the left foot of the smaller feet had stood alone, the person was standing on one foot, very close to Sarah's head.

They'd been stamping on her with the other.

She looked at the footprints and imagined the people who made them standing there, arms down, as blank-faced as men in a line-up. They'd be interviewed separately. They'd blame each other, they always did. It didn't matter and they'd both be convicted, but this time maybe one of them would be telling the truth when he said he was innocent.

She went outside for a breath of air and found Leonard on the step. "Where was Kay Murray working yesterday?"

Morrow paused for breath at the gate. It

was a lovely garden. The ground in front of the house was a sea of raked white gravel with a stepping-stone pathway that arced around to the front door. The border plants were brightly colored, pink and blue, hanging over the watery white-marble chips. A high fence protected it from the view of the neighbors, a trestle of brilliant orange flowers disguising it.

Leonard had referred to Mrs. Thalaine's house as "the old Glenarvon stable block" in the written report. Looking at it now, Morrow could make out a portion of the path to the big house, a stripe of worn ground at the head of the hill beyond the cottage.

It didn't look like a stables anymore, it looked like a brand-new, whitewashed house designed as a picturesque drawing of a stables. She opened the spindle-topped gate and held it behind her for Leonard. She had been here before and it seemed sensible to bring her back, so Mrs. Thalaine would know who they were and wouldn't feel the need to waste time with preliminaries.

Morrow rang the bell.

After a short pause a slim woman opened it; a neat woman, her gray hair streaked with blonde, dressed in beige slacks and a matching stone jumper, a blue silk neckerchief loose at her throat, tucked into her crew neck. She looked out at them over half-moon reading glasses and recognized Tamsin Leonard.

"Well, hello again!"

There were no preliminaries. Leonard had promised to come back and inform jittery Mrs. Thalaine if there was a murderer roving around the village and she and her husband should evacuate. She was very keen to establish whether or not this was the case and didn't offer tea or coffee or a wee plate of nice biscuits but sat them down in the living room and quizzed them about the progress of the investigation so far.

"No one yet, then?"

"No," said Morrow firmly. "We're quite sure that whatever led to Sarah's death was a personal matter and there's no ongoing threat."

"So, it doesn't concern me?"

"No."

"OK." She seemed relieved at that until it occurred to her: "What are you doing back here, then?"

"I was looking for Kay Murray."

Her eyes narrowed. "Kay?"

"Do you know her?"

"Indeed I do. She's my lady-what-does." She tittered at that. Morrow declined to tit-

311

ter back.

They looked at each other for a moment. A bird pecked at a feeder hanging in a window, tuck-tuck.

"Did you know Sarah?"

Mrs. Thalaine wasn't enjoying this. She seemed to realize that Morrow was a different sort of police officer, not the nice sort either. Tuck-tuck-tuck.

"Sarah grew up here. Went away to school obviously, and we keep ourselves to ourselves, but she grew up nearby."

"What sort of a person was she?"

"She was an only child. Shy growing up. Kept away from the local children . . ."

"She kept away or was kept away?"

"Well, my children were invited up for birthday parties but we always felt that they weren't very welcome: they were padding really. My older son liked Sarah very much. Said she was funny. She did impersonations of her nannies. They were all French. She made them laugh."

"The family fortunes had declined recently, hadn't they?"

"*Everyone's* fortunes have declined recently. Look at someone like Kay Murray, I mean, people get desperate, don't they? Four children and no husband —"

Morrow snapped at her, "Have your

fortunes declined recently?"

Mrs. Thalaine touched her neckerchief with her fingers, at the jugular. She opened her mouth but snapped it shut again. Tuck-tuck-tuck and a flutter of black wings at the window as the bird flew away, sated.

Mrs. Thalaine filled her lungs. "We invested our savings in shares, through a brokerage firm, AGI. They lost it. All."

"How much was that?"

Mrs. Thalaine tapped her jugular again. "Six hundred thousand. More or less."

She began to cry but refused to give in to it. Her lips quivered and she pulled a silk handkerchief out of her sleeve and dabbed at the corners of her eyes, trying to preserve her make-up.

Morrow would have been ashamed to admit it, but it was quite boring to watch. Thalaine was crying about money while the stairs in Glenarvon were carpeted in chunks of Sarah's face. When the sobs and hiccups abated Morrow spoke softly, "And AGI lost the money?"

"Did they? Where did it go?" She slumped, as if it was all too much for her, and looked coldly at Morrow. "Do you have *any* idea who did this?"

"Who do you know in the village?"

"Most of the older residents."

"Is it quite mixed around here?"

"How do you mean?"

"Old people, families with children?"

"Yes, quite mixed."

"Many teenagers?"

"Some."

"Who do you know with teenager children?"

"The Campbells have two daughters, nineteen and fifteen."

"No boys?"

She stopped, looked at Morrow, knew, somehow, that this was what she didn't want to hear: "Kay Murray has three boys. Teenagers."

"I meant in the local area."

Mrs. Thalaine started crying and couldn't stop herself. "We're moving anyway!" She pressed her hankie to her mouth in between fractured exclamations. "We're going to have to sell our family home and live with our children. We've been here for thirty-two years. Now we have to go and live with our children."

Morrow was sorry for being so dismissive of her loss. She reached forward and touched her arm, apologizing for unkindnesses committed in her head.

"Ye no coming up?"

TWENTY-FIVE

Kay was plating up mince and potatoes when the buzzer rang and made her flinch. John was expecting his pal Robbie to come up. Robbie had the guilty look of a wee boy who wanked all the time, possibly not at normal things. John had told her three times this evening that Robbie was coming up to do homework, so she knew they weren't planning on doing that. Still, as long as they were hanging about the house she could keep opening the bedroom door and walking in without warning. Robbie's brother was on tags for fighting as well. Nasty family.

The buzzer rang again and she shouted, "John!"

He came out of his room, looking paranoid, and saw her holding the big pot of mince over the plates. She worried suddenly that he might be smoking a lot of hash and made a mental note to smell for it.

315

"Buzzer. Might be Robbie."

John picked up the receiver and turned away from her. "Aye?"

The person on the other end spoke too long for it to be monosyllabic Robbie. He was making his excuses, maybe. John pressed the button for the lobby doors and hung up.

"Is he not coming up?"

"Eh?"

"Is Robbie coming up?" she said slowly, and nodded at the mince pot. "Does he want some tea?"

John looked vague. "No, it's the polis."

"The polis? Again?"

"To talk to you." He tucked his T-shirt into his jeans at the back, as if he had a gun, and walked away.

Moving quickly, Kay slapped a ladle of mince on all five plates and dished up the boiled potatoes and beans. She was squeezing tomato ketchup onto four of the plates when a knock rattled the glass pane on the front door.

Stepping out into the hall, she banged quickly on Marie's door and opened it to an indignant "Hey!"

There were two warped faces behind the mottled glass on the door, and neither one looked like Alex. One was shorter than the other, neat hair, looking down the corridor, the other staring straight at the glass as if they could see through it.

"Tea's out," called Kay, watching the front door while moving around the hall. "No ketchup."

"I don't want any —"

"Don't give us any shit, Marie."

She didn't have time to knock before she opened Joe and Frankie's door. "Tea's up." She heard them stir, grunting as they got off their beds. She opened John's door and shouted, "Mince!" over the noise of his stereo.

The police could see her moving around. The smaller one lifted a hand to knock again but Kay opened it before they made contact.

"Yes?" she said.

A man and a woman. The man had a tiny wee mouth too small for his face, and wiry dark hair. She knew the woman from Mrs. Thalaine's the day before, small, dark, big hooked nose, but she looked different at Kay's front door, familiar, like a woman she might be friends with.

They introduced themselves — the man, Harris, for the first time, and Leonard smiling, holding her neat little hand out — and asked if they could come in and talk to her

317

for a moment about Sarah Erroll.

Kay sighed, kept a hold of the door so that her arm barred their entrance to the hall and turned back, exasperated and shouted to the kids, "Tea's UP!"

Joe called that he was coming and Marie arrived at her bedroom door, looked out, seemed annoyed. Kay pointed her into the kitchen. "Your dinner's in there getting cold."

Marie sneered at her. "I'm not hungry."

Joe and Frankie trotted out of their rooms, nodding hellos to the police and John came out, ignoring them, keeping his head tipped down so his skip cap hid his face.

"Well, Marie, you're getting nothing later," said Kay, inappropriately angry because she was ashamed of how rude Marie was to her. "So don't be thinking you're going to skip your dinner and eat shit all night."

Marie went into her room and slammed the door so hard that it bounced open again re-revealing her like a magician's assistant. Mortified, she used both hands to shut it again. Joe and Frankie saw it as they came back from the kitchen with their dinner plates and laughed fondly at her.

The fight went out of Kay suddenly, as it did sometimes at the end of a day. She turned back to face the police —

"Thanks, Mum," called Joe from behind her, and her mood softened.

She leaned against the door. "What is it you want?"

The man, Harris, made a chopping motion with his hand towards the living room. "We'd like to come in."

Kay sucked her teeth, reluctant. This was her time, her hour or so, when all she had to do was iron and smoke and watch telly and burst into John's room every time she went to the loo.

But they were the polis. She stepped back and waved them towards the living room. She let them go in alone as she went to the kitchen, picked up her plate and brought it into the living room with her. She was not going to let her dinner get cold while she made them cups of tea, she told herself. No fucking way.

The woman was sitting in the armchair with Kay's pint of Bru and fags and lighter arranged around it.

"That's my seat."

The woman looked to the guy for an order. He gave a little nod to say yes, you may move. They were worse than the fucking kids. Leonard shuffled around the omnipresent ironing board to the settee and

319

Kay sat down, balancing her plate on her knees.

The ironing board was right between them so she reached over with her foot, pushing it towards the telly, careful not to tip it: her ashtray and a half-ironed shirt were balanced on it. *Hollyoaks* was just starting on TV.

She cut a boiled potato in half and looked at the man. "What is it?"

Harris sat forward on the sagging settee. "OK, Miss Murray, as you know, Sarah Erroll was killed on the . . ."

He went on, but Kay found her mind yearning for telly and her thoughts wandering, speculating about the *Hollyoaks* characters and what would happen to them.

"Put that telly off, would you?" Kay was looking at Leonard. "Remote's on the ironing board."

Leonard stood up, found the remote and switched it off. She stood there for a minute.

The man looked none too pleased. He caught a breath and started again, "Why didn't you come up to Glenarvon today?"

She should have. She had said she would but she couldn't face Alex again. She was still angry with her for coming up alone, knew she wouldn't have approved of the place, of the house, of her still smoking.

She put a potato in her mouth and shrugged. "Was I supposed to?"

"Yes, you were. You said you'd come up and tell us if anything was missing. You told DS Alex Morrow that in front of DC Wilder and we were expecting you."

Kay forked a nugget of mince, dipped it in her ketchup and put it in her mouth. She chewed and looked at them. They'd sent two police officers, plain-clothed, higher wages, she was sure, sent them up to her house to tick her off for not pitching up to help them. She raised her eyebrows, daring them to give her a row. "The day fell away from me. What do you want me to say?" She looked from one to the other. "Are you here for a sorry?"

He didn't answer. He reached down to his briefcase and took out a pen and a clipboard as Kay ate and watched. It was the same clipboard form they'd filled out at Mrs. Thalaine's house. It must be a standard form they got everyone to fill in.

"Can I have your full name?"

"Kay Angela Murray."

"Marital status?"

Kay dropped her eyes to her plate. "Not married."

He filled out bits of the form without asking her — she could see him fill out the ad-

321

dress and guess her age at 45–60. She was thirty-eight.

"Have you always been alone?" Leonard smiled a little, not unkindly but pitying nonetheless.

"How do you mean?"

"The kids . . ." She looked sad.

Kay stared back at her. "I didn't conceive them on my own, if that's what you're asking."

Leonard smiled dutifully. "Must have been difficult . . ."

Kay was sick of answering that. She was sick of people assuming her life was hard and she was unhappy just because she didn't have a husband to hog the remote and shout at her, but she said nothing.

Harris asked for her mobile number and date of birth and she saw him change the approximate age accordingly.

"And are they all your children?" He nodded back out to the bedrooms.

Kay snorted, still smarting from the humiliation in the hall.

"You don't think I'd let someone else's kids speak to me like that?"

"No, I mean, none of them foster kids or anything?"

"No."

"There's Marie and she's . . . ?"

"Thirteen. Youngest." He wrote as she spoke. "Then John, fourteen. Then Frankie and finally, Joe: fifteen and sixteen."

"Quite a cluster." The stupid woman nodded sympathetically.

Kay ate some more dinner. "You got kids?"

The woman shook her head. She was in her early thirties, Kay thought, just the right age to be panicking.

"You don't know what you're missing," said Kay.

That line only worked on people who didn't have kids. The man did have kids, definitely. He looked skeptical. "You're not with their father?"

"No."

"You in touch with him?"

"No."

He held her eye, wanted her to admit there was more than one father but she wouldn't. It was none of his fucking business. Sarah Erroll had died, not her. She turned her attention back to her dinner.

"Miss Murray, we've been investigating Sarah's murder, as you know, and all of the carers we've spoken to have said that you were in charge of the staff in Glenarvon."

"Right?"

"How did that come about?"

He said it as if she was up to something. "What do you mean?"

"Well," he smiled, "are you qualified?"

Kay licked a burning smear of vinegary ketchup off her lips. "No. I got on well with Sarah and she trusted me to look after her mum when she was away at her work. Me and Mrs. Erroll: we got on well."

"Did Sarah tell you what she did for a living?"

Kay shrugged, she'd never wondered about that actually. She'd assumed that it was something technical that she wouldn't understand so she hadn't asked. "Never told me."

He watched her face to see if she was telling the truth, which she found insulting, and moved on. "In the kitchen, the table in Sarah's kitchen . . ."

They looked at each other. He seemed to be expecting an answer. "Is that a question?"

"Did you notice anything odd about it?"

She tried to think. "Couldn't get it clean? It had marks. Is that what you're asking me?"

"Did you mop the floor in the kitchen?"

"Sometimes."

"And you went under the table?"

She was really puzzled. "Well, I myself

didn't climb under the table but I did reach under it with the mop if it needed it. Was there a trapdoor underneath or something?"

He didn't answer. "The dresser in the big hall is missing —"

"Sarah sold it."

He wrote it down.

"At Christie's, I think it was Christie's auction house. They had the name painted on the side of the van. It took four of them to get it in the back."

"Did she sell a lot of things from the house?"

"You've been listening to gossip in the village, haven't you? They were angry that she was selling things off, like the house belonged to them or something, but do you have any idea how much it costs to nurse an old dear at home? It's a bloody fortune."

"She sold a lot of things from the house?"

"Yeah. She was leaving after anyway, soon as her mum was away she was leaving to live in New York. She said I could visit her there."

He seemed surprised. "Were you that close to Sarah?"

She was irritated that he seemed so surprised. "A bit." But they weren't. The invite was one of those meaningless invites, as if she'd want Kay pitching up in New York in her cleaning tabard.

"What sort of person was Sarah, in your view?"

Kay shrugged. "Good to her mum."

"Was she nice?"

She thought about it for the first time and hesitated. "She looked after her. Spent a lot of money she didn't have looking after her."

He tried to prompt her. "Was she clever? Was she depressed about her mum? Was she lonely?"

"I dunno." Kay didn't have the time to speculate about what went on with other people. "I take people as I find them. I liked her company. She was quiet. We only talked about Joy, what she'd eaten, when she'd slept."

"You must miss the money?"

"Course. But I'd have done it for nothing. Me and Mrs. Erroll . . ." she moved the food around her plate, "best friend I ever had."

"Wasn't she confused?"

"Oh, aye." She felt again the sharpness of her loss. "But when you're confused it sort of strips away a lot of shite about ye. All the stories you tell about how great ye are or where you've been; she couldn't remember those things. She just *was*. And what she *was* was lovely."

She looked at her half-eaten plate of food.

Remembering Joy had given her a knot in her throat that she couldn't swallow past. She put her plate down by her chair, picking up her drink. The hall buzzer rang briefly and she heard John pad out to the hall, lift the receiver, snigger into it and press the button to open the front door.

"Hmm." Harris looked at his form. "A couple of the carers we interviewed said you sacked them."

"Who's that? Anne Marie Thingmy and someone else, skinny lassie?"

He looked a blank.

"Anne Marie was a lazy, torn-faced cow and the skinny lassie was late every day. You can't have people not turning up. Joy couldn't be alone for a minute. She was still mobile when it suited her and the house was full of stuff to trip over. I mean there's a steep drop not fifty feet from the house. If she got out —"

"Did Sarah have anything of value lying around the house?"

"Not that I saw."

"Hmm." He nodded as if this was significant.

Out in the hall Robbie had arrived at the front door, she heard him and John whispering out there. She wanted to go and tell the wee cripple-dick bastard to fuck off back to his own house.

Harris saw that her attention was on the hall and he nodded out there. "These boxes, out in the hall, where are they from?"

Kay lifted her pint of Bru, glaring at him over the rim as she took another drink. When she had finished she put it down. "Where do you think they're from?"

"I don't know. Why don't you tell me?"

"You think they're nicked? That I'm a thief? Reduced to stealing empty cardboard boxes?"

He blinked slow. "Why don't you just tell me where they're from?"

"Because the insinuation's insulting. Why don't you ask Alex Morrow what I said when *she* asked where the fucking boxes came from?"

Kay watched him look back at his clipboard and realized that he hadn't known Alex had been up here, on her own. She hadn't meant to tell on her. A principle was a principle, it couldn't be a question of how much you liked the person you were applying it to. But he was smart and he knew now.

Outside, in the hall, John shut his bedroom door very firmly. Kay stood up abruptly. "I'm going to ask you to leave now. If you don't mind."

She walked out into the hall and leaned over to John's door, opening it and shoving it wide. "Finished your dinner?"

A pause was followed by John calling in a guilty, sing-song voice, "Finished!"

"Bring your plate out and wash it then." She glanced back into the kitchen. Marie's dinner was untouched, congealing on the plate.

The police were in the hall, the man, Harris, putting his clipboard back in his bag. Joe and Frankie came out of their room, Joe carrying the stacked plates and cutlery. She was embarrassed to see that the top plate had been licked clean, big tongue marks around the rim and she saw both police officers looking at the boys critically, sizing them up.

"Well, Mother," said Joe, oblivious, "another culinary triumph! Is that you guys off?"

Harris didn't even have the courtesy to look up when Joe spoke to him. His eye shot from Joe to Frankie. "We'll need to speak to you again."

"Any time," said Kay, hating him for looking at her boys like that, head to toe. She took his elbow and pushed him gently towards the door. "Any time at all."

She shut the door on them and saw them

329

linger there, behind the glass, not speaking. They moved away and she waited until she heard the lift doors open and shut.

From the corner of her eye she saw John's bedroom door swing very slowly shut.

Furious, she turned to it, kicked it with her foot so it bounced off the wall, and hissed, "I know what you're doing in there."

Joe was behind her. "Let him have a wank, Mum, it's nature's way."

Frankie laughed loud at that. She even heard Marie laughing in her room. She hadn't heard that for months.

Morrow and McCarthy weren't sure the hotel manager could see them but they could definitely see him: lean and cold, with an attentiveness that was a little overpracticed. He stared unseeing through the webcam, still, as if he was in an Edwardian photographer's neck clamp. He blinked rarely as he answered their questions about Sarah Erroll, seemed haughty and irritated. Morrow hoped he couldn't see her too well, she didn't think she'd pass muster.

Morrow and McCarthy had to speak very, very slowly, to overcome the problem of accents, sieving their language for Scottish words and enunciating their *t*'s. Morrow felt that she was being ridiculous: "WhaT can you tell us abouT SarAh EErroLL?"

He spoke without hesitation, as if he was reading a monologue from an autocue: Sarah Erroll had been a guest at the hotel many times. She had never been anything but a charming guest. *No,* there certainly was *no* suggestion of her engaging in prostitution. She always met with the same gentleman when she came here. Occasionally, he would stay over with her.

"I see," said Morrow slowly, picking her words for clarity. "By 'staying over' you mean sleeping together?"

"That would seem likely."

"Did you know the man?"

The manager smirked but he actually looked a little offended. "The gentleman called himself 'Sal Anders.' That was *not* his real name."

He left a pause for her to ask, which she found a bit annoying. "What was his real name?"

He gave himself a single disapproving nod. "Lars Anderson. I can tell you now because that gentleman has passed."

"Passed what?"

He looked confused. "Um, Mr. Anderson died."

"When?"

"This week?" His disbelief was tangible

331

across the Atlantic. "The story has been in all the newspapers over here. I believe it happened in England."

"Was he famous?"

"Very famous." He paused. "Here. He died in *Eng*land."

"Yeah, we're in *Scot*land. Scotland's a different country than England so it's maybe not a big story here."

His intelligence insulted, the manager blinked and spoke again, his tone exactly the same as before. "I'm aware of that. This is a very big story, can you really not have read about it? Allied Global Investments? Billions of pounds lost? Lars Anderson?"

Morrow thought she had heard something about that but looked to McCarthy who guessed, "Is he the financial guy?"

"At the center of the financial scandal," nodded the manager. "He hung himself two days ago. You know, it's a rumor over here but we heard the British press published photographs of him hanging. We don't have that kind of press over here. It's quite different . . ."

Morrow asked him how he knew the man's real name was Lars Anderson, had he seen a card or something? The hotel manager shifted in his chair and said it was his business to know such things.

"Do you have any proof it was him though?"

"I have credit card receipts from the hotel shop."

"In his real name?"

"Yes."

"Why would he change his name to check in and then pay with his own card?"

He looked very arch at that. "I don't think that particular gentleman was concerned with keeping his identity a secret. I think it was a token. He was telling *us* to be discreet."

McCarthy sat up as it came to him. "Oh, aye, I remember he was married?"

"So I believe . . ."

Morrow began to recap his evidence, making sure they had it right so that they could write it up and fax it over for him for notarization: Sarah and Lars Anderson were having an affair — No. He stopped her dead. It was not a love affair. They may have been sleeping together but this was not a love affair. He bought her a gift from the hotel shop, a bracelet. A lover doesn't do that. A hotel present means that he remembered her on the way into the hotel, not that he had been thinking about her when he wasn't with her. Morrow said maybe he was forgetful. His face remained neutral. How

333

did he know the bracelet was for Sarah? He smirked again, genuinely amused this time, because Sarah gave it to the maid as a tip.

"So the relationship was, what? Stormy?"

"Possibly, it was an accommodation . . . ," he suggested.

Morrow was tiring of him and his subtle social nuances. "What the hell does that mean?"

The manager blinked slowly, tired of her too. "They were using each other."

"OK." Morrow stood up. "I'll let my colleague here recap your statement with you, and he can fax it over for you to sign."

She left without saying goodbye and went out to the incident room.

Routher was looking over someone's shoulder, watching them work. "You," she said, "I want a newspaper search on this name." She wrote "Lars Anderson" on a scrap of paper and handed it to him. "I want a printout in twenty minutes." He took it from her.

She went into her office. A scant ten minutes later Routher knocked on the door and came in with today's newspaper and printouts still warm from the printer.

"I've been following this story," said Routher, excited. "He was a right bad yin."

Morrow nodded, pretending she'd heard

of Anderson, but she wasn't prone to reading the newspapers.

"Ma'am? See like 'here' and 'hair'? 'Lars' sounds like 'liars.' "

She looked at him. He was right. "Good. You're not a waste of skin."

Routher smiled, and went to leave.

"Come back here," she said. "Shut the door."

Suspicious, he did as he was asked and stood in front of her.

"So," she nodded at the door behind him, "what's going on?"

"In what way?" he said stiffly.

"What are you guys plotting?"

His chin trembled and he began to sweat.

"Routher," she said quietly, "if a face could shit itself then yours just has."

He didn't find it funny. He looked as if he might cry.

"Get out," she said.

He scuttled out and shut the door. He'd go and tell them she knew something was up, might flush something out.

Morrow turned to the first story. She was shocked at the front page showing him hanging from a tree — she didn't know they could print that. She knew the one rule about reporting suicides was generally not to report them because they encouraged so many copycats.

The sum of the articles seemed to be that Lars Anderson was a City financier who had become the focus of a hate campaign in the press. She read a *Sunday Times* explanation of his scam three times but didn't understand what he had done to lose so much money; it ran into billions. The most she could gather was that he had given people mortgages at a rate they couldn't afford, but she didn't really understand why this made him so evil. She thought maybe the people who took out the mortgages should have checked whether they could afford it.

Whatever he'd been doing, he'd made a lot of money at it. His Kent house was pictured from the air and the ground. There were aerial images of his holiday home in South Africa and estate agent photos of the interior. It didn't look that nice. His wife was pictured driving, walking, always with dark glasses on, frightened but prim.

Several of the photos of Lars were the same one. She wondered why. There were a few in which he hurried into a car, came out of an office door with his face hidden behind a rolled-up newspaper or hand. But the posed photo was glamorous.

In it, a silver-haired man with a tall forehead stood in front of a manned helicopter. His coat was open, he carried a briefcase and he looked as if he had stopped for a snap to be taken before he got into the helicopter and went somewhere important. It was a carefully setup photo, he was carefully posed and made up but still his slight belly and raspberry nose weren't entirely disguised. Lars looked straight to camera, haughty, malevolent. Most people would have smiled and tried to look pleasant, but this was how he wanted the world to see him. She found that telling. The newspapers detailed his wealth and belongings, they seemed dazzled by him.

According to the reports, AGI and his personal bank accounts had been frozen by the fraud office, awaiting investigation. Mrs. Thalaine had mentioned AGI, that's where she'd heard it before. Two days ago Anderson had left a civil court hearing which disqualified him from ever holding office in a limited company again. A Serious Fraud Office investigation meant that he wouldn't be able to operate under any capacity. He'd gone straight home and hanged himself. He was found four hours before Sarah Erroll was killed.

Calling up the thumbnails from Sarah's iPhone, she found the New York pictures of the silver-haired man. It was out of focus but if she squinted she could see it was Lars Anderson.

She picked up her phone, chose an outside line and called the Serious Fraud Office in London. Shut. The message said they were only open until five fifteen. Nice shifts.

A sharp, familiar knock on the door.

"Come in, Harris."

He opened the door and stuck his face in.

"Harris, you OK for going to London tomorrow? I was trying to make an appointment with the SFO but they're shut."

He looked excited, still had his coat on. "Ma'am: Kay Murray's got antiques in her house, Leonard says they're worth a lot of money, rare things, and her kids have got matching black suede trainers. She's as hostile as buggery. We need to get her in."

TWENTY-SIX

Morrow sat in her office, nervously chewing a nipple of raw skin at the side of her mouth. She had a foreboding that something awful and wearing and sad would come out of Kay's interview, that it would be a keeper.

For Morrow, the cases that kept her burning eyes blinking into the dark were not the bloody ones, not the vicious ones when eyes were gouged or fingers snapped or children hurt. Morrow's keepers were those where events seemed inevitable, the cases that made her doubt the possibility of justice, the value of what they were doing. Sarah Erroll was starting to feel like that.

She stood up and shook off her sense of dread, opened the door and paused outside the incident room. They were more comfortable now, thinking the end was in sight. The scene-of-crime photos were no longer the focus of anyone's attention, no one was

339

avoiding it. They thought they had solved it.

Bannerman's door was open a chink. She knocked and stuck her head in before he had the chance to ask who it was, and was surprised to find him talking to their boss, McKechnie. Morrow didn't even know he was in the building.

McKechnie was an old-school procedure-priest. A politician, broad around the middle, small about the chin.

Bannerman was leaning over his desk, grinning, McKechnie smug, hands on stomach, leaning back in the hard chair. There was always a bond between them. McKechnie had brought him on and was here to witness his prodigy making the kill at first hand.

"Sir." She nodded.

"Good work on this, Morrow," he said, looking to Bannerman for confirmation.

Bannerman smiled encouragingly. "Very good work. Tomorrow, I need Harris here."

They had already bought Harris's plane ticket for London and it wasn't transferable.

"But we're only going for the morning, we'll be back mid-afternoon."

"I want him in the morning. You'll take Wilder."

Bannerman was keeping her away from

Harris, isolating him. And he was bringing it up in front of the boss so that she couldn't object, because any complaint would make her part of the rebellion. Without fanfare or warning the war had begun.

"Fine," she said, blinking to cut him off. "I'm not going into the interviews, sir."

Bannerman nodded. "I've already explained that you know the suspect."

"No, um," Morrow held the edge of the door tight, "Murray's *not* actually a suspect."

Bannerman nodded a concession. "Point taken: the suspects' mother. Although," he looked at McKechnie, "she *may* be a suspect. We'll have to see when we get up there."

"And the boys are in the back?"

"Yeah, we've sent their shoes off and brought in all the antiques she had kicking around the house." He explained to Mc-Kechnie, "One of our new recruits spotted them on a routine visit."

He was talking as if they'd found the British Museum up there. Morrow hadn't seen a lot of antiques in the house. "What was there exactly?"

Bannerman pushed a sheaf of color photos printed on copy paper over his desk towards her. She stepped in and fingered through them.

The ink had smeared a little. That the items were pictured next to a ruler and had an exhibit number next to them made them seem stolen.

The first item was a silver eggcup. It had been found on top of the cupboard in the kitchen, covered in a greasy dust. She could still see the tiny hairs stuck in it at the upper rim.

The next one was an art deco watch with a rectangular face and diamonds on the surround.

"Found that in a sock under her bed," Bannerman told McKechnie, helping Morrow to the next picture, the site of the discovery. The dust was thick under the bed. Random lost items were scattered around the navy blue carpet, a pair of tights rolled into twin doughnuts, an empty light bulb box, a celebrity magazine. The orange sock was lying by the skirting board.

Then there was a bowl with enameling on the outside. It had been found on the ironing board and was photographed next to a brown burn mark on a vivid flowery pattern. Kay'd been using it as an ashtray. A cursory search of the internet suggested it was worth thousands.

"There's not that much," said Morrow, sounding sour.

The men didn't say anything but she knew what they were thinking about her. It didn't bother her. She never felt she had their good regard in the first place and she'd be out of here soon. Her hand strayed to her belly for reassurance but she caught herself and dropped it to her side.

Politely, Bannerman changed the subject, looking at McKechnie. "Right?"

McKechnie smiled at his protégé. "Whenever you are."

They stood up, coming past her at the door; McKechnie happy because a high-profile case was about to be wound up, Bannerman because he was doing the winding. Morrow followed them out at a distance.

A single row of chairs was set out in the remote viewing room, four in all. McKechnie took the middle seat.

"Sir, this is DC Tamsin Leonard. She spotted the ashtray that led to the search."

Morrow was furious with Leonard. She was wrong to be: Leonard had spotted the bowl, she hadn't put it there, but she felt angry at her. Overcompensating, she gave Leonard credit when it was usual not to, introducing her to a boss three grades above her, saying her full name.

They sat down, Morrow next to McKechnie, Leonard on his other side.

Routher came in from checking the camera in the interview room and switched on the boxy television, tuning it to camera one.

A fuzz of snow evaporated and the tall narrow room was pictured. The camera was angled towards the door and the two empty facing seats, Bannerman and Gobby seen from behind so their faces were hidden. They busied themselves taking off their jackets, putting the cassette tapes on the table. As Gobby poured three plastic cups of water out, Bannerman turned back and smiled at the camera. It was too flippant for McKechnie — he shifted reproachfully in his seat.

Everyone waited. The room looked suffocatingly small, high walls, a narrow table and two big men sitting on one side, facing the door, waiting and willing the next interviewee to fail.

The door opened slowly and McCarthy's face appeared. He looked concerned, didn't speak, seemed to be checking that the chair was there. Kay shuffled in and sat down on the lonely side of the table, clenching her hands on the surface in front of her. She met McCarthy's look of concern briefly, blinking to let him know she was all right. Morrow wondered if they knew each other.

Kay looked at Bannerman and Gobby in turn. "Hello," she said formally.

Gobby's head bobbed. Bannerman reciprocated her civil tone but it sounded facetious. "Good evening, Ms. Murray." He held the tapes up. "We're going to put these tapes in the cassette recorder to record the interview."

Behind Morrow, McCarthy came into the viewing room and pulled a seat out from the wall, watching the TV screen. Morrow looked at him and he raised his eyebrows, asking if it was all right for him to stay. She nodded a yes. He looked back at the screen, frowning, concerned, and Morrow was touched: McCarthy didn't know Kay. He just liked her.

In the interview room Kay looked around as Bannerman and Gobby undid the cassette wrappers, putting the tapes into the players. Thinking herself unobserved, she seemed to look up, searching for a window, another door, a way out. Her eyes flicked up to the camera. In the second before she saw the red light and realized the camera was on, she looked frantic and cornered.

Bannerman sat back, told the tape who was there, what the day was, where they were. He told Kay that they were filming and might be watched remotely by officers in another part of the station. She looked straight at the camera, eyes hateful, as if she could see her accusers through it.

Morrow blinked at the screen to swipe the brutal glance away.

"So," Bannerman began. They could see from behind that he was smiling. "You understand why we're here, don't you, Kay?"

Kay didn't smile back. "Because you found things in my house that you don't think I should have?"

"No." He broke eye contact. "No, because of Sarah Erroll's death. That's why we're here, because Sarah Erroll was murdered in her house, you had access to that house and her accounts and," he paused for emphasis, "because you have things in your house that don't seem to belong to you."

"Like what?"

"Hmm." He looked at a sheet of his scribbled notes, opened his folder, flashed a photocopied image of the eggcup at the camera. He decided not to do that bit right now. He shut the folder and looked up. "Let's start at the beginning."

McKechnie murmured "oh no" under his breath and Morrow sympathized: Bannerman was going to drag it out. Two hours, by her estimation. That's how long it took for a suspect to break under prolonged questioning. Two hours of personal details and bus timetables and getting phone numbers slightly wrong before the ennui became unbearable and they gladly put their hands up. It was already five to eleven.

"How did you come to be working for Mrs. Erroll?"

Kay blinked, paused and said, "No," very firmly. "Let's not start at the beginning. Let's get down to the main —"

"No." Bannerman knew McKechnie was watching. "We'll start at the beginning —"

"No, we won't." She was firm. "And I'll tell you why: because I've got four kids, two of them are down the stairs and they're terrified, and the other two are sitting in a neighbor's house and they've all got school in the morning."

"I think this is a bit more important . . ." His voice was loud.

"Right? See, I don't." But hers was louder.

Morrow leaned forward, elbow on knee, her hand pressed over her mouth to cover a smile.

"Because," continued Kay, "I know what went on. I was there. I know my boys and I know there's nothing to this." She might have won the point if she'd pressed it home but, suddenly, her courage failed her. A bubble of panic seemed to rise through her chest, pushing her back in the chair, twisting her voice to a weak whine. "And I know you're going to find that out. And you're going to let my boys go home. And get some sleep." She was crying, her face contorted. She slapped a hand over her eyes, shook, her mouth contorted wide.

"There's no need to be afraid." Bannerman sounded annoyed.

Kay kept her eyes covered and caught her breath. "The fuck are you talking about?"

It wasn't the floor wipe McKechnie had been expecting. He had stopped looking at the screen and was checking the crease on his trousers.

Mouth bubbling, eyes wet, she dropped her hand. "There's every fucking reason to be afraid."

"What have you done, Kay? You can tell us."

"No! I'm not." She stopped to wipe her nose on the back of her hand. "I'm not scared because I've done anything. I'm scared because *I don't trust you.* Any of ye. And I know I've done nothing and my boys have done nothing and I *don't trust ye* to find that out."

It was a bad start. Bannerman hadn't expected Kay to be so articulate. He sat back heavily, watched her give a shuddering sniff. When she had calmed down he said quietly, "Let's start at the beginning."

Kay sniffed again, terror subsiding and anger setting in.

"How did you get the job with Mrs. Erroll?"

Kay licked her lips and looked around the table top. She looked at the camera, she looked at Gobby and then at Bannerman. "OK," she conceded, "here ye are: I worked at Mrs. Thalaine's and the Campbells' doing cleaning. I met a cleaner called Jane Manus, young lassie, another cleaner, on the train station platform one night and she said Sarah Erroll was advertising for carers for her mother —"

"Who is Jane Manus?"

"— ten quid an hour. So I missed my train and went up the house and knocked and Sarah answered and I said to her, I heard you're advertising, I don't have any qualific —"

"Who is Jane Manus?"

"— qualifications *or* experience. But I'm a grafter and I like old folk. Gave me a tryout. I worked for nothing for three days. Half shifts. And me and Mrs. Erroll got on well

349

and she gave us the job."

Morrow glanced beyond McKechnie to Leonard and saw a tiny smile on her face as she took Kay's side.

"Miss Murray, you don't understand what happens here." Bannerman held a stilling hand out to her. "I ask the questions and you answer the questions because this is a matter of us collating information. We know what we need to ask —"

"You need my whole work history?"

"We need *context*."

Morrow had seen him do this before: he was using words he assumed Kay wouldn't understand. The split second it took someone to work out the meaning gave him the advantage, made them lose their conversational footing. But he hadn't the measure of Kay at all. She was sharp and thought fast.

"You can get context from someone else. I've got responsibilities. I need this to be quick," she said.

"Well," he chuckled unpleasantly, "I think it's fair to say that our needs take precedence here. We're conducting a murder inquiry —"

"And I'm helping you with that. I'm happy to help."

"You don't seem happy."

At that Kay looked at him with eloquent

disgust. "And who would be happy? My sons are downstairs waiting to be asked about this. Fifteen and sixteen. They shouldn't even know these things go on. And don't you dare show them any mucky photos of dead people. I've spoken to you guys four times already, this is my fourth time talking to you —"

"Third time." He checked his notes. "We've only spoken to you three times. DC Harris and DC Leonard came out to your house, you met Morrow and Wilder in the avenue and now this."

Kay sat back and sucked her cheeks in, glanced at the camera.

"Are you prone to exaggeration, Kay?"

She said nothing and Bannerman felt he'd found a weakness. "Did you exaggerate how rich Sarah was when you spoke about her to your boys? You must miss the money she was paying you?" He left a pause. "Did you know there was money in the house?"

"No."

"That's not true, is it, Kay? You certainly knew where some of the money was. You paid the other women wages in cash. You've filled out the accounts book, we compared your handwriting."

"Sarah left the money out for me. I wrote it into the accounts book and she left what we needed out."

"She left out the exact amount?"

"Yes, in wages packets. I didn't even touch that money."

"Maybe you got the boys to come up to your work, you showed them the money and they went up there for it and they panicked and Sarah got hurt."

"My boys have never been to my work."

"Well, let's see. How much were you making when you worked for Sarah?"

"Tenner an hour."

"How many hours did you work a week?"

"Eight hours a day, five days a week."

"So, about forty. That's about four hundred quid before tax? That's a lot. Was it a lot to you?"

Sad, Kay looked at the camera.

"Ms. Murray, *was it a lot to you?*"

He was asking if she was poor. She looked at her hands. "Yes," she said quietly.

Kay seemed tamed after that. She answered the questions monosyllabically, rarely looking up, making no more appeals for decency or understanding. She missed the money badly but managed. She didn't get any money from the kids' fathers. Yes, there was more than one father. Yes, they were all born about a year apart. She didn't react beyond a lip curl when he muttered

352

that she must move on fast, and went on to ask her about their behavior and school attendance.

Morrow could have written a note and sent Routher into the interview room with it, telling Bannerman that she had been at Kay's house and that, adding all those times together, she was telling the truth: it was four times. But she didn't. Sending a note in would tell Bannerman one thing only: Morrow was on Kay's side. If he knew that he'd question her even more vigorously, not to spite Morrow, just because he'd think Kay was winning the audience vote in the viewing room.

Kay described Joy Erroll's death in a monotone: the old lady was getting ready for a bath, Kay was alone and she had gone to get the hoist, leaving her sitting in her dressing gown in the bathroom. When she came back Joy had fallen off the chair. Kay put her in the recovery position but Joy'd had a bad stroke and was already dead when the ambulance got there.

Bannerman asked what she did then, but Kay was still back in the bathroom on the floor, holding her friend's limp hand.

He had to tap the table to snap her out of it. He asked about the money under the table.

"Under the table?"

"The kitchen table, we found seven hundred thousand pounds on a shelf under the kitchen table."

Kay did a bad thing then. She didn't exclaim or seem surprised, but rolled her head in realization. "Seven hundred . . . ?"

"Thousand pounds."

"That much?"

Bannerman, seen from behind, brought his shoulder blades together. "Yes," he said. Morrow knew he thought he was on to something. An innocent person would drop their jaw, ask more about the table.

"Did you know that was there?"

"No."

He shuffled through the photographs, took them from the back of his notes, set them on the table in front of her. He pointed to the first one.

"We found this watch in a sock under your bed. Where did you get it?"

She picked it up and looked at it. "Sarah gave it to me when her mum died."

"How did that come about?"

"After the funeral she took me up to her room and showed me a box of jewelry —"

"What did it look like?"

"Green silk, was old. A bit tatty." She looked up at him, seeing if she should add

354

more. "Hexagonal shape?"

"And what did she say?"

"Take one thing."

"Was the watch the most expensive thing there?"

"I don't know. I don't know much about that sort of thing."

"What sort of thing?"

"Art deco jewelry."

"But you knew it was art deco?"

"Sarah said it was."

"Why did you choose this one?"

She looked very sad. "The shape."

"But you didn't wear it?"

"No."

"Why did you keep it in a sock under your bed?"

"Case we were burgled."

"This" — he put the picture of the enamel bowl in front of her and she sighed at it — "where did you get that?"

"Mrs. Erroll wanted me to have it. She gave it to me because she knew I liked it."

"But Mrs. Erroll was confused —"

"And when Sarah came back I asked her if I could take it and she asked her mum and then said yes."

"And this? The silver eggcup?"

She shook her head. "I don't think I've ever seen that. I don't know where that came from."

"It was on top of your kitchen cupboard. You didn't put it there?"

Kay slumped, defeated. "I don't know what to say. I need a fag."

Bannerman wound it up, told the tape they were stopping for a comfort break and McCarthy hurried into the room to take Kay out for a smoke.

McKechnie couldn't resist putting his oar in: "Morrow, get the eggcup tested for the boys' prints. Conceivably she didn't know it was there and the boys brought it back afterwards and hid it."

"No," said Leonard, "it was covered in oily dust. It left a mark on the top of the cupboard where it was sitting. It had been there for months."

McKechnie looked and saw her for the first time. He expected her to wither under his gaze but she didn't. She met his eye until he got up and walked out of the room.

Morrow sat back and smiled. It was pleasant to watch someone else fucking up.

TWENTY-SEVEN

Thomas stepped down into the dark, feeling his way with his toes, Ella keeping tight behind him.

"Tom! Tom! Put the light on," she said, excited and frightened and annoying.

But the string for the light was at the bottom of the stairs. He slid his hand along the bare plaster wall, his fingertips sensing the tiny smears of perspiration rising up from the soil foundations behind it.

He tugged the string.

The bright light blinked twice, searing snapshots of three bright white coffins onto Thomas's retinas before it came on. Ella was being another character, another girl she'd seen in a film or a ballet. She gasped at the freezers, stepped around in front of him, still holding his shoulder as if for protection. This character touched him incessantly, not in a wrong way, just a clingy way, as if she was *en pointe* and needed him

357

for balance. He suffered it because her moods were sliding about all over the place and he didn't want to upset her.

"What is there?" Moira was looking down from the top of the stairs, pointing to the chest freezer with the ready-made meals in it.

Ella opened the lid and fell back a step at the sight of all the food. She ran her hand along it, frost crackling at her fingertips. "What is everything?" She smiled back at Thomas for an answer.

"Everything is food," he said flatly. "Moira, what would you like?"

"Is there any mushroom pappardelle?"

He looked along the top layer. All the lids were neatly labeled. No mushroom pappardelle. He raised the basket shelf to look below. Five portions marked "mushroom pappardelle" were sitting in a row.

"Yeah." He leaned into the deep body of the freezer and brought three containers out. "Got some."

Ella lurched forward, snatched them out of his hand and ran upstairs giggling as if she'd done something terribly funny and daring. She skipped past Moira, laughing into her face as if she was in on the joke, and disappeared from view.

Moira smiled passively. As she turned to

go after Ella into the kitchen the grin dropped and her eyes fell sadly, as if she'd been smiling along to bollocks like that for a long time.

Thomas shut the freezer, pulled the light string and stepped carefully up the steps to the kitchen where Moira and Ella were standing on opposite sides of the black granite island. Ella saw him emerge and squealed, jumping back as if he'd caught her.

"I'm not chasing you, Ella," he said carefully.

Ella waited for a moment, looked out of the big window, and then laughed as if he'd said something terribly witty. Moira smiled automatically, like the light in the cloakroom.

Thomas turned on his sister. "What's so fucking funny, Ella?"

She stopped laughing, cocking her head.

"What's funny?" He walked across the room and stood in front of her. He was very close to her but she just looked straight over his shoulder.

Thomas lost his temper, poked Ella in the shoulder, harder than he meant to. Afraid of the heat rising up the back of his neck he stepped away and glared at the frozen food on the counter.

"Food? Is the food funny?" He picked up a portion and threw it, missing her, the tub landing heavily and skidding across the floor.

Ella didn't move but she'd stopped smiling.

"Am I funny?" he shouted.

In the silence of the kitchen his voice reverberated off the granite worktops. Ella's fingers were shaking.

"What the fuck is wrong with you, you mental cow?"

"Tom, stop picking on her," said Moira, silky voiced. "Let's defrost these in the microwave and have supper."

A high-pitched alarm trilled gently.

"What's that?" asked Ella.

Thomas stepped over to the freezer room and looked back down the stairs in case he'd left the freezer door open. "No."

"Car alarm?" suggested Moira.

Ella pointed at a red light on the wall, blinking in time to the intermittent noise.

"House phone," she said triumphantly.

Thomas reached for it. "See? And you're back in the fucking room, Ella."

"Tom," said Moira, "if it's a journalist hang up at once."

"Hello?"

A woman's voice. She sounded angry.

"Yeah, hi. Who am I speaking to?"

"Thomas."

"Yeah. Would it be possible to speak with a member of the Anderson family?"

Moira's eyebrows rose in a question.

"Whom shall I say is calling?"

"I'm Lars Anderson's other wife."

"Hang on." Thomas dropped the phone to his belly.

"Who is it?" Moira was coming over to him, hand out to take it.

He faked a weak smile. "It's only Donny McD from school pretending to be a fucking journalist. I'll take it in the front room."

"Oh." She seemed to know it wasn't, but she retracted her hand and backed off. "Stop swearing, it's common."

"Yeah." He nodded Moira over to the food as he walked out to the hall.

"Hang on," he told the receiver and went into the living room. His hand hovered over the light switch but he left it off and stood in the dark to speak. "Hello?"

"Who is this?" demanded the woman. "Who *are* you?"

"I'm Thomas Anderson, Lars Anderson's son. Who are you?"

"I see, I see, I see." She sounded very much in charge. Thomas felt a bit intimidated.

"My father told me about you."

"Did he?" She softened. "Did he tell you I have a son your age?"

"He said. Phils, isn't it?"

"Yes, Phils. Phils . . ."

"Dad told me about him."

She sniffed at the mention of Lars, mumbling something about him being gone as Thomas wandered across the room to the window. It was dark and had been raining. The lawn was as sleek as a badger's pelt. He shouldn't be intimidated. He should try to sound normal. "Sorry, what's your name?"

"Theresa." It was a low name, Irish, but she made it sound Spanish by putting the emphasis on the first syllable and rolling the r — *Ther*esa.

"What's your second name?"

"Theresa Rodder."

It wasn't a posh name, but she certainly sounded posh. He could see the drop of her jaw as she drawled her surname.

"*Ther*esa," he said, mimicking her affected tone respectfully, "might I come and visit you?"

A pause. He thought she was horrified by the prospect until he heard the bottle chink against the glass and the trickle of wine or whatever it was. "Yes, Thomas, I should like that."

Thomas stood with his cheek pressed to the cold windowpane. "Shall I come tomorrow?"

"Sure."

"Will Phils be there?"

"No, he'll be at school."

"Oh, I see. What's your daughter's name?"

"Betsy."

"So, *Theresa*, what's your address?"

She gave it to him. He didn't recognize it but mouthed it over and over to himself in the dark: 8 Tregunter Road, SW10. She hung up without making a specific time.

Thomas walked through the hall, sweating lightly as he tried to remember the name of the street, clutching the phone to his chest. He hurried into Lars's office. It wasn't his actual office, just a big room with a massive bookcase installed, even though he never read anything. The desk was matching yellow glossy wood with spots, poplar burr. Thomas went to the desk and looked in the top drawer for a pen, jotting the name of the street down on one of Lars's embossed memo cards. Then he called 1471 and got the phone number, in case he got lost on the way.

As he wrote he glanced back to the drawer

and saw a black sheen. Thomas reached into the dark drawer. Soft, warm skin. Lars's wallet. Lars always had his wallet with him. Thomas imagined him standing exactly where he was standing now, his feet where his feet were now. He imagined his father reaching into his pocket, pulling the wallet out and tucking it away, his very final gesture before hanging himself.

Thomas pulled the wallet out and flipped it open. It was crammed with big notes and credit cards, the leather worn smooth from being in his father's back pocket, rubbing against his left buttock. Thomas shut it slowly and slipped it into his left-hand back pocket, just to try it. It felt heavy, tugged at his trousers, but the weight of it was comforting, felt like a morsel of Lars's certainty. Very suddenly, Thomas missed that.

The light snapped on above him. Moira was standing in the doorway.

"What are you doing in Daddy's desk?"

Casually Thomas folded the memo card and put it in his pocket. "Lost Donny's number, just jotting it down. I said I'd meet him in town tomorrow."

Moira folded her arms and looked skeptical. "Why isn't Donny at school?"

"He was sent home before me. Stepdad's got cancer."

She knew it was a lie and narrowed her eyes. "I don't think it was Donny at all. Why haven't I heard his stepfather's ill?"

Thomas cleared his throat unconvincingly. "They're keeping it quiet. Worried about stock prices or something."

Moira considered it and then said, "I don't believe you. That's a wicked lie to tell, Thomas — cancer."

Thomas shrugged and came around the desk.

As he pushed past her at the door she was smiling and sang after him, "I think someone's got a girlfriend."

TWENTY-EIGHT

Bannerman made short work of interviewing Frankie and then Joe but it wasn't difficult: they had no evidence, no witnesses against them, nothing concrete to ask about at all. It was a fishing expedition. Since it was so late he took twenty minutes for each of them, asking them where they had been on the night of Sarah's murder, who could confirm it, what they were wearing that night, had they ever been to their mum's work, where they thought the ashtray, the eggcup and the watch had come from.

Both boys had been in for the early part of the evening and out for the second part, and since they couldn't definitively say what Sarah Erroll's time of death was, it left them as possibilities. Neither had heard of any money in the house.

McKechnie had pissed off home but Morrow and McCarthy stayed in the viewing room and watched Kay sitting next to

Joe first and then Frankie. They saw her pretending to be calm for her boys, as if it was routine for them to be questioned in the middle of the night about a brutal murder. A couple of times when they looked afraid, she repeated the same phrase:

"They just need to know it wasn't you, son, so they can find out who it was."

But even on the grainy camera set high up on the wall, she didn't look as if she believed it.

Joe came over very well. He met Bannerman's eye and tried hard with Gobby, addressing his answers to him a couple of times, failing to draw him out of himself.

Frankie was younger by a year but a lot less mature. He was frightened and met the questions with a sulky glower, needing to be prompted by his mum several times. He should have been more forthcoming because he was the one with the alibi: he'd been at work, delivering pizzas, sitting in a car with a fat guy called Tam all evening. They needed two guys because Tam was the shop owner's brother-in-law, needed the job, but was too fat to walk up stairs, so he gave Frankie a portion of his wages to do the leg work. Frankie made ten quid a night and got a pizza at the end.

By the end of the interviews, as Bannerman was telling Frankie and Kay that he'd need to see them all again but they were being sent home tonight, Morrow knew in her gut that they were innocent. Morrow knew what a cover-up among family members looked like: no eye contact between them, well-rehearsed answers to the important questions, often phrases echoed from person to person. When people were colluding no one had to check their phone or ask their mum where they had been on the night in question.

It was midnight when Bannerman shut off the tape and ejected it, bagging it for evidence. McCarthy went down the corridor to show Kay and her boys out, leaving Morrow watching the remote screen herself.

Bannerman and Gobby stood up and stretched their legs, pulled their jackets off the back of their chairs and gathered their papers. McCarthy was waiting by the door but Kay put her arm around Frankie's shoulders and made him stand up. "What happens now?" she said.

Bannerman was magnanimous. "You can go home."

"How can I go home? I left my purse on the kitchen table."

Frankie looked at her. "I've got my Zone Card, Mum."

"But that won't get me home, will it? Or Joe." She looked expectantly at Bannerman. "How am I to get home?"

She wanted a lift home. They'd never give her one.

Bannerman had his jacket on and was halfway out of the door. "Can't you get a minicab and pay when you get to the other end?"

McCarthy touched her elbow, nodding her out.

"I'm eight floors up, they'll not let me out the cab."

"Send one of the boys up and you can stay in the car."

Bannerman and Gobby jostled past her, bully-buffeting her and Frankie as they made their way out into the darkness of the corridor.

Morrow turned the car radio off. She was flying to London in the morning, catching the six-thirty flight, and should just go home, but she couldn't just drive past them. It was a wild area. Blank walls were punctured with dark alleys and feral bushes grew over bits of wasteland. It wasn't a place to walk at night. She saw them, one boy on either side of Kay, walking down the dark road, Kay's head hanging forward, shoulders slumped low and Joe nudging his huddled mum and making a joke. They were taking the straightest path to walk the four miles to Castlemilk. Kay didn't have taxi fare.

Morrow drew up ahead of them, pulled on the handbrake. She shut her eyes for a moment's respite. This wasn't going to be nice.

When she opened her eyes again she saw Joe looking in the window at her, frowning. She nodded to the back seat. He stood up and consulted with his mother in a whisper. Kay bent down then, glared in, angry and wet eyed, and stood up again. She told the boys something.

Frankie opened the passenger door and leaned in. "What do you want?"

"I'll run you home."

He slammed the door but they didn't walk away, they were whispering. Morrow watched Kay's hands adjust her handbag strap across her shoulder.

The back door opened and Joe got in first, climbing along to the far window, then Kay, then Frankie. He shut the door and they all pulled their seat belts on, managed to find the clips for them, though they were squashed up hard against each other.

No one spoke before Rutherglen. Morrow

was afraid to look in the mirror. She wanted to put the radio on but was afraid a cheerful song would be playing and it would make her seem even more callous.

Finally Joe snapped, "This is good of you."

Kay whispered, "Shut up."

"But it is, Mum, it's decent of her."

"Nasty fucking arsehole." Kay didn't specify exactly which person in the car was the nasty fucking arsehole, but she didn't need to.

It felt like a very long drive. Kay was crying at one point, sniffing, careful not to make too much noise. Morrow checked the mirror out of long habit and saw the shadow of Frankie's arm moving over his mum's shoulder. She looked away. She could be home now. She could be in her warm bed with Brian, sorting it out in her head, coming up with justifications, convincing herself that she was just doing the job, that she needed to make these hard choices for Sarah.

When they finally arrived at the steps from the main road to the high flats Kay said, "Here's fine," as if she was in a minicab.

Morrow was too tired to fight so she said nothing, drew up the hill and stopped.

Frankie opened the door and climbed out before she even had the handbrake on. Kay followed him. It wasn't in Joe's nature to leave without saying something.

"I do think that was decent of you. Thanks."

Morrow didn't wait to watch them open the door to the lobby. She pulled out and drove away, a little too fast.

TWENTY-NINE

Thomas turned into Tregunter Road and stopped. His hands were balled in his pockets, angry sweat prickling his palms. Big cars, big houses with big windows.

He had been hoping that it was a mess, one of those sudden shifts in tone that happened in London, when you turned a corner from a perfectly decent area and found yourself in a shit hole. This was the opposite of that.

He'd just left a crescent of absurd opulence, of massive country houses jostling on a city street, and it must have been a beacon to robbers because the houses were metal-shuttered, cowering behind walls pitted with alarms and video cameras. He'd turned from that into a habitable street built on a human scale.

The houses on Tregunter Road were big but some of them were semi-detached and none of them even had garages; most of the front gardens had been changed into parking spaces. One that he could see had a double buzzer on the door, which meant it was converted into flats. The doors had letter boxes on them, doorbells next to them. Members of the public could walk straight up to them. People lived nice, modest lives here. She lived here.

Thomas already knew this area. Lars liked to take him for lunch in Fulham. Twice at least, Lars got his driver to come down this road. It seemed an odd route. It wasn't on the way. Thomas remembered it because Lars explained his order, which he never did. He said they'd miss the traffic on the Fulham Road, and all the fucking pedestrians on the Kings Road. Thomas remembered looking at the yellow houses and wondering why Lars was explaining himself and had a funny smirk on his face as he did.

It made sense now. She lived here. The other Thomas — Phils — he lived here.

There was no one in the street. Thomas walked heavily, keeping his face hidden under the skip cap he'd bought from a market stall outside Charing Cross Station, his eyes flicking this way and that, scanning for movement and approaching people, noting that there were concealed video cameras on the properties.

He found number eight.

A low stone wall separated it from the street. In the front garden he could see a discarded skateboard sticking out of a bush. It made him double check the street number: they were never allowed to leave their belongings in view, he and Ella.

But it was number eight. The house was semi-detached, tall, yellow brick with white plaster trim, like all the other houses in the street. It was nice that they were all the same, like a uniform. The curtains in the front window were open, the lining draped perfectly uniformly. She hadn't done that herself. She still had house staff.

Thomas saw a car coming a block away and hurried to open the gate and walk up to the stairs, jogging to the privacy of the top step before the car came past.

A black door with serious brass fittings: a post box and a spy hole and a heavy lion's head knocker. He couldn't hear anything from inside. He lifted the brass knocker and banged twice on the door.

Steps shuffled, and the light changed on the spy hole. He had assumed she had staff but it wasn't a maid who opened the door.

She was younger than he expected. Slim with suspiciously round breasts. She wore white jeans and a pale gray sweater. Her brown hair was pulled up in a high ponytail and she had no make-up on. He couldn't imagine Lars with this woman: she didn't look formal enough, or old enough. She looked like Sarah Erroll, except very tall and pretty.

"Hello?" She didn't recognize him, put her hand on her hip and sighed, annoyed, when he didn't answer. "Look, can I help you?"

Thomas saw behind her, into the hall. It was tall, grand, with a high bookcase running the length of it, but it was messy: kids' and grown-up jackets were thrown on chairs and over banisters, a telephone lay off the cradle, lying on the stairs as if she'd just been speaking to someone and had dropped it and walked away. A used mug with a dried dribble of brown tea down the side had been left next to it on the stairs.

Thomas couldn't believe it was the right house. All of these tiny infractions were crimes to Lars, dreadful crimes, behaviors that had caused blazing rows. He was a stickler for form and formality. Thomas and Ella were never allowed to play in the public rooms. Even in their own areas of the house, the moment they had finished playing with anything they had to get the maid to tidy up. Thomas had once been screamed out of

376

a room by Lars because he cut a slice of Brie de Meaux across the nose and they didn't even have company. If Lars was a different man here, he wanted to know that man.

He looked up the wide stairs and suddenly, from nowhere, he saw blood splattered on white jeans and her scalp hanging off, Sarah Erroll afterwards, but only in details, split skin, hair stuck in open cuts. He felt sick and frightened.

The woman was looking at him and rapidly losing interest. He looked back at the hall, certain he had the wrong house.

"OK." She began to shut the door but Thomas suddenly saw that the mug was a Chelsea mug and the bookcases were poplar burr, like Lars's study at home. He stuck his foot out, catching the door, jamming it open.

The woman looked at his shoe and then at him. He could see that she was angry but she didn't shout.

"Sorry," she said lightly, looking him in the eye while she reached behind the door with her right arm. "What's your name?"

"You called me last night," he said.

She seemed to frown at him. Her skin was amazingly smooth, like paper. He couldn't work out how old she was — she looked young but was dressed older, moved like an older person.

"No, darling," she drawled slowly, "I think you're at the wrong door."

"But I'm Thomas Anderson."

"Oh. My. God. Thomas!" She grabbed his sleeve and pulled him into the hall. "I'm so sorry, I didn't recognize you. You're taller than your father. And handsome."

He saw then what she had reached behind the door for: she had a baseball bat in her hand.

She propped it up behind the door again. "How did you get here? Does your mother know you're here?"

Thomas was standing quite still. The hallway was dark now that the door was shut. He stood still and listened and heard no one else in the house, no shifts of air or radios anywhere. They were completely alone.

She touched her chest, pressing her hand into the cushion of her strangely spherical tits. "I'm Theresa."

He looked past her, nodding, taking his time before muttering, "Fucking Catholic."

She leaned in. "Sorry?"

He didn't want to say it again so he said nothing at all.

"Did you ask whether I was RC?" She

smiled tentatively, a little twitchy smile, as if she was hoping it was a quip or a joke or something.

He didn't answer.

"Well, I am — Catholic, if that's what you're asking." She made a silly sad face and crossed her eyes. "Failed."

Thomas didn't want to look at her. He kept his eyes down but she reached out and took his chin in her hand as if she was holding a dog's paw and looked at him, at his eyes and mouth and nose, at his build. "You don't look a bit like your father."

He liked her for that, because he did look like Lars, he knew he did. He had a lot of the bad bits of Lars, his thin mouth and bushy eyebrows.

"I do a bit."

She screwed up her eyes. "Maybe a titchy bit . . ."

"Kids not in?"

"No." She lurched across the hall and picked up a photo: a boy and girl, both with Aryan white hair and sun-kissed skin. The boy was about Thomas's age but taller and better-looking. He didn't smile but he looked confident, he had every reason to be. He probably knew girls his own age and kept up with music and saw bands and things like that.

The girl was older than Ella, not as pretty but less awkward and not nuts. They were standing on a white beach with a crystal blue sea behind them, shoulders pressed tight together, friends.

"Is this South Africa?"

"Plett, yes." She stepped away, wary. "Yes. The house . . ."

"Oh," Thomas looked at the picture again, "I never went there . . . was in school."

"It's pretty but I prefer France."

"I like France." He sounded almost normal.

She smiled at him. "Look, I'm sorry about the telephone call. I must have sounded very . . . unfriendly."

He thought back to it and shrugged. "It's OK." He looked into the house.

"I didn't think you'd come . . . I thought you were at school."

He cringed. "Got yanked out and sent home . . ."

"Because . . . ?"

"Yeah."

She sighed. "Why did he do it, Thomas?"

Thomas didn't answer. He really thought Lars did it to upset everyone, particularly the businessmen who'd conspired to have him removed from office. That was his style. He'd even use his own death to win a point.

380

But he didn't think Theresa wanted to hear that.

He hesitated for so long that Theresa filled in for him, "He just couldn't take the pressure anymore."

It was a very kind interpretation. He thought that she might not see much of Lars, really. He chewed his cheeks, glaring down into the house.

"Poor, poor man." She nodded and followed his eye down into the house herself. "Thomas, I know you've been away at school for a long time and it makes you grow up terribly fast but tell me this . . . ," she said seriously. "Are you much too mature to be a fan of pancakes?"

It was a pretend Dutch pancake house, wooden tables strewn with clogs and tulips. Everything was orange. She ordered three black coffees for herself and waffles with syrup for him. She didn't want to eat, she said, but she'd have a corner of his if she got hungry. The way she watched the plates of food moving around the room made him think that she was already hungry but dieting.

His waffles came on a plate with a picture of a windmill on it, but they were delicious and it was a long time since breakfast. He kept his cap low as he ate and she drank the mugs of coffee in quick succession.

She did the talking. She'd met Lars at a party a long time ago. She didn't like him at first. He kept correcting people and talking loud and she thought he was ill-mannered and boorish. She was leaving, looking for a taxi when his car stopped and he offered her a lift. She never thought she'd see him again so she told him to sod off, that she'd rather walk home than get into his car. He sent her flowers the next day and every day for ages. It got dull, actually, she said and Thomas sneered at that, no, it did! She didn't have anywhere to put them! She was living with her sister and the whole house was full of dying roses. They were melting onto the carpets and staining them. She phoned to tell him to stop and one thing led to another. She looked ashamed then. She didn't even know he was married for a long time, not until she was pregnant. He might understand a little better when he was older but sometimes you did things that looked really wrong from outside but she'd never meant to hurt anyone.

He nodded at that, felt tearful and she held his chin again and made him look at her. "You know what I mean, don't you?"

He didn't answer, but he didn't pull his

chin away either.

"Sometimes," she said gently, "it's nice to talk to someone outside your immediate circle." Then she flattened her hand to his cheek, stroked it and let go. Her hand was warm and soft and he wanted to grab it as it retreated across the table, tell her about Sarah Erroll, ask her what the fuck he should do about it.

But he didn't. Instead he asked her how she felt after, when she realized Lars was married and already had kids. Theresa said well, he didn't have kids, Moira was pregnant just like her. She said she had to accept that it happened and move on. But, Thomas asked, weren't you angry with him for putting you in that position? She shrugged; some people make you complicit, she said, it's a mistake to think they do it deliberately. It's not even about you, it's just who they are.

Thomas finished eating and she'd had enough coffee. He paid the bill with money from Lars's wallet, saw her looking at the wad of crisp notes, her eyes as fixed on them as they had been on the plates of pancakes.

They went for a walk. She took him for a wander around a furniture shop she liked and then they went into an antiques shop and decided what they liked and hated.

She took him across the road to a garden center, talked about gardening and smelled the plants. Her parents were keen gardeners. They had an ornamental garden that was open to the public for many years. Theresa said that she was so bad at gardening she could kill mint. He didn't really know what that meant but he laughed along anyway because she was laughing. It was nice, like they were friends. If she had been his mother things might have been different. He might have been calm and cool and done skateboarding. He might have had hobbies and been confident with girls.

He began to think he was wearing thin on her. They had been together for almost an hour and a half when he saw her checking her watch behind the bonsai trees.

Anxious not to outstay his welcome, he went over and said he'd have to go soon, could he walk her home, and she said yes, she'd like that, and it was charming of him to ask her.

She slipped her arm through his as they walked back.

THIRTY

The Walnut was on a curved, tall street in the City of London that had no shopfronts, just offices. The exclusive club barely declared itself on the street: a small plaque on the wall with an etching of a walnut on it and a buzzer. They went up a flight of inauspicious stairs and through a door manned by a bodybuilder in a sharp black suit. His accent was posh, his manner firm but courteous at the same time.

He checked their credentials, buzzed in to check that Howard Fredrick was expecting them, and then let them through the velvet studded door with a dramatic sweep.

It was tiny, very small for a public space, just a small room really. Three semicircular black velvet benches were set against the wall, joined to one another in a continuous wave. All the free walls were smoked glass, making the virtually empty area seem busy and warm. A small man with a ponderous belly was sitting on the furthest bench, his arm around the back, listening, bored, to a very pretty young woman chatting happily between sips of white wine. In front of each bench sat a small, low table with an opaque glass top, light radiating from inside and a cut-out in the center for a champagne bucket. Facing the tables was a short, well-stocked bar, again in glass, again up-lit, giving the woman serving a radiant glow.

She was dressed primly, in a white shirt and black bar apron, and her blonde hair pulled up in a high ponytail. Morrow thought she looked a little bit like Sarah: long faced, slim, little make-up. She smiled up at them, surprised at the sight of Morrow and Wilder in their bad suits and provincial haircuts but hiding it as she moved to the bar to greet them, her mouth open in readiness to smile, hands flat on the bar top, open to them.

Howard Fredrick swooped in from the back office and intercepted them. He pumped both their hands, looking them in the eye pointedly, tipping his head as if committing their names to memory, as though he'd been waiting to meet them for ages. He waved them to a door at the side of the bar, inviting them into his office.

It was a nice office. Almost the same size

as the bar itself, this room had two long windows onto the street, a beautiful walnut desk and matching chair, a small safe, and filing cabinets. He'd been expecting them: Sarah Erroll's employment file sat on his desk, next to a glass of water.

He didn't offer them a drink, or tea, or anything, but directed them to the chairs in front of his desk while he sat behind it.

"Thank you for coming," he said, possibly out of habit. "You're interested in Sarah Erroll?"

"Aye," said Morrow, feeling herself on the back foot, unclear how to take charge and not certain she needed to. "She worked here?"

"I have her file here." He flipped it open. "She worked here for seven months, and left to move back to Scotland because her mother was ill —"

"How many hours a week did she do?"

He looked at the file. "Five shifts a week, about seven or eight hours each."

"What shifts was she doing?"

"Eight till two." He looked at Wilder. "Our license is until four but we rarely stay open that long."

Wilder nodded, as if that was what they had come here to ask and he was satisfied.

"You here much?" asked Morrow.

"Every minute of every day." He smiled at that, a hollow smile. Morrow didn't feel she was getting past a pre-prepared statement.

"Were you fucking her?"

"No." It didn't throw him at all. "I don't fuck my staff."

"Who was she fucking?"

Fredrick sat back, crossed his hands over his stomach and looked at her. Morrow looked back. His hair was dyed dark, possibly covering gray, but it sort of suited him. His skin was quite olive but he was most definitely London, his accent just working class enough to be genuine, not so working class that he'd adopted it. He was fit for a man in his forties, not smoker-lean, not cocaine-thin, but muscled and fit. She guessed he spent a good bit of his time at the gym.

His lip curled with disdain as he reached forward and touched the manila file. "I don't keep notes of that sort of thing."

"Could you tell us off the top of your head?"

"No," he said, and she felt he was telling the truth. "I've had this bar for nine years, we always employ girls who look pretty much alike and, being honest with you, they blur into one after a while. I don't remember her much."

He left it at that. Crossed his hands over his flat stomach, raised his eyebrows for the next question.

"You got a national insurance number for her?"

"She said she was a student." He pushed a number scribbled on a sheet of paper across to her. "This is the student number she gave us. UCL. Check it."

She heard what he was telling her. "It's phony?"

"Yeah, phoned the uni this morning, turns out it was someone else's."

"She friends with any of the other girls?"

He shrugged and looked at the file. "She got the job through her friend Maggie, they knew each other from school."

"Where could we get hold of Maggie?"

"That's her behind the bar now."

"She's still here?"

"Not *still,* she's back."

"Where's she been?"

He stuck his tongue into his cheek, eyes amused. "Married. Bloke she met in here. Turns out he's a twat. She's come back. Briefly."

"How do you know it's briefly?"

Fredrick looked at her, seeing her for the first time. He paused, considering, she felt, the wisdom of being honest with her. "Being honest with you, I don't like the girls to stay too long." He waved his hand vaguely. "Makes the bar . . . stale."

"They get bored? Their work suffers?"

"No, the clients get bored. You know, girls in a room, day after day, they can shut up at first but after a while, they get to talking, becomes all about them, doesn't it?"

"What do they talk about?"

"Their problems, their boyfriends, their family, who gives a shit." Fredrick clearly didn't. He sounded bored even listing the things that bored him. "The men here want to drink and escape their work, a lot of them have got wives at home, they don't want to have to listen to that shit here, do they?"

"What do they want here?"

"Drink, bit of glamour, everything taken care of." He puffed his chest out. "We're a private members' club more than a bar; you have to be recommended to get in here."

"Lars Anderson drank here, didn't he?"

The question stopped him dead. He considered Morrow and Wilder again, looked at their clothes, at her shoes, at her red-rimmed eyes. He glanced at the door. "Rocco checked your ID, did he?"

"The doorman?" she said.

"Yeah."

"He did, aye."

390

He reached forward, flipped his fingers at them. "Can I see them again?"

They showed him their warrant cards and he checked the photos, asked them to take the card out of the wallets and looked at the back, tried to bend Wilder's to see if it was made of sturdy plastic. He gave it back, seemed pleased with himself. "D'you know how I actually know you're not journalists?"

And he waited until they answered. "No, Mr. Fredrick," said Morrow, burning eyed, getting annoyed, "how is it that you know we are not journalists?"

" 'Cause you're in charge." He smiled. "You know, a woman. Pregnant. A pregnant woman."

He sat back, very pleased with his deduction, whether it was that she was a woman, or a pregnant woman that made her not a journalist, she didn't give a flying fuck. Fredrick owned a club people wanted to get into and he spent a lot of time in drinking company. Those twin factors seemed to have prompted him into mistakenly thinking himself interesting.

"Lars Anderson drank here, didn't he?" she said, echoing her intonation from earlier to show she was getting impatient.

"Yes."

Morrow looked at him. He looked at her.

She would have launched into the details of her day so far, getting up at five for the six-thirty flight, feeling sick, Wilder almost missing the plane because he'd gone to the toilet, the heat on the underground into town, the noise and confusion of rush hour in London, all to get here and be treated as if she'd come from the cleansing department. She could have told Fredrick why he should tell her what he knew, what the consequences would be if he didn't, but she felt bored even contemplating a rant. So she sat back.

"Fuck's sake," she muttered, shaking her head. "Cough it up."

Fredrick liked that, smiled at that. "Him and Sarah?"

Morrow nodded heavily. "Him and Sarah."

"Got on well. Saw his car pick her up from work a couple of times."

"She ever say anything about it?"

"No. She wouldn't. Discreet. Nice girl." He nodded approvingly.

"See her getting picked up by anyone else's car, ever?"

He pursed his lips, thought about it. "No. She wasn't escorting when she worked here." He read Morrow. "You knew she was an escort?"

"Aye."

"She left here once she started all that."

"How did you know that?"

He slapped the manila file shut. "That's why she left here. She was in with a girl, Nadia. I knew what she was thinking. I said to her, not here, Sarah, can't have it. If you're gonna do that you can fuck off. So she did."

"Who's Nadia?"

He looked past them to the door, pursed his lips again. "I'll get her in if you like."

"Why would you do that?" asked Morrow, just because she wanted to know.

Fredrick shrugged. "I'll always help the police if I can," he said, but he couldn't look at her.

Maggie Back-briefly-behind-the-bar was not upset particularly about Sarah Erroll's death. Morrow wondered if she'd understood that she'd been murdered, maybe she hadn't read the papers, but after quizzing her for a bit it became clear that she had. She said the things people say: it's awful, how terrible, but her expression remained blank and apathetic.

Maggie had left the job to get married to a businessman she'd met here through the bar. A party had been organized on a boat

393

and all the Walnut girls were invited. He was younger than her by two years and already a millionaire. She really thought he was going to make it. But then the crash came and he handled it badly, didn't get out and now he had nothing, minus nothing because he was trading with their own money. She was glad to have her job back; Howard was a good friend. She didn't seem to know it was temporary.

Morrow asked her how she met Sarah.

"We were at school together, I was a few years older than her. I met her at my sister's and she needed a job, looked the part, I knew Howard was looking. I brought her in and got her an interview. She started that night."

"What sort of person was she?"

Maggie looked blank. "Nice, quiet person, worked hard, helpful . . ."

"What was she like at school?"

"Quiet." She corrected herself. "Actually, I didn't know her, you'd have to talk to my sister."

"Can you give me her number?"

Maggie had to fish her mobile out of her pocket to find it. After Morrow had jotted the number in her notebook she glanced back up and saw Maggie looking at the back wall of the office — her cheekbone was lit from the side. She had laughter lines, wrinkles on her forehead but they looked stale, unused, traces of facial expressions she seemed unlikely ever to make. It hit Morrow suddenly: Maggie's face was paralyzed. She wasn't a cold bitch: she'd had her face pumped full of Botox.

"How old are you?" she asked.

Very slowly, Maggie's shoulders rose to her ears. "Twenty-seven."

"Very young still," she said flatly, wondering why she felt such a strong urge to save Maggie from herself.

Deep in Maggie's eyes, Morrow thought she saw a twinge of disdain. "Not really," she said.

Fredrick was angry with Nadia, very angry. He let her into the office in front of him, jostling her with a prod in her back, curling his lip as he pointed at his desk chair, telling her to sit down. Nadia let him boss her as though it were a sexy game. She looked as if she could buy and sell him. Her coat was blonde mohair, ankle length, her jewelry was spare: matching necklace and earrings in a textured zigzag yellow gold. Her swarthy skin was flawless and her hair was black and chocolate, not cheap-looking or wig-like in the way Jackie Hunter's hair had been, but thick and rich.

As she sat down her coat slid open across perfect brown knees, revealing a red woolen dress and perfect legs. She gave Fredrick a reproachful smile.

"Are you Nadia?" asked Morrow, feeling that they must look very plain to her.

Nadia turned to her with a practiced smile. "I am Nadia, yes. Howard tells me that you would like to talk about Sarah and her business?"

"Hmm, did you know Sarah?"

Nadia looked to Fredrick for direction and he scowled at her. "No, I'm afraid there has been a mistake on Howard's part, unfortunate, but I didn't know Sarah." Her accent sounded Middle Eastern, or Brazilian, Morrow couldn't tell for sure.

"He said you did."

Nadia looked at him, a smile playing behind her eyes.

"Fucking stop it," he said. "She's only fucking dead. They don't want you."

Nadia conceded flirtatiously. "OK, Howard, I tell it the truth: I knew her, she was a friend of mine, OK?"

"How did you meet her?"

She waved a hand over her shoulder. "At a party. She was serving the drinks, Howard, he sometimes give them extra work . . ."

They looked at him for confirmation but he was glaring at Nadia. "So we meet, we talk, she pretty and short of money and I say to her, you can set up a business, legal, on the internet, no one know your business, all private dealings. *Just for fun.*" She emphasized the last part as if it was an absolute legal defense. "Yes? For *fun.*"

"How did she react to that suggestion?"

Nadia glanced at Fredrick. "Very happy about it —"

"No, she wasn't," said Fredrick flatly. "She was in bits."

"She talk to you about it?" asked Morrow.

But Fredrick wasn't even looking at Morrow. "Nadia has a problem telling truth from fantasy. It's a big problem." Nadia smiled sweetly at the desk top. "She don't know if she's fucking lying or not, do ya?"

She gave him a look, so old and knowing that Morrow knew that Nadia had played Fredrick and won.

"Can we talk to Nadia alone, please?"

He didn't like that. Tried to think of a way around it and then pushed himself off the wall with his shoulders, stalked to the door, turned to say something and thought better of it, opened the door and walked out. The door fell shut.

Nadia pursed her lips, an echo of Fredrick's gesture earlier. "He's a very emotional pers—"

"Aye," interrupted Morrow. "Nadia, I don't give a fuck what's going on between you two and I don't give a fuck about what you do for a living, all right, hen?"

Nadia read her, took in her cheap suit and pregnancy bump, her neat hair and saw that they were so opposite there was no threat here. She nodded softly.

"I want to know two things: how did she get into it and what Lars Anderson was to her. Clear?"

Nadia straightened her dress. "He was a friend of hers, Lars, a gentleman friend."

"A client?"

She shrugged a yes.

"He good to her?"

She widened her eyes. "Very good."

"No, I'm not asking if he paid her well or gave her presents, I mean was he good to her?"

She shrugged again, ambivalent this time. "He's a rich man, he's not so good but not bad. You know men . . . what they are like . . ."

"Misandry," said Morrow.

"Miss who?"

"Misandry. It's the opposite of misogyny. A blind prejudice against men on the basis

398

of their gender. It's not healthy, Nadia. It makes for unhappy relationships."

"Oh," she said politely, "that's interesting. I didn't know there was such a word."

"It's the long-term damage of your profession, isn't it?"

She shook her head. "I don't know —"

Morrow leaned towards her. "Will you ever trust a man again?"

Nadia saw that she understood her a little. "You don't know how the money draws you in . . ."

Morrow sat back. "Miners get lung disease."

They smiled at each other for a moment.

"Maybe you're less damaged than me: I'm a police officer, we don't trust women either."

Nadia smiled, thought about it, huffed a little laugh. "Even girls who don't do this . . . Not everyone's happy in relationships. At least when I'm lonely I'm *rich* and lonely."

"What was Sarah like?"

"Nice girl. Didn't want to do it at first. Her choice, but she needed the money very bad. Her mother was ill, she couldn't afford health care. She asked me how to start. I told her."

"What did you tell her?"

A little regret flickered around her lips. "I invite her to a party, with party girls. She fuck a couple of guys there. Then she get into it."

"Was she upset after? Howard Fredrick said she was in bits."

"She wasn't happy but it wasn't rape. She wasn't crying. She was fed up afterwards but we all are fed up afterwards, at the beginning. Is a hard job. That's why everyone doesn't do it. Is hard sometimes. A lonely job. And it affect you." She looked at Morrow. "Mis-antry?"

"Misandry," corrected Morrow. "Did she come into work afterwards?"

"For a couple of shifts. She talk to Howard about it. He very angry with me. Tell me to stay the fuck out of his bar after. It's silly really because I didn't meet her here, I met her in a party but after he says not more parties with the girls, he didn't know who they would be meeting, so on." She glanced at the door. "He thinks they are thoroughbred horses, the way he treats them."

"The bar staff?"

"No, is just . . . he doesn't like what I do for a living." She touched her hair, a self-soothe gesture, and Morrow could tell she cared what he thought.

"You and Howard . . . ?"

Nadia frowned quickly and nodded to her shoulder. "We were close for a while."

"He's very angry with you."

She looked at the door to make sure it was shut. "They can fuck me," she hissed, her face hard and angry, "but they can't own me." She sat back and smiled at Wilder, resuming her party girl persona. "Drive them crazy."

The streets of the City of London were so quiet it felt like Glasgow during an Old Firm Game. A few tourists followed the brightly colored maps in their hands, snapping pictures, filming on their phones. What little traffic there was consisted mostly of buses and black cabs.

Morrow was glad to get to Heathrow, glad to be sitting in the departures lounge with the other Glaswegians heading home with sunburn and summer clothes on, talking to strangers and laughing with their mouths open, watched by the cabin crew in smart uniforms.

Wilder sat next to her, reading a tabloid newspaper as solemnly as the Bible, and she sat and imagined Sarah Erroll at a party, on her back and thinking about the money and her mum as a red-faced businessman rutted over her. It was an accident of fate: Sarah

401

needed the money, she happened upon Nadia, she found that she could do it. She might have met a stockbroker and been good at that instead.

THIRTY-ONE

Kay wiggled the key in the door but it didn't work. She tried jabbing it in and out of the lock and blowing on it. It had never happened before: the key did fit into the lock but it wouldn't turn at all. She wanted to kick the door, punch it and shove it with her shoulder.

She stopped, took a breath and counseled herself to caution. She was tired from the night before. When they got back she'd gone next door to collect Marie and John, taken everyone home and made them go straight to bed. Then she sat up until five in the morning, smoking in front of the telly. She knew they were lying awake, blinking in the dark. She heard Joe and Frankie whispering when she went to the toilet at ten to four. She sat up smoking and drinking herbal tea, too embarrassed to go to bed, thinking about her family and how they looked to the police.

403

She knew they looked working class, herself looked a little disheveled sometimes but she always thought they looked decent. Maybe they didn't. Maybe they looked envious and covetous and low. Maybe she did look 45–60, Frankie seemed odd and John was a rapist in the making. Maybe Marie was fat and Joe was smarmy. She had never had a crisis of faith in her children before. It made her sick.

To prove to herself that she was decent, she rose after three hours' sleep and made them all get up and eat breakfast and go to school in clean and ironed clothes. Then she dressed herself, brushed her hair and caught the bus to Thorntonhall. On the top deck she leaned her head on the rattling window, the condensed breath of strangers running into her hair, and vowed to listen to Margery without saying anything about the night before. She would pat Margery's hand and tell her not to worry. She'd forget herself, do her work well and in good grace.

But Margery's key wouldn't fit. When she opened her eyes again she had taken several deep breaths and relaxed her body a little, twisting at the waist so that she was facing the French doors of the kitchen.

Margery was watching her. Her arms were crossed. She was wearing her yellow slacks, the expensive ones she regretted buying but loved. She wore them rarely, kept them for special. Banana yellow flares, thirty years out of date.

Kay raised her hand in a static wave, but Margery didn't move. She stood perfectly framed in the windows, looking straight at her. Kay waited for her to gesture at the lock or invite her through the French doors. Instead, Margery uncrossed her arms and pointed back at the gate.

Kay glanced back. The gate was shut, she had shut it properly. Still Margery stood stiff, pointing at it, mouthing "No" or "Go."

Someone was in there with her.

Dropping her plastic bag into the deep gravel, Kay rushed over to the French doors and rattled the handle, pulling when she should have pushed, trying to open it. Realizing her mistake, she turned the handle and shoved, banging the glass door against the worktop inside.

Margery fell back, clutching the sink. "Get out!"

"Who's in here?"

Kay headed for the living room.

"No one."

She stopped. She listened. She knew the sounds of this house and there was no one here but Margery.

"Get out."

Kay was sweating, panting, felt vulnerable in front of Margery who was standing, cool against the sink. "Why?"

Margery stepped over to the table as if it was a matter of great urgency and adjusted the position of a small crystal vase with a single yellow rose in it, shifting it slightly. She looked at Kay, pulled her lips back in a pitiless smile. "The police have been back. *You know why.*"

For a moment Kay couldn't hear anything in the world but the dull thump of her own blood. She felt the blood in her cheeks, in her eyes, across her face.

She saw Margery Thalaine, standing in her thirty-grand kitchen, baring her teeth at the help and she understood completely what Margery was seeing: a failure and a mess.

"You're wrong," she whispered when she meant to shout. "That's wrong."

"Get out." Margery's voice was flat and she meant never come back, not later or in a year.

Kay had things to say that could hurt Margery, she could cast up that she had been a friend to her, that she had been needlessly kind. She could cast up that she was owed money for mopheads and detergent. Even, in a weak moment, she could bring up Mr. Thalaine's flight from Berlin in 1938 and ask how Margery could side so easily with the authorities.

But she did none of those things because she was too upset to speak. Instead she walked out of the French door and shut it gently behind herself, looking at the handle, not into the room.

Then she walked over to the front door, slid her hand through the handles of her poly bag, reaching up to her like a child. Kay walked out of the gate, keeping her head high until she reached the bin recess around the corner, and lit up. She turned to the hedge to hide her face as she smoked.

A deep scratchy breath halted the tears pressing behind her eyes. She had barely exhaled the smoke when she took another draw. The panic was not because Margery had been mean to her or belittled her. The panic was because she now didn't have that job and she had four kids and they needed shoes and food and the rent needed paid and the fucking council tax. It was just about money. Just money. I can get another job, she told herself, knowing that they were few and far between, that she was being paid well and the hours suited her. Another job would be a night job at Asda, she'd be out all night and the kids would be alone in the house — she wouldn't even know if they were in or out. Or who was there with them.

She took another draw. No. There would be other jobs. She still had the Campbells. Maybe they would know someone else here who needed a cleaner. Maybe.

She dropped the cigarette, quite impressed that she had managed to finish it in four draws. She stood on it, gathered herself, straightened her hair and walked around the lane to the Campbells' house, slipping through the garden, keeping off the lawn, until she got to the kitchen door.

Molly Campbell was in the kitchen. She was waiting for her, watching, and Kay knew. Margery had been here, blowing off about her and Molly was going to ask for her key back.

Miserably, Molly smiled and opened the door.

"Hello, Kay." She tilted her head to the side, sighing, stepped back to let Kay into the kitchen, pointed to a chair that she had pulled out from the table for Kay to sit on. Kay sat and tried to listen while Molly Campbell sacked her, went through the details of her tax, explained why it was better for everyone if Kay never came back here. It's the tax: Margery had explained that Kay was "leaving" her employment and without that job this one just wasn't worth it. Best for everyone. She'd put out a plate of biscuits.

Kay tried to listen but she felt the loss of Joy Erroll rise in her chest as a wave of warmth and sorrow. She felt a bony little hand in hers and saw Joy's tea-stained teeth as she laughed happily. She had five teeth left by the time she died, little pegs. Her gums had shrunk and she wouldn't wear her false teeth anymore. Kay felt the weight of Joy as she lifted her off the loo, both arms around her skinny body, Joy's little arms around Kay's neck, and Joy, startlingly appropriate, singing an old big band tune and pretending they were dancing together.

Kay burst out crying. She gathered her things and stood up, got the door open and stepped out into the garden.

"Oh, no." Molly Campbell reached out for her. "Kay, I'm so sorry, please come —"

But Kay waved her away. "No, I'm fine."

"Please come back in and sit for a minute."

"No, no." She fumbled in her bag, still crying, wishing for the warmth of Joy's body against hers, for the deep love she had lost, and she found the key and put it in Molly's outstretched hand. "It's not this," she said, feeling ridiculous because it was two mornings a week, for God's sake, "it's not the job."

She scurried away, skirting the lawn again, desperate to get away and hide her face.

She smoked at the bus stop, something she never did. Margery Thalaine could be driving past and see her but she didn't care anymore. She'd never see her again.

She managed not to cry, pushing to the back of her mind the realization that this could well be the last time she would ever come here. She didn't have any jobs now and wouldn't even get the Asda job without a reference. Maybe Molly would feel bad and would give her a reference.

As she waited, her face numbing in the wet, her phone rang in her handbag and she didn't answer it but waited until the bus came and she was settled in a window seat.

Donald Scott wanted her to call him, please, regarding the settlement of the Erroll estate. She had to dredge her memory for the name. He was the Errolls' lawyer. He used to come to the house to see Joy. Always asked for biscuits with his tea and never ate them. He sounded snooty in the message, and said something about the police and the bowl and the watch. Kay tutted at her phone. As if a watch and bowl were going to make any fucking difference to the final settlement of the estate. But it occurred to her, she could call Scott and get a reference off him. He'd known she worked well for Mrs. Erroll. Maybe she could get a good reference and get a job in an old folks' home. She might even get trained.

The spark of hope snowballed: Scott was a lawyer too, that would be a good reference. Kay watched the road this time, seeing the familiar hedges and turnings and trees. Calmed, she could see what her mistake had been: Margery regretted confiding in Kay. Kay had listened to her and crossed the line from employee to intimate and it was easier to justify being mean to an intimate. Margery had probably been looking for an excuse to sack her, as if Kay could be tied up at the handles and thrown in the bin.

The job would have ended soon anyway. Margery was broke and the Campbell job would hardly cover her travel on its own, so she'd have left that too.

She sat back, feeling the burn of cigarettes and grief in her lungs. A new beginning. She felt able and competent again. A mother of four. The only shadow on her mood was last night. They would be brought in for questioning again. It could happen at any time of the day or night. The police could come to the boys' school and whip them out. They could turn up at a friend's house and whip them out, and smears like that stuck to a boy. She thought of the teachers looking at the boys differently, of them being asked not to come back to friends' houses, being excluded.

Kay decided to do something about it because she had never learned the skill of being passive.

She was back at the house with Frankie and Joe, sitting squashed together at the tiny kitchen table. Joe and Kay had taken the seats, leaving Frankie to perch on a step stool that sat him too high for the table.

"Now, I'm going out for the afternoon," she said firmly, knowing she seemed in charge and certain. "Does everyone know what they're doing?"

Frankie looked at his list of tasks. "I don't think you needed to drag us out of school to do these things, Mum."

"Aye," said Joe, looking at his list. "Most of these guys are in school. I need to wait until they get out before I can talk to them anyway."

"Boys," she said, "don't tell the wee ones but I got a fright last night and I need to sort this out *today.* I've phoned the cops and we're going back in at teatime so you need to be back here at four thirty to meet me to get the bus."

Joe blinked at his list, looked at her, quizzical. "We know you got a fright, Mum."

"We all got a fright," Frankie said quietly.

"How are you not at your work?" asked Joe.

It hadn't occurred to Frankie that Kay would normally be at Mrs. Thalaine's.

Kay reached for a cigarette, changed her mind and looked back at them. "I'm going for a career change. I'm going to be a nurse."

Kay got off the bus at the Squinty Bridge and walked across the river to Broomielaw. A brisk wind streamed across the river from the broad plane of Govan, rising up the boom of the flats. Even in the deep doorway, it lifted the tail of her coat and blew her hair up over her ears. Cars passed quickly, anticipating the motorway five hundred yards away.

Kay told herself that this was a mistake but she pressed the buzzer anyway.

The receiver was picked up and a woman

413

spoke. "Who's it?"

Kay said her name and the woman made her repeat it. She hung up and Kay waited. A bus passed and slowed, stopping a hundred yards down the road. Kay considered running for it but the receiver crackled to life again: " 'Mon up."

She looked at the glass doors, expecting a signal, but none came. She pressed the door with her fingertips and it opened in the lobby.

These were private flats, expensive, but the lobby was filthy compared to hers. She found herself tutting at the sticky floors and fag butts in the plant pots. They shouldn't be smoking in there, not in a communal space. Someone had even burned cigarette holes in the leaves of the fake plants. The kids around theirs wouldn't do that. They'd get chased.

She called the lift and stepped in, pressed the button, turned to face the doors and watched them close. As the lift took off she cleared her throat and straightened her hair, saw her reflection in the door and saw that she looked old and dowdy and worn, 45–60. The lift stopped, the doors hesitated before opening and she suddenly wished she hadn't come.

At first she thought it was another lobby

because it was as big and high as an airport.

A wall of windows two stories high looking out onto the river, facing down it to the sea. The surrounding walls were yellow sandstone and there was hardly any furniture, just a big settee. But then she saw the woman. She was standing ten feet away, diagonally across the room. It was a strange place to greet anyone coming out of the lift, not where your eye would fall. She wanted people to look for her.

Bleached hair, pink lippy, heels. She waved like a child, raising her arm at the elbow, hand nodding from side to side. "Hiya."

Kay nodded and looked around for someone else.

"I'm Crystyl."

"OK." Kay didn't have the fucking time for this. She just wanted to make a mistake and get out and get home and smoke in peace.

"Danny's in here." Crystyl held her hand up to a door on the same wall as the lift and Kay walked over to it. It was open a little so she pushed and the woman hurried over, hobbled by the heels, making a big deal of it.

"I'll tell him —"

Kay held her hand up. "I'm fine, hen." She stepped into the room to get away from whatever the fuck was going on with her.

It was a low room, a den. Startling halogen lights were punched into the ceiling. The carpet was thick, the walls clad in pine shelves with a big mirrored bar inset into one. The biggest telly she had ever seen took up the far wall. The footballers on it looked life size.

Danny McGrath had not aged. He had not spent long nights nursing temperature spikes that came to nothing, or stayed up sewing last-minute costumes for school concerts. He had never worked double shifts back to back, the first to pay for child care, the second for rent money. He had done none of these things. He had pleased himself and worked to get the things that he wanted, like the big telly he was sitting in front of now, like the leather recliner armchair he was lying on. The expensive bottles of drink, all of them full, glittering on the glass shelves behind him. He looked young and fresh and rested.

He sat his chair upright when he saw her and used the remote to pause the football match he was watching. He didn't bother standing up and didn't invite her to sit down. He wasn't expecting this to take long.

"Kay, hen, how are you?"

She kept her hands in her pockets and

nodded around the room at all his things. "Nice." But Kay had a good eye and knew the furniture was vulgar and factory made and wouldn't last.

"What can I do for ye?"

It was a mistake, she was making a mistake. She held her breath.

She looked at the far wall and said what she had rehearsed in her head on the bus over here: "I need to ask you a favor."

They looked at each other. Danny nodded. "What is it?"

"Your sister," she said, looking at the moonlight whiteness of the belly peeking out from under his T-shirt, "I need you to speak to her. She wants my boys for something and they're good boys, they didn't do anything."

Danny cleared his throat. "I don't see Alex."

"She wants them for a murder. They didn't do it."

"Kay, hen, I don't see her. I leave her alone, she body-swerves me."

But Kay was tearful. She was stupid to have come here. She was panicking and being stupid. "You'd think with her expecting . . ." She began to cry. She'd have hidden it better if she'd been in front of someone she respected.

Danny watched her cry. "She's pregnant again?"

"Twins."

"I never noticed . . ."

"She's showing already."

His eyes flickered towards the television. "Ah, well, she'd a coat on."

"You're not going to say anything to her, are you?"

Danny tutted, shifted his backside in the leather chair. "Alex is nothing to do with me. If I could help I would. If there's anything else I can do . . . I'll pay for lawyers if they charge them, how about that?"

Kay managed a deep breath. Beneath her feet the thick carpet creaked as the fibers shifted. Kay wanted to get out of here. She had never asked Danny for anything and it was a mistake to come here now.

"OK." She stepped back towards the door.

"Sixteen?"

Kay caught her breath. "Eh?"

"Sixteen, is he?"

She had her hand on the door. "Who's this?"

"Joseph. Is he sixteen?"

She turned square to him. "Yeah, Joe's sixteen."

They looked at each other. Danny's eyebrows rose slowly.

Kay tutted. "Don't flatter yourself, Danny, Joe's good-looking."

But Danny wasn't to be put off. She'd never told him but somehow he knew Joe was his. He looked away from her, cleared his throat. "What sort of a boy is he?"

He was thinking about JJ. Kay suddenly saw him properly. His eyes were red-rimmed, his paunch was settled, his ankles looked a bit swollen. Danny: 45–60.

Kay stepped towards him and cupped his cheek in her hand, startling him, and she said, "Danny, Joe's a lovely, lovely guy," and she held his face in both her hands as he fought off a crying pang like a child.

Embarrassed, he stood up, brushed her hands off and turned away, drying his face on his sleeve, sniffing.

"Pet," said Kay. "Pet?"

He couldn't turn back to her. "Wha?"

"I shouldn't have come here."

"No. I'm fine."

She opened the door, wanting to get out before he got it together but he was by her side. He was holding a chunk of twenty-quid notes, trying to press them into her hand.

Kay looked at the money, keeping her

hands in her pockets. "Stay away from us," she said, and left.

THIRTY-TWO

They ate their sandwiches in Bannerman's office and she talked him through the Walnut interviews. He wasn't listening. She stopped short of telling him about the party, feeling it was too personal to Sarah to tell someone who plainly didn't care. He was waiting until she was finished so that he could talk through his theory. He was excited by it, she could see that it had come to him as a realization and he was glad of it. Bannerman didn't want to get stuck in the endless gathering of information and getting nowhere and his theory was their means of escaping that fate. It seemed very unlikely to Morrow.

What Bannerman was suggesting had happened was this: the Murray boys had broken into Glenarvon through the kitchen window, possibly at their mother's instruction. Breaking in would make it look as though it had nothing to do with her, since she had a key. Once in the kitchen they left no prints until they climbed the stairs to Sarah Erroll's bedroom and Frankie, the younger one, broke off and went to the bathroom. He touched the toilet seat lid with his thumb, leaving a perfect print. They then committed the crime and threw their clothes away on the way home. Unable to find the money, they left with nothing but an ashtray and a watch. The silver eggcup had been discarded as the proceeds of a theft now because it wasn't silver, but electroplated, and had been on top of the cupboard for years.

Morrow shook her head, "Saying they broke in to make it look as if they didn't have the key sounds a bit convoluted. Maybe whoever did it just didn't have a key?"

"But it would make us think they didn't when they did."

"That's a bit sophisticated for robbers who lost it and kicked her head in, don't you think?"

"And then they panicked and grabbed the watch and the bowl."

"Again, a bit sophisticated. They put the watch in a sock under their mother's bed and use the bowl as an ashtray."

He could see she wasn't buying it. "She

said they hadn't been there." He slid a photograph of a fingerprint over to her. "We found Frankie's print on the toilet seat."

"But nowhere else?"

"Nowhere. Wearing gloves?"

"Why would you wear gloves and take them off at the loo?"

Bannerman had been preparing this, she could tell by his smirk. He reached his hand forward, palm down, thumb opposing, and mimed lifting a toilet seat up to the wall. He raised his eyebrows. "Having a pee. Break in, very excited, need to go . . ."

"Not a pee," she said, sounding vague because she was thinking. Harris would have known what she meant by that but it wasn't obvious to Bannerman. Burglars and home intruders often voided their bowels in a house, often in strange places like the living room floor or in a kitchen. Adrenaline made everything move, speeded up the small intestine. Usually they got in and the wave of excitement passed and they found they couldn't walk for needing the toilet, couldn't even get to the bathroom. It wasn't, as many victims thought, a statement of disrespect or defiance. It wasn't a statement at all, just a biological imperative. It seemed unlikely that they would urinate in a loo and then flush it away, nice and tidy, and put gloves back on and then carry on to commit a murder. They'd found prints on the phone anyway. They weren't Frankie's. He'd have said if they were.

She looked down at the photograph of the print on the white plastic. It was verifiably Frankie's thumbprint: the fingerprint analysis stapled to the back had sixty points of identity and it was only a cursory examination.

Bannerman added, "She says on film that her boys have never been to that house."

He was right, Kay had said that, but it was a hell of a big case to base on a single fingerprint.

"Shirley McKie," said Morrow quietly. He looked at her as if she had threatened to kick his balls.

"I'm just saying," she said, "it's just one print, we don't want to bring that up again."

The DC Shirley McKie case was a police horror story. The Strathclyde Detective Constable's thumbprint was found at a murder scene that she had never been to. It wouldn't have mattered but forensic evidence against the murder suspect consisted of a single fingerprint at the scene as well. His conviction was overturned and McKie's disputed suspension had thrown the service into a tail spin: if they didn't prove she was lying and had been there then all fingerprint evidence over the past forty years would have been open to question, opening up a huge number of cases for retrial. It was ignominious, but the bosses decided to eat their own. Then Shirley McKie got a lawyer and won the case anyway. Everyone was waiting for the second shoe to fall.

Bannerman turned a page of his notes, signaling a change of conversation. "Leonard's 'friend' . . .." He looked up. "Is she . . . ?"

"Is she what?" said Morrow, belligerent, as if she hadn't wondered herself. "Friendly?"

He smirked and dropped it. "Just, they don't look like they do in films."

"What, you mean scratching at each other with big, dirty-looking false nails? What about her friend?"

He seemed irritated by the implication that he'd ever had access to pornography. "Spoke to her on the phone, she's preparing a presentation for us. We had the photos enlarged and it seems there's a scar on the sole of one of the shoes. She thinks she can separate their movements. Work out who did what."

"Good. We can charge them both with conspiracy if you think she'd be all right on the stand."

"She's very giggly."

"Ah." That was bad.

"She sounds about fifteen."

"What age is she actually?"

"Twenty-three. I saw a picture of her online."

"Was she young-looking?"

"Her Facebook picture is of her topless on a beach. But she did look very young."

They couldn't use her as an expert witness if she seemed young or silly. Juries wouldn't like her, the prosecution case would look foolish by association, and the papers loved an excuse to print a topless picture in the news pages. They'd use it if her evidence became material. "No one else in the lab who's presentable that we could use?"

"No, she's developing the technology herself, it sounds interesting though."

"Why," pondered Morrow aloud, "are we discounting the possibility of a client attacking her?"

He nodded, considering it seriously. "Something goes wrong, a young man maybe, can't get it up, angry with her, comes back and kills her?"

"It's possible, isn't it?"

"No, it's silly. She never met clients in her

house and she'd stopped answering the emails. The fact that it's in her house probably means it's something else, doesn't it?"

A knock on the office door interrupted them and Harris opened it. He couldn't even look at Bannerman.

"Ma'am, there's a journalist on the phone. He wants to talk to someone in charge."

They both frowned at him. Journalists phoned all the time. Harris was supposed to bounce them off to the media and press department.

"He's from Perth."

"Why would I talk to him?"

"He's telling us about Sarah Erroll having no knickers on when she died."

Greum — he spelled it for her — Jones sounded middle-aged but enthusiastic for his job. He worked on a small local paper, had retrained after being made redundant from some job she had no interest in. He had relatives in the force. He hadn't published the story yet but wanted to pass on the information immediately, in case it was useful.

He'd been doing a small story about the closure of a community center. Normally he wouldn't bother going there, they were a small paper and only had four staff so they didn't have a lot of time, but it was near his aunt's house and he thought he could fit in a visit there too. So he went. The center held tea dances for pensioners but had to stop because the priest who organized them had got drunk and taken the petty cash and bought vodka with it. It could be a big story.

Morrow was starting to wonder why she'd agreed to take the call when he got down to it: he went to see the priest and found him pissed, crying and reading a copy of a paper and he pointed out the story about Sarah Erroll's murder. He said that she was asleep in bed when they came for her and she didn't have any underpants on. Greum had checked back on all the newspaper articles printed about her and it didn't mention that in any of them. Was he right? Was she asleep? Did they find her naked from the waist down?

Someone involved in the investigation was talking. That was clear. But that could be any number of people: the officers, the bosses, the scene-of-crimes, secretaries, the scientists and doctors, anybody. They could have been talking for money, or it might have been some small power play related to Bannerman and Harris.

Greum repeated the question: was she naked from the waist down? Morrow said she couldn't comment.

The priest also insisted that nothing had been stolen from the house. Morrow started to make notes as she listened. They kicked her face beyond recognition, that was how she died. And a bit of her ear had come off and was on the stair beneath her shoulder.

Morrow stood up abruptly and hurried across the corridor to the incident room, looking at the board, the scene-of-crime photos, keeping Greum on the line by asking him for the priest's name, where he worked, was he a habitual drunk? None of the photos had the earlobe detail in them. She walked back into her office and pulled out the full set of photos. Only one of them had the earlobe in it. It was taken after Sarah Erroll's body had been moved. None of the coppers had seen these pictures.

"Greum, I don't think this is leading anywhere." She tried to keep her voice flat. "These facts are widely known."

He was disappointed but tried to be a gentleman about it. "Oh, really?"

"Yes, I'm afraid so. But thanks very much for phoning us."

"Auch, I had my hopes up there. I thought I'd stumbled on a story."

"Well, never mind. Sounds as if the man's in enough trouble as it is."

"He certainly is that."

They said their goodbyes and he hung up.

Morrow remembered the holy water font inside the door at Glenarvon. Just to be sure Greum wasn't still there she picked another line and called the local coppers, getting through to her equivalent officer in Perth.

DS Denny was surly and unhelpful. He would send some coppers out to speak to the priest but he knew for a fact that the man was a drinker and you would hardly take the word of a drunken priest against anybody, eh?

She rang off and went to see Bannerman.

"Sir." She was breathless as she hung in the door.

Bannerman glanced up.

"There's a priest in Perth who's describing Sarah Erroll's injuries in detail . . ."

He sat back, raised his eyebrows in a question and she knew what he was asking. "Not in the press, no. Definitely, even if Leonard's pal's leaky, what he's saying isn't in the photos."

"Is that what you think?"

Bannerman's mood seemed to have shifted utterly since she had left the room four minutes ago. He was angry, not with her, but with someone specific.

Morrow sighed and slumped at the door.

She was in no position to challenge him about anything, least of all his moodiness, but she shook her head. "I'm going to Perth —"

"No, you are not."

"I can't do this investigation —"

"You can do what I tell you to do."

They looked at each other for so long that the twins began to stir.

"And what are you telling me to do?"

"We'll pursue the Murray line until we find out what happened there," he said.

Morrow imagined a luxury ceiling seen from a luxury bed. "Sir, I'm entering the Perth lead into the notes. If it turns out to be significant, it's your lookout."

Bannerman flicked his hand dismissively, telling her to fuck off. "Yeah, why don't you just do that."

She shut the door between them before he could change his mind. Out in the corridor she allowed herself a triumphant smirk.

THIRTY-THREE

Kay sat at the table next to Frankie, waiting. She looked around the cold room, cold in its colors and the furnishings. The architecture of this whole building seemed designed to communicate hostility, from the buttresses on the street to the cell-like plainness of the office they had to wait in.

Frankie sat hunched over, his back so bent it looked unnaturally round. She traced the curve of his spine, as if she was checking he was all there still, from the nape of his neck down to the little bumps of fat on his hips. It was the pizzas. He was eating three pizza dinners a week at the moment, enjoying having money and working, feeling what it would be like to be a man and make his own way. He was a good boy. She rubbed his back, correcting his posture under cover of an affectionate gesture. He shook her off and looked up at the camera in the corner of the room.

"No." She pointed. "The light's not on yet, darlin'. Camera's not on."

Sure her hand was gone, he slouched further over the table, his hands out.

"Let's get this over and done with," she said, half believing it herself, "and then we can go home and get on with our lives."

He gave her a look then, searched her face to see if she believed it and saw that she didn't. She shrugged, exasperated.

"It was your idea to come in here," he said.

Kay held her hands up. "I just thought, you know, we can sit at home with our fist in our mouths and get yanked in at ten o'clock or we could come in at a reasonable hour and get it over and done with."

But it wasn't that. She was here with her boys, brushed and washed, with the papers they had prepared and the statements she had gathered to prove to someone that they were good-living people. She was smart enough to know who she was trying to prove it to.

"I'm going to miss my work."

"I know, pal." She loved him for that. "I know. It's just one night."

They heard a noise behind them in the corridor and turned to see the man, Bannerman, with Alex Morrow tripping after him, her eyes down, a wee bundle of papers in front of her. Kay stood up to meet them and prodded Frankie to make him get up too. Alex looked small and round today, standing behind her tall slim boss, and Kay wondered if he knew she'd driven them home in her own car. Probably not.

He sat down and then Alex Morrow sat down and neither of them made eye contact with her or Frankie, or said hello or thanks for coming or anything. They busied themselves with cassette tapes. A woman came in and checked the camera and gave them the OK and left without meeting Kay's eye.

They were ignorant people. That's the only way she could account for their lack of warmth or social decorum. Margery Thalaine, Molly Campbell, Alex Morrow and this tube sitting at the table here. Ignorant.

The man introduced himself again, Bannerman, as if they'd have forgotten. He said it was an informal interview and thanks for coming in but he didn't look grateful and it didn't feel informal. Frankie's face was blotchy pink and he was scratching the back of his hand. He looked guilty.

She poked him at the waist, making him bend towards her, and gestured to him to sit up. He flashed her an angry look and she was pleased, it was better.

"First of all," said Bannerman, as if it was nothing at all, "what shoe size are you?"

Frankie looked at Kay. "Seven," she told him.

He relayed it to them: "I'm a seven."

Bannerman wrote it down. He wanted another rehash of the night Sarah Erroll died, where Frankie had been, how long everything had taken. Frankie handed over the brand-new red folder Kay had given him.

"What's this?" asked Alex.

"Um," Frankie looked at her again, she wished he'd just say. "It's, um, stuff my mum made me get . . ."

Frankie had been to Pizza Magic in the afternoon for a photocopy of their delivery receipts for that night. Fat Tam had given him a written statement, more of a note really, saying Frankie'd been with him all night and he hadn't been out of the car for longer than ten minutes. It was written on the back of a pizza order form, on cheap paper that was supposed to fold around a carbon slip, and didn't look very official. But Tam signed it with a big flourish, as if that made it a more compelling piece of evidence. He also said, and underlined it, that Frankie's brother had never been in the car with them and they hadn't seen him all night.

Bannerman looked at Tam's statement, his lip curling up at the side. He unfolded it and finished reading. His eyebrows shot up at the end as he looked at Fat Tam's big signature.

"This," he held it up, "is actually worse than useless. You can't go around getting people to write statements for you."

Frankie touched the folder defensively. "How not?"

"Because it could be construed as coaching a witness."

"What am I meant to do then?"

"Just let us do our jobs." He gave a bitter little smile, first to Frankie, then to Kay.

"The polis at our bit are bent," Frankie told Alex, annoyed now, sounding like himself.

Alex craned forward, encouraging him, glancing to the left, up to where the camera was filming, telling him to go on.

"When there's a break-in at the flats they send one officer up to take a statement and look at the doors and that, and we found out that it meant they weren't even processing the complaint 'cause it was making their numbers look bad."

Bannerman did not want to hear it, his

eyes were open wide. "How is this relevant —"

"So you'll excuse me," interrupted Frankie, fifteen and a gentleman already, "if I seem a bit wary of you 'just doing your jobs,' it's 'cause my experience with the polis has been mostly bad."

Alex sat back. "Is there any record of that, Frankie?"

The way she said it made Kay feel that she had looked into it and knew there was. She felt a shock of sudden gratitude towards her.

"There is a record of that, yes, the local police station —"

Bannerman leaned in between them. "This isn't what we're here to talk about."

Frankie got stuck and looked at Kay. He'd trusted her about the folder and it hadn't panned out. She didn't know what to do now.

Bannerman started again: "Are you and your brother close?" It sounded like a threat, the way he said it.

Frankie looked nervous again. "Aye."

"Would you say you're very close?"

It sounded sinister and he hesitated. "I would, aye."

"You hang about together? Do stuff together?"

"We share a bedroom. We've no option."

"You're of a similar mind?"

Frankie shrugged his shoulders up and looked confused. "Suppose."

Bannerman nodded and wrote something down. Alex licked her lips.

"You wear the same sorts of clothes?"

Frankie looked at him. He looked at Alex and then at his mum and the nervousness left him suddenly. He laughed, boyish, merry.

Bannerman wasn't joining in. "What's funny about that?"

"What, you mean the shoes you took off us, the trainers?"

"Yes, you had the same trainers — d'you dress alike?"

Frankie laughed again. "I'm fifteen," he said and looked at Kay, deferring. She was smiling too now, not because it was funny but just because she was so relieved to see him smile.

"Mr. Bannerman," she said, "I'm their mum. I buy their clothes."

He seemed embarrassed. "Where did you purchase those particular trainers?"

"I got four pair at Costco, one pair for each of them."

He scribbled it down. Kay said, "They're actually pretty chuffed you took them because they all hate those trainers."

"Mum, they look medical," Frankie told her.

"They're well made," Kay told him, "and they're waterproof."

"Teenagers don't care about *waterproof,* Mum. They're diddy shoes."

"Well, fine." They were smiling at each other and Kay saw Alex was smiling along with them. "Diddys don't get wet feet."

"You've no style, Mum. That's why I got the job, to buy us some decent gear."

They grinned at each other. He didn't spend the money on clothes at all. He blew it every week on taking his brothers or his sister out, or buying knock-off movies, but it was a relief to talk to each other.

Bannerman took charge, asking details again, very annoyed, but the spell was broken. Frankie was back with her and confident again, himself again.

No, he'd never been in a gang. His attendance at school was flawless. He'd cooperate in any way he could. He was happy for them to come to the house if they needed to, they could look through his things if they wanted to, speak to anyone about him.

Alex asked him if he'd ever been to Perth, which Kay thought odd. Bannerman did too, apparently, because he listened to her asking questions about it and was interested in Frankie's answers. Frankie had never been to Perth. He did not attend a church, though he had been to a disco at the local Orange Lodge two years ago but that was only because his friend had tickets and did that count as attending a church? Alex said it didn't. Frankie got embarrassed and said he wouldn't go now, he thought that was wrong. He actually supported Celtic now, they could ask anyone.

Kay interrupted, "Are you allowed to ask about religion?"

"Yeah," Alex said, kindly. "You're thinking of job interviews: they're not allowed to ask you about religion."

Bannerman asked if Frankie had ever been to Glenarvon? Just once, he said. When was that? Well, it was half term and Mrs. Erroll had died and he was off school anyway. He went to the funeral and they left from the house because there was room in the car. She didn't have a lot of family and his mum was so upset that he wanted to go with her.

Bannerman acted as if this was hugely significant. "Where did you go in the house?"

Frankie didn't remember. They'd been in the front room mostly —

"Did you go upstairs?"

He nodded.

"What?" said Kay. "When did you go upstairs?"

"I went to the loo."

"How?"

"I couldn't find the other one."

Bannerman asked him personal questions: how did he do the toilet, did he sit or stand? Frankie got embarrassed because his mum was there but answered anyway: he stood. Was the seat down when he went in? He couldn't remember. Did he usually lift the seat when he did a wee? He supposed he did. Kay saw his right hand push out under the table as he thought about it.

They stopped abruptly and took Frankie out, and Joe came in and sat down next to her.

He was feeling insecure, she could tell, because he was doing a charm offensive. He shook hands with both Alex and Bannerman and asked how they were this evening? Alex smiled and said she was fine and how was he? Joe misunderstood the pleasantry and said he was a bit nervous and felt a bit tired after last night. He'd had to come home early from school and he was a bit dizzy.

They walked him through the same questions as Frankie: Joe knew his own shoe size, a size nine. He'd spent the night with his pals and he had a blue folder full of coached witness statements that might go against him if the case came to trial. Bannerman told him he'd done the wrong thing too.

"We were trying to save you time," explained Kay, hoping she sounded reasonable.

Bannerman was frosty about it, slapped the folder shut and pushed it back across the table to Joe. "Don't do it again."

He'd never been in a gang, his mum would have killed him.

Morrow asked, "Have you ever been to Perth?"

He was definite. "Yes."

Kay looked at him. "When?"

"Couple of months ago," he told her. "An away game for the sevens."

"I don't remember that."

"Yes, you do. You made me sandwiches. Remember we had a fight about the fare because I didn't book it in advance and there wasn't room on the bus?"

"No."

"I had to pay the full train fare because I didn't book it in advance and you said I should have known that I wouldn't get a place on the bus —"

"That was Carlisle."

"Oh. Was it?"

"Yeah, that was Carlisle."

"Have you been to Perth?"

He looked to Kay for the answer. She shook her head.

"No," he said, "I've not been there."

"Know anybody there?"

"No."

He'd never been involved in religion of any kind, although he supported the Gers and once fancied a girl who was Catholic, did that count? No, Alex said it didn't. Joe said that was good because he never even spoke to her and it would be a shame to get done for murder for fancying someone he'd only seen in the street. He laughed, expecting them to join in, and looked sad and frightened when they didn't.

Kay sat and listened, touching his arm when he looked vulnerable or worried. Her anger began to recede. She realized slowly that Margery would have turned on her whether or not Alex went to see her; that Margery was a snob and a funny old bird. She'd probably have sacked her soon anyway. She couldn't afford a cleaner anymore, certainly not five days a week.

She saw Alex touch her stomach sometimes, saw her sitting over on one buttock

443

and smile to herself when the babies shifted; Kay's eyes slid across the table top to her tummy. She couldn't find it in her to hate her anymore. And Joe was right: last night, dropping them home, had been decent of her.

By the time the interviews were over and they were being shown out of the station and having the bus stop pointed out to them up the street, Kay had decided to go and see Danny the next day and tell him just to forget it.

THIRTY-FOUR

They were planning the funeral. Moira and Ella lay on the bed with a throw over their legs, in bed together, but not in bed. Moira with a pen and a notepad balanced on her knees, Ella cross-legged, a giant packet of marshmallows standing upright in the bowl of her thighs. They'd found a dry-store cupboard, big as a walk-in wardrobe, full of food that the family had never even seen and the staff must have been keeping for themselves: cheap biscuit assortments and marshmallows and boxes of Wotsits.

Thomas didn't want to sit on the bed with them, even though there was room, it felt wrong, so he wandered around the periphery of his parents' bedroom, an unfamiliar room, glimpsed through the open door but never explored in childhood. He had never been told not to come in here, and couldn't have said why he hadn't. Even now he felt a frisson of fear that Lars would walk in, open his eyes wide wide wide and roar a reproach.

The big yellow poplar-burr sleigh-bed sat in the middle of the room, the massive window looming behind it like a bedstead.

Moira had decided to bury Lars in Sevenoaks. It felt a little spiteful to Thomas. He said that maybe Lars would prefer to be buried in town, since they would be moving when they sold up and he loved the city, but Moira was insistent. She said that since he loved this place so much, it was fitting, but she had a smile behind her eyes when she said it. She was trapping Lars in the place where he had trapped her.

Ella ate marshmallows slowly, getting eight bites out of each, as Thomas wandered slowly around the room, touching things that had belonged to Lars, wondering if he had exactly the same things in his other house. He looked up at Moira in the bed. She was happy, lying there with Ella, jotting notes about the funeral and who should come and what should happen. He felt bad for her, knowing that Theresa would call soon. Moira might already know but she didn't like facing things. She might start taking antidepressants again and they'd lose her again.

"Anyone from school you'd like to invite to Daddy's funeral, Tom?"

Thomas shook his head.

"Not Squeak?"

"No." He touched a hairbrush. " 'S too far."

"Hmm." Another day she might have sent the Piper for Squeak, just so he could be there for Thomas, but this was a different time. They couldn't afford things like that anymore.

"His daddy might send a plane for him?"

"No, I'd rather not."

"How about Donny? Did you invite him?"

"Donny?" He looked at her as if she was mental.

Moira pursed her lips at him. "Donny, stepdad has cancer, you spent this morning with him . . ."

Thomas blushed, felt horrible and sick, but Moira thought she'd tripped him up and smiled, nodding at him as if to say she knew.

"You could invite her, if you like, your girlfriend."

He tutted at her and looked away, embarrassed because Theresa couldn't be his girlfriend. It was creepy to think about it and yet he had. On the train home he'd thought about little else. He didn't think about actually touching her. He thought instead warm soupy thoughts, her thick hair, the way she rolled her shoulders when she walked, eating breakfast in the stupid pancake place after a night together. He went to the toilet on the train and had a quick tug, thinking about something else entirely, a film he'd seen, so that he could go back and sit and daydream in safety about her.

"Don't you want to invite her?"

"No."

Moira watched him, became serious. "You weren't meeting Nanny Mary, were you?"

"Fuck off!" he spat, angry that she knew about that and had mentioned it.

"Because that woman sold those pictures of your father to the paper."

"I'm not meeting Nanny Mary, for Christ's sake —"

"She's a snake."

"Fucking hell, shut up about that."

Moira read his face and saw he meant it. She turned back to her pad.

Exhausted by not being the center of attention for a minute and a half, Ella curled up on the giant pillows. "OK, what songs?"

"*Which* songs," corrected Moira.

"No," Ella kicked her little heels on the bed, "I think you can say 'what songs.' "

Now she was being cute, talking kind of babyish. Thomas was staying away from her.

She was laying it on so thick he'd found himself on the verge of punching her. Her moods swung around all the time — she laughed during pauses, and she asked stupid questions: will it rain tomorrow, what is that color called.

He thought of Phils and his sister, Bethany. They'd be cool about this. He imagined himself as sulky Phils, skateboarding Phils, growing-up-in-Chelsea Phils. Thomas tried to imagine an equivalent person in his class at school but there weren't any because Phils went to day school and they were always different. And if Ella was Bethany she'd be cool too. She'd be honest with Thomas-Phils. She'd say she was sad that their dad was dead, as well as glad. Bethany probably trusted Theresa, she wouldn't lay it on with a trowel or copy characters in the movies to know how to behave. Bethany would know already.

" 'Star of the Sea'?"

"No," said Ella, "something . . ." she couldn't think of the word but pushed her hands in the air as if she was throwing confetti, "UP!"

"Rousing," said Moira.

"Yes, something rousing. Rousing, rousing."

" 'Jerusalem'?"

"Is that a hymn?"

Moira wasn't sure. "He liked it though."

Ella nodded. *"Rousing."*

"OK." Moira wrote it down. "And afterwards. Should we have a funeral supper?"

"Is that what people do?"

Thomas didn't know about this bit, he'd never been to a funeral, so he was actually listening.

"Well, we can get some caterers. But would anyone come? It's a diplomatic uncertainty. Daddy was in trouble and no one's scared of him anymore . . ."

Far away, down the stairs, the phone rang softly. Thomas was quick to the door. "I'll get it."

"No." Moira leaned over to the bedside table and lifted a receiver.

"Hello?" She listened, looking pleased at first and then puzzled. Thomas's heart tightened into a fist. He glanced at the bedside clock. It was only six thirty, he'd left Theresa at one. It was only five hours since they'd parted, five and a half hours, and he'd thought of little else. Maybe she had too. Maybe she thought about him the same way and it was meant and they could overcome the obstacles that lay between them, the way she and Lars had overcome his other family.

Moira looked at Thomas with cold clear eyes. "Just a moment." She smiled and held the phone out to him. "For you."

He took the receiver from her hand and retreated to the other side of the room before he lifted it to his ear.

A wheezy breath hit the receiver. A man's breath, not Theresa.

"Thomas. Is that you?" The voice was slow and tired, a broken man's voice. Lars, his voice changed from the hanging, calling from the morgue. "Is that you?"

Thomas walked out onto the landing, shutting the bedroom door carefully behind him. "Who is this?"

"Thomas, this is Father Sholtham."

Thomas caught his breath. The name came from a million years ago. Father Sholtham was the school's priest. There were rumors that he'd been a drunk, that he'd been in the navy before entering the priesthood, been a boxer, killed a man. He had charisma and didn't give a flying fuck about Doyle or any of them: Thomas had once seen him, on stage during a parents' assembly, reach into his trouser pocket and blatantly scratch his balls.

"Father?"

"Thomas, are you there?"

"Um, yeah, Father, I am." He was flat-

451

tered that Father Sholtham should phone him. There was a pause on the other end but Thomas didn't want him to go. "Did you — how did you get my number, Father?"

"Mr. Doyle . . ."

"Oh, I see."

"Thomas . . . I don't know how it is . . ." The sentence tailed off to deep breathing. He sniffed then and it sounded wet, as if Father Sholtham was crying, as if he was in trouble.

Thomas didn't want to speak to him here, on the stairs in the hall, he wanted to concentrate and speak to him without watching the bedroom door. "Father, will you stay on the line and wait for a moment?"

"I will."

Thomas held the phone and ran down the stairs. He knew that voices carried up the hall: he'd heard Lars and Moira say terrible things to each other in the living room. So he hurried into the kitchen, taking the steps down to the freezer room, leaving the light off and sitting in the dark on the bottom step.

"Father?"

Father Sholtham was crying now, spluttering like a child. "Tom, Tommy? Can you talk to me?"

"Father, why are you crying?"

"Oh, God!"

Thomas held the phone away from his ear and realized abruptly what it was: the priest was pissed. It was pathetic, disappointing.

"Thomas," whispered Father Sholtham, "I *know* what you did."

Thomas froze at that. "Sorry, Father, what are you talking about?"

"To her, the woman," he broke off to sob, "God in heaven."

"Father, where are you?"

He was angry about that. "Nowhere! Don't even think . . . I don't want you thinking . . ."

He really was very drunk. He'd be easy to confuse.

"You're a bit drunk, Father, aren't you?"

"I am, yeah." Big sniff. "I am."

"Father, you shouldn't be talking about it, should you?"

"Thomas, there are sins . . ."

"You could be excommunicated for talking about this, if you heard it under certain circumstances . . ."

"I am already lost, Thomas. I'd rather be lost than let you —"

"OK. Look. I think, drunk or sober, you need some help. I think you need to seek some spiritual advice about this, Father, and you need it soon."

The priest caught his breath. "Right, you're right."

"No harm's been done so far, Father, I'm going to forget this conversation —"

"No harm?" He could barely speak. *"No harm's been done?"*

"I mean about this." Thomas was very firm. "About *this,* the matter of you saying this. You need to see someone and soon."

"I was going to, I was waiting —"

"Until you'd stopped drinking? Well, maybe you won't stop until you do."

Thomas was curled over his knees, pressing them tight into his chest, squeezing the breath from himself, his eyes shut tight.

"Thomas?"

"Hmm."

"I'm afraid for you."

"Hmm."

"I'm worried you won't make a confession."

It was laughable. "How likely am I to do it now, do you think?"

Father Sholtham had nothing to say about that.

"Father?"

"Yes?"

"When did you hear?"

454

"Why?"

"I need to know." He didn't seem moved by that, he snorted, so Thomas added, "I'll confess, if you tell me."

"Really?"

"Yes."

"Because Thomas, it's not enough to confess, you have to be truly penitent —"

"Father, how could I not be?"

They were whispering now, as if through a confessional screen, as if a chapel full of nosy fuckers were four foot away.

"I can't take a confession over the phone, Thomas."

"I know, I'll go down here, I'll find someone here. When did you hear about this, can you tell me that?"

Sholtham considered his position for a drunken moment, which was longer than a normal moment. "Lunchtime. Choir meeting."

"That's a Tuesday, isn't it?"

"Twelve, yeah, why?"

"Were you drinking then?"

"God forgive me, yes. Will you confess, Thomas?"

"I'll go to confession if you do."

The old man cried at that. He cried for a long time, half reciting stock phrases dredged out from a priest's trousseau, bless you, God have mercy.

Thomas talked him down, made him promise to confess and swore he would too.

After he hung up he didn't move. He stayed doubled over in the freezer room, looking at the concrete floor, stunned motionless.

By the time they met on the pebble beach Squeak'd already told Sholtham. He found Sholtham drunk and confessed to him and he'd told him that Thomas killed her. Squeak had always been planning his escape.

Thomas didn't want to get caught now, not now that Theresa was going to phone. What would she think if she knew that about him? She'd be afraid of him. She'd think he was a monster and he'd never ever be able to explain what happened in that hall. Not even to her.

Anyone would do that to you if they got you down, but Squeak more than most.

THIRTY-FIVE

Brian Morrow was contemplating the back hedge as the washing machine finished its cycle. He'd loaded the clothes in wrong and the final spin was noisy, the weight of the clothes pulling the machine off center, the vibrations rattling the big kitchen window. That hedge needed plant food or something. The leaves were yellowing and it was supposed to be an evergreen. He turned back to his list on the table, found a pencil and wrote "see to hedge" at the bottom. He stopped and ticked off the things he had already done: the washing, sort linen cupboard, eat lunch. He didn't forget to eat anymore, he just put lunch in there so he would have another thing to tick off, give himself a feeling of accomplishment. The counselor had said it was important to achieve things in the day and advised him to make up a list the night before, a modest list, and then try to fulfill it. It would give

457

him a sense of purpose and accomplishment. He didn't really need the list now, but he enjoyed it.

The noisy spin cycle abated and Brian heard the doorbell through the rattle. He put his list on the table and walked out to the hall. A shadow behind the glass door. A man, not carrying a package, not delivering anything. A bulky man.

Brian opened the door.

The man was tall, a bit fat, dressed in dark tracksuit trousers and a sweatshirt. "Can I help you?"

He nodded and Brian suddenly saw his wife's face in him, the dimples, the chin, the stubbled halo on his head was the familiar honey yellow. It was Danny McGrath. "I'm —"

"I know." Brian pulled the door shut a little, letting him know he wasn't welcome. He had come here when he knew that Alex would be at work, knew that she wasn't there to tell him off. He knew Brian was at home. He knew, Brian felt, that he'd had a breakdown and was vulnerable. His mind ran through the house: they kept no money in the house, Alex didn't like jewelry, he had no social security books.

"What are you doing here?"

"Heard something about you," said

Danny. "Brought you something."

He stepped back from the doorway. Behind him on the step was a giant box with Mamas and Papas tape around it and the receipt sellotaped onto the top. It was a buggy for twins. They'd looked at buggies online and Brian knew it was the most expensive one.

"Oh." But he pulled the door shut a fraction more.

Alex didn't want baby furniture in the house in case they lost the babies. She didn't want Brian to meet Danny. She'd be upset that he'd been here.

Danny stepped in front of the box again and looked over Brian's head into the hall. "Can I come in and talk to you?"

"No, Alex wouldn't like it."

"No? Doesn't want me here?" Annoyed, he looked away.

Brian looked over his shoulder to the street. "Would you like her coming to your house when you weren't in?"

Danny didn't answer.

"You wouldn't like it. You'd be suspicious if she came to your house specifically when she knew you'd be out."

Danny looked down his face at Brian, his mouth turned down as though he found him sickening. He rolled his head away, looking back out into the street. "Wee man at nursery?"

"Wee man?"

"Your son."

"Are you here to threaten me?"

"I'm not threatening ye," he leaned in, "I'm just asking how your son is."

Brian nodded. "My son?"

"Aye, what's his name? Gerald, is it?"

Brian stared at him. *What's his name.* He stared too long at Danny's mouth. He was scared but he squared up to Danny McGrath in honor of Gerald. It was a moment stolen from the future he and Gerald would never have. It was the gesture of a good dad, the shooting of the mad dog in the street with a single shot, scaring the bullies off, putting down the spiteful teacher. Brian pointed to the box with the twin buggy in it. "Get that out of here."

Astonished, Danny looked from the box to Brian, awaiting an explanation.

Brian kept his eyes on the box. "Gerald died. Two years ago." The box was navy blue and gray, blurred, a photo of two smiling identical babies on it. "Meningitis. Sudden."

Danny couldn't look at Brian. He coughed and covered half his face with his hand.

"Yeah," said Brian who was used to it. "So, you can imagine how nervous we are about this pregnancy, twins and so on. I don't want Alex getting upset. We can well do without this." He pointed Danny up and down, realized it was insulting and shifted his finger over to the buggy.

"Aye," Danny looked at the box, "and, um, some people don't like to have baby stuff in their house before it comes."

"It's not just that," said Brian. "You, coming here, what's your business here? Leave us alone. Go away."

But Danny shook his head. "I can't go away," he said heavily, "I need your help."

They sat in the kitchen sipping instant coffee and eating malted milk biscuits. Danny was trembling and Brian hadn't the heart to leave him on the step. It didn't seem to be about Gerald — Danny had never met him — but about some grief of his own.

He sipped his coffee, which he took weak with three sugars. He seemed smaller in the kitchen. Not threatening, just poor, as if no one had ever shown him how to dress properly. He looked much older than Alex, not on his features, but his skin looked tired and dry. It looked like a smoker's skin.

"This is a nice house."

Brian looked around the kitchen. It was a plain house. A nineteen thirties semi with a circular window in the hall and long wide windows front and back.

"I always wanted to be from a house like this."

Brian was from a house like this. That's why he liked it so much when they viewed it. Alex liked it because of the light — the garden was south facing and they were on a hill so it streamed in the back of the house — and the area was quiet.

They did nothing to it when they moved in, happy to settle for what was there; the wooden eighties kitchen, the plain bathroom, the orange walls in the hall.

"Quiet here," said Danny.

Brian pushed the plate of biscuits over to him. There was only one left. Danny looked at him and Brian nodded him on. He took it. It was a child's biscuit. They bought them for Alex's indigestion.

"She doesn't want you here."

Danny took another bite. "I don't want to be here."

"Why are you?"

He chewed the biscuit and sipped his coffee. "My son," he said.

Brian nodded. "Young John?"

"Aye," said Danny. "I need her to speak to the woman, she needs to know what the boy's been through and I need you to tell

Alex something from me —"

"I don't know if I'm going to," interrupted Brian.

Danny took it in, nodded. "OK." He finished his coffee and put the cup down carefully on the table, turning it by the rim. "There's a case she's involved in, someone involved in it came to see me. They came to me, want me to pressure her to stop looking into it."

Brian didn't understand. "You asking her to stop?"

"No," said Danny sincerely. "I'm warning her. If they're coming to see me they'll maybe see other people. I want her to know she's getting warned off the Murray boys."

Brian was reluctant to suggest it so he left a pause. "Are *you* warning her off?" he said as if he was guessing.

Danny looked skeptical. "I'm not stupid, as if that would work."

They smiled at each other until Danny broke it off. "Just tell her: there's stuff going on in the background she doesn't know about. The Murray boys are good boys. But someone's desperate."

Brian watched through the front window as the Audi pulled away. It was a four-by-four and the windows were shaded: a gangster's

463

car. He watched it drive slowly out of the cul de sac and stop at the end of the road, signal and turn back into the city.

THIRTY-SIX

Morrow was keeping out of Bannerman's way, staying in her quiet office, following up loose threads of inquiry. She listened to the ringing, half expecting to be put through to the answerphone, but the call was answered by a light-voiced girl speaking in a sing-song.

"He-llo?" A classical music radio station played in the background.

"Oh, hello, um, my name's Alex Morrow, I'm with Strathclyde Police, I was calling about —"

"Oh, God, Sarah! I'd forgotten for a minute, Sarah-farah, God . . ."

"Yeah, could I talk to you for a minute? Have you got a minute?"

"Yeah . . ." Morrow could hear her sitting down, turning the radio down to a murmur. "Yeah, sure."

"Um, I really just wanted to ask about what sort of person she was."

"Sarah?"

"Aye."

"Hasn't anyone told you about her? You must have talked to people who knew her . . . ?"

"Hmm." Morrow wasn't sure what she wanted from her either. "Sorry, let's start again: could I take your name and address, just for the record? All I have at the moment is that you're Maggie's sister —"

"*Half* sister. She's my half sister."

"OK."

"I'm Nora, surname Ketlin. Her surname's Moir. Different father."

She seemed very keen to have that made a matter of record so Morrow repeated the names as if she was writing extensive notes. She wrote down Nora's address and swapped email addresses in case anything came up later. "So you were all at school together?"

"With Sarah?"

"Yeah."

"Yeah, she was in my year. Not in my house, we didn't know each other very well at school, different groups, but we got to know each other once we'd left. We were hanging around in London, wondering what to do, sort of thing. Our school sort of trained us to be wives, really, not very academic . . ."

"What was Sarah like?"

"A very nice person."

Morrow dropped her pencil. "Nora," she rubbed her eyes, "that's all I'm hearing about Sarah — niceness. Was she really bland?"

Nora stumbled at that. "No . . . she's . . . no, she wasn't *bland.* Sarah was . . ."

They listened to each other breathe for a moment.

"Look" — Morrow heard Nora sit forward; her voice became low and sounded closer to the receiver — "what you have to understand is the sort of people Sarah came from: not an old family but a good one. Reserved. Well mannered."

"Did you know she was working as an escort?"

"I did, actually."

Morrow was surprised by that.

"She didn't tell me, I was looking for a bookshop on her phone once and stumbled on her emails. We argued about it."

"What did she say?"

"That she needed the money and she had no skills and she wasn't bright but she wouldn't marry a wanker from the City and pump him for money. She said she could stop escorting any time. If she married for money she'd have to get a bloody divorce. And this way, the money was *her* money. She needed it for her mum's care —"

"She was making about three times as much as she needed for that, you know."

"I do know. She saved a lot of it for her next life, when she stopped. She was going to move to New York and reinvent herself. Don't get me wrong, she wasn't a martyr. She had lovely clothes and always traveled first class."

Morrow found herself smiling at that. "She sounds quite ballsy."

"No," said Nora simply, "she wasn't. Thing about Sarah was she was honest. She said she got that from her mother. Her mother called a spade a spade. To do with being older when she had her."

"Did she love her mum?"

"She worshipped her mother. It was as if she was the only person in the world for Sarah, except, well . . ." she stopped herself. "They were really close, yeah."

"Except who?"

"Well," Morrow could hear her wincing, "um, she's —"

"Lars Anderson?"

Nora tutted and huffed.

"Did Sarah make you promise?"

"Yeah."

"Promise not to say?"

"Yeah."

"He's dead too, you know."

"I saw that."

"Do you think their deaths are related?"

"No. Lars was a *shit*." She spat the unaccustomed word. "He didn't give a toss about anyone but himself. I can't see him caring if she lived or died, frankly."

"But she loved him?"

"Really loved him. That was what was so despicable about him — he made them all feel they were the only one, that he really needed to take up space in their lives, you know, declared his love. It was a cheap trick. I told her so at the time, I said, 'He's a shit, Sarah, a fat old shit,' but she wouldn't hear me. I think she just needed someone to love and decided on him."

"Did she take money off him?"

"No. She wouldn't even accept jewelry. She wanted him to know that she loved *him*, not his money. He knew that. He was skimming money and giving it to her to hide it for him. He knew she'd never touch it on point of principle. She wanted to differentiate herself."

"From who?"

"All of them, the other women, the families. He had two families. Not been in the papers but everyone knows. Had one filed away in Sevenoaks and another one in London."

"Did he have kids?"

"Yeah, four that I know of."

"Any boys?"

"Probably. I know one of them was at his old school in Scotland."

"Where in Scotland?"

"Um, Perth, I think."

She saw Harris watch her from the incident room as she crossed the corridor to Bannerman's door. She knocked and bent back to catch Harris's eye and smile at him. He didn't smile back.

Bannerman called her to come in. He was reading a manila file incident report.

"Sir," she said firmly, "remember the priest in Perth?"

He sighed, reluctant to discuss Perth again.

"Well," she carried on, "Lars Anderson, the man in the iPhone photos? He has two sons. One of them is at boarding school in Perth."

She stood back and smiled at him. Waited. She saw his eyes glaze over. He looked back at the sheet of paper in front of him.

"I want you to call the Serious Fraud Office. Get some background on Anderson."

Background gathering was a DC's job, a chore.

"You're determined to ignore this."

"Morrow, you got to ask everyone if they'd been to Perth, we've phoned Perth, Sarah Erroll never went to Perth, you've made extensive notes about what little we've got from the Perth lead, give it up."

Morrow backed out and slammed the door. When she turned away she found Harris standing at the door of the incident room, watching.

A skeptical Met officer took her name and said he'd have to phone her back through the station switchboard, for verification that she was a Strathclyde police officer. He sounded very up himself, not at all collegiate, and made it clear that the information he'd be prepared to share with her was very curtailed and she was lucky to get it.

He was relieved when she made it clear she didn't want specifics about the company. He was even happier when she said there might well be hundreds of thousands to be reclaimed from Sarah Erroll's estate.

"So, what's the paper trail?"

"Um," she tried to think of a way to bullshit him and then lost the will, "what does that mean?"

"Receipts for the money, transaction notes, that sort of thing. What have you got?"

"What, like from a till?"

"Or handwritten would do."

"Um, there's almost certainly none. Is that bad?"

He laughed at her. "Yes, it is, if there isn't any evidence the money can't be recovered."

"I see, probably why it's there, eh?"

"You've got nothing?"

"Well, we've got sightings of them together in a hotel in New York."

"No use at all. Can you fax over a photo of her?"

"Yeah, you got anything you can give me in return?"

"Hmm, how about records of missing funds?"

"Good — specifically chunks of euros missing from New York?"

He hesitated, she could hear a keyboard in the background. "Well, I'm going home in a minute but, straight off, I can tell you I've got several big euro cash withdrawals from a Manhattan bank branch?"

"Why would he do that? Why not just take the money out here?"

"Less tracking there and he knew we were

watching him."

"So New York was the easiest option?"

"Safest, probably. But he'd have to smuggle it into the UK." He read something, she heard him whispering "let's see" to himself. "Yeah, this account is a personal one. An expenses deposit account."

"What does that mean?"

"Slush."

"Slush? It's a hell of a lot of money for slush."

"You wouldn't believe how much these people get through."

"Is it like petty cash?"

"That's exactly what it is."

"But there's hundreds of thousands of it."

"I know. Businessmen are emptying these accounts all over the world right now. No one in the office watches them all that closely. The amounts are peanuts to them usually so there are few safety checks. The office just tot it up every so often and make sure no one in the bank is siphoning it off. As long as he took it out consistently and admitted he did there would have been no checks at all."

"So, with no receipts, where does that leave us?"

"Well, out of our investigations anyway. We'd like as much as you have on Sarah Erroll though, where they met, how often and so on."

She managed to get off the phone and call Perth CID to ask about the drunken priest. She got bounced around from department to department. She knew the sound of a ricochet well enough: no one had been to see him. She was hanging on the phone listening resentfully to classical music when Harris knocked briskly and stepped in, shutting the door behind him.

He thought she was through to someone and made a big thing of signaling that he wouldn't say anything but would just wait here until she was finished.

"I'm listening to a recording of Vivaldi."

He looked at the shut door. "Ma'am, Bannerman wants to know what you're doing."

She hung up.

Harris was looking at her expectantly. Bannerman had made a tit of himself over Frankie and Joe and he was throwing his weight around the men, picking on her to make it seem fair. He was hassling the good workers, questioning everything they did. The injustice of it was infuriating. It didn't seem to occur to him that police officers, more than office workers or insurance salesmen or any other profession, might have an

474

innate sense of the rightness of certain things.

Harris raised his eyebrows and muttered under his breath, "You know, ma'am, you're not the only one who feels that way. The men —"

She held her hand up abruptly. "Ah!" She'd had other people's fights made hers before.

"Sorry, you seem a bit annoyed."

"I'm always a bit annoyed." She stood up. "This isn't about Bannerman for me. I've hated every boss I've ever had." She gathered a pen and notebook from her desk, put her handbag in her bottom drawer and made sure it clicked locked as she shut it.

Harris was still nodding when she looked up again. "I haven't."

THIRTY-SEVEN

Thomas stayed in the freezer room for a while, thinking about the phone call from Father Sholtham. He couldn't say how long, but it felt like a long time.

Squeak was an altar boy but he wasn't religious, he said he did it for the trips. He was devout like Lars was. For Lars religion was like a membership of an afterlife country club: he despised people who weren't Catholic, and really believed they were going to hell and good riddance to them. Thomas struggled against the reflex to prayer, especially now, when everything was so mixed up. Maybe Squeak was going through that too. Maybe he genuinely confessed to a drunken priest the morning after. It was just possible that Squeak had found his faith again in a moment of despair. Thomas shook his head. Squeak was scheming. He was scheming even before they met on the beach. Squeak didn't want to get caught. He was so far ahead of him, Thomas was defeated before the fight began.

He stood up and walked heavily up to the bright kitchen.

Theresa still hadn't phoned. Thomas glanced at the wall clock. Ten past seven. She might call yet, but she wasn't in a hurry. He'd have called her hours ago, if it was up to him. The lightness of the morning in town left him, making everything seem bleaker.

He poured himself a Coke from the bottle in the fridge, drank it down and went back upstairs, gathering himself on the traipse up the staircase, getting his story right for Moira. He'd say the phone call was the girlfriend in town's father. He wanted to ask Thomas about him meeting her because she'd been late back to school lessons and the father'd had to write her a letter explaining her absence from PE. Thomas supposed that's what happened at day school. You had to write to them about everything. The PE detail made the lie more believable, he thought, and it had to be good because Moira was so used to being lied to.

He walked back into the bedroom and knew immediately that he'd walked into the middle of a catastrophe. They looked so utterly detached from each other they might have been in different rooms.

Moira was sitting on the edge of the bed, facing away from Ella, pale and scared, as if something horrible and sexual had happened. He thought of the depressed girl from Kiev in the miserable room in Amsterdam.

Ella was over by the window, behind the bed, looking out over the lawn.

Moira looked up at Thomas, ashen, and said why didn't he take Ella downstairs to the family room and maybe they could watch a movie together? Confused, Thomas sat down next to her, put his hand on her back, tried to read beyond the horror. "Mum?"

Moira attempted a smile. "Ella's . . ." but she didn't know what Ella was.

Thomas stood up and looked at his sister's reflection in the window, just beginning to form as the sun set. She was crying, her mouth open, turned down like a mask from a Greek drama.

She began to flap her right hand, small shakes, like she'd eaten something hot, and then the shakes got bigger and she started hitting the glass on the window, louder and louder with the back of her hand. It was time for this nonsense to stop.

"Ella?"

She didn't listen. She started to say something but he couldn't make it out over the noise of her hitting the glass.

Thomas went to her, yanked her shoulder, turning her around to face him and shouting "Stop it!" but she didn't. She carried on crying and shaking her hand and upsetting everyone. So Thomas shouted again, even louder, "Ella! Fucking stop it! We're all sad, for Christ's sake. You can't make it all about you!"

He was feeling pleased because that was exactly the problem, he'd articulated it perfectly. But she was shaking, her whole body trembling now, as if she was getting into it. Thomas raised his hand and slapped her hard across the face.

Ella stopped shaking.

Thomas glanced up and saw himself in the side window. He was tall and broad-chested, the sinews on his arms tight, looming over the small girl. His face was twisted with annoyance. He looked like Lars.

Ella dissolved to the floor, arms in front of her. He looked down. Her wrists were scarred, badly scarred with long scratches up and down them.

He tried to pick her up. She flopped onto the floor again and curled around his ankle, sobbing, tears rolling into her yellow hair at the temple, her cheek maddened by the slap.

Thomas bent down, crouching right down on his haunches and waited until Ella got tired and stopped writhing, until she was staring at his ankle, seeing nothing. He knew that this was the real Ella.

Suddenly, he understood the worried calls from the school over the year. This was why Lars and Moira went to visit her so much more than they went to see him. This was why they dropped their voices when they spoke about her. This was why they kept them apart. She had been ill for a long, long time. She was mad and baffling and scary. He looked at Moira and he understood why she made certain that he was the first one home.

They should have told him. He didn't know, he thought she was snooty and spoiled but he didn't know that she was nuts. They should have told him.

He touched Ella's shoulder, the way Doyle had tried to touch him, and he said to her, "I'm sorry, Ella, I thought you were faking." And then he didn't say anything after that.

Ella waited until Moira went to the bathroom and shut the door. Then she slowly got up and stood slack, occasional tears

480

dripping from her nose onto the floor, leaving deep dents in the thick carpet.

"Come on," he said, and took her hand and led her out of the bedroom. She saw her own door, her bedroom door, and stopped, bringing a toe towards it, pointing at the bottom of the door frame and Thomas said, "Do you want to go in there?"

But she didn't answer and he was afraid to leave her alone so he took her downstairs, helping her on the steps, walking in front of her, holding both her hands as if she was a very old lady. He saw the ridges on her wrists then, and saw that some were very old and healed white and some were so new they were still sealed with crusty scabs.

They were at the bottom of the stairs when Moira called down to them that she was tired and going to bed and they'd sort this out tomorrow. All right? Thomas? Darling?

"OK, Mum." He heard her shut her door tight and imagined her locking it, though he didn't actually know whether there was a lock on that door.

In the family room they sat next to each other, squashed up shoulder to shoulder on the frosty white sofa, watching *Mission Impossible II*. Ella sat with her hands palm up, showing her scars, and Thomas felt like

481

tutting because it was so dramatic but he looked at her face and saw that she just didn't give a shit if he saw them or not. She didn't speak but she nodded to herself at the movie when the characters peeled their faces off.

"You're not well," said Thomas as the credits rolled.

Ella dropped her head to her chest as though she was very tired. Thomas didn't think he had ever seen anyone as sad as her.

"Ella?"

She didn't look at him.

"It's all going to be all right. I'm going to look after you now."

She didn't answer but he could see that she had heard and understood and that it mattered to her that he had said that. He could do that for her. He could be Theresa for her, a proper parent, someone who was there all the time and made sure she didn't do anything to hurt herself.

He walked her upstairs, to her rooms, his arm through her arm, guiding with his elbow. They walked through the pink sitting room and through to the bed. She sat down on the edge and he lifted her little feet and made her lie down. He sat in the other room and left the door open, watching her chest rise and fall until she fell asleep.

Thomas put the lights off in there but kept the side light on in the sitting room and left the door ajar. He stopped outside for a moment. Through the master bedroom door Moira's television laughed loudly. He knocked but she didn't answer.

And Theresa still hadn't phoned.

THIRTY-EIGHT

Morrow pulled her car into the steep driveway and crunched on the handbrake, leaving the Honda in first gear. She didn't trust
it on the gradient.

The living room curtains were drawn.
Orange light bleeding around the edges,
shining bright and warm into the night. The
light was on in the hall as well. This was her
second favorite moment in the day, drawing
up to the house, knowing Brian was in
there. Her first favorite moment was climbing into bed. Rock and roll.

She opened the door and stepped out,
locked the car and looked around the quiet
neighborhood. A nice area for a family to
grow up in. She smiled to herself and
walked up to the door, fitted her key and
opened it, calling, "Hiya," as she put her
door keys back in her pocket and hung her
coat up in the cupboard.

"Hiya." Brian came out to meet her. "How

was London?"

"It was grim. Bannerman wouldn't let me take Harris because he's seeing revolutions everywhere . . ."

"What was the bar like?"

"Good-looking women, ugly men. Saw Kay again though, and her boys."

"Go OK?"

"Yeah, they did really well."

He was standing half in the hall, half in the kitchen, holding on to the door frame. It was an odd posture for him. He looked secretive, coy, as if he was blocking her way, as if the kitchen was full and he was about to spring a surprise party on her.

She nodded at him. "What?"

Brian balked at conflict. Morrow quite liked a fight but not in the house. Brian didn't like any kind of antagonism. He took a deep breath. "Come in here."

She followed him into the kitchen, expecting a surprise as soon as she walked in. The kitchen looked the same, same table, same bland fitted units the old couple had left, usual kitchen cloth draped over the tap to dry, usual bowl of dinner waiting for her in the microwave.

She smiled. "What's going on?"

Brian looked worried. "I want you to sit down."

She took a chair. He sat next to her and chewed his bottom lip. "Danny came here today."

She looked around suddenly as if he might still be in here, and when she spoke she found she was whispering. "Here?"

"Yeah."

"You met him?"

"Yeah."

"When?"

"Teatime, about five, five thirty or something."

"Why didn't you phone me?"

"Didn't want to bother you."

Brian wasn't injured. He didn't even look scared or bothered. She touched his cheek and he smiled at her, seeing how protective she was of him. They sat close, huddled, suspicious.

"I don't like him coming here."

"I know."

"I don't want him knowing you."

He took her hand. "I'm all right."

She squeezed his fingers. "I'm sorry."

He squeezed hers. "No need."

"Was it about JJ?"

"Yeah, and Kay Murray."

"Kay Murray?"

"Someone came to see him, told him to pass on a warning to you: you've to lay off the Murray boys."

"He's warning me off?"

"No, he's telling you *someone else* wants you warned off."

She snorted. "He can't come here and tell me what to do."

"Is that what he was doing?"

Morrow shrugged. He'd never done anything like this before. She sat back and thought her way through the possibilities. Danny could be telling the truth, but that would be out of character. If he was lying she had to wonder why he would tell that lie. He wanted her to lay off the Murray boys but wouldn't say it directly. Then it hit her: Joe was sixteen. Alex had lost touch with both of them but Danny and Kay probably still knew each other back then. She considered for a moment the possibility that Danny was Joe's dad. But Joe didn't look much like Danny. He didn't act at all like Danny. And then she remembered the flat, how little Kay had, buying four lots of shoes at Costco, all the same, because they were waterproof and would last a winter. She was working as a cleaner and a carer and clearly supporting herself and her kids. She wasn't taking anything from Danny. But Kay was proud. She wouldn't have taken anything from Danny.

It could have been true, Danny could be warning her that someone else, not him, knew they were related and wanted her to lay off the Murrays. It could have been Kay herself.

"She doesn't trust us," she said.

"Who doesn't trust us?"

"Kay Murray. She doesn't trust the police." Alex shook her head at the table. "Could Danny be his dad? Joe's lovely."

"Is he?"

"Does he know Joe?"

"He didn't sound as if he did."

"Why, what did he say?"

Brian shrugged. "The Murray boys, he kept calling them the Murray boys. Someone wants you to lay off them."

She was lost in her thoughts for a moment until Brian said, "I made a nice lamb stew. Will I heat it up?"

"Please."

Brian stood up, shut the microwave door and put it on for three minutes, watching, waiting with a spoon. Morrow saw herself and Kay in the avenue that first time they met and how pleased Kay was that she was a police officer and how she might have gone home, or sat on the train and thought about her, being an officer, and how that was an alternative life for her son.

Joe might be her nephew. She laughed to herself. If she was related to Kay in a distant sort of way she wished she'd known. She'd have loved an excuse to stay in touch.

The microwave pinged, Brian opened it and stirred and then shut it and put it on again. When he sat down he was smiling. "He looks like you."

"Think?"

"Yeah," he touched her lips, "same chin."

"He can't warn me off anything —"

"Alex." Brian leaned forward, put his hand flat on her stomach. "He isn't warning you off anything. He's calling a truce."

"You don't know him —"

"No, I don't but I can see that he's asking you for help and you're saying no."

THIRTY-NINE

Thomas sat down in the family room, holding the phone receiver and told himself that, for fuck's sake, a hundred years ago people emigrated at his age. They lied about their date of birth and joined up and fought in the First World War at his age. It wasn't that big a fucking deal. At school they were always talking about resilience, developing resilience, Duke of Edinburgh and all that crap. This was a Duke of Edinburgh. He should get a Duke of Edinburgh for this.

Making plans, he decided to ring a doctor in the morning about Ella. And at least now he knew that on or off the medication, Moira was a feckless prick. He was holding the phone receiver so that he could get to it before Moira. He'd been holding it for so long that the cold metal handset was body temperature now.

Theresa wasn't bothered about talking to him. She'd have called by now if she was.

He still really wanted her to phone and speak to Moira though, wanted her to break the news to Moira that she wasn't that fucking special. She wasn't so fucking chosen that she could ignore a twelve-year-old having a breakdown and pack her off to school or to watch a movie.

He stood up, went into the hall, and found the jacket he'd worn this morning. In the inside pocket, folded in two, was the stiff embossed memo from Lars's desk and it had Theresa's address and number on it. He stopped at the bottom of the stairs, listening. No noise from Ella's room. Moira's television was still on, still loud.

Tiptoeing for no reason, he snuck down to the freezer room, put the light on and sat in whirring warm as he dialed the number.

He listened as it rang out, his heart beating loudly in his throat. It was answered by a boy. "Yeah?"

Thomas opened his mouth but the words took a moment to form. "Is this Phils?"

"Yeah. Who's this?"

"Thomas Anderson."

They listened to each other breathing for a while, half brothers, each waiting for the other to say something. Phils pulled the phone from his mouth and said in a drawly posh-twit voice, "Mummy, it's that boy —

the *son*."

Theresa took the phone. Her voice was clipped. "How did you get this number?"

He looked at the card. "I 1471'd it last night."

"To what end?"

He didn't know what she meant. She was like a different person. He'd meant to make conversation, ask how her day had gone, work up to politely wondering aloud why she hadn't phoned Moira. He'd meant to give her an excuse, maybe she was feeling too tired to phone? Not to worry, she could call tomorrow.

"*To what end,* Thomas? What are you up to?"

"Nothing really, you said you'd call my mum . . ."

"*Her?* Why would I call *her?*"

"Well, I don't know, you said you'd call —"

"A woman," she sounded furious, "so wrapped up in herself that she was complicit in the sexual abuse of a child?"

For a moment Thomas thought Phils had been abused, by Lars, but it made no sense. "What are —"

"Did you or did you not fuck your nanny?"

It sounded as if she was talking to some-

492

one else, as if she was someone else. But she was waiting for an answer.

"Theresa?"

"Do you or do you not know Mary Morrison?"

"Nanny Mary?"

"And she fucked you, didn't she? She says Lars ordered her to. That he threatened her if she didn't. What kind of people are you? Don't ever call here again." She hung up.

Thomas stared at the floor, the phone still on his ear, listening to the burr of the dialing tone. What the hell had happened?

He ran through their parting — had he done something to offend her? Had he said something about himself, something about Lars that was shocking? She'd said Lars was a bit of a prick and he just agreed. Well, actually he didn't agree but he didn't stand up for him either. Maybe that was it. Maybe she expected him to disagree. Maybe she was disappointed about that. He thought of her lovely messy hall and her nice round tits and was sorry for whatever it was he had done.

She quoted Nanny Mary. Nanny Mary must have gone to her house and told her that stuff, chasing a payment, but it was utter bullshit. Lars might have paid her to fuck him but he wouldn't threaten her. And he was fifteen years old, he wasn't a child.

He got up and turned the light off. As he climbed up into the kitchen the phone rang again.

"Hello?"

Theresa, still crisp and unfriendly. "Look," she said, "I've been having a think. We've got to get this sorted out."

"No one threatened Mary."

"You're a child, Thomas."

"I'm fifteen years old."

"You're still just a child."

"Yeah." He thought of her today, putting the baseball bat down, linking arms and brushing her nipples across him as they walked along the road. "Didn't stop you shaking your tits at me this morning, did it?"

She paused at that, kind of acknowledged it, and spoke confidentially. "It makes your mother sound very bad indeed, all that Mary stuff. So far she's come off as the victim, but if people *knew* . . ."

"And, plus, you were going to hit me with a baseball bat before you realized you knew me, how does that fit with me being a poor little kid?"

She heard the steel in his voice and shouted, "Phils and Betsy are *not* going to be pulled out of their schools, you can bet on *that*."

"I never said they should —"

"And I want a share of the proceeds of the house."

"Which house?"

"The one you're standing in."

Thomas had told her they were going to sell. He saw suddenly that she'd been pumping him for information all morning. She'd been saying how funny it was that everything had changed, where would they holiday now? Where were the children going to school now? Would he study abroad, when he went to uni? She'd even sympathized when he said they only had the Piper left. She probably knew Nanny Mary before, knew all that stuff, was working him from the beginning.

"Tell your mother that she'll be hearing from my solicitor in due course."

"Tell her your fucking self, Ther*ee*sa," he said, and hung up.

He dropped the receiver on the worktop and stepped away, staring at it. Bitch. A fucking bitch. Sarah Erroll had died in her place and it was her fucking fault, all of it.

What else had he told her? He didn't know what he was doing, he couldn't look after Ella or worry about Squeak, he didn't have a clue what he was doing. Looking up at the high ceiling he felt defeat creeping through him like a chill. He was just a kid. He didn't know what he was doing. His loss was private now but soon, when she went to a lawyer and the papers heard, it would all be made public. Stander.

Panicked, he went upstairs to his mother. Her television was still on but he tiptoed past Ella's door and knocked gently. Abruptly, the television fell silent and the light snapped off under the door.

Thomas tried the handle and found it open. He didn't look in, afraid she might be naked or something.

"Moira?" he whispered.

After a long while she answered, faking a sleeping voice, "Hmm?"

"Ella's . . . asleep now."

Moira was determined to see the pretend-sleep through. "Wha . . . ? What are you saying, darling?"

Theresa had spent the morning smiling and sharking around him for information. He honestly believed she liked him. Moira couldn't even tell a convincing lie about being asleep.

Angry, he reached in and turned on the light.

Moira was fully clothed, sitting on top of the bed with an ashtray on her lap and a

496

curl of smoke snaking out of it. He was surprised. He didn't know she smoked. He forgot what he meant to say for a moment.

She smiled weakly. "I must have nodded off . . ."

"Ella's asleep."

She tried to smile but it looked really bitter. "As should you be." She said it like a mother in a story book.

"What's Ella got?"

She seemed surprised, as if she hadn't noticed really.

"She's nuts," he said carefully. "What is it she's got?"

"Ella's . . . nervous."

"She's really not well."

Moira grinned, her eyes slipped his and then came back, her smile sadder than before. She was trying hard. He could see that she was trying and she'd been on a high dose for a long time.

Thomas wanted to tell her everything. A woman died in Scotland. Ella is floridly nuts. Theresa is Dad's other wife. She is a shark. She is not stupid. She has round tits and handsome children. She will eat you alive while we watch and I cannot save you because I am a child.

But he didn't say those things. Instead he said what Moira wanted and needed to hear: "Good night, Mum."

A warm grateful smile broke over her face and she slid down a little in the bed. "Good night, darling."

Carefully, Thomas shut the door and stood alone in the dark hall.

FORTY

It bothered her. As Morrow stepped out of the front door into the brisk morning, walked down to the car and unlocked it, slowly and gracelessly fitted her odd shape into the driving seat and tucked her coat in before shutting the door, something nameless weighed on her. She started the engine, using only the mirror to reverse into the street, already uncomfortable when she turned from the waist.

She stopped at the bottom of the hill. Took a breath, shook her head and wondered what was wrong. A sense of discomfort but not the usual, this had a different quality. She started off again, pulling down the road, slower than usual. The radio buzzed with news of traffic jams and children's birthdays, rumors of an accident on the M8. She punched the switch, turning it off, and drove into town, the roads quiet because it was so early.

She felt, she realized, as if she was driving with someone she'd had an argument with. But she was alone. Stupid.

She let it go, losing herself in the commands of the road, the red lights, the give ways, performing textbook brakes when pedestrians crossed the road thoughtlessly or other drivers made silly turns.

By the time she got to the station she knew she was angry with herself, but not why. It wasn't that Danny had been in her house or met Brian, she wasn't feeling soiled by that. It was Perth, something to do with Perth.

She parked up in the yard, walked up the ramp, through the booking bar, calling hellos to all the night shift, trying not to let the thread of the thought drop from her mind.

Through the lobby, into CID, she found Bannerman's door open, his light on and the man himself in, reading over papers.

"Sir?"

"Morrow? You're in early . . ."

"So are you."

He waited for her to speak but she didn't know what to say. "You want something?"

She didn't know if she did. "Umm. Perth. This Perth thing is bothering me."

He gave a little sigh and tapped the papers in front of him, eager to get on. "Fine, call it up and check it out."

"Yeah," she said, wondering why it felt wrong, "I'll call, yeah . . ."

"Could you leave me alone now?"

"Sorry."

She retreated, shut his door, stood looking at it. He'd say it was to do with her pregnancy. Anything she did that needed explaining was to do with her pregnancy. She wasn't even annoyed about it anymore.

"Ma'am?" She turned and saw Harris walking into the incident room.

"You're nice and early."

"Yeah, my eldest is going to France with the school. Had to drop him early for the bus."

She watched him disappear into the room, still feeling bothered and detached. She went into her office and opened her computer for the contact details for Perth. A blank email from N. Ketlin nestled among the departmental spam in her in-box. It had an attachment with a numbered title. She opened it, downloaded a fat file and clicked.

It was a twenty-four-second video of Sarah Erroll, alive, sitting at a table in someone's garden with a fat gray cat lolling on the table in front of her, its tail curled around her wrist.

Sarah's face was quite hard to make out

because the day was so sunny and the shade so deep, but she was smiling and singing quietly to the cat as it purred and writhed on its back and she rubbed its tummy: you are my sunshine, my only sunshine.

Sarah looked like a child, moved like a child with the awkward grace of someone who had not yet fully flowered. Next to her on the table was a yellow packet of Kettle crisps and the iPhone they had found on the bed.

She finished singing and leaned forward, still not knowing she was being filmed, and kissed the cat's furry side and then she sat back and saw that she was being filmed and her face looked dismayed and her shoulders fell and she shouted, "Nora! Fuck off with that bloody phone!"

Behind the camera Nora gurgled a laugh and Sarah looked straight into the lens and laughed back. The image froze.

Morrow covered her mouth with her hand, felt the bile rise high in her chest. She was letting it go, trading Sarah for peace with Danny, peace with Bannerman, ticking out her time. She was staring at the ceiling and doing it for the money.

She drew a deep breath, stood up and pulled her door open, screamed for Harris to come here.

He arrived at the door, startled, as if he expected her to be on the floor, delivering her babies.

"Get your fucking coat, Harris. We're going to Perth."

FORTY-ONE

The gate buzzer rang as he was standing in the kitchen and Thomas hurried to the video screen by the front door, watching the blond man hang out of his Merc window and shout into the microphone.

"Hello?"

Thomas dropped his voice to make himself sound older. "Who is this?"

"I'm Dr. Hollis." He looked Scandinavian, big, nice discreet black car. "I have an appointment with Mr. Anderson this morning."

Thomas pressed the entry button and watched the gates swing open in front of the car.

The doctor slid back into his seat and the car pulled out of shot.

Thomas used the joystick to move the camera around the entrance. There was no one else there. He'd half expected a gang of angry protesters to reassemble there now that Lars's suicide was off the front page but they must have someone else to hate now. There wasn't even any new graffiti, so they hadn't been back.

While he was standing there he heard the car draw up, heard a door open and shut and a leather sole scuff the steps. He opened the door.

"Mr. Anderson?" Dr. Hollis had white hair and eyebrows, though he was young. He had a mustache as well, but a cool mustache, and a little tiny bit of beard under his bottom lip. He was dressed in country casuals, in a gray tweed overcoat with a flash of pink lining and a nice white shirt. He looked clean and friendly.

Thomas opened the door wide. "It's good of you to come so early."

"It's not a problem." Hollis brushed his feet on the doormat and stepped into the hall. "How are you today?"

"Fine," said Thomas, wary the psychiatrist would see his past or his future or something.

Dr. Hollis wasn't trying to see through him. He dropped his satchel and let his overcoat glide off his shoulders.

"Um, my sister's upstairs." He led the way, taking the steps two at a time.

Dr. Hollis followed, hurrying at his back.

"Have you seen her this morning?"

Thomas nodded. "Yeah."

"Has she eaten?"

Thomas stopped at the top of the stairs, looking back at the fit mountaineer coming after him. "No."

Hollis took the last three steps in one. "You said on the phone that you think this is ongoing, why did you say that?"

Thomas didn't want to say why. Everything he'd hated about Ella was why: the many visits by his parents to her school, her coming home in the middle of term, family holidays he wasn't invited on. He wasn't sure he could say those things without sounding like a bitter twat. So instead he said, "Well, she's got scars," and he gestured weakly to his wrist.

"Nothing else?"

Thomas shrugged. "She's weird?"

Hollis nodded, as if he didn't understand but was trying to. "And your father has recently . . ."

Thomas slumped against the banister, mumbling, ". . . isn't an easy way to say it . . ."

So Hollis just said it the hard way: "Killed himself?"

"Yeah." Thomas was aware that his mouth was hardly moving. "On Monday." He looked at the carpet and couldn't think of anything else to say about that. "So . . ."

Hollis waited for a moment and then nodded once, not making a big thing about it. He grunted and dipped his head up the landing, telling Thomas to get on then.

They went through her sitting room to the open bedroom door. They could see her tiny form in the big bed. Thomas knocked and waited and turned back to explain, "In case, she's decided to talk . . ."

But she hadn't. He pushed the door further open.

Ella was in bed, on her side, facing away; it wasn't clear if she was awake.

Hollis was looking at the room, at the big window and the furniture. His mouth was open in a little appreciative smile. Lovely place. Thomas had to gesture him to Ella, to remind him why they were there.

Hollis walked around the bed and pulled up a chair.

"Hello, Ella, my name is Jergen. I'm a psychiatrist." He had changed the tone of his voice, dropped it, and it took on a special quality, a kindness about it that Thomas found unbelievably touching. He had to blink back tears as he listened, move himself from the door to a position near the windows where Hollis wouldn't see him unless he looked up.

"Now, Ella, we haven't met before, have we?"

She didn't speak or move but she must have given some signal because he took it for a no.

"Have you seen a psychiatrist before?"

Again, Thomas could see no response.

"And who was that?"

She mumbled something. Hollis wrote it down and showed it to her. He corrected it and showed it to her again. "If you would like I can arrange for that person to come and see you again." He left a moment for her to blink or knock or whatever. "Or I could see if I can help. Do you have a preference?"

He watched her for a long time, expressions flickering across his face as if he was having a silent conversation with her. Then he leaned in and said something quietly and stood up, looking over to Thomas, stepping around the bed.

In the hallway Hollis told him that his sister wasn't well and he would like permission to contact the doctors she had seen before, to get some background.

"What's wrong with her?"

"I can't tell yet. Do you know if she's on any medication?"

508

"I don't know. She's all over the place though, she laughs a lot. I hear her talking to people who aren't there. Mood shifts . . ."

"And your mother?"

"Yeah, she's a bit nuts too."

"No, I mean where is she?"

"Oh, she took a cab into Sevenoaks."

Hollis nodded. "I see. I need her consent to access Ella's medical records. When will she be back?"

"She's making arrangements for the funeral, so, I don't know." Thomas didn't want Hollis to think he'd been abandoned and he certainly didn't want his pity. "Dad's funeral's in three days . . ."

But there wasn't a flicker of pity on Hollis's face.

"We all have needs," he said seriously. "It must be a difficult time for you, *all*." He said it like that, with the emphasis on *all*, but Thomas knew that he'd added it on so that Thomas didn't feel singled out. He sounded a bit like Theresa, saying just the right thing at the right time. It made Thomas uneasy. He suddenly considered the possibility that Hollis might be an undercover journalist, snooping around the house, secretly taking photos. It didn't seem likely but the possibility made him want to get him out of the house.

He stood tall and looked away. "You leaving . . . ?"

"Come downstairs with me, please."

Hollis led the way this time, along the long hall, down the stairs, hurrying as if he was in a hospital corridor, on his way to somewhere urgent. At the bottom he waited for Thomas, swiveling his head, looking for directions. Thomas held his hand up to the front door but Hollis said, "I want to talk to you."

Thomas took him into a big blue day room and they sat at a corner of a huge white dining table.

"Thomas," said Hollis, "your sister is very unwell. Those scars on her wrists. What do you know about them?"

"Nothing."

"How old are you?"

"Fifteen."

"I need to speak with your mother right away. Do you have her mobile number?"

"She hasn't got a mobile."

"Well, what's the name of the undertakers?"

"I don't know. 'Brothers.' Something 'brothers.' "

Dr. Hollis searched "undertakers," "brothers" and "Sevenoaks" on his mobile, called a number, asked for Moira and found her.

510

"Mrs. Anderson, this is Dr. Hollis, I am here with your son. I'm afraid you must come home now."

As she answered, Hollis's eyebrows crept slowly up his forehead.

"I need consent and a medical history — I see . . . yes . . . it is — I see. Can you possibly — I see, yes." He looked at his watch. "Five? But just now Thomas is alone. Can someone else —" He turned away from Thomas, turning his face to the wall. "He is far too young to do that. No — yes he is. He is far *far* too young to be left alone with this situation . . . No." Suddenly he was very firm. "I can do nothing until I have seen her medical records — I really don't care, Mrs. Anderson. I don't care about your husband's funeral. You must come home to your children at once."

She hung up on him. Thomas could hear the dead tone. Hollis held the phone to his ear and sort of pretended she was still there for a moment. Then he looked at the phone, tutted and was a bit pink, a bit angry when he spoke to Thomas.

"Thomas, I have said to your mother that you are far too young to be left with this situation. It's — it's really not good." He looked angry. "So she is coming as fast as she can back to the house."

He looked around, sucked his teeth in frustration, slapped his hands against his thighs. Thomas understood. He said quietly, "Look, you can go."

"I have a patient that I have to see," explained Hollis. "But I must say, if your sister is not under adult supervision in this house then I will have to take her to hospital for observation because I cannot leave a child in charge of a suicidal child."

"Look, it's OK to leave me."

"No, it really *isn't.* You're misunderstanding me. I am not asking for permission, I am telling you: it really isn't OK. I may have to telephone the social services department. Ella might not be OK. She has tried to kill herself before, a serious try. She has cut her wrists, she knows what she is doing."

All Thomas could hear was "social services department." They'd take them away. The papers would hear. "She won't kill herself."

Hollis stood up, readied to leave. "You know, in a family, if a parent kills themselves a child is much more likely to do it. *Much* more likely."

"Please . . ." Thomas's voice was high and wavering, "don't phone the social services department . . ."

Angry, Hollis fixed on Thomas as if he had done something to Ella. "I would ask you to stay with your sister until I get back. I will be as quick as I can."

FORTY-TWO

Morrow wouldn't explain the trip to Harris,
or what the consequences would be for her.
She didn't want him involved or for the trip
to turn into a tedious bitching session about
their boss. She could tell, though, that he
was delighted to get out of the office. He
was so pleased he seemed a little bit agi-
tated, said it a couple of times, God, it was
good to be out. He seemed to know that
she had defied Bannerman, seemed a bit
nervous about it.

The sky was a wide expanse of picture-
book blue as they passed through Stirling's
flat valley floor. Morrow watched as the
castle on its sharp spur of rock appeared
around the side of a hill and wondered why
she didn't come out of the city more often.
Her phone was in her hand and she knew it
would ring any minute now, that Bannerman would be livid, that she would defy him
and go on to Perth anyway. There would be

a lot of fall-out when she got back to London Street. Even if she single-handedly brought in a gang of murderers this afternoon she'd still get her arse felt when she got back but she was fine with it. She knew she was doing the right thing for Sarah. She could get suspended for the rest of her pregnancy, sit at home with her feet up. She wouldn't mind that.

Harris saw her glancing at her phone. "Waiting on a call?"

"Aye." She looked away.

"I've an awful druth," he said. "Can I . . . ?" He looked ahead to a petrol station.

"Aye, pull in."

He went into the shop and bought them a can of juice each and a bag of toffees to share on the forecourt. The motorway was only separated from the petrol pumps by a strip of grass and lorries passed at seventy miles an hour, kicking up the wind. The day was cold but beautiful and clear, bright enough to squint at.

Morrow took a toffee and downed her fizzy orange.

"You shouldn't be eating rubbish like this," he said to her over the roof of the car. "You should be eating a sensible lunch."

"That's the nicest thing about being pregnant . . . ," she said, and didn't have to finish the thought because it was Harris.

"Everyone's got an opinion." He chewed.

"It's worse later," she said, "when every-one wants to paw you."

He nodded down the road, back to Glas-gow. "Wonder what we'll be coming back to?"

She shrugged, conscious of the silent phone in her jacket pocket. "Shit storm. Thought I'd have a call by now."

She took another toffee out of the bag and looked over at the road. It was a flat low valley, green and rich, and the road snaked through and around the ancient river, find-ing its way in the deep shadow in a cleft of abrupt hills.

Neither of them wanted to get back in the car and drive through it, but eventually Morrow groaned, "Oh God, let's lever ourselves back in."

They were pulling their seat belts on when Harris said, "Ma'am?" He waited, making her answer.

"What?"

He was looking at the hills.

"Harris? What is it?"

He took a deep breath. "We're not sup-posed to be here, are we?"

"Never you mind about that."

"Bannerman . . ."

"I'll get the bollocking." She took a breath. "You know, it doesn't matter —"

"No, the men . . . They can't stand him."

She snorted. "They'll just have to learn how."

"You won't be getting any call."

She felt sick, didn't want to know and tried to make a joke of it. "Did you order him killed, Harris?"

He didn't want to tell her and looked away. "Safecall."

"Calls about Bannerman to Safecall?"

He didn't start the car, seemed afraid to move. He stayed, elbows on his knees, fingers resting on the bottom of the steering wheel, looking at the speedometer.

Morrow looked at him. "My God, Harris."

Safecall was an anonymous helpline for officers who were being bullied or who wanted to report police corruption in safety. It was a great and decent idea but, like a lot of them, had a terrifying dark side. Reports could lead to instant suspension, demotion, and an officer being whipped out of their posts, all with no known accusers. Even if the case was found not proven, it spat officers out the other side, bitter and paranoid and ruined.

"Who's calling Safecall?" She realized immediately that the question was illegitimate.

Harris could phone Safecall and report her for asking it. "Oh fuck, forget it."

"Different . . ." He hesitated. "Lots of people. He took a laptop home, never brought it back . . ."

"Bannerman stealing? Fuck off!"

"Not just that —"

"That's ridiculous, at least meet him head on."

"He is a bully, ma'am."

She turned and shouted at him, *"He's your boss!"*

Harris looked away out of the window. It was a low trick. She didn't know what to say to him. "Oh, Christ. Start the fucking car and let's get to Perth."

He did, pulled out onto the motorway and built up speed, pulling out into the fast lane just in front of a lorry that was threatening to overtake a truck and block the lanes. She took another toffee and unwrapped it angrily. "You shouldn't have told me that. I don't want to know those things."

He didn't say anything but she could see he was glad he had. He'd meant to tell her all along. He was implicating her and he would only have done that if the end was in sight. He was marking her for their team.

As they drove on into the shadow of the hills Morrow tried to imagine the station without Bannerman. She couldn't.

It was hard to remember that Glasgow was not Scotland. Morrow grew up in Glasgow, lived there and worked there, but this was Scotland outside the attention-hungry central belt: mild gray stone houses, built low and graceful, set on wide streets, vivid with history.

They took a wrong turning and skirted the Tay, passing pretty bridges and public buildings with fat, fluted columns and pediments. She wished Leonard was there to tell them what they were looking at.

It was after lunch and the traffic was heavy so they took a while getting back through the town. Divisional Headquarters was a nineteen sixties white cube punched with windows, squat, the edges rounded and of slightly comedic proportions. Harris drove in and parked in a reserved parking space next to the front door.

Morrow raised her eyebrows at him.

"They must have known we were coming." Harris opened the door and stepped out.

They waited for twenty minutes in reception to be told that DCI Denny was unavailable at the present moment but someone else would see them. The duty officer neglected to give them a name. Fifteen minutes later he came back to them, lifted the counter and told them to come through. A ginger DC with tiny eyes led them upstairs, through long corridors and up a fire escape stairwell into a small room. Then he sat down at a desk and gave them a three-minute report which he read off a typewritten sheet.

Father Sholtham had been visited by his officers and was too inebriated to be questioned. He'd been unable to answer questions about Sarah Erroll.

"Was he rolling drunk or fast asleep?"

"Doesn't say."

Morrow was pissed off about it but had to be gracious. They were from Glasgow, were expected to be rude and pushy.

"It's a shame you didn't go back to interview him again," she said, "because we really think he has some significant information."

The DC looked through her. "We did go back. We went back twice. Three times we went and three times he was passed out or pissed."

"Have you ever met him before?"

"Oh," he was suddenly animated, off the page and passing on gossip, "he's well known. He was sober for a long time, he's a good bloke."

"How long was he sober for?"

"Ten years or something."

"Does anyone else have any information?"

"About what?"

Harris sighed audibly and she decided to cut it short. "Where can we find him, then?"

The DC told them that Sholtham had been moved from the parish house to a local house used for visiting clergy. He snickered at that. "Guess that they didn't want parishioners turning up at the doors and being greeted by a drunk priest walking about in his underpants."

"That's hilarious," Morrow said flatly. "And you've been a great help."

FORTY-THREE

It was a modern council estate, neat little houses fitted together like a puzzle, built in the same gray as the older houses in the town.

The door was answered by a young man with very short hair and haunted eyes. He was wearing slacks and a shirt, neither of which fitted him terribly well. He welcomed them and brought them into the kitchen, insisted on serving them tea in a steel pot, and a plate of Happy Shopper custard creams. Father Sholtham was upstairs and would be down in a minute. He knew they were there.

They were left alone.

After a short while they heard steps on the stairs, the shuffle of slippered feet. The feet paused outside the open door. Father Gabriel Sholtham walked in and introduced himself.

Morrow stood up to meet him, introduced

herself and Harris and shook his hand. She looked down: his hands were big and soft and she saw a blue swelling on the back of his right hand where he must have knocked something incredibly hard.

He had a square face, big features, the sort of face that in a healthier man would have commanded trust and obedience, a police face. But he wouldn't look at either of them and kept his eyes cast down to the worktop, pouring himself a black tea from the pot, adding in two sugars as they explained that they had come up from Glasgow.

He wore a gray jumper over a gray T-shirt, black trousers and blue slippers. The slippers were telling a story. They were suede and speckled with dried drips and splashes. Morrow didn't want to speculate what they were splashes of.

He pulled a third seat up to the table and sat down.

"We're the officers investigating Sarah Erroll's death," said Morrow. "We understand that you have some information about that."

He winked at his tea as he stirred it, a micro-tic. She didn't know if it was a needle-pin pain through the eye from his hangover or the mention of the name. When he spoke his voice was a low rumble, west coast with a trace of Irish. What he said sounded very considered, as if he was giving evidence in court.

"I read about it in the newspaper. I talked about it. I was foolish. I've wasted your time, making you come here. I'm sorry."

"I see," said Morrow. She didn't know how stern to take it. He seemed very brittle. "That's not enough, Father, because you know things about that girl's death that weren't in the papers."

He knew that already. He sipped his tea noisily, taking care not to look up at them.

"So," she said softly, "you've either been part of her murder or you know someone who has."

He glanced towards her, looked away quickly, hiding in his tea. "Maybe I am part of the crime," he said. A deep sadness flared in his eyes and he drank hot tea to shove it back down.

"Part of the crime?"

"Yes," he told his mug of tea.

It was interesting. Morrow had a talent for spotting lies and liars. She knew how to trap someone who was pretending to tell the truth, ask for details and then ask again later when they'd forgotten what they said, confront them with the inconsistency. She knew how to spot a suggestible person, someone who lied and didn't know they were lying, ask outlandish questions, see if they agreed they'd shot Kennedy. But this man was attempting a different kind of deception. He was taking a theological approach to it, treading very carefully, he was tiptoeing around a big fat bloody lie and was willing to be charged with murder rather than give it up. She felt that he'd tell the truth if she asked him but the question would have to be the right one.

"What did you do?" Her voice was very soft, hangover-respectful. "Father, what did you do?"

He frowned and shook his head.

"What 'part of the crime' did you do?"

He hadn't prepared an answer for that question. "I don't know."

"Well, let's go through it: did you break into her house?"

"No."

"Did you creep through her house and go up to her old nursery room?"

"No." His voice was flat but his eyes skittered around the table, trying to map the angles to the questions, work out where the ambush would come from.

"Did you then find her asleep in her bed after a long day's traveling and wake her and frighten her?"

"No, I didn't do that either."

"Did you chase her downstairs until she fell on the steps?"

"No."

"Did you stand over her and bring the heel of your foot down over and over again on her face?"

"No."

"Did you use your body weight to break her nose, stamping so hard that her eyes burst —"

He was weeping and whispering, "No, didn't do those things. No."

She let him cry. Harris clasped his hands tightly together on the table. She handed Father Sholtham a hankie. He took it and thanked her and wiped his nose. She started again.

"OK: did you drive the people who did it away from her house?"

"I can't drive, I lost my license . . ."

"They'd just brutally murdered an innocent woman. I don't imagine they'd be stopping to check your license." She took a custard cream and bit it. Chewing it, she kept her face to him, innocent. "Did you drive the people —"

"No. I didn't drive them. I wasn't — I was in hospital when it happened. Having my teeth out."

"Did you leave the hospital at any time

526

during the day of —"

"No. I had eight teeth taken out. They gave me a general anesthetic. It was day surgery and I got out at eight that night."

"Where did you go then?"

"Back to the parish house. I was still living there . . . then."

She bit her biscuit again, chewed again, watched him wiping his face. He pushed the tissue so hard into his eye that it was compressed as small as a mint.

"Can I ask about the drink?"

He nodded.

"You've had a problem before?"

"I have." He seemed more deeply and sincerely ashamed of that than implicating himself in a murder. His voice had dropped to a whisper and he looked almost too sad to move his mouth.

"But you haven't drunk for a good long while?"

"That's right. Good long while."

"How long?"

"Eight and a half years."

"It's a dark place, isn't it?"

He looked her in the eye, searching for sympathy and found none. Disappointed, he went back to examining the table top.

"When did you start again?"

"Few days ago."

"How many days ago?"

He tried to answer but couldn't work it out. "What day is it?"

"Thursday."

She could see him working backwards. "It started on Tuesday, I think."

"The day after Sarah was killed?"

"Was it? I lifted the drink because I'd had surgery . . . they gave me opiates . . . I was confused."

He knew the excuse for drinking was bullshit and he knew it was the day after Sarah was killed. Morrow gave him a reproachful look and he dropped his eyes in shame.

She watched him for a moment, and he felt her watching him, sipped his tea, smacking his lips at the bitterness of it. Clearly a man shackled by conscience, he was protecting someone. She didn't know why he would do that and she was finding it annoying.

She tapped her fingertip on the table and said, "You wait here." She stood up and motioned for Harris to follow her.

They went out through the hall. The young man who had let them in was coming through the living room and waved, trying to catch their eye, wanted a chat but Morrow shut the front door after them–

selves. They went back to the car and got in.

"He's lying to protect someone," she said, "I think it's another priest."

"No," said Harris, certain. "Someone's confessed to him, he's drunk, blurted it out and now he's trying to save his soul by taking the blame."

"How would you know that?"

Harris smiled. "I'm a Pape."

She didn't know what to say. It was easy to get these things wrong and she had a poor enough track record with tact. "Well . . . good for you."

Harris laughed because it was a ridiculous thing to say and he could see how hard she was trying.

She held her hands up. "I don't know what to say, I didn't know."

"Aye, well," he said awkwardly. He didn't know what to say either.

"Good for you," she said again. "So . . . how does it work? He has to take the blame because someone confessed to him?"

"No. He's sworn never to repeat what people tell him in confession. But he's done that now and it's a terrible sin, breaking that. Cardinal. He's trying to make up for that by martyring himself."

"Is it not a defense that he was steaming?"

"When was being steaming ever a defense?"

They looked back at the house and saw Father Sholtham standing at the kitchen window, watching them in the car.

"No, but it's mitigating, isn't it?"

"Not for something like that."

"So, Mr. Pape, what do we do now?"

Harris reached back for his seat belt. "Find out who confessed."

Morrow looked back as they drove away, saw Sholtham watching them drive off: a big sad man in a picture window that came up to his knees. His hands hung at his sides, loose, fingers curled limp, waiting for judgment to be made upon him.

The parish house was altogether finer than the council house. Sitting next to the chapel in a city center street, it echoed the needle spire in its narrow pointed windows and the sharp point of the door. The stone didn't match though. The chapel was made of the native gray stone and the little house next to it was red with blond tracery around the windows.

"You ever talk to Leonard?" she asked as they got out of the car.

"Sometimes."

"What do you think of her?"

"Nice. Smart." He didn't mention her sexuality and Morrow liked that. "She knows her buildings and antiques." Morrow fell into step next to him and waited to cross the busy street. "She's smart."

The front door had two steps up to it, steep, loiter-proof. Harris reached up and rang the bell. It sounded like a death announcement.

"Think she's a prospect for promotion?"

Harris didn't want to answer. "Suppose."

"Bannerman'll be suspended on suspicion and we'll need someone to step up and take the DS position," she said, referring to the conversation at the petrol station. "I want you, but, you know . . ."

They watched the door.

Harris cleared his throat, "I get more . . . you know, with overtime."

"Yeah." They heard someone coming down a stone corridor towards them. "You worried about starting a coup when there's no one to take over?"

"How d'you mean?"

"Well, I'll be off on maternity. We need a DS. That . . . calls thing." The lock scraped back behind the door. "They'll ship someone in. Don't know what they'll be like, do you? Creating a power vacuum."

Harris smiled. "That's word for word what

531

Leonard said. She said that's what happened when Napoleon came to power."

He was just passing on an interesting comment of Leonard's, but he'd admitted to talking to other officers about Safecall. That made it a campaign. They looked at each other.

"So, you admit it's a coup?" she said.

Harris looked frightened.

The door opened. "Can I help you?" A tiny, elderly woman with a rayon blouse and unflattering pleated skirt looked out at them.

"Strathclyde Police," said Morrow. "We'd like a word about Father Sholtham."

The housekeeper was delighted to give up every detail she had on Father Sholtham's movements the day after Sarah's murder. She was very angry with him, though she seemed like someone who woke up angry anyway. She kept asking them what would make a man of faith drink like that? Why would he do that? Make himself ridiculous, like that?

A sober Father Sholtham had breakfast and took morning mass next door at eight. He didn't take confessions after mass, they weren't until five p.m., and he began to drink that morning. She noticed he was acting strange but he said he had flu. He left to attend a meeting at a nearby school and she thought he had flu. He seemed unsteady. He had lunch at the school. Then he came home and did some praying in his room. He hadn't taken any phone calls, she knew because the phone was in the hall. Morrow was keen to get the details of the teatime confessions but the woman kept talking about the prayer in his room, maybe that had sparked him off, why would someone drink like that, to hurt themselves — Morrow cut her off.

"Who was at confession?"

"Father Haggerty."

"Is that all?"

"No," Harris interrupted, "she means who gave a confession to Father Sholtham?"

"No one," said the woman. "No one did. Father Haggerty took the confessions."

"Father Sholtham didn't?"

"No. He was scheduled to take confessions at five p.m., but he went out for a walk and when he came back it was obvious he was very drunk. Didn't have flu at all. He'd lied earlier. Father Haggerty found him changing for confessions and brought him here. We put him to bed. He's been drunk ever since."

They couldn't get a list of names out of her for the people who had been at mass the morning before he drank. She only came in at nine and although she often attended mass in the morning before work she hadn't that morning.

When they got outside Harris told her that there would be a core group of people who went to morning mass every day and they could ask them if anyone had taken the priest aside afterwards or spoken to Sholtham at length.

It was only as a long shot that they went to the school.

FORTY-FOUR

On the GPS St. Augustus's was out of town, fourteen minutes on a stretch of motorway that took them over a ridge of high hills and down into a lush valley of rich farmland, big fields and pretty houses nestled in copses of trees.

As they drove over the head of the hill, a curtain of rain rose towards them, the sunshine behind it lighting it yellow. They could see it race across the valley, the cars and lorries drive straight into it, bright drops exploding on their roofs and bonnets as it washed the dust from the road and passed overhead. Everything they saw seemed brighter afterwards.

The GPS directed them from the motorway to roads that curved sympathetically around the landscape, around the edge of thick woods, skirting a hillock. It brought them to a single-track bridge, built from the local stone, and down a winding road of low laborers' cottages, with deep windows and heavy black thatch roofs. A high red wall gradually emerged from the trees and approached the roadside.

The wall curved into a wide circle framed by twin curved gate houses on either side and black iron gates that lay open.

"Fucking hell," said Harris as he turned down the drive, and he didn't tend to swear.

Beyond the gates the red gravel drive snaked through first a wood, then immaculate lawns up to a big elegant house. The house wasn't square to the gate but faced away, slightly diffident. Built on three levels, with a modest columned portico at the front, it looked grand and cozy at the same time. It had been extended but all the new buildings were clustered behind it so as not to spoil the view.

In front of the house the lawn sloped away, dipping down to meet a small burn with a little arched bridge over it, leading to the tennis courts and playing fields beyond.

Harris stopped the car. The main door was shut tight and there were no other cars there. As he looked around for clues to the parking area, Morrow watched a troop of small boys coming across the bridge. They were dressed in their gym clothes, tracksuits and big blue fleeces, all flushed, some with sweat-dampened hair. As they were only about ten or eleven years old, the athletics equipment was too big for them to carry comfortably: they struggled with the hurdles, holding them high to their chins and over their shoulders.

"There must be a car park around here," muttered Harris. "Unless there's another way into the grounds."

Now that the wee boys were closer Morrow could see their excitement, chatting and hurrying in groups. They took the path that cut diagonally through the lawn, to a changing room entrance around the side.

"Weans are weans, though, eh?" said Morrow to herself.

A boy, smaller than the others, came running up behind the car, hurrying to catch up with his friends. He passed them, breathless, pink faced, pumping his little arms at his sides to help him go faster. He saw the last of his companions walking in the door ahead of him and redoubled his efforts, running fast, kicking his feet high behind him, spraying red gravel.

The soles of his trainers had a familiar three-circle pattern on them. Morrow hurried out of the car as fast as she could and shouted after him, "Son!"

He twisted, still running, slowing, jogging

backwards.

"Come back here."

He didn't. But he stopped still outside the changing rooms, looked to the door and spoke to another boy who was scraping mud off the side of his black shoe. The boy shouted into the door. A sturdy woman in a red tracksuit came out. She had a whistle and a stopwatch hanging around her neck.

Morrow flashed her badge. "We're from Strathclyde Police. These shoes, are they part of the uniform?"

"Yes."

"We'd like to see the headmaster, please."

She started at that but didn't ask why. "I'll show you," she said and led them through the changing room door.

Harris and Morrow followed her through the corridor past the changing rooms. The teacher kept her eyes down as she hung in at the door and shouted like a sergeant major, "McLennan!"

A tiny high voice came back, "Miss Losty?"

"You're in charge for the next ten minutes!"

"Very good!"

Miss Losty exhibited tremendous self-control as she led them through the narrow servants' corridors and upstairs to the school secretary's office. She never once asked what they were there for but led them and dropped them in the capable hands of a lady in a tan blouse, flashed a smile and left.

The secretary asked them to wait in the corridor and shut the door while she made a phone call. Moments later she took them down a long, dark corridor with a black and white checked floor to an office with a sign on the door that said "Mr. Doyle — Headmaster."

She knocked and opened the door, hung in and said the police were here.

Wallis Doyle came to the door, shook their hands and introduced himself, examined their ID photographs closely and then welcomed them into his small office.

The room smelled of air freshener and new carpets. It was very orderly. The window sill of Doyle's office was lined with stacks of papers and folders, but all the piles were tidy and everything seemed to be where it should. He even had a recycling center in a corner, homemade from empty boxes of crisps, the circular openings color coded: one for newspapers, one for cans and the bottom for glass. Inside each box the rubbish for recycling was tidy, as if it wasn't really being used but was just there as an example.

He was courteous, sitting them down in comfortable seats and offering them tea. They said no thanks and the secretary left, shutting the door carefully. He watched the door close and stood at the side of the desk, his hands clasped one in the other. "Well, welcome to St. Augustus's," he said as if addressing parents. "What can I do for you?"

"Yes, Mr. Doyle," said Morrow. "Sorry, it is Mr. Doyle? Not Father Doyle?"

"No, no," he smiled at that idea and showed her his wedding ring, "Mr. Doyle."

"We wanted to ask about Father Sholtham's visit here on Tuesday?"

"With regard to . . . ?" He cocked his ear.

Harris looked at Morrow.

"What time did he get here, who did he speak to, when did he leave?"

"And why would you be asking that?"

Morrow cleared her throat. "Because I want to know."

They stared at each other, Doyle's expression cooling towards her. He unclasped his hands and put them in his pockets, leaned his bottom on the desk. "Father Sholtham arrived at twelve thirty-five. He came to the side chapel to tell the choir that the funding for their Malawi trip had been met: one of our parents had agreed to match the money already raised. For every thousand pounds they raised another thousand would be added —"

"You're very sure about the time."

"We were expecting him at twelve but he was late. The bus was late."

"What happened then?"

"We had a celebratory drink of tea and then he left. I saw him out."

"How did he seem to you?"

He thought about it. "Fine, a little under the weather. I'm assuming this has something to do with his drinking, he certainly wasn't drunk then. He had a general anesthetic the day before so he wasn't well, but he didn't smell of drink. I saw him half an hour later, leaving for the bus and he seemed fine."

"Hang on," interrupted Harris. "You saw him out and then you saw him leave half an hour later?"

"Yes, from the blue room. It's on the first floor and I saw him on the driveway."

Harris frowned. "Why the time lag?"

"The buses are infrequent. He would have waited downstairs in the hall. It was raining."

"He didn't take confessions?"

"No."

"And who would he have spoken to while he was waiting down there?"

"No one."

"No one could happen past him?"

"Oh, sure, easily. It's free association until classes start back at one fifteen. The boys could come and go but they'd have to be looking for him down there. It's not a part of the school they hang around in. The games rooms and dorms are over the other side of the campus."

Harris nodded. "You didn't leave him with anyone or see anyone approaching him?"

"No."

"Confession . . ." Harris shifted in his seat. "It's not like when I was a boy. You can do it anywhere now . . ."

Doyle said nothing but smiled, confused. He'd assumed they were here about the priest.

"But," said Harris, "it's still confession if you can see the priest, if it's not in a confessional . . ."

"Sure. Well, it's a sacrament but if the priest uses the sacramental forms, they can take it anywhere. A lot of priests prefer to keep it more casual now, especially with younger people, don't they?"

"Less intimidating," suggested Harris.

"Sure." He was looking from one to the

other, hoping for clues. Morrow sat forward. "On Monday afternoon, the day before, were any of the kids missing from the school?"

He thought back. "No."

"Were there any school trips to Glasgow that day? Sports events or debating teams or anything?"

"No. Could you tell me what this is about?"

"Have you heard of Sarah Erroll?"

Doyle blinked. "No. There aren't any boys by the name of Erroll here. I could be wrong. Sometimes the parents have different names now, the mothers . . . What is this about? Who is Sarah Erroll?"

Morrow didn't like him. She didn't like his attitude, she didn't like that he ran a private school and she didn't like his tidy-as-a-minister's-conscience office. "Mr. Doyle, I don't think you're being honest with me. You know who Sarah Erroll is."

He shrugged. Irritated. "Has she been to visit this school?"

"You're not answering my questions. Don't start pitching your own."

Doyle was not a man used to being disagreed with. He bared his teeth in a cold smile and slid off the side of the desk, moving around to sit in his chair, keeping the broad oak surface between them.

She pointed at the tower of recycled crisp boxes. "There are newspapers in there which covered the story extensively. I think you are worried about answering openly in case it'll reflect badly on the school."

Doyle looked guiltily over at the crisp boxes. "I don't recall that particular story."

"The uniforms the boys wear," said Harris. "Are they the same for every year?"

"Yes."

"Trainers: where are they from?"

"Which 'trainers'?"

"The trainers. The trainers all the boys wear for PE, the black suede ones."

"They're just normal gym shoes. I don't know the make —"

"Where do the boys get their uniform — is it a special shop?"

"No. It's just Jenners."

"In Edinburgh?"

"Yes. But look, every part of the school uniform is manufactured for general sale. The blazer badges and evening jackets are the only things made for us. Anyone could buy those gym shoes."

"You're not being very helpful, Mr. Doyle."

They sat in silence, Morrow scanning the office, Harris staring at Doyle. Doyle was the only person in the room who was uncomfortable.

He hatched a plan and stood up. "Well, thank you again for coming. I will go through the class records for that day and see who, if anyone, could have been in Glasgow. Our boys are not allowed to keep cars, so it might be worth you checking with the local train station."

"I know my job." Morrow stayed resolutely in her chair.

"I can access the records but I must ask you to leave now."

Harris looked at Morrow. Morrow looked at Doyle and took her time deciding. "I'm phoning you in three hours. If I don't get the information I need or if I think you're not cooperating, I'm coming back in uniform with a squad and we're doing a search. Clear?"

Doyle held his hand out to his door.

Morrow stood up and Harris followed her. Doyle tried to get around to the door but Morrow beat him to it and opened it herself. "We can find our way out."

"Not at all," said Doyle and ushered them, shutting the office door and locking it after them.

The ratchet sounded loud and definitive in the quiet.

He waved them in front of him and took them in silence down the dark corridor, away from the secretary's office, through a large door into an oval central hall. It was very cold and empty apart from a gleaming rosewood grand piano and an empty white marble fireplace. The floor above had an oval balcony, overlooked by a domed glass window.

Doyle shook their hands, avoiding their eyes, and showed them through a door to the top of a short twin staircase that arced down either wall to the front door. He stayed on the balcony and watched them leave.

As Morrow shut the front door after herself she heard the lock click firmly. The car was parked right outside and Harris had the keys in his hand. "Are we going home?"

But Morrow stopped him. "Where's the chapel?" she said, looking back up at the house.

They stepped away, looked left and right. They walked ten feet to the doors of the changing room. The chapel was behind it, a tall blond barn of a building, pushed back from the main façade, with red glass windows coming to a point at the top, like those of the parish house. They stood and looked at it. Harris looked back at the front door for Doyle.

"Let's go for a wander," said Morrow.

There was a logical time frame to the extensions: the first-built and worst-worn buildings were close to the back of the main house: a wooden corridor and a hall that looked as if it had been thrown up during the war. Beyond them were the red-brick builds of recent years, what looked like classroom blocks and a swimming pool with big sliding windows on metal frames. Tucked far around the back was a white concrete block, the regular windows and uniform navy blue curtains lending it the feel of a cheap hotel.

Behind that was the startling latest development. A series of corrugated-iron rectangles, shipping containers, two stories high, each spray-painted subtly different tones of white with a gray mesh staircase leading up and around the building. Each had a wall of windows with frosted portions to afford privacy but they could see that the lowest one housed a common room: five boys lounged in armchairs, and a darts board and a plasma TV hung on the wall. Above and around the others were classrooms with jolly furniture, multicolored recycled-plastic desks and chairs. A boy sitting in a chair by a window on the first floor looked down at them and pointed.

A door opened in his block and a tall thin man stepped out onto the gangway one floor up. He shouted down, "Can I help you?"

Harris shouted back, "Strathclyde Police." He showed his badge. "We've just seen Mr. Doyle. We're looking around the grounds."

The teacher went back into his room and they saw him through the glass wall as he told the boys something that made them all stare out of the window. The boys at the back came over to the window to see them.

Morrow and Harris backed up the side of the common room block.

It was then that they saw the notice: a sign bolted onto the side said that the buildings were composed entirely from recycled materials, were carbon neutral and solar powered, and they had been kindly donated by Sir Lars Anderson.

Morrow and Harris hurried around to the front, past their car and found the front door locked. Morrow tried pressing the bell but she couldn't hear it ringing inside.

"Changing rooms," said Harris, and headed back the way they had come.

"We'll get lost," said Morrow, turning to him. Then she saw him, a boy running around the corner from the extensions, tall, about sixteen, head swiveling, looking frantically for someone.

He stopped, his shoulder to them, taking them in. He was thin, his nose was short, eyes baby-round. His head was shaved, his skin sunny-summered. Morrow had seen him in the classroom with the nosy teacher. He'd come to the window to look at them.

"Hey, son," said Morrow. "How do we get back in? We need to see Mr. Doyle."

"You don't need Doyle." He was panting. "You're here to see me."

FORTY-FIVE

Thomas sat in the corridor on a hard chair and listened to Moira opening the front door downstairs. She had a bit of trouble, tried the wrong lock twice and finally, fitting the key in and turning it, the door fell open and she stood there for a moment. "Hello? Anyone?"

Thomas let her wait. "Up here," he said quietly.

"Thomas?" She came to the bottom of the stairs. "Thomas? Are you there?"

As she approached he felt the hairs rise on his arms, on his neck.

"Tom?" She was smiling, as if it was a game of hide and seek, coming to the bottom of the stairs. "Hello-ho?"

They were both still, Thomas on the hard chair outside Ella's open door, Moira at the bottom of the stairs. She shifted and he heard a small brittle noise amplified by the stairwell, the light crumple of tissue paper.

Tissue paper in a bag.

"Up here," he said, his voice flat.

"Oh." She took a tentative step, wary because of his tone, because he hadn't moved to where she could see him, because she sensed the fury in his voice. But still she came and he heard the soft whisper of tissue shifting in a bag as she took the stairs, and she muttered as she came, "Good heavens, the traffic was terrible in the town." And "These stairs seem to get steeper every time . . ." making pleasant conversation, willfully pretending that they were happy friends having a jolly little fucking conversation.

She arrived at the top of the stairs and saw him sitting sentry outside Ella's door. She was carrying a bushel of bags, cardboard with ribbon handles, from posh clothes shops. She saw him look at them.

"For the funeral."

He said nothing.

"Sales . . . my own money . . ."

Thomas looked away and folded his arms. She didn't move, shifted her hips awkwardly, opened her mouth to speak but drew a blank and tittered nervously as she glanced at her bedroom door. She wanted to go to her room and try on her new things, he knew that, but she was afraid to pass him.

"Have you been there long . . . ?"

Thomas turned to look at her. "The fuck is wrong with you?"

She flinched at his tone and his manner, looked hurt, raised a shoulder against him. "Your father's funeral . . ."

"She's suicidal, Moira. You went out and left her here with me."

Moira dropped the bags to the floor. "Tom, you don't know —"

"I shouldn't be left in charge of her." He was shouting now, and glad he was shouting, enjoying the release.

"Darling, you don't know the first thing about it."

"You're right, you stupid bitch." He rose to his feet. "The doctor's here, I know nothing about her condition, I'm talking to him like a prize prick. *How the fuck do I look?*" They both froze at that. It was Lars's phrase. Thomas should have stopped there but shame propelled him on, "What kind of fucking mother are you?"

"I had to arrange your father's funeral, my husband's funeral!" She was tearful, stuck at the head of the stairs, the bags at her feet wilting onto their sides from the weight of the contents and he saw her do what she always did when she argued with

552

Lars: roll her shoulders inwards, her head drooping to her chest. She was making him the bad guy.

He stomped over to her. "I couldn't even phone you —"

But she turned to face him, tears streaming down her face, her voice whiny. "Imagine how I feel, Tommy: I'm in an *undertakers'*, with people looking at me, they know who I am, and then he calls the desk and asks for me."

"I haven't got a mobile number —"

"Why?" she shouted, flailing her arms wide. "Why? Why haven't you got a mobile number for me? Because I had to throw my mobiles away. Journalists were phoning every minute. *I can't even have a mobile.* How do you think that feels?"

He was close to her now, and he saw how near to the edge of the step her heels were, how far she had to fall. "It didn't occur to you in your tiny mind that you could just have not answered when journalists called? It says 'unknown' when someone you don't know calls. You don't have to throw the whole fucking phone away."

Moira glanced at her feet, was suddenly aware of the drop behind her, looked accusingly at Thomas who had stopped three feet away, and turned her back to the wall.

They glared at each other, Thomas leaning forward, making himself the predator,
Moira feeling behind her for the wall, face
turned away.

"What's the fucking *point* of you?" he said,
giving her the cue to run.

Moira covered her face, splaying her
fingers so she could see, and turned to run
downstairs, but the clothes bags were about
her feet and her heel pierced a thick blue
ribbon handle, becoming entangled, making
her stagger unsteadily.

"Thomas?" A small voice behind him,
Ella, not even on the landing but half in the
doorway, keeping covered. She was still
wearing the clothes from yesterday, still had
sticky pink and white smears of marshmal-
low stuck to the front of her T-shirt. She
watched Moira slip and tumble, her arms
sliding down the wall, fingers flexing, looking for purchase.

Thomas spun back to a dull thud. Moira
was on the floor in front of him, splayed on
her side, the ribbon handle on the bag still
skewered on her heel, the bag gaping crazily.

Black tissue ripped with a hiss and a pair
of brown leather trousers dropped out,
slowly unfolding as they cartwheeled down
the staircase and came to a stop.

An alarm sounded, the soft, gentle trilling

of the house phone, like the end of a round in a genteel boxing match.

Moira pulled herself upright and looked down the hall to her bedroom. "If that's the doctor, I'm not in."

Ella looked to Thomas, one eye visible, pleading with him as she hung on to the door frame.

Thomas smiled at her weakly and walked down to Moira's bedside, picked up the phone and said, "Hello?"

"Hello, Thomas, is your mother there?" It wasn't Dr. Hollis.

Numb, he walked down to Moira in the hall. She was sitting on the top step, untangling the ribbon from her heel and saw him hold out the receiver. She took her time, standing up, patting her hair to make sure it was straight, and took the phone. "Hello?"

She listened. Theresa's voice on the other end was harsh, loud, haranguing. Moira's face hardened as she listened. "Did he?" she said at one point, glaring angrily at Thomas. She listened until the monologue ended and then waited, pinching her mouth. "Is that all you have to say?"

She listened again. Thomas looked back down the corridor and saw Ella still in the doorway, watching, curious and forgetting herself. He smiled to see her like that and she met his eye and gave a half smile. She knew he'd stayed with her and it mattered. For a moment Thomas felt proud and honorable.

"Hmm," said Moira, as though she had been told something only quite interesting. "Well, if this is indeed the case then I'm very sorry for you and your children."

The voice on the other end shouted but Moira spoke even louder and drowned her out. "You must remember, dear: the world is full of whores but in England a man can have only one wife."

She hung up, and handed the phone back to Thomas as if it belonged to him. Looked him up and down and then bent to pick up her shopping bags.

When she stood up again she looked older. "I have a headache and I'm going to my room, darlings. Perhaps you could just see the doctor yourselves."

FORTY-SIX

His name was Jonathon Hamilton-Gordon. He stood in front of the changing rooms, eyes on the horizon, and told them the story as if he was being sick: he and his friend Thomas Anderson skived off after athletics. They drove to Glasgow, to Thorntonhall. They broke into Sarah Erroll's house, through the kitchen. They were supposed to frighten her but his friend lost it and kicked her face in and killed her. Jonathon stood, breathing unevenly, holding his chest.

"Have you got asthma?" asked Harris.

"A little bit," said the boy.

Harris got him to bend over, asked if he had an inhaler but he didn't. As he held the boy's shoulder and let him catch his breath, Harris looked over at Morrow.

Neither of them wanted this: their adrenaline was up, their fingers were tingling, they were ready for the chase but the fox had come over and shot itself at their feet.

The boy stood up, his breathing more regular. Morrow looked for a spark of emotion on his face but found nothing.

Harris was the first to speak. "Where was she when you went in?"

"Asleep," he said, calm now. "Upstairs, in a room. It was round, the room."

"Did you kill her there?"

"No, no, no." He fell back a step and Harris lurched towards him, thinking he was about to run but the boy held his hands up and made it clear he was giving himself up. "No, I mean, *I* didn't do it."

So Harris rephrased the question with exactly the same intonation: "Did *your friend* kill her there?"

"No." The boy was speaking to Harris and Morrow took the chance to move around behind and block him, why she didn't know, she wasn't in a fit condition to run after him or tackle him. "She ran downstairs. He did it there, at the bottom of the stairs."

"How do we know you're telling the truth?"

"My car. I've got baby wipes covered in her blood."

They all turned towards the sound: someone approaching from the far corner, walking quickly. A big square man in a gray suit came around the far side of the building and stormed over to them, taking charge.

"Hamilton-Gordon, get back inside." He swung his shoulder between them and the boy. "Officers, what are you still doing on the school grounds? Mr. Doyle asked you to leave."

Morrow was catching her breath. "Sorry, you are . . . ?"

"Mr. Cooper."

"OK, Mr. Cooper. We're bringing this boy upstairs to talk to him, and Mr. Doyle or yourself can sit in."

"No." Cooper held a massive hand up flat to her face. "Here's what's going —"

Morrow was full of adrenaline and disappointed at the chase being cut short. She spoke so loudly that Harris and the boy cringed.

"We are detaining this boy in connection with the murder of Sarah Erroll. You can participate in the process. If you do not choose to participate an alternative responsible adult will be found to sit in on the process. The purpose of the appropriate adult is to clarify events, step by step. Is that clear to you?"

Cooper's hand withered back down to his side. He looked from Morrow to the boy. "Jonathon, I'll phone your father —"

"We did it," said Jonathon, but he couldn't

look at Cooper. "We did it, sir."

"You . . . ?"

"And Thomas Anderson."

Back up in Doyle's office the boy was more cowed. He listened to his rights, nodding, as if he knew them already. Then he began to talk again. He hung over his knees, hugging himself as he told them the details. He didn't waste time emoting or making a case in his own favor but stuck to the bald facts of how and where. Morrow watched, able to because the boy had decided that Harris was in charge and told him. The confession sounded rehearsed. He didn't hesitate or wonder, wasn't dredging up facts. He had practiced this confession and it bothered her that he had.

Doyle gave her a slip of paper with Thomas Anderson's home address. She handed it to Harris and he slipped out to the corridor and made some calls to the other boy's local cops.

Morrow made them sit in silence until he came back, upping the tension, making them itchy to talk. When Harris came back he looked lighter, gave her a nod, and she motioned for him to start the questioning again.

"How did you get there?"

"I've got a car . . ." Doyle and Cooper sat up at that, "in the village."

"Where's your car?"

"In a garage behind the Co-op."

"Where did you get the car?"

"Dad got it for me."

Doyle was furious. "You're sixteen years old!"

"Well, Dad got it for me."

Cooper flared his nostrils at Doyle. Morrow made a note to ask about the father.

"Jonathon." She sat down near him. "Did you tell anyone about this? After it happened, did you speak to anyone?"

The boy looked up, his eyes red from being rubbed with his knees and he looked past Morrow to the window. "I did," he said lightly, "I made a confession to Father Sholtham."

"And what did he say?"

"He told me to call Thomas and get him to give himself up with me."

"Will Father Sholtham confirm that?"

He almost smiled. "Well, I don't know if he can say what I said but he will admit that I spoke to him."

"Did you call Thomas and ask him to give himself up?"

He was staring into the distance and chewing his fingertips.

"Jonathon, did you call Thomas?"

"He wouldn't answer after the first time. He's the guilty party. He didn't want to give himself up. If you check his phone you'll see that I called and called."

She looked at his feet. He was wearing leather shoes, class shoes not sports shoes. "Have you got trainers, son?"

He shrugged. "I've ordered new ones from Mrs. Cullis in the linen room. They'll be here any day. Might be here today."

"I see. What size did you order?"

"I take an eight and a half. She'll have a record of it. She had to write it down and everything."

"Right." She nodded, watched his face, saw an expression in his eyes, triumph or amusement, she couldn't tell.

"What happened to your other ones?"

"Lost them."

"When?"

He smirked at that. "This week some-time."

"You ordered the new ones this week?"

"Yes."

Harris asked: "And Thomas has those same shoes?"

"Yes, he does." He was too quick with the answer, much too quick. "His shoes are in my room."

Morrow interrupted. "Why are they in your room?"

"Oh, I must have picked his up thinking they were mine and then mine went missing so I had to order new ones. His name's in them, I realized, after I took them to my room."

"I see," she said flatly. "Can I see one of the shoes you're wearing now?" She held her hand out. He was reluctant, gave himself time to think about it. He bent down, pulled his laces loose, took the shoe off and handed it to her.

The leather instep was worn but she could still read it. It was a size nine and a half.

"What size were your previous pair of trainers?"

"I don't know."

"Would Mrs. Cullis have a note of the size?"

"No. I got them in the summer from Jenners."

"I see." She leaned forward. "You wouldn't be ordering shoes in the wrong size to try and confuse us, would you?"

"No." He seemed stunned that she'd managed to put it together. "I wouldn't . . . ever."

"You wouldn't have taken your friend's shoes and got rid of your own shoes so he'd get all the blame?"

"No." Too quick.

"Jonathon," she said slowly, "we're going to take you to Glasgow and interview you formally. Would you like us to call your parents or would you like Mr. Doyle to call them?"

"Mr. Doyle."

"You need an adult to sit in on the interviews — who would you like that to be?"

Without considering it, he pointed straight at Doyle. He didn't need time to think it through because he'd already thought about it. Jonathon knew he'd dropped his guard; he scanned the room to see who'd spotted it and the eyes he met were Morrow's.

"See, because my dad's in Hong Kong," he told her, a little flushed, "but he'll be back next week ...."

Morrow looked hard at him. "Where's the motor, son?"

It was a small lock-up behind someone's house. Built at the end of the garden but with a path to the street and the door at the side affording absolute privacy. Jonathon gave them the key and they opened it, and he told them the light switch was at the side, higher up than you would expect. Morrow flicked it on.

Harris stayed outside with the boy and Morrow stepped in for a look. She put her hands in her pockets as a reminder to touch nothing — it was easy to forget. The car was a black Audi Compact. An A3, chrome trim wheels. It was brand-new. She stepped back and looked at it. It was high spec, for a boy racer, but she could see that for a father with an infinite amount of money it would be a small car, a modest beginning.

She looked into the cabin. On the passenger side the footwell was full of brown smeared cloths, the door pocket stuffed full of them. The driver's side was clean.

The garage door behind her rattled open, the sudden slap of light startling her. Tayside coppers were outside with a van they were loaning them to get the car back to the lab. Morrow bent back to the vehicle, looking in from the front of the bonnet, and she could see that the thin veneer of dust on the dashboard stopped in the middle. The driver's side had been wiped clean.

Harris walked in, smiling, nodding at the Audi. "What d'you think?"

Morrow shrugged.

He was a little annoyed. "Oh, don't look so happy."

"I'm getting a bad smell off that wee guy."

FORTY-SEVEN

Thomas sat on the sofa in Ella's sitting room, facing the big window. A brutal shaft of light was coming over the lawn. He thought sometimes of moving. Getting up, getting a drink. He was hungry too. But there was so much to do that he couldn't move. He should go into the bedroom and speak to Ella. There must be something he could say to her, something that would make her snap out of it, beg her to get up, shout at her to stop loafing around. There had to be some single phrase that would help but he couldn't think clearly enough to work out what it was. And he needed to talk to Moira, apologize for knowing about Theresa, make her get a lawyer to protect them. He should call Squeak as well, find out what he was doing, telling Sholtham. He should chase up Dr. Hollis and ask when he was coming back to see Ella. He couldn't stand guard outside her bedroom for the rest of his life. And he was hungry.

Small tasks all, but they seemed insurmountable to him. He couldn't focus hard enough to identify the first action towards either of them.

Please don't kill yourself, Ella. That wouldn't work. It'll hurt Moira. No, that wouldn't do either. The phrase came to him, abrupt and heartfelt: *please don't leave me here.* He started to cry, his face yawned open, silent. *I can't do this anymore.*

He ordered himself to think other things.

He sat, blinking into the blinding light from the lawn, listening to the gentle burble of the television in Moira's rooms. Adverts.

She knew about Theresa now. And she knew that he knew as well. She'd be in there, in front of the telly, crying, gouging her scalp with her nails, feeling let down by Lars and him and everyone. Smoking certainly, maybe even holding a bottle of antidepressants. It was going to get worse. Theresa was smart and nasty. She'd sue Moira and get all the money. Other people must have known too, not just him. Lars must have taken Theresa to formal receptions and they'd feel the same as he did: he preferred Theresa.

He looked through the door to Ella's bedroom. She was on the bed, pinned to her back, her bare feet visible through the doorway.

The minute he went to the toilet or fell asleep Ella'd creep downstairs and get the gun and shoot herself. Lars had shown them all where the safe key was. She probably wouldn't do it right, either, just blow her eye out and bleed to death, shoot her nose off or something. Then people would laugh about it and say they couldn't even get that right, this family, couldn't even shoot themselves in the fucking face. Stander.

People emigrated at his age. It was up to him. Indignant self-disgust propelled his head up until he was looking straight into the sunshine. He stared into it until his eyes flashed white and ached. It was up to him. He stood up and walked out of the room.

Vision blurred from the brightness of the sun through the window, he ran his hand along the dado rail to guide himself to the top of the stairs, and stepped down, holding the banister until he got to the bottom. He blinked hard to restore his sight.

Lars's office was a cushion of quiet. Thomas stepped inside, looking left to right, which was silly because he knew exactly where the safe was. He walked halfway across until he was just past the desk, and stopped to brush his fingers over the desk top, where Lars's hands had been just before he walked out to the lawn. He felt better. As if Lars had given his approval or something.

He stepped over to the bookcase, to the phony book that looked no different from the real books because they were just as likely to be read. He pressed the sky-blue leather with gold writing on it and the spine of the book sprang towards him. The keys sat in a small, green felt insert.

Two keys, not big, old-fashioned, shackled together with a ring. Thomas took them out and found that he was sweating, for no reason really, and his mouth was filling up with saliva, as if he was going to be sick. He wondered if this was what Lars felt as he unloaded his wallet to the desk drawer and wrote his nasty suicide note, blaming Moira for what he was about to do, laying the blame at her door for him choosing to excuse himself from the coming years of humiliation.

Thomas shut the spine, hiding the fact that he had taken the keys, in case Moira glanced in and saw that he had been in the safe. He stepped over to the desk, crouched down to the footwell underneath and lifted the edge of the rug, revealing a brass handle fitted flush to the parquet. He flipped it up, lifted the small section of floorboard out and set it to the side.

There, the beige metal lid with red plastic finger holes. He slipped his fingers in and lifted it off like the lid on a cookie jar and found the safe lid. More beige metal, a cheap-looking brown plastic handle and the keyhole in the middle, like a navel. He fitted the key in, turned it and took the lid off. He dropped down, snaking his hand in through the narrow neck to the two-square-foot space underneath. Papers. A book. Some jewelry in suede envelopes. Thomas reached further down, leaning in so that his whole arm was swallowed by the floor, and felt the sharp edge of a box. He pulled the box out and, reverently using two hands, took off the lid: the snub Astra Cub, a solid, heavy handgun, the handle and barrel a single molding. Next to it, like bridesmaids, two spare magazines to match it.

A silly gun. Girl's gun. He looked at the barrel: Guernica, it said, Made in Spain. He saw Picasso's horse screaming at the sky, seen it in a book at school, Beany showed it to them but Thomas wasn't really listening. What he did remember was the image of the horse and he knew that the horse with the cartoon eyes was dying, that it didn't live to see the horrors of the Second World

War, and that seemed relevant somehow, a mercy.

He sat back on his haunches and looked at the gun. Guernica.

Playing a part, he stood up, put the gun in his back pocket and adjusted his stance. Wide legged, sneering, taller. He reached back and pulled the gun slowly — because he didn't know if it was cocked — pulled it slowly out of his pocket and held it in two hands, pointing it at the door to the hall.

"Ptchew," he said, lifting his hands in a slow-motion recoil. He smiled to himself. Felt better. He did it again. *"Ptchew."*

Still smiling softly he looked at the small black gun. Weighed a ton. A solid little friend. He put it on the desk and bent down, shutting the safe door but not locking it, leaving the keys sticking out and stacking the lid and floorboard panel under the desk.

He shouldn't leave the spare rounds lying around though, in case there was another gun somewhere. He put one in each front pocket of his jeans. Heavy. Maybe six rounds in each? Maybe eight in each, plus what was already in the gun. The gun. He lifted it, looked at it closely.

The trigger was silver and as solid as a knife. He squeezed it a fraction, felt it come to the point, graze the firing mechanism and let it fall back.

Do not, he remembered from somewhere, a film or a documentary or something, *do not* lock your elbows or the recoil will shatter the bones. Was it a sci-fi film? Maybe that was laser guns that did that. He should keep his elbows soft anyway, if he fired it, which he wouldn't.

He stopped suddenly and gave a small surprised laugh at himself. Why would he fire the gun? He only had it to keep it from Ella. He shook his head at the floor. What was he thinking?

His gaze bounced around the crescents and dots of the poplar-burr desk top. He was thinking about shooting someone. Part of him was thinking about it. A bad deep-down part. He didn't even know how to shoot.

It couldn't be that hard. In Uganda kids were soldiers in the army. They handled guns, shot people, cut arms and legs off, and they were drunk or on glue. Couldn't be too hard.

He was getting stuck here, the way he'd been stuck on the sofa upstairs. His eyes came to a rest on an inverted comma on the desk top. He was getting stuck. *I can't do this.* But he was doing it. He had saved

Ella from this gun. He was doing it.

He looked at the gun in his hand.

Solid. It had one button on it, a sliding button right next to the trigger, and he guessed that was the safety lock. He pushed it up and felt it click, pushed it down and up again, and down and up and down and put the gun in his back pocket.

Better. He felt better. His trousers were heavy now though. He took a few steps towards the door and found that the weight was comfortable to walk with. Better actually. He felt tethered to the ground, as if he was sinking into the earth.

He stood by the study door, hands gunfighter-wide at his thighs, elbows bent so recoil couldn't shatter his bones.

From upstairs, a whisper of sound, the voices and music from Moira's TV.

I am doing it, thought Thomas, and he walked off up the stairs.

FORTY-EIGHT

When she arrived at the station she was called straight into Bannerman's office. McKechnie wanted to brief her about the investigation into Grant Bannerman.

McKechnie wanted to make it clear that nothing had been proved against her boss. He had been found with the laptop in his home but they couldn't show intent to steal. The other claims against him were more serious though: bullying, mistreatment of junior officers, sending staff out to get him his lunch . . . Morrow lost her patience at that.

"Who?"

"Who what?" asked McKechnie keenly, hoping for a clue, she suspected.

"Who did he send out for his lunch?"

He looked at his papers. "Doesn't say."

"He brought in sarnies, every day. He's a drawer full of health bars, for f—" She caught her breath. "Look, sir, I've got two upstairs needing grilled and I don't believe any of this. Can we talk about it later?"

He slapped the folder shut. "Yes."

"Where is he now?"

"Suspension."

"He's sitting at home watching telly and I've got to do all this myself?"

McKechnie widened his eyes. "We have legal obligations, Morrow."

"I need to go back to London to question the other accused as well."

"People have a right to work in safety —"

"Safety? He's guilty of nothing but being unpopular, sir."

"Well, we have to investigate these things, the complaints —"

"With respect, sir, the complaints are bollocks. He's not coming back here, is he? After this. Even if he's innocent of everything, he's not coming back here. And unless you can get someone in, I'm the only senior officer and I'm about to go on maternity."

McKechnie knew all that already. She stood up, feeling reckless. "I'm gonnae" — she stopped herself — "get on with my job."

McKechnie stood up to meet her, a glint of an apology about him. "Morrow, this is the world we live in now."

"Aye." She opened the door and stepped

575

into the briefing room. Everyone was there. The night shift were gathering, the day shift hanging on to get the gossip. Everyone looked at her and most of them were smiling, thinking they'd done her a favor.

Morrow looked around at them. "You cowardly shits," she said, imagining her words being read out before a disciplinary committee, tempering them, keeping it vague. "You've no compassion for the bosses because you'll never be us." She saw them continue to smile but hide it under hands and cups. "We'll be an army of nothing but soldiers 'cause none of you'll step up."

She looked around to see if she'd gotten through to them and knew that she hadn't. Something snapped inside her. "Harris?"

He stood up at the back. "Ma'am."

"Get upstairs," she said, and a sudden flare of anger made her add, "you fucking arsehole."

Although Jonathon Hamilton-Gordon had asked for Doyle, his family had intervened and sent a friend to sit with him, just a friend, someone Jonathon knew personally. The man was ringing all sorts of alarm bells in Morrow. His clothes were too neat, he didn't make eye contact with the boy.

Though they sat next to each other at the table, their body language was cold. She felt sure he was a lawyer. The appropriate adult's job was to tell the person they were with what was going on, explain what the big words meant or read out things they couldn't if they had a learning disability. It was not to hand them slick legal advice, or give them tips on how to avoid charges.

She watched them on the remote view, worried about going in there with Harris. Leonard stood behind her; she looked worried too.

"That jumper is cashmere," she said, looking at the neat man's jersey.

Morrow looked at the jumper. It looked ordinary. It was green and had a crew neck. He had a shirt on underneath it. "Have you got X-ray vision or something?"

"It's the way it hangs," she explained. "It's thinner. I bet that cost about two hundred quid."

"No! Jerseys can't cost two hundred quid."

But Leonard was nodding, certain.

Morrow looked again. "They said he's a family friend. I don't think they've ever met before, what do you think?"

The boy and the man could have been strangers sitting next to each other on a bus. In London.

Harris appeared behind them, his mouth pinched, avoiding her eye. Morrow, still angry, turned and squared up to him. "Yeah?"

He looked past her to the screen. "We going in?"

"Aye," she said. "Come on." She swept past him and led the way down the corridor.

This interview room was big and clean.

The man was next to the wall and the boy on the outside. They stood up as Morrow and Harris came in, shook hands. Jonathon's hand was dry and he seemed very calm.

She let Harris take the inside seat, put her folder down in front of her chair and they fitted the cassettes, started the recording, drew their attention to the video camera. Neither of them asked for anything else to be explained to them, not for time frames or what was happening next. The man asked for no clarification on the charges as she read them out and the boy barely listened to the caution.

Then they all sat in silence for a while until Morrow looked across at the man as if she'd just realized he was there. "Sorry, what is your name again?"

"Harold."

"Whereabouts are ye from, 'Harold'?"

He blinked and cut her off. "Stirling. I live in Stirling."

"That's right, we have your address downstairs, don't we?"

Again he blinked and cut her off.

"Nice part of the world, out there, nice. What is it you do for a living?"

Harold sighed at this, and glared a prompt at Jonathon, who responded, "Aren't you supposed to be questioning me?"

She cocked her head at him. "Really?" She turned back to Jonathon. "Can you really have more to say after all that you said in front of Mr. Doyle? All that stuff you told us and physical evidence you gave us . . .."

Harris smirked next to her and she could see it made the boy angry.

"I do want to get this over and done with," he said, trying to appear helpful.

Morrow looked languorously through her notes. "Son, see whatever happens here? *Whatever* happens here, this is not going to be 'over and done with' anytime soon —"

"I didn't mean that," Jonathon said, "I meant these questions. I want to get these over and done with."

"What do you think is going to happen when these questions are over and done with?"

He shrugged carelessly, glanced at

Harold's hands, which were folded one gently over the other. Harold looked straight at her, defiant, proud. He genuinely thought he was getting bail for Jonathon. He'd told him he was too, which seemed unprofessional. Jonathon hadn't told him about the car or how much he'd said already, she realized.

"Hmm." She continued looking through her notes. "D'you watch a lot of cop shows on TV?"

He checked with Harold and Harold nodded him on. "No. I'm at boarding school, we don't get to watch much TV."

"You don't get to have a car either." She smiled at him. He didn't smile back. "No, the reason I'm asking is because I wonder if you've ever heard of 'the prisoner's dilemma'?"

"Is that a cop show?"

"No."

Jonathon looked quite amused by this train of conversation and pushed himself away from the table, swinging on the back two legs of the chair. "What is it then?"

"Two guys in two rooms being questioned about the same events. Yeah?"

He nodded.

"Both want to keep it a secret. Suppose, for example, they've done a bad thing." She

580

gave him a hard look. "If you can imagine that scenario."

He sucked his cheeks in as though killing a smile.

"These two guys in the two rooms have done a bad thing together. And they've been caught —"

"Or given themselves up," he said.

"What's the difference?"

"Well, in one scenario they're sneaking off," he smirked. "In the other they've — you know — done the deciding."

"I see." She nodded at Harold. "An interesting distinction. So the two guys are in two different rooms and neither of these guys knows what the other one is saying about what happened. They give different versions. I was out of the room the whole time, say stuff like that." She dropped her voice and smiled, conspiratorial, as if she was sharing a family receipt: "We work out what happened from the contradictions."

He let his chair drop forward onto all fours. "Don't they just blame each other?"

"Well, that can happen, yes, sometimes, classic episode." She nodded happily. "They give each other up. One says 'he did everything, I'm innocent,' the other one says, 'no, it was him, I'm the innocent party.' Quite the conundrum for the police. Then we have to fall back on our physical evidence, try to piece it together. Work out what happened. Course, it costs more because the case goes to court, everyone pleading innocence and that, but ye get that pay-off, you know?" She smacked her lips. "Sentences are much longer. The feeling that everything's been looked at and looked under, cross-examined, pulled apart . . ."

Jonathon smiled and licked his lips, pushed back, rocked his chair again. "Is that what's happening here?"

"No. Here you're saying he did it and you happen to have lots of physical evidence that he did it. In your version you did nothing and all the physical evidence about what you did is missing. Isn't that a stroke of luck? Apparently you were off saying your prayers while it happened."

He sat forward and nodded seriously. "OK."

She looked at him and at Harold and found them both looking smug. She turned a page of her notes. "Oh." She looked closer at the page. "Oh, dearie me. Two sets of footprints are stamped all over Sarah's soft face." She looked up and smiled. "What kind of prayer is that? I'm not religious so —"

Jonathon shot forwards. "No —"

"OK." Harold stood up. "We're stopping here for a comfort break."

Morrow looked confused.

"That," he said, "is aggressive, intimidating questioning of a minor."

She stood up very slowly, holding her stomach and giving him a wolfish smile. "Harold, are you a lawyer?"

Harold snorted indignantly through his nose. "We want a comfort break."

Morrow slapped shut the folder on the desk. "Take as long as you like. I'm finished. You'll be taken downstairs now and charged."

Jonathon stood up. "Then can I go home?"

Morrow widened her eyes at Harold. "No, Jonathon, you'll be taken to court and they decide."

"And they'll let me go home?" Suddenly panicked, he looked tearfully from Harris to Morrow to Harold.

No one answered. In the pause Morrow saw something die in Jonathon Hamilton-Gordon's eyes.

She slipped his gaze, ashamed of the glee she felt at the death of hope in a child. She picked up her folder. "You'll be taken downstairs now and charged with Sarah Erroll's murder . . ."

FORTY-NINE

A wall, a gray wall, not the car. Not in the car now, out of the car. A gray wall in a bare cell. Nothing in it but a short bench attached to a wall. When he sat down on it he was facing the door with a handle and a lock, a big lock that had screws in it and a slat for looking through and it was too much information so he shut his eyes and didn't look anymore and found he could breathe. It was a small room. Thomas nodded to himself. It was a small room.

Outside, in the corridor, people moved around, shuffling, speaking sometimes. That was too much. He was sliding.

Feet moved towards his door, a hand slid over the metal, precursor to a key jabbing blindly at the lock. Thomas sat with his eyes shut and shuddered.

The door opened, light burned into him, his chin buckled at the horror of being looked at, and a commanding, fatherly voice said, "Out, mate. Come on."

He was shivering. His hands were welded to the bench, his ankles soft at the thought of having to stand up, step out into the world and be seen. *I can't do this.*

"Come on, *out.*"

Thomas stood up. He staggered once but managed to stand, opened his eyes wide enough to look at the ground in front of him. He shuffled over the threshold, into the day, into the corridor with other people in it.

"They're waiting for you upstairs. Scottish. *Two women.*" He said it as if it was lucky, as if he'd lucked out having two women to question him. Thomas stood still. The man seemed to be looking at him, he saw his feet pointed towards him. "Got an appropriate adult to talk to you. Tell you what's going on."

He was staring at him; Thomas felt he needed to show him that he wasn't mental. He looked up at the policeman, a fat man, and was surprised to hear himself say, "OK."

Relieved, the officer jolted forward to a side door, keeping Thomas in front of him. He showed him around the corridor to the meeting room, pointing him in the right direction with jabs of his fat finger.

Into a room, a bigger room, no windows.

585

A camera in the high corner, sitting on a corner shelf made of plywood. A man at a table. Gray hair, gray face, gray fingernails.

The man smelled of cigarettes. He slumped the same way Thomas slumped. They took either side of the table, knees avoiding the table legs, facing away from each other. Thomas found it hard to listen. He was to be questioned by officers from Strathclyde Police about a murder. He could answer or not answer but both would damn him. He'd had a gun and bullets on him. This was bad. He would have to explain. Explain. He, the cigarette man, the stale, smoky, depressed man would explain when things happened. Thomas stopped listening. When he tuned back in the man told him he could ask. He didn't really know what he was supposed to ask about but his lips were too heavy to ask for clarification.

"THOMAS!" The man wanted his attention. Thomas gave it to him. "Do you understand me?"

His teeth were as yellow as kippers, as if he'd been sucking his cigarettes, dipping them in yellow wine and sucking the brown tar and rolling it between his teeth. He was disgusting. His gray eyebrows were raised in a gray question. Thomas nodded to make him stop asking him things. He nodded and nodded and then knew it was too much and stopped.

The man got up slowly, moved around to the wall behind Thomas, pulling a chair over. Thomas didn't turn but heard him sit down by the wall. When he turned to look the man had a spiral notebook flipped to the first page and a pen poised over it, ready to write. He leaned his head back against the wall and shut his eyes. Thomas turned away.

They waited in the silent room for a long time.

Ella came to see him off. The police arrived. Moira let them in and brought them upstairs and said "There he is," or "He's there," something simple, and they stood over him reciting a sort of prayer, monotone. They waited for him to react and then they took him, lifting him from Ella's sofa by the elbows, telling him "Up" and "Come on, up onto your feet."

It felt so right for them to come. Like hall monitors finding a lost first-year in a corridor and taking him to his classroom. Like an unaccompanied child holding the hand of a pretty stewardess. It was too much for him to take in, all the flight boards when he couldn't read very well, all the time zones, because Mexico City was a long way away and he didn't even know when to eat. Lars left on business the day after he arrived.

The hall monitors noticed his trousers sagging. What is this in your pocket. Sorry, spread your arms, yes, just a moment, no, stay that way. Thanks. Anything else? Any needles on you?

Ella got out of bed. She was in the doorway between her living room and her bedroom and she looked at him and she caught his eye and she saw then, that he was where she was, but he'd never had the chance to say it or tell her. They spoke to each other as two strange men in uniforms patted his legs and pockets and found the clips. She watched them take the gun from his pocket and she licked her lips and glanced back at him. She looked hurt, too depressed for palliative lies. She looked hurt but she blinked and pressed her lips together, part reproach, part apology.

Moira had changed her clothes. She had changed into the leather trousers from the stairs and a cream blouse with ruffles all down the front. She was gulping for air and tugging at the ruffles and a price tag hung from the label at the back.

She couldn't come with him, she told the

police stewardesses, because her daughter was gravely ill and she had called the doctor and he was due at any moment. There was no one else. To go with him. There was no one else. She tugged the ruffles on her shirt so hard the front of her bra was visible and beneath that, on her stomach, a wrinkled crease like a smile. There was no one else.

He was outside then, suddenly, in the open air, a hand on his head, pressing hard, making him corkscrew at the knees, until they sat him in the back seat and shut the door. He looked back up to the door and saw her, Ella. Tiny. She stood in the huge entrance, watching him drive away, her mouth slack, tears rolling down her cheeks. Moira behind her, putting a hand on her shoulder and Ella, feral, snapping her teeth at Moira's hand.

In the still room, the door opened. Two people came in — one round like Santa Claus, one a slim woman. He looked up. Two suits, navy blue and black. Slim was small, big nose, pretty. The other, blonde hair, tall, big shoulders, dimples. Amazonian. Pregnant. Stern.

Folder on the table. A green cardboard folder with sheets of lined foolscap, scribbled on, handwritten. Photos of things.

He could see the top of the pictures.

Introductions. Names. Cassette tapes. He'd never seen one before. Out of the cellophane wrapper, into a machine. A waspish buzz filled the room and the pregnant one asked him his name.

"Thomas Anderson." He was surprised by how well it had gone, his speaking. His voice sounded fine.

She asked him another question, did he know what was going on, or something, and he said yes. But then it was dates, and that Monday, and he didn't really know what she was asking about. The sentences were too long, he couldn't hold the head until she got to the tail of these great snaky sentences.

They looked at each other for a while. She asked if he was all right. He said he was.

"Do you know Jonathon Hamilton-Gordon?"

He caught a breath and shrugged with one shoulder.

"The boys at school call him," she glanced at her notes, " 'Squeak.' "

"I'm at school with him."

"Do you know him?"

He looked at the women. The pregnant one was looking at him intently, blue eyes heavy-lidded. The pretty one looked hard at the table. This was an important question. His future might hang in the balance but he couldn't focus. This was a trap.

"No. I don't know him." This was a trap trap trap.

"He says he knows you."

"We don't know each other." That was true.

"Have you spoken to him since you left school on Tuesday?"

"No."

"You didn't phone each other?"

Just say no. Say no. "No."

"Did he call you?"

The sim card was in the toilet in Biggin Hill airfield. They couldn't prove Squeak had called him or that it was his mobile number. It was in the toilet.

"We don't know each other." But Donny McD had the same number for him. Lie to them. Just say no. "He phoned me but I don't know him, I didn't even answer the phone. I don't know him." That was true. That bit was true.

"You don't know him?"

"No." He said it certainly, knowing he was on safe ground, knowing it was true.

"How did you know he phoned you if you didn't answer?"

"Well . . ." How did he know? "Well, his

name came up on the screen."

"What did it say?"

"Said 'Squeak.' "Thomas blushed because what she said next was obvious:

"You don't know him but you had his number in your phone, listed under his nickname?"

Thomas blushed and shuddered. Stander. Vulnerable. Things to hide. Found out. He felt himself slide sideways, as though he was melting, as though the heat of shame had melted half his face and he was melting sideways through the room like a pool of mercury flinching from her touch. But the questions went on as he flowed downhill, about Monday night and Sarah Erroll until he felt the words pop from his mouth.

"Her address was on Lars's phone."

A pause. "When did you get it?"

"January."

"Months ago. Why did you go to her house?"

"Lars —"

"Lars sent you?" She was hungry now the answers were coming, interrupted him when he was fishing a sentence out from deep down. He looked at her hands, rolling his eyes back to tell her how hard it was, speaking, and she sat back, leaving him room.

"Lars took me out. Sunday. Sunday before

that Monday. *Ice cream.*"

Lars took him out for ice cream. *For ice cream.* As if he was Ella. And in the room were other men in suits with kids, unhappy men and unhappy children who bore a faint resemblance to one another, like a grooming parlor for incestuous pedos. Thomas was the oldest by years. Lars bought him the biggest ice cream and he knew the news was going to be bad. He thought Lars had cancer. But it wasn't cancer.

"What did he say to you on that Sunday?"

The memory made Thomas feel so heavy he could barely shrug.

At the sprinkles: I have another wife. Digging through vanilla and bloody sauce, crystals of ice binding the balls of ice cream together. Other children. Very much want you to meet. Philip. Fillip. Fillip. And a photo, smiling fillip. Beachy smiles. Down to the fruit, pointless, as if the damage of the sick-making cream could be mitigated by tinned pineapple, cut small into little rays of syrup-sun. Coming to St. Augustus. You and he will be friends. And everyone will know you are a cunt. And everyone will laugh in your fucking face because you were never the One Son, never the only begotten. And Thomas asked his father, why have you forsaken me? And his father told him not to be a child and waved to the waitress for the bill.

In the present, in the room, the women were looking at him, craning in to hear his thoughts. He spoke:

"Got another family. Another son. Coming to *my school.* I was upset. Thought it was her." He looked at the green folder. "Sarah."

"Did you tell Squeak about it?"

"Only because he had the car. We don't know each other." And they didn't. They really didn't.

"Did you go there to kill her?"

"No. Scare her. Lars." He fell away to muttering the middles of words floating in space — impress him — stand up — don't take shit — know he'd love it.

Did he kill Sarah Erroll?

Floating off in words, a cloud of mumbles, a stormy cloud churning words and smack on the table and a loud shout — *Did he kill Sarah Erroll?*

Thomas looked at the pregnant woman, at this virgin filled with the promise of a new life, blonde, like Mary in the nativity, blonde and his face began to cry, his eyes began to cry and he told her what he thought. "Worse. Standing. Watching. Doing *nothing.* It's worse."

She showed him photos of the house, the bedroom, the kitchen, of Sarah Erroll at the foot of the stairs, her face gone, her head gone, her life gone, and he thought of the horse in Guernica and he thought of the lucky wasps dying and he lost all his words. Except one word. And he said that one over and over, always with the same intonation, an incantation: *worse.*

And then they put him back into the small room and let him sleep.

Morrow stood in the security queue at Gatwick airport, seventy people in front of her, but ready, holding her laptop and a zip-lock plastic bag with a lonely ChapStick in it, waiting. Last flight home. They were lucky. Leonard was behind her, carrying the notes. The babies were leaping hard on her pelvis, cheerleaders for life, telling her not to give up, not to get sucked down.

It was the hardest interrogation she'd ever done. Low before she started, tired before she started, she saw the despair in Thomas Anderson and knew what he was thinking though he said very little. Lars had killed him over the ice cream. Lars had wiped out his significance and his identity over the ice cream. He had wiped out the meaning of his mother. There was another. He had wiped out the significance of him by having another son, loving another son, and she knew from her own experience that what haunted him more than anything was the suspicion that his father loved the other son and was kind to him and proud of him. Danny had that same look in his eye, a lack, a suspicion that there were children in the world who were beloved when he wasn't. That's what she couldn't look at in him. That's what she had avoided all these years.

The queue shuffled forward. Around her people began to unpack, loosen belts, undo their laces in preparation.

The carnage was her father's fault. Lars Anderson's fault, not Thomas's, not Danny's. They were told too early that they didn't matter, that their God-like mothers were just shags. Sarah Erroll wasn't Thomas's fault. She couldn't be his fault because he was too young to know that the only real defiance would be to stop the cycle of damage, stop it all and make the other boy his real brother.

The queue moved closer to the security arch and Leonard leaned towards her. "Did he tell the truth?"

She didn't pad her sentences. Morrow liked that about her. She shrugged back. "I think he did. Do you?"

Leonard leaned away and smacked her lips, thinking for a moment. "You think he just watched?"

"What do you think?"

"I don't know . . . he could be off his head because of his dad dying as well."

"His wee sister's ill too, the attending officer said." She saw herself abruptly as a small child and Danny watching her in the playground with those haunted eyes and she began to cry like a small girl, covering her mouth and sobbing and trying to slap it off with her sleeve. "For fuck's sake."

Leonard handed her a packet of tissues and pretended not to notice.

When they got through the arch the security officer called Morrow aside for a search. She was sun-wrinkled, a maternal fifty-something, and stroked her carefully across her stomach. Morrow saw her glancing at her red eyes. When she moved down to stroke her legs with long, pronouncedly non-sexual sweeps of her hand she asked, "You all right, love?"

"Aye, I'll be all right."

The woman stood up and looked at her stomach. "How far on are you?"

"Five months."

She held Morrow's eye. She didn't believe her, thought she was sneaking on to have

597

the baby on the plane.

"Twins," explained Morrow.

"Oh," the woman smiled. "No wonder you're crying."

The search finished with a pat on the back and a call of good luck and Morrow collected her bag. They walked around to the café nearest to their gate.

"Coffee?" asked Leonard.

"Get me a tea. I've got a call to make."

Leonard went off and Morrow took out her mobile. No answer. It was late so she left a message:

"Hello, this is Alex Morrow, leaving a message for Val MacLea. I've changed my mind about talking to you about John McGrath . . . my nephew, John McGrath. If you think I can be of any use I'd be happy to talk to you, any time. Call me back."

FIFTY

Thomas was in the library reading a book about the Second World War when they came for him.

"Anderson, Thomas," shouted McCunt from the door.

Thomas stood up immediately, reflexively, and turned to face the call. McCunt was a nice man, they called him that fondly, to hide the fact that they liked him because he never tried to pretend he was anything other than a prison guard and always gave a warning before putting anyone on report, gave them a chance to dodge it.

"Out," said McCunt, stepping back, making room for him to move.

A hand on the table slid over to Thomas's place, asking for the book he'd been reading.

Thomas pushed it across the table. The other boy had a shaved head to show off his fighting scars. They were both reading the same book, didn't often have library time together and Thomas had got in first today. They'd talked about the book but Thomas suspected they were reading it for different reasons, that they were taking different sides.

"Move," said McCunt, louder this time.

Thomas went over to him, slipped out into the dark corridor and turned back for further directions. McCunt shut the door, listened for the lock and then turned to him, gave a friendly nod that looked like a head-butt.

Thomas swithered left and right. "Where am I going, sir?"

McCunt nodded left. "Visiting, son."

It was the wrong time for visiting but Thomas didn't want to seem insubordinate so he took a couple of steps down the corridor before he said, "But it's not visiting though."

McCunt grunted and came after him, shepherding him down the corridor. "Yeah, you're wanted in visiting, though."

Thomas's stomach tightened and he stopped still. McCunt almost bumped into him. "It's not my mum, is it?"

"No," McCunt was reassuring, "no, it's a lawyer's visit, son, just a lawyer's visit."

"Oh."

Thomas walked on, down the corridor, keeping his eyes down. The lino had been buffed to a glint by the cleaning crew but the smell of heavy disinfectant they used for mopping still clung to the skirting. The smells in the remand block were all pungent, the smell of shit or piss or cum, the stench of onions or mince or pine, all of them concentrated, overwhelming, engulfing. He hated it when he first came, felt as if he was drowning in smell, but he liked it now.

Thomas wasn't due a lawyer's visit. His court-appointed lawyer was lazy and slack. Something must have happened. He wondered if Squeak had killed himself.

They took the full length of the corridor to the far door, passing a kitchen vent, walking through a cloud of eggy sponge. The warm wet of spring was in there too, the miracle smell of grass growing. Through the breeze-block wall on their left the Seg boys were running in circles. Through the thunder of their feet Thomas imagined Squeak hanging, lying, bleeding, and felt sad for him, glad for everyone else, but sad for Squeak, stupid, broken, canine Squeak. *I won't tell them what you did,* as if they themselves didn't know who had done what to Sarah Erroll, as if moral guilt was like playing tag and Squeak could pass it on by

601

saying it. His thoughts were broken by the instructor's hollering through the wall.

They reached the locked door at the end of the corridor and McCunt called a redundant, "Stop!"

Thomas smiled and turned back, saw a little smirk on McCunt's mouth as he reached for the pad and looked up at the camera.

The door buzzed and McCunt pulled it open, stepping back to let him through. Nicer corridor. Less smell, less buff on the floor too because they were timed here when they cleaned, weren't allowed to linger because it was less secure.

Paler gray walls, windows looking out over a courtyard with grass in it, paintwork less chipped.

They walked down to the visiting rooms' doors. At the far end was the communal visit room, firmly locked because it led straight out of the prison. Before that, five doors, all the same gray with a bigger than normal window, down at waist height, frosted in parts.

McCunt pulled the keys from his trouser pocket, feeling along the chain at his belt for them, and unlocked the door marked "3," holding it open.

Thomas stopped in the doorway. It wasn't

his gray-faced crumpled lawyer. Sitting at the table, so big and healthy and prosperous-looking he almost filled the room, was Squeak's dad.

He stood up. "Thomas." No trace of tears in his eyes, no redness, no grievous blank stare. Squeak not dead. "Hello," he said, his voice a cigar smoke rumble, rich as brandy sauce, and the accent a welcome, unfamiliar, RP lilt. Everyone in here spoke in ragged cockney and Manc., some rolling west coast African, some London West Indian, no newsreader Estuary.

McCunt nodded him into the room. Thomas took two steps and the door shut behind him, locked, but McCunt's shadow stayed in the glass.

"You're not my lawyer."

"Sit down."

Thomas moved around the table, took the seat Mr. Hamilton-Gordon was gesturing to, reflecting that he had the habit of obedience now. He went where he was told, sat for as long as he was told. He was fully conditioned now and should be careful about that.

Mr. Hamilton-Gordon was a lawyer, Thomas remembered. "Oh, you're *a* lawyer," he said.

Mr. Hamilton-Gordon sat down too.

"How are you, Thomas. Well, I hope?"

It was nice to hear the creamy accent, the soft lyrical timbre of his voice. Thomas had known Squeak's dad for most of his life, through photos mostly. He always looked cross and didn't alter his dress according to climate. He wore uncompromising tweed jackets to dinner in St. Lucia, on yachts off Monaco, at dinners in Hong Kong. He was fat but wore bespoke, which did him lots of favors. Today he had a green tweed jacket and pink trousers on. No tie. Weekend home clothes. His hair was a silvery white, touches of black still there, but thick and strong hair, quite long for a corporate lawyer, quite lush. He seemed too colorful for the drab gray room.

He looked at Thomas thoughtfully. His eyebrows grew skyward but had been pruned by a barber: wiry antlers, blunted.

"You're not my lawyer," said Thomas again.

"No, I'm not." He crossed his arms.

"Why are you here?"

"Talk to you. This," he flicked his finger back and forth between them, "bad blood. No use. Got to stick together. Work it out between us." He crossed one leg over the other, the outstretched foot boxing Thomas in against the wall, claiming him back from

604

the prison. He swung the foot slowly, a pendulum on a venerable clock.

"Agree? Thomas?"

He gave a reflexive "Yes, sir," sharp and quick, but Mr. Hamilton-Gordon wasn't a PO, Thomas didn't have to call him "sir," it was a stupid error. He said "sorry" and the big smart man nodded, frowned at the table as if he understood. "Army," he said, somewhat irrelevantly but Thomas understood him too — Squeak's dad was putting it in a frame of reference he could understand.

"Thomas, let me say firstly how sorry I am about your father." He had one hand on the table, the leg across Thomas on the other side, circling him, a formalized embrace. "He was an amazing man."

"You knew each other?"

"We did," he said sadly. "We did, we did."

"From?"

"School."

"Oh, yes."

"I was at St. Augustus two years below your father. He was always an extraordinary man. But flawed." He looked up through his eyebrows to check that Thomas thought that fair and he did. "He was, he was flawed." He tapped a forefinger on the table top. "His mother was very ill when I knew him."

"Was she?" Neither Lars nor Moira had much time for family recollections. He didn't know anything about Lars's mother but that she was dead.

"She killed herself." He was looking at Thomas through the gelded eyebrows again, tense.

"I didn't know that."

"Your father was younger than you are now. He was at school at the time. It was very difficult for him." He watched his finger tap out a rhythm and stopped. "Don't remember the old man too harshly, is what I'm saying. He was flawed but he had a lot to overcome. And he did so. Magnificently."

Thomas nodded to be agreeable, but thought that whatever Lars had been through, he was still a big shouty fucker.

"You must understand what he over-came."

"Yeah," said Thomas. "OK."

"Are you angry with him?" He flashed a joyless smile.

Thomas considered the question. "I don't think about him at all now."

He smiled again, a flash of teeth, gums, eyes unmoving. "Yes. Are you well in your-self?"

"Fine," he said and wondered about Squeak, was he fine? Was he dead? "Why?"

606

"Well," the breath left the big man's body through the jungle of his nostril hair, noisy, "runs in families, suicide, yes?"

"Really?"

"Yes." Matter-of-fact. Scientific observation. "Generation to generation. Once the thought is there, it's always a possibility . . ." It sounded as if Mr. Hamilton-Gordon was suggesting Thomas might like to kill himself.

"I'm not going to do it," said Thomas and watched for a reaction. There was none.

"I've spoken to your mother. She's very worried about you."

"I'm in prison, charged with a disgusting murder. She should be worried."

"She's also worried about your sister. Ella has been taken off the antipsychotics."

"Oh, thank God." She couldn't even speak on them. Thomas called her once a week and the nurse held the phone up and she breathed and even from her breathing he could tell she was sad.

"She's been moved to a private clinic."

"They took her off them?"

"It's private. Very expensive. A work colleague of mine is on the board." He looked up again. "Your mother is without funds at the moment, I don't know if you're aware of her situation, if she spoke —"

"She won't speak to me."

"Hmm." He wasn't surprised at that.

"Have you spoken to her?"

"Yes. She's as well as can be expected with you in here and Ella so . . . ill."

Thomas smirked to himself. Moira's main concern was never himself and Ella, he could see that now. Moira's main concern was always Moira. And still he craved her attention. Even though she wouldn't answer the phone or hung up when she realized it was him calling. Even though he knew she had no real excuse for abandoning him as she had. There were boys in the Segs for sex crimes whose families came once in a while. She wasn't even that far away. He'd mapped it during a moment of longing for her.

"The care Ella needs is very expensive. She may be there for some time."

"Who organized that?"

"I did."

"Well, thank you —"

"I'm very angry with you, Thomas." It was abrupt, but his voice was flat. "I'm angry with you for taking Jonathon with you to that house. You can understand that, can't you?"

Thomas saw then that Squeak's dad wasn't angry with him. He was fucking furious with him. He was so angry he was sweating lightly. Tiny globes of perspiration prickled out of enlarged pores on his forehead. His forefinger began to tap out a jig on the table again. "You shouldn't involve others in your personal problems, Thomas. It's bad form." He stopped speaking, grunted lightly at the back of his throat, stopping the things he mustn't say from coming out. And took a deep breath. "But we're here now. Who's going to represent you?"

"When?"

"Who is your lawyer?"

"Why are you asking me that?"

The eyebrows rose slowly. "You need a good lawyer. One always needs a good lawyer. Do you have a family law firm?"

Thomas was sure they couldn't afford them, even if they had. "I don't think we do, anymore, no."

"It's expensive."

"Probably."

"Mother selling the house, yes?"

"I think so."

"It will be on the market for months. The market's very slow. Big houses, fewer buyers, harder to sell."

"Yes."

Mr. Hamilton-Gordon leaned in, very intimate, finger tiptapping the table near to Thomas's bare arm. "Let's talk outcomes," he said seriously. "The difference for someone on this charge with a good lawyer, as compared with a lackadaisical one, is twelve years. Are you aware of that?"

"That much?" Thomas affected surprise and Mr. Hamilton-Gordon responded warmly: "Yes, twelve extra years in prison, without the possibility of parole. Instead of getting out at twenty-five you'd be leaving prison at thirty-six, if you don't have a good lawyer." Mr. Hamilton-Gordon sat back. He cleared his throat and made his play. "Thomas, I am going to get you a lawyer. And pay for Ella's care. In return, I want you to do something for me. Yes?"

Thomas looked blank.

"Yes?" Prompt, prompt. Hamilton-Gordon looked at Thomas's mouth, willing him to move his lips in the affirmative. Thomas didn't say anything. Far away, through walls and doors, a trolley wheel squealed like a stuck pig.

"What?" asked Thomas.

"Because you are going to tell them that you're responsible. That you took Jonathon there. That he stood by and tried to stop you. Do you understand? In return I will support Ella and your mother, maintain your family until you are able to do so yourself. You're a bright young man by all accounts, and this is by no means the end of everything — you have a future, rest assured. Does that seem fair to you?"

"It does." And it did, it really did. He'd taken Squeak there, so he was responsible in a way. It did seem fair, even if something about it bothered him. He couldn't think what it was but it was a sharp annoyance, insistent, urgent as an angry cold sore.

"Well, Thomas, I'm very glad we've reached this accommodation, I think you'll find, when you look back on these events later in life —"

He talked but Thomas was distracted by a tiny movement on his head: Mr. Hamilton-Gordon's hair was moving.

A thick strand of silver was shifting on his crown, left, up, on its own, he was sitting perfectly still, talking in his low rumble about how much sense everything made to everyone and how everything would be fine and it would all be over soon.

The hair slowly rose to an upright position, like a car aerial, pointing at the ceiling. It looked so bizarre Thomas couldn't hear what he was saying for watching it.

". . . many men of substance, looking back on the misadventure of youth . . ."

And then, as Thomas watched, through the hair, a face appeared over the horizon of his head, so completely lit and perfectly crisp that Thomas could make out the Rorschach inkblot on its face.

A wasp, crawling through his thick hair, a wasp.

Mr. Hamilton-Gordon saw him looking at his head, felt the movement suddenly and panicked. He swatted his head, slapping himself. A little black and yellow body tumbled off, legs wriggling, falling upside down. It landed on his shoulder, bounced, fell again, under the table. Thomas could hear it: *Bzzbzz*.

Thomas stood up suddenly, letting his chair fall behind him, and looked down at the floor, at the wasp, dazed but struggling to its feet. *Bzzzbzzbzz*. Thomas couldn't stop watching it.

A slap on the table. Hamilton-Gordon was very angry. ". . . Trying to have a serious conversation with you . . ."

Thomas grinned and looked down at Squeak's dad, looming over him, aware that he was frightening the powerful man. He reached over slowly and slapped the table himself, loud, the flat of his hand *bzzbzz*ing with the force of the blow.

Hamilton-Gordon stood up to meet him. But he wasn't as tall as Thomas, only came to his chin and Thomas looked down at him. It wasn't even an analogy. He had been waiting, somehow, to see another wasp, as if when they came back it would all go away, this bubble of time, make sense, but the wasp was just a wasp. It wasn't epiphany, it wasn't an analogy.

"Thomas!" shouted Mr. Hamilton-Gordon. "It's just a wasp."

Thomas began to laugh. It meant nothing. It was all just random stuff and deaths. He laughed and laughed until Squeak's dad banged on the door and asked to be let out. He laughed all the way back to the library.

And even lying in his bed that night, as he fell asleep, a fat warm smile nestled on his face because none of it meant anything else. It was all just random stuff that happened.

FIFTY-ONE

Leonard's friend had taken months to draw up her initial findings over the blood splatters. She had submitted them on a DVD with a forty-page explanation that amounted to a thesis. Every point was footnoted, every authority cited. She had even put a cover letter in with the DVD and the thesis explaining that her graphics had been borrowed from the computer games department and she would, in the fullness of time, devise her own graphics, but, for the sake of time efficiency, for the benefit of the particular case in which they were engaged, she had resorted to —

Morrow left the letter in her in-tray with the thesis and put the DVD into her hard drive.

A screen, offering her a selection of episodes, all blank blue except the first one marked "Case I*." She clicked it with her mouse.

A photograph of the stairs at Glenarvon, seen from the foot, a doctored version of the scene-of-crime photos with Sarah's body wiped out and replaced with a graft of green from further up the stairs. The screen was still for a moment, and then an aerial view of the stairs with three sets of feet at the top, imprints of feet. Bare feet, Sarah, next to the banister, toes deep in the carpet, quite distinct from the soles. At the other side of the stairs, next to the wall, one pair of shoes with the three circle marks of the St. Augustus shoes. A slash across one sole, the left sole. Slightly behind Sarah, between her and the slash shoes, another pair. This pair had a distinctive dot at the heel. Morrow knew what it was: a black pebble from the Glenarvon driveway. They'd found it in Thomas's right shoe, the pair Jonathon had bagged carefully and hidden in his room.

She wasn't ready for it when Sarah's feet took off down the stairs — jumped slightly in her chair, glanced, embarrassed, around the office.

When she looked back at the screen it was happening in slow motion: Sarah's feet flew down the stairs, two at a time and then, out of nowhere, hair fell from her invisible head, she didn't see it but Morrow felt Sarah's head yanked back as someone grabbed her hair and pulled out chunks, letting them drop gracefully to the ground. The slash shoes had grabbed her hair and then Sarah's invisible bottom impressed itself on the carpet, her feet twisted against the green and then her back landed on the steps, like a ghost sinking into green marzipan.

Feet were by her, kicking, sending graceful red splatters over the carpet, settling like scarves over one another. And one set of feet moving by her, keeping balance by shifting their weight, taking a stair, going back up, holding the banister. And the other set, creeping down, keeping by the wall, tight to the wall.

Jonathon Hamilton-Gordon's heels clung to the skirting board, keeping as far away as he could, trying to pass at one point, and retreating, as Thomas Anderson kicked and kicked and kicked the red out of Sarah, until she was wiped out.

FIFTY-TWO

Kay waited in the outer office, sitting on a settee that was too low to the ground for there to be any dignity on it. The receptionist was nice enough but Kay knew and she knew that she was better than her: better dressed, nicer hair, better clothes. They were about the same age, 45–60.

"Could I get you some tea? Some coffee?"

Kay waved her away. "Fine, thanks."

She wanted to get in and out and away.

It was a nice office anyway, wood paneling everywhere and the carpets were nice, plain. The place seemed very quiet, which Kay liked, everything seemed muffled. It had taken so long, she was pleased. She'd have a reprieve to enjoy the bowl. She had stopped using it as an ashtray.

She slipped her hand into her open handbag, face still pointing innocently up to the window but her mind and heart were with her fingertips. She traced a snaking silver coil through pools of brilliant blue and red, red as deep as an embrace, as deep as blood, as deep and luminous as love. Her fingertips bumped over the round dots around the top and she thought of a woman, a washer-woman or a farmer, coming home with cold tired hands and sewing that pattern on their runners and looking at them in the morning and knowing they were beautiful, that they had made something beautiful. She thought of a big woman walking along a mud track, in big boots and gray clothes, a long skirt trimmed with heavy mud and a beatific smile on her coarse face because she had wrought something beautiful and it meant something about her. She knew it was a good and godlike thing. And she loved what it said about her, because she was more than the beasts of the earth or the indignities of being alive. This woman wouldn't mind that her work was copied by others and that she was forgotten, she would glory in the journey of her creation. She didn't need to own it for it to continue to exist. She had brought a beautiful thing into an ugly world.

Kay withdrew her fingers from her bag, and she hid her face at the window until the sadness had passed. Cars passed below the window, a bus, a man on a bicycle struggled up the hill and panted as he stopped at the lights.

"Miss Murray?" Kay turned to the receptionist. "If you'd like to go through now."

She gathered her things, her ever-present poly bag, her coat and handbag. She wanted to touch the bowl again, just once more but told herself that was enough now. The receptionist stood at her desk and held out a hand to the wood-paneled corridor behind her.

"First door," she said, watching Kay, making sure she found it.

The door was open and Mr. Scott was standing by his desk, looking himself, a neat wee dick, expression hidden behind his stupid wee glasses.

He shook her hand like a doctor. "Miss Murray, won't you sit down?"

Kay didn't. She dropped her bags on the chair and reached into her handbag, bringing out first the watch. She'd wrapped it in kitchen roll so she wouldn't have to see it again, because it reminded her of Joy and the Day She Died. She didn't think she would feel so sad about the watch here, in the dark wee office, handing over that last thing of Mrs. Erroll's. She didn't even like that fucking watch.

And then she took a deep breath, saw the

coarse Russian farmer woman smile a consolation, and reached into her bag for the bowl. She put it on the desk without looking at it. She tore her hand away and picked up her things, cleared her throat.

" 'S that it?"

"Miss Murray." Mr. Scott seemed pleased it had gone so smoothly, that there had been no tussle for the goods. "Miss Murray, I have some surprising news for you."

She looked at him, saw the dawn of a happy smile break on his face. He took a deep breath. "Joy Erroll left you everything."

She didn't understand. "Everything what?"

"Oh, the house, the money, Sarah left a lot of savings, a *very* large amount of cash was found in her house, all the movables, the ownership of the land leased to the kennels, the balance of Joy's savings which again, were not inconsiderable . . ."

Kay busied her face with the far wall as he spoke. She was crying, her face awash, blinded and seeing nothing but the face of Joy.

"Joy's will — in the event of Sarah dying intestate, the entire estate defers to you."

No. No, no way was that possible. "Joy Erroll was nuts. How does that work?"

"Sarah had power of attorney and she cosigned the will in the first year you were there. Everything comes to you." He slid into his seat, a hungry little smile on his face. "Aren't you lucky?" He had a page in front of him and his index finger was drawing an eight in the top corner.

Kay pointed at the bowl. "That?"

"Yes, that's included in the estate."

Kay reached out, her hand hovering over the rim. She picked it up without looking at it and held it tight.

A coarse Russian woman collapsed on a dirt road, buried her face in her mud-splattered skirts and sobbed.

ACKNOWLEDGMENTS

A great many thanks to Jon, Jade and Reagan for sorting out the second half of this book, which was, ahem, a bit messy. Also everyone at Orion for generally jollying me along and Peter and Henry for all their hard work and support.

Also thanks to Stevo, Edith, Fergus, Ownie.

To the Jocks in their eyes: may you burn in hell for what you done to me.

ABOUT THE AUTHOR

Denise Mina is the author of *Slip of the Knife, The Dead Hour, Field of Blood, Deception,* and the Garnethill trilogy, *Garnethill, Exile,* and *Resolution.* She won the John Creasey Memorial Award for best first crime novel. She lives in Glasgow, Scotland, with her family.